TESTIMONIALS FOR HAVE IT YOUR WAY BY VERNON GLENN

"...Glenn's tale is often humorous. A diverting misadventure about a legal representative's illegalities."

—KIRKUS REVIEWS

"Glenn writes real lawyers, courtrooms and secret settlement conferences better than anyone in the business! Eddie Terrell is back oozing southern charm in a rip roaring crime novel full of surprises with road trips, romance, family sagas and the RJR Reynolds heir's plane crash and death to boot. You Have Your Way is an action packed, hard drinking romp that will make you laugh out loud and want to join in the fun."

—LAURIE HUTCHINS, NORTH CAROLINA DISTRICT COURT JUDGE

"Another wild romp with flamboyant attorney, Eddie Terrell, who slithers effortlessly between upper-crust Southern society and its seamy underbelly. A cast of eccentrics join the likable antihero in an illegal scheme that may cost him both career and freedom. Dive in and enjoy the fun!"

—MORETON NEAL, AUTHOR OF

Remembering Bill Neal: Favorite Recipes from a Life in Cooking

"Trial attorney Eddie Terrell does mid-life crisis like nobody's business in E. Vernon F. Glenn's You Have Your Way. This crime caper, written by a twelve-cylinder mind, pulls you right in and delivers one hell of a return on your investment. Fans of Glenn's first book, Friday Calls, will delight in the return of Terrell and some of his cohorts who rise to the occasion in You Have Your Way."

— SARA JOHNSON, AUTHOR OF

Molten Mud Murder and The Bones Remember

YOU HAVE YOUR WAY

E. VERNON F. GLENN

You Have Your Way

ISBN: 978-1-732906617 (paperback)
ISBN: 978-1-732906624 (hardback)
ISBN: 978-1-732906631 (large print)

Published by:

MPG, who dearly and clearly always pays attention
KSK, my brilliant mentor and dearer friend
PBG, who never gives up on me, even when I do
FJB and JEH, none ever better

ACKNOWLEDGEMENTS

Special thanks and enormous gratitude to my editor Alice Osborn and my publicist Hannah Turner who both navigate my confused self around these strange twisting tracks. Last, but never least, my dear friend and original law partner Terry Crumpler who took a flyer on me and then we went out and did it and so many stories grew from all of that and still do.

And a big tip of the hat to the marvelous and talented Cheryl Ann Lipstreu who created the portrait of Eddie Terrell which graces the back cover of this fun meandering. She's cool!

CONTENTS

From the *Montana Standard*, Police blotter
Butte, Montana, Summer 2019

Police arrested Derek Grady, 30, of Butte at about 4 a.m. Saturday on the 3400 block of Hill Avenue for a misdemeanor count of resisting arrest.

Police stated that Grady was walking around in an empty lot in his underwear with a beer box over his head. When police initially tried to talk to Grady, he allegedly ran away.

Just y'all remember: one person's crazy is another person's business as usual.

CHAPTER ONE

THUNDERSTRUCK

AC/DC

HE LOVED HER voice that sang and twanged out of her angel lips. She was built like a long, lovely country road he loved cruising up and down with his eyes. Gigi Faye Erin, independent insurance investigator, was a blonde, real honest-to-God looker, born Irish, raised Southern white trash, who climbed out to power and glory but never let the hick in her get away. And she could whoop your ass in a New York minute.

Gigi Faye had been hired by big money Chubb Insurance out of New York City to look into some heavy-duty jewelry thefts in the monied venues of Winston-Salem, North Carolina. Significant insurance claims had been paid out on "special items" policies and a couple of the companies smelled more than one rat.

She needed a wingman to legit her, so she had called on Eddie Terrell to be her shade moustache. They had tussled often here and there in the past, always enjoyed the push and shove, always got the claims settled and had plenty of respect for each other. Now they were on the same side and since she had requested Chubb to put Eddie in the game with her, Eddie was getting paid fat by the hour too. It would be fair to say they looked at each other as pros and also knew that they should not dip their quills in the company ink well. Still they thought about that from time to time but kept it mostly to themselves. Sometimes there would be a Martha White "hot rise" moment, fueled by a few post-settlement pops, but these were quickly doused by Gigi Faye's arched eyebrows which flashed, "Get your brain outta there and keep your hands to yourself," though she never said never. Sometimes Eddie was encouraged, and sometimes he just thought he was delusional.

Eddie Terrell had picked Gigi Faye up at her condo out on Peace Haven Road. The complex was so full of good-looking ladies that the wags had renamed it Piece Heaven. Gigi Faye cheapened not a bit of those blatantly sexist play-on-words. They talked about diddling their marks and how they wanted to play it. Soon they settled on the old "we are just friends having a nice time" bit. She was going to be an independent insurance agent selling multiple lines. Eddie was just going to be Eddie the Lawyer, out for a good time with an attractive friend.

Eddie would take care to compliment Gigi Faye on how nice she looked and Gigi Faye would return the words. It would be nice to be taking a run together in the name of business. Eddie had been getting erratic among billowing doses of weirdness at home lately. *No doubt climate change was for real*, he thought as he grimaced and drove on.

They arrived at The Alley, a high-class steak house joint. Everyone there acted like Eddie and Gigi Faye's BFF, squeezing their arms or necks. A white tie and tailed Vietnamese piano player low-crooned over his white baby grand tucked in the corner. Eddie and Gigi Faye sat at a community table with plenty of open seats, eying the crowd slowly while nursing their weak drinks.

The clientele fell into two basic categories: tourists who read a review online and dutifully made a reservation and the regulars, who were girls on the make or match and older guys whose bellies hung over their cowboy belt buckles. The regulars always dressed to the nines and the gals jeweled up and wore tight, tight leggings and bare midriff tops. The Alley had great food, hustling service, and a good vibe. It was always crowded. They minted money.

Two tarted up gals came in, looking pretty good but obviously on the lookout for better times and days. They parked across from Gigi Faye and Eddie. Everyone nodded at everyone expectantly. The gals had on the big bling of rings and bracelets.

Gigi Faye and Eddie knew those two could not afford such baubles, so the ice had to be from sugar daddies or dead husbands. Gigi Faye, never shy, regarded the two.

"Now y'all are looking strong this evening!" Her down-in-the-holler croak cloaked a twelve-cylinder mind.

"Oh, excuse me. I'm Faye and this feller here is Eddie. And you?"

"Thanks for noticing! Pleased to meet you. We're here to...well... look around. I'm Tina and this is my friend Mitchell. Y'all from around here?"

Eddie leaned forward and getting a better look at their jewelry, whispered conspiratorially, "Sometimes..." and he winked. They all giggled.

"Let's get you ladies a few pops. What'll it be? It's on me."

They tittered and Gigi Faye encouraged them. "Y'all come on now. He's good for it so far!"

Now at ease and loosening up, the two in unison asked for kettle bomb cosmos that were soon delivered.

As they ritually sipped away, Eddie happily inquired, "Now am I correct in assuming that you two beauties are here to see what the merchandise looks like this evening? There's some pretty stout businessmen in here and I ain't just talking waistlines. I'm talking wallets and Gucci loafers and cashmere sport coats if you get my drift." He winked again and smiled gently and sweetly.

The gals took it straightforward and nodded demurely in assent.

The one named Mitchell said, "Well, Eddie, it appears that none of us are in high school anymore and I think we appreciate the observation. Looks to us like you and Miss Faye here are paired up pretty good, so no chain breaking there. We heard this was a good fishing hole to dip a hook into. You know some of these folks? Introductions are always appreciated." She grinned slyly as her buddy shook her head in mock disapproval of the hussy forwardness of it all. Tina had her waders on too.

Gigi Faye said, "Sure. We'll introduce you two honeys and I expect within thirty minutes we'll be giving our seats up to a couple of swell guys. And let me ask you this. That's some killer good-looking jewelry y'all are sporting. Where you get that? It's nice!" Tina and Mitchell brightened and looked at each other coyly.

Tina said, "It's all gifts from good friends. Isn't that right, Mitchell?"

Mitchell nodded and for a split-second gazed at the floor. Gigi Faye mouthed, "Nice ice," and the gals were pleased. The conversation galloped along nicely now. More drinks were ordered. Tongues were loosened, addresses and numbers exchanged, ham-it-up photos were taken, and Eddie went hunting for bait.

A few minutes later, Eddie tow-boated back to the table a couple of older bulls in sheep's clothing. They simply glowed of money, dressed and draped by the best haberdasheries in town. These were the types who always let their money dress them, everything matched and mixed and paired to make the impression.

"Ladies, I'd like you to make the acquaintance of these nice gentlemen. This fellow here with this spectacular blue necktie is Tommy Notes. His partner in this evening's fun and games is Ron Padgett. Guys, these lovelies are Mitchell and her friend Tina. And do y'all know my buddy and unindicted co-conspirator Gigi Faye?

"Unfortunately or fortunately as the case may be, Gigi Faye is avec moi ce soir and thus y'all will have to just do without us once we have one more drink together to help celebrate new friends and old." Eddie nodded and smiled to each as he set a table of prospective hedonism. Gigi Faye rolled her eyes at Eddie an ambiguous set of signals: "Yes, you are an asshole but with an effective touch."

A waiter sailed up expectantly, ready to take orders which were received and soon effected. More whiskey and white water all around. Mitchell efficiently opened the bidding with, "Hey y'all! We are glad to meet you. Tell us about yourselves." She leaned forward with all the interest of a bird dog on point.

Ron Padgett, in his mid-fifties, sporting a full head of silvering hair and a few jowls, was locked and loaded. "Well, let's see. I'm in construction, have my own outfit. Not married, no gal pal, grown children. Lived here all my life and my picture hasn't been pinned up in the post office yet, but there's still time you know..."

The gals tittered. Eddie and Gigi Faye glanced at each other. If the other guy could hold his own, the ship of liquor lust would sail. Mitchell winked at Tommy Notes. "Now it's your turn, good sir."

Notes was no amateur. A big, broad man, also in his mid-fifties, he had sweet brown eyes and a receding hairline with the graying upsweep at his back collar. "Well, first of all, Ron here has done way better than all right. His is one of the biggest construction firms in the state. First class operation too. Plays a nice game of golf, holds his liquor well, is most welcomed at the bank too." Notes plowed on, nods and winks abounding. "I'm in the trucking business, try to haul just about anything and everything; been at it ever since I can remember, divorced, with grown children. I like to gamble a little, travel, not much on the golf side—am just bad at it—but I do have a few other redeeming qualities." His speech was followed by an aw-shucks-toe-dragged-in-the-dirt head tilt.

Padgett rejoined, "If I've done better than okay, my friend Tommy here lapped me a long time ago. He's probably the second or third largest hauler in the southeast, right, Tommy?"

Tommy slapped his hand just a little and acknowledged, "Oh, something like that. Now, ladies, tell us about you all? Miss Gigi Faye too. Eddie here we already know plenty about, the lawyer's lawyer. Mitchell, how about you go first?"

Mitchell was in her late forties with long legs, a fine face and figure and a charmingly forward manner that was complemented by her B-52 coif of dark hair. She was a presence. "Well, I'm married, have been too long but we're settled in our ways. He really doesn't care much about anything I do as long as I keep the house straight and make sure his dinner is good to go. He's pretty boring to tell the truth. About half the week at nights, I'll go out with gal friends. I'm Tina's wingman this evening. Children are grown and I'm bored with being a stay-at-home sitting duck. So, let's have a few laughs and some fun!"

Padgett low whistled and murmured, "Count me in." Notes just smiled the smile of the fellow who saw gold in his pan. He motioned for Tina to introduce herself.

Tina, fortyish, blonde, and very pretty, had slightly hooded eyes and an exceptional décolletage. She spoke clearly but softly. "I'm recently separated, couple of kids all grown up, allegedly..." It was her turn to wink ruefully. "I've always been a homemaker too but need to find some work, so I won't be so bored. A night out like this is a real treat for me. It's always nice to meet nice people and have a little fun."

A round of amens nodded forth as the waiter appeared for the next order. Eddie turned to Gigi Faye and asked, "Whaddaya think?"

Gigi Faye grinned. "I think you, and thus we, have done some damn fine work here this evening and I'm good with one more but then, no more, okay?"

"Another round, it is." He handed the fellow his black Amex card and said, "When you come back, bring the ticket to me. After that, y'all are on your own!"

They were all happy, for reasons seen and unseen. Mitchell looked across the table and asked Gigi Faye, "Now, since you two are leaving us soon, out with it. What's y'all's story?"

Eddie introduced himself and said, "Plain and simple, we're just good buddies. I know a lot of these folks in here, have run across Tommy and Ron in here from time to time." He pointed to the two men.

"I'm a lawyer. I try cases, try to fix things, been at it a while. My friend Faye here has a few independent insurance agencies scattered about the Piedmont. We're both local talent. Now we gotta move along. Nothing to see here and we gotta go! It's a school night for me. Y'all have a good time!"

Big swallows drained down and Eddie signed the ticket, took Gigi Faye's arm, bowed gracefully to the four winning contestants who waved happily back. The duo swept out the door, leaving behind the piano notes, the clinking and rattling of ice in glasses, and the swelling and murmuring of the night's many conversations. As they turned to walk up the sidewalk to the valet parking, they saw the two pairings in bloom.

They walked in silence for a while and then Gigi Faye stopped, looked with lowered chin and eyes raised wide open and said, "Now it's my turn. what did you think?"

Eddie grinned. "Can't wait to take a look at the photos we all took. Probably some good pictures of the goods." Gigi Faye whipped out her digital camera and clicked it a few times and there they were.

"Yup, those are stolen goods on both of them. Now, how did they get to where they were blinging on those boobs?"

"Good eye, Miss Erin! Let me see if I can help fill in another piece of our puzzle. Those two broads are not bereft and lonely housewives. I believe they are high-end working girls, in the service of Mama Bunny also known as Madge Roberts. Madge serves up the most high-toned poontang in this town. Bored, money hungry, like to fuck, whatever, the word gets around that if you are reasonably good looking and have an acceptable skill set, you can ply the trade as one of Mama Bunny's chosen. Now let's noodle this out."

They got in Eddie's car and he began driving Gigi Faye home. She asked, "How do you know all this? And do you know Mama Bunny?" The latter question was much more than professional curiosity.

"Yeah I know her a little bit, mostly from male clients I've helped out on other matters. And, no, Miss Killed the Cat Curiosity, I have never availed myself of her services.

"It's pretty much common knowledge in lawyer and money circles. Top cops know about it too, but the johns are high-powered and influential; many of whose family names adorn plenty of big buildings and companies around here and it's pretty much a victimless crime, so best not to poke at it with a stick. No telling whose name is on Madge's list. Now, here's what's intriguing to me. Her girls almost always do day work, stay in the shadows so to speak, and get on home by late afternoon to resume the meat and three domestic goddess routine and here we have two of 'em out galivanting at night, wearing all that stuff. Now, why is that?"

It didn't take them long to begin the "if that, then that" algorithm. Gigi Faye's feminine instincts kicked into a higher gear. She began a solving dialogue with herself. "Gotta keep our eye on the prize. Did your gal Madge give them to those two? Highly doubtful. Did those two steal them from their original owners? Again, highly doubtful. Those two may be big fun, but inside job thieves they ain't. Here's what I think we got. And if I'm right, pressure will have to be applied."

"Keep talking. Tell me more."

"First of all, if they are Mama's girls, and they probably are, then they have jumped the reservation and are out wildcatting, either to score some extra dough or just have some fun... nothing like some good old-fashioned networking."

"What about the jewelry?"

"I believe..." Gigi Faye's voice tailed off as both her head and Eddie's jerked to the rear of the vehicle where a large, very bright blue strobe light pulsated closer and closer to them. It was a motorcycle cop.

"Oh, shit...oh, fuck...oh, damn," murmured from their mouths.

"What you gonna do?" Gigi Faye whispered with just enough whimper to make Eddie momentarily forget the trouble walking toward him.

"Not much I can do 'cept play it straight, I guess," he sighed.

Eddie eased the car over to the edge and steeled himself for the spear. It was late and there was no way he could gandy dance through this one.

He rolled his window halfway down, reached in the glove box for the registration and pulled his license from his wallet as the approaching footfalls crunched a little louder. A large, tall motorcycle policeman now stood at his window, a long Maglite flashlight at his side.

"Evening, officer," said Eddie, eyes straight ahead. The officer asked for his license and registration which Eddie handed him through the window.

"I'll be right back, sir. Please be at ease." He turned to go radio the information in.

Gigi Faye leaned over to Eddie and whispered, "How bad off are you?"

"Not as good as I ought to be. And remember, I signed the ticket for about how many drinks? It's in my wallet. I thought my driving was all right, but he'll say he had probable cause. I went over the yellow line, was tapping my brake lights erratically, was weaving, whatever suits him."

"Damn."

"Yeah, damn is right. I'm sorry. You okay?"

"I'm okay, just worried for you. Can you beat it?"

"Dunno yet..."

They sat silently in the puddle of apprehension that waiting for the shoe to fall always brought. And this was just the first shoe. The dark night and random cars swooshing by proved to be no sedative.

They didn't hear him come back. He was now on Gigi Faye's side of the car, shining his light in on her, sweeping up and down and across. She was frightened. And then he went back around the rear of the car and said, "Eddie, how about roll your window all the way down."

Eddie exhaled a querying "Huh?" Gigi Faye stared a sharp question at him. Eddie shrugged and complied.

"Eddie, my friend, what have you been up to this evening and who is your lovely friend?"

Eddie then recognized Bobby "The Topper Copper" Allen, all six feet six of him, resplendent in knee-high gleaming motorcycle boots and a glistening white helmet which made him appear even taller. Eddie and Allen went way back, to the earliest days of State District Court, Traffic Division.

Eddie had always been imploringly solicitous and polite without beggaring on behalf of his wheeled offense clients and Allen respected and enjoyed that. Sometimes, he'd let Eddie cut a lesser offense deal with the assistant DA. Sometimes if it worked out, Eddie never gloated and made sure the client didn't either and if it didn't, well so it goes, try it, take your chances, or just take the medicine.

He sensed a whiff of some sort of miraculous salvation wafting nearby but he was also wary. Topper Allen always worked days and here he was at night. Had his quotas (and, oh yes, they all had quotas) come up short or was he working off some sort of disciplinary problem?

Eddie inhaled and looked at the big man and said, "Hey, Topper. Been a while. How you doing? Well, this is my friend Gigi Faye Erin. She is a top shelf insurance investigator and I've been paired with her by a big insurance company to try and unravel some probable jewel fraud. We've been downtown at The Alley doing some watching and digging and are making headway. I'll admit we've had a few but needed to in order to not be marked as stiffs but I thought I was okay. Really. I'm just taking her home now. We've put in a good night's work."

Topper responded, "No kidding? For real? That's pretty interesting. I've been good. No complaints." He then stuck his head inside the car and said, "Ma'am, sorry for the inconvenience but I do have a job to do. Where do you live?"

"Just about a half mile here down Peace Haven up in the back rows of The Regency." Topper Allen's eyes brightened and a Cheshire Cat smile flickered briefly on his lips.

"Well, Eddie, step on out of your vehicle and come on back here with me. Gotta field test you."

Topper opened the door. Eddie sighed, his imagined harbor of safety beginning to dry up. "Yessir."

They went to the back of the car, where Topper asked Eddie to recite his ABCs, count backwards from twenty, had Eddie wobble on single legs, put his big index finger just beyond Eddie's nose and made Eddie follow it back and forth while shining his light on Eddie's face. Then he instructed Eddie to walk heel to toe five yards out and five yards back. Once these tasks were completed, Eddie ventured, "I wasn't too bad, was I, Topper?"

"I've seen worse but you ain't gonna be on the medal stand neither." Eddie grimaced. "But Eddie, let's do this. That's a pretty gal. You like her?"

"Well, yeah, sure," Eddie replied puzzled.

He took Eddie's arm and walked him not to the driver's side door, but around the front of the car to the passenger's door. Topper opened it and said, "Miss Erin, is it? Here's what we are gonna do. You look all right to me. You are gonna drive this vehicle to your home."

Gigi Faye nodded and asked quizzically, "What about Eddie? Are you gonna take him in? I wish you wouldn't."

Topper grinned and said, looking at them both, "Every now and then, I get to give a get-out-of-jail card. Tonight is y'all's lucky night. Miss Erin, you are gonna carefully drive your passenger, Attorney Eddie Terrell, to your place. This is his car, right? I'm going to follow you so just take it slow and easy. Now, he is to spend the night with you. He is not to leave and neither are you. I'm on patrol out here until the 7 o'clock shift change. If I see either one of you out on the road, I will bust both of you. Do you understand?"

They both slowly, silently nodded. Gigi Faye's mind churned a little bit, and she started to speak, but then thought the better of it. Eddie just murmured, "Thank you, Topper."

"Let's get on with it. Miss Erin, get behind the wheel, please."

In a few minutes, they arrived at Gigi Faye's apartment. Nearby in the pool house, a good slamming kegger was raging along with lots of loud voices and laughter and equally loud music. Topper walked them both to her door. "Now y'all have a nice, quiet, good night. No trips out until seven. And by the sound of what's going on just down the way there, I expect I'll have plenty to work and call in as the night goes on. Remember, I gotta call a roller, can't take a drunk in on the back of a cop Harley." He laughed.

Eddie asked, "Topper, why are you out working nights? You are a daylight guy, aren't you? Everything okay?"

"I appreciate the interest, Eddie. Just catching up on required night training. Have to do it every few years. Now, y'all go take care and solve your mystery. Good night."

Topper gave a little salute and cranked the bike and rumbled away.

The couple went inside. Gigi Faye switched on some lights, turned to Eddie. "Never saw that one coming. Did you set that up?"

"No. No. He just...he just did it on his own initiative. Glad he did."

"Oh, I bet." But Gigi Faye smiled peacefully.

"Let's have a big drink. My nerves are a little jangly."

"Sure, you wanna talk about your theory some more? I think that's maybe a good idea."

"Yes, let's do that."

She pulled a fifth of bourbon out of a cabinet along with a couple of glasses and motioned for him to come and sit down on a small couch. Her place was neat and orderly, not at all schlocky or tricked up. She had good taste. There were no overhead lights so the lamp lights exuded calm. Gigi Faye poured two and kicked off her shoes and tucked her long legs up under her and said, "Okay, where were we?"

Eddie just stared and waited. It was hard to not notice his breathing was a little shallow.

"I think the jewelry is being 'stolen' by husbands, sometimes with the complicity of their wives or vice versa and then claims for big cash come through. I think some of these randy fellows hand things out like party favors in return for flesh favors. Or new cars or whatever. They get the money. The pieces go off into places where most folks don't go or don't care. And things just sorta disappear. And it's a lot of effective, disposable, tax-free moola. And remember, pieces can be transacted over and over again down the line. Those two tootsies tonight could both go out first thing tomorrow and trade out or hock stuff for cars, clothes, travel agent services, whatever is of value to them or just put everything in cold storage for a while. The stuff is a moving target and hard to keep up with." She took a long pull of brown water.

"Makes sense to me. How you gonna get the stuff back? Those two birds made the mistake of being in public with some fine pieces. If it weren't for the tip we got, we'd never seen it." Eddie drank and then drank a little more.

"Seems to me you can be a big help here." She reached over and topped him off, then stiffed herself up good as well.

Eddie could feel his nerves a touch unsteady. She was gorgeous. They got a good ID on some serious stolen rocks. They almost went to jail. The blue light in the rear window had scared the bejesus out of him. And now, he was sitting here in her place, unspooling the deal, drinking more than a little bourbon with her and on top of it all, had to have a cop-mandated sleepover with her nearby. Oh so close and yet so far. Damn, she was a smart gal!

He wondered if she'd like to go to law school but it fleeted past him. "Here's how I see it. We, of course, can track Mitchell and Tina down with a little footwork, scare the shit out of them, get the stuff back and recommend to the insurance company that no charges be filed in return for the ladies telling us from whom did they got the stuff. They generally do it that way, no publicity. They just cancel the policies and refuse to write them again. Sometimes a heart-to-heart visit will be made to the original claimants to put the fear of God in them." Eddie could feel the bourbon up in his head, lapping against the shores of his brain.

"Hang on. I've got another idea. Let's say you're right, that these are Bunny's girls. Let's go see her. What does she do for her "real" job?" She poured some more. The room was now inescapably warm and comfortable.

"I believe she's a seamstress. Works out of her home but also does much contract work for the nicer ladies' stores like Montaldo's and Nitsa's. Hear she's pretty good at it too."

"Hmmmm. Interesting. I want you to do this. Go to Madge Roberts. Or let's go together. Show her the pictures we took. Ask if the two gals are familiar to her. If they are, I expect she won't hold back. She don't want no trouble. She'll call her two fence jumpers in. We'll pay a 10-percent finder's fee too. Tell her we don't want to get her in trouble. Get her to give you a five-dollar bill and now she will have 'retained' your services, so lawyer-client confidentiality. She'll get our stuff back for us which we can recover most if not all earlier lost value on the resale market and you will have a nice, interesting new client. Then you and I might just have access from time to time to nice, interesting new information."

"Jesus, you are a fine thinker!" Eddie continued. "What if the two aren't in her stable?"

"Well, if we don't ask, we ain't gonna know, right? And if they're not, we can always go chase them down and play it the way we first talked about. So, you in? This is the sort of thing why we wanted you playing with us."

Eddie confirmed with a "yes" and then said, "How about a toast?"

Gigi Faye clinked his glass and asked, "How about one more drink before bedtime?"

"Sure. Uhm. You know I can't leave here until in the morning. You got an extra blanket and pillow? I can just rack out down here on your couch. You mind if I watch a little TV after you've gone on?"

She poured out the rest of the bottle for them and eyed him with obvious mischief. "Eddie, you're coming upstairs with me once we swill this last. You've earned it, boy!"

Eddie's head spun silently and he grinned and blushed. "Damn. Thanks!"

Later, after they had talked about all sorts of stuff and laughed and did all the things that often happen when this sort of thing blossoms, they stepped quietly up the stairs. Eddie realized he had not thought about Lee Ann Jepson one iota all night and knew in a few minutes he might forget about her entirely.

CHAPTER TWO

THE THRILL IS GONE

B.B. King

EDDIE LAID HIS half-sodden head into the crook of his right elbow as a sniper would, albeit an exhausted one tighter than Dick's hatband, and squinted through the prismatic bevels of his rapidly-emptying brown water glass to sight in on the only really good-looking gal in the joint. As steady as he might shakily achieve, he pulled the dreamy "Bang!" trigger in both his brain and in his pants. It was a clean shot. He hit at least four of her and he grinned a goofy smile. Lucky for him, she was a duck in a barrel, perched with one leg crossed like a man. He raised his head and asked her, "Whatcha say your name was again? Man, you a pretty girl!"

She had one hand cocked on a high hip and a thoughtful finger toying with her lips. She looked at him with a mixture of wry amusement and wondering watchfulness and smiled. "Hey, tinhorn Eddie Terrell, like I said about forty times before, my name is Mikey Riewey, like 'Get Mikey to eat it, Mikey will eat anything' and maybe you're gonna rue the day you met me. Ya wanna write it down or somethin'? Hell, I can remember your weird-ass southern fancied-up name from the get-go."

"Well, okay, fine. Got a piece of paper and a pencil because I don't want to forget you."

"Damn, son, you're a lawyer. You're supposed to have that kind of crap with you all the time, aren't you? And just by the way, you ain't gonna forget me anyway."

"Well, I am a little drunk. Well, maybe more than a little but I can see you good and I'm thinking."

"Yeah, I can hear the gears grinding in there for sure!" She laughed and he sat up and laughed as well.

Eddie asked, "While I'm resting my weary brain here, I'm wondering what you do when you're not hanging out in here?"

"Can't you tell?"

"No."

"Hair. I do hair. Fix the ladies up. Make 'em prettier. There ain't much else to do around here and I'm not interested in doing much else."

"Will you do mine?"

"No."

"Why not?"

"Easy answer."

"What?"

"You're hopeless. No way to make you prettier!"

Mikey laughed. Eddie feigned a hurt.

"You don't think I'm at least a little bit pretty?" He winked. She smiled.

"Well, maybe..."

They had been flirting with each other for a good twenty minutes now at the far left dark side corner of the big horseshoe bar at Chick's in the great metropolis of Alder, Montana, a tiny crossroads town in the heart of the Ruby Valley.

About a week ago, Eddie had come home early one morning after being surprisingly and happily sequestered with his insurance investigator friend at her place by a clever cop. It was a fine time, but the due bill was being presented and Ms. Lee Ann Jepson was beyond raging hot. She laid into Eddie with both barrels and he knew he had it coming. She screamed, cussed him out, roared imprecations, wept, moaned, sighed, and cried and smelled him like an agitated bloodhound, and then cried and shrieked and hollered some more. It was the high opera of domestic dissolution.

"You smell like a cheap whore, you shit-eating bastard! I hope your cheating-ass dick falls off!" And so forth.

It wasn't close to the first time such an avalanche of vocal depredation had engulfed him and he knew, like being in a riptide, to stay still, afloat, tread water and the tide will eventually go out. She slammed many doors. She was good at it, very good.

Eddie shaved and showered and dressed, grabbed a big sheath of papers off his home desk, stuck his head into the guest room where Lee Ann was balled up in anger and dark fear and resentment to offer her the biggest of leaves, "Look, honey, I'm sorry. I didn't realize my phone was off and a cop made me stay off the road until dawn. I've been killer busy. You know that. It's all weighing on me and us pretty good. I'm sorry. It's a long story. Nothing happened, I swear. I'll tell you about it tonight. I've got to be in court at nine. Hope you feel better. I love you."

She replied smolderingly, her voice rising, "You are a lying motherfucker. Go fuck yourself!"

"Okay, well...see you later then. Again, I'm real sorry."

"Fuck you!"

Eddie thought to himself, *Well, at least a lot of it is true...* as he headed first to the drugstore for his swelling steel banded fat head. And therein lay the nubs of the matter. No matter which it was, the chicken or the egg, Eddie was the gerbil and his life had become the wheel and it was simply impossible to Rosetta Stone the poultry thing. They were both rotting each other out.

He was backpedaling stupidly and ham-handedly and nothing was getting better except his law practice. Money and cases were pouring in. They were very well-to-do, on the verge of wealthy. His prestige was climbing. Lee Ann really didn't need to work but they decided some time ago they'd have no children and she wasn't about to sit around playing pretend Junior League or lining up a game of hit and giggle tennis with the girls. He had a sour, ominous continual sense that he was on his way to a big Icarus moment. She knew he was off the chain and not sure whether that was a bad or good thing. Their lives, once so pleasant, had become sulfurous nightmares.

Things had occurred. They kept occurring with ever-growing intensity and often fury. They just blossomed like mushroom clouds, a spark, a flash, and the world was a roiled, spoiled mess. Glass doors kicked out. Dishes hurled, the bigger the better. She obsessed about her weight and looks and constantly inquired of Eddie about them. No answer was correct or even helpful. She often flung herself to the floor, kicking and screaming like a child. He began to not give a shit.

He was working all day and into the evenings and then drinking with pals and other hard drivers. Some nights he would not come home, flopping at old friends' pads, or burrowing in with new friends. One night they went to an annual Bachelor's Club party. He talked to lots of girls. She got pissed and left.

He then went to a raucous all-night party and got a cab home as the sun rose, delivering two lovelies to their apartments along the way, then directing the cabbie to his place. As they pulled up to the mailbox so stylishly labeled "Edward Terrell," he was, head down, rummaging in his pockets for the fare when the cabbie dryly noted, "Those were two good-looking gals we just took home. Now, who is this woman standing in your yard looking like she wants to scream at us? What do you want me to do, mister?"

Eddie looked up into the devil's eyes of a crazed Lee Ann and said, "Drive on." It was but a temporary fix.

There had been the Sunday night after a long weekend of them both carousing with friends, warily watching one another and now worn out, when she started to pick about some piece of furniture she wanted. Eddie said, "Look, I'm really tired and just don't have time for this. I've got a long day ahead," and he turned out the light.

She turned it back on. "I want to talk." He turned it off. She turned it on again and then sweeping about their bedroom, turned all of the lights on. He got out of bed and grimly turned them all off. She turned them all on again. He silently unscrewed each bulb, opened a window, and tossed them out where they exploded in a "pop pop pop" as they crashed and burst onto the driveway. She sullenly relinquished the field and they fell into a fitful sleep.

Fifteen minutes later, there was a hard pounding on their door. Eddie, dully roused, went to the top of the stairs, and peered down the front door's sidelight windows. There were two policemen shuffling their feet and a coiled-up elf-like guy in a ratty tartan bathrobe standing well below the head level of the cops. Eddie, curious and perplexed, hustled down the stairs. He could hear Lee Ann on the landing, swishing her robe and patting her hair.

"Evening, officers. And to what do I owe the pleasure of this visit? Oh, and Mr. Lowrance? What brings you to my porch with these gentlemen on this dark and cold night?"

Mr. Ed Lowrance was their next-door neighbor, an engineer at the local plant that assembled Nike missiles, a gnome-like, obsessive compulsive snoop whose skin was translucent tallow. He was as hairless as one of those nasty Chihuahuas and his pate gleamed silver under the porch light. He never looked at you but rather myopically squinted and peered at everything. He was an enormous ever-present pain in the ass. And adding to his annoying mien, he spoke with a very pronounced lisp.

Eddie glanced up behind him. At the top of the stairs stood stone-faced Lee Ann, arms folded, jaw set, the executioner in waiting. She had already passed the "J'accuse!" marker and was just waiting for the tumbril to be sent around to take Eddie's shit-ass neck to the block and blade. "Now what has this bum done?" She thrilled at his looming problem.

"You Eddie Terrell?" one cop asked. "I'm Griffith and this is Best." Eddie nodded. Beyond them on the curb a black and white with a cycling red and blue strobe bar idled.

Eddie thought in a mental grimace while his smile was on high beams, *Oh the neighborhood is gonna love this shit.*

"This your residence? And who is the young lady at the top of the stairs there?"

"Yes, this is my home. The young lady is my friend Miss Jepson." Eddie looked around but couldn't figure it out. He could feel Lee Ann's laser beams burning a hole in his head.

"You know Mr. Lowrance here?" The cop jerked his head toward the fidgety gerbil.

"Yessir, I do. He lives right over there across my driveway."

"Well, Mr. Terrell... you're a lawyer, right? Think I've seen you around the courthouse from time to time."

"Yessir, that's right." Everyone was waiting for the punchline.

"Well, Mr. Terrell, we got dispatched after Central got a call from this Mr. Lowrance here. He reported the sounds of gunshots here at your place."

Before Griffith could inhale anew, Lowrance started with his Elmer Fudd staccato recitation of "shots fired" with the urgency of the righteous, stabbing the air with a string of exclamations.

"Yes, tha' tha' that's right! We were sle' sle' sleeping. We heard ex' ex' ex' plosions! It was gun gunfire. I know it was. There were ma' ma' many shots! These people fight and shout a a lot! I know know there is some some something wrong here!" Lowrance rested his case, crossed his arms across his shriveled chest, nodded in self-affirmation and looked up defiantly.

Officers Griffith and Best looked at Lowrance with narrowing eyes and then turned to Eddie. If there had been gunplay, it looked like everybody in the shoot-out was a damn poor shot unless there was a third-party stiff stowed away in the house. That seemed unlikely. There weren't even any signs of domestic violence. Everyone was neat, orderly, and responsive and still. No hysteria on the horizon.

"Well...what say you, Mr. Terrell?"

Eddie smiled quietly and prepared to stick it in Lee Ann and Lowrance together. One knife, two kills.

"Officers, I believe Mr. Lowrance here has misapprehended the situation and has jumped to irresponsible conclusions that have wasted your time, our time, and our taxpayers' money."

Eddie shot a withering look at Lowrance who peevishly peered into the vacuum of his knowing truth and said, "There were were were gunshots. I know know know it!"

Eddie calmly paused before continuing and looked back up behind him at the glowering Lee Ann. He gave her a flat line smile. She knew he was getting ready to be publicly flayed. The whip hand was at the ready.

"Officers, there has been no gunplay, no shooting, nothing at all such as that. Now, there has been a disagreement between myself and my friend (it dripped like a venom from his lips), but as domestic discord goes, it sure wasn't much. I know you, Mr. Lowrance, snoop and spy on us all the time and judge judge judge us terrible sinners unto the gates of hell, but you completely and badly missed your target here."

Eddie saw the cops were beginning to be bemused so he decided to help the humor of the moment along. Lowrance's taut little vessel of a face was beginning to sag with the discomfort of uncertainty. Eddie was going to lay it on thick with dismissive good humor.

"Officers, here is what transpired. Miss Lee Ann up there," he sharp gestured over his shoulder with his thumb in the manner of an umpire emphatically calling the runner at home out, "wanted to argue tonight with me about something else she wanted to buy. Not an unusual occurrence. But it was getting late and I have to be in court on a number of pretty serious matters first thing tomorrow morning," he continued and gestured to two bulging briefcases that sat next to the front hall table, "so I declined to be disputatious and simply turned off the lights and tried to begin to sleep.

"Miss Lee Ann was not satisfied nor pleased with my response and she turned the lights back on to vent and I then turned them back off and then she turned them back on. I think you are all getting the picture."

The cops were nodding. Who hasn't been in a hot over and over again tit for tat with a crazy woman? Lead dog cop Griffith was openly smiling, Best was just grinning. Lowrance was mystified, knowing his Ship of Truth was taking on water below the waterline. Eddie continued.

"I had to break the cycle, of course. So I got up, unscrewed every lightbulb, I think there were six, opened the upstairs window and threw them out down onto the driveway where they popped, all broken on impact. My friend, now in a dark she could not light, finally relented and allowed me to seek sleep...which I did." He glared at Lowrance.

"Please, please go take a look down the back of the driveway and you'll find the detritus of the bulbs and if you'd like to come in and look around, I'm happy to make y'all a cup of coffee or get y'all a co'cola." He flipped the front hall light switches and the walkway light and burglar lights instantly lit the front and the side of the house up.

Griffith said, "Best, how 'bout we go down there and take a look, please? Ma'am, Lee Ann, is it? You all right? Is that the story""

She croaked a nodding "yes" and turned swirling in her silks and fled to the bedroom, hangdog and hating. While Best was beaming the drive, Eddie asked, "Y'all busy tonight?"

Griffith replied, "Not very and this sure doesn't seem to be much of a heavy load either, now does it?" He looked at Lowrance.

Best hollered up the drive, "Affirmative on the light bulbs."

Eddie asked again, "Y'all want anything? Y'all wanna come in and look around?"

He hoped they would come in and nose around. Would serve that bitch Lee Ann right. He knew his thought pattern was unchristian, but he was just about fed up to here with her drama.

Best returned. Griffith said, "I don't think that'll be necessary. We'll be going on now." There was a slight pause and then he looked wearily at Lowrance who had pretty much become a pillar of salt.

"Mr. Lowrance, you need to go on home now. But before you go, I'll need to visit with you in our cruiser so I can begin to write up this very unnecessary incident report that we are required to prepare. Please go get your driver's license for identification purposes. And I will volunteer this as well—keep your nose out of these people's business. Do you understand, Mr. Lowrance?"

Lowrance whispered the required "yes" and padded away on his assigned errand.

Eddie quietly called, "Have a real good night, Mr. Lowrance." He was sick of that little prick too. "Well, officers, nice to meet y'all. Sorry it was under these petty circumstances."

"Sorry to have troubled you, Mr. Terrell, but we think you understand."

"I do. Y'all have a good night. Be safe out there."

They had all parted and Eddie turned out the lights. He could see Lowrance silhouette in the squad car as the cops' stern faces were turned to him.

Eddie stood still, thinking. It just went on and on. And he wasn't helping.

Recently there had been the fraternity brother's wedding up in Maryland where too many of the boys from college had gathered. Booze-fueled laughter turned to hysteria and hijinks while Lee Ann was the maid of honor who'd spent the two days glaring with high bludgeoned hate at all of them.

Lee Ann had become a frenetic harpy and Eddie had become a workaholic, self-possessed, schizoid, a ducking and diving bastard.

The clock kept ticking. The last straw, and there was always a last straw, came when he was standing in line at the Walgreens down at the foot of the massive, sprawling Wake Forest University Medical Center. He wanted to buy some legal pads and pens. He always had too many and felt a need to always have a few more. Trial lawyers almost have this chronic penchant.

Two people stood in line in front of him. One was a sad looking, obviously lonely bedraggled woman buying many packs of discount cigarettes and a liter of Mountain Dew. The salesclerk was a chirpy, teenage girl, deeply focused on effusive and cloying customer service. The old broad loved the attention. They gabbed about everything from the fine value of the DVDs to the weather to something about some soap opera info tease mag that arrayed the checkout counter line along with gum, candy, and cheap gizmos. They were chewing up time and in the same instance, dragging it out to render

Eddie's worsening impatience morph into a quiet frantic panic. He knew this wasn't just them, as annoying as it was; it was him too. He was beating himself down. He felt he was being emotionally strangled.

The lady finally paid and left, the counting out of random dollars and spare change and the flurry of the clerk's bilious gratitude for the lady's patronage further burrowing into Eddie's deteriorating soul.

And then now there was just a tall, snappy dressed, well-groomed, and coiffed fellow before him. Oh, thank God, he would be out of there soon. Eddie was riven with the idea of an escape, but he was frozen. And so he waited, drew long breaths, looked around, glanced up and down, and suddenly the fellow squealed in a swishing falsetto and loudly exclaimed, "Oh! Look! The Queen has abdicated! It says it right here! I had not heard it! Oh, my God! The Queen has abdicated! Did you know?!"

He was speaking to Eddie as he waved the most recent edition of the *National Enquirer* above his head.

The sycophant salesclerk whizzed an affirmatory, "Oh! That's terrible! What happened?!" The commiseration of idiots was fully joined. Eddie's patience snapped and he knew he must somehow hold his tongue.

Eddie went blank, then black, then bleak.

He opened his mouth and forbade words to run out and then stealthily, deep low-voiced measured it out.

"No. Queen Elizabeth II has not, I repeat NOT abdicated. This is all the usual trashed-up fiction that the drugstore checkout line provides. It's not true. She still is Queen of the United Kingdom and the other Commonwealth Realms."

"But it says right here that she has!"

"No! That is not true. She has not!" The "not" cracked like a pistol shot.

The clerk's open mouth clamped closed while the tall fellow's high-pitched, whining supplication totaled a disbelieving, "But?"

Eddie paused, looked at the two, reached for his wallet and pulled two twenties out. He handed one to the guy and one to the clerk. He growled.

"Look, I've got to get out of here, I have an emergency. If I'm lying I'm dying. I'm as serious as a heart attack. Here, this is for me to get to the head of this forever longer line and if you like, you can buy that lying rag to enjoy at your leisure. And, young lady, this is for two legal pads and two pens and you keep the rest. I appreciate your help on this. I gotta go." And he did.

They gasped as he hit the door. He got in his car, started it, and slumped against the window. He was breaking. His heart was pounding. He was pouring sweat. He knew the fuse was lit.

The tall fellow walked past his car with a Walgreens plastic bag, the *Enquirer* sticking out the top. He glanced at Eddie, sneered, and kept on going. The sun was glaring bright in Eddie's eyes. As he pulled out of the lot, he saw the young salesclerk standing at the doors, looking at him as some weird, improbably rude creature. She was right. He was evolving in an ugly way. He was getting out of there as fast as he could before his brains started bleeding out of his ears.

CHAPTER THREE

AMAZING GRACE

ONCE I WAS LOST AND NOW I AM FOUND

Aretha Franklin

EDDIE WENT HOME and Lee Ann was there. They had one of those "Look, honey, this is not working out" talks, the kind that lasts about five minutes max only if the participants are drugged. He told her it was time for her to go settle someplace else and gave her a credit card with a ten-thousand-dollar limit, telling her to please use it to get squared away. She looked at him with the anger of knowing resignation. But no tears, no raised voice.

"So, that's it? Just like that? Kicked to the curb?"

"Honey, I'm sorry but you know this thing ain't working out; all we do is fight, disagree, argue and worse."

She swallowed and nodded slowly. "You know I thought you were the guy, but of course I guess I knew all along you were not him. I don't hate you but I sure as hell don't like you very much right now. What are you going to do? Stay here?"

"Yes, I am, but I gotta get away for a while. This has chewed me up, work is chewing me up, we are chewing each other up. So in just a few minutes, I'm gonna throw some clothes in a bag and get out of here, to where I'm not quite sure, out West somewhere, I think."

"It's not just me?"

"I think that's right. It's a lot of stuff."

"So aside from me, you're basically fucked up about everything else too?"

"I think you're right."

Her face hardened. "Damn, you turned into a fucking lightweight! Go on with yourself. Get your shit and get out. I'll be gone in a few days. Fuck you. Don't never come around me again." She growled hard but did not cry. She refused herself that release in front of him.

"Fair deal. It was great while it lasted. It really was. Sorry it didn't. Feel free to burn that credit card all the way down from 10K to zero. Then please cut it up into little pieces and throw it away. And when you leave, please leave your keys on the front hall table. Obviously I don't want you here when I get back."

"Don't worry. I'll be gone in a few days." They both spoke in the flat monotone of unhappy endings.

"Thanks, Lee Ann. I guess I won't see you around but no matter what, good luck. I mean it."

"Oh, for Christ's sake, Eddie, go fuck yourself."

He went to pack while she went to think about where to find the next new brave world. Eddie called his all-world, all-pro legal assistant, Patty.

"Hey, how you doing?"

"Fine. What's up? You know we got some motion hearings coming up this week. You ready? You need anything prepped?"

"No, and yes, probably. Lee Ann and I just blew it up. I gotta get out of here for a week or so. Settle my head. How about just let the court know I need say, a two-week continuance. I've got a personal matter to attend to. Call opp counsel and apologize, grovel, exaggerate, whatever... just handle it all, please."

"Don't worry. I will. Sorry it didn't work out, but..." He could hear her taking a Goodyear Blimp-sized drag off her long Winston, then exhaling a swelling blue gray cloud across her office. She could have been a fog machine in the navy. "You saw it coming, I know. Last many months, you've been wound up tighter than a shitty two-dollar watch. Haven't been right on your game. Lacking focus. Good thing you can bluff. Sorry, but it's true."

"Yeah, you're right. Good cases can assist a bluff. I'm sorry." She was the boss trace horse. She always pulled and pulled well. She was good to him. He was good to her. He felt bad he had been letting her down. It also occurred to him at that instant that he did not feel bad for letting Lee Ann down. It was a healthy marker, albeit a sad one.

"Eddie, go somewhere to screw your game back into place. Where you thinking you might head? And for how long? Just trying to get an idea."

"Thinking out West, Montana maybe, gone a week, ten days."

"Keep me posted. They got cell service out there?" She laughed.

"I expect there'll be some sort of Alexander Graham Bell apparatus in the sticks that will let us talk if we need to. I'll let you know."

"Thanks. Keep in mind we've got a couple of cases going on that need good hauling and pushing here sooner rather than later."

"You talking about Reynolds and what other one?"

"How could you forget?" She laughed again. "The Pussy Preacher case! Geez, you dope!"

"You're right. The Pussy Preacher is all right with me! How about you prioritize our 'get 'er done' lists and I'll get on them when I'm back, at your guidance of course."

"I will. Anything else?"

"Yes. You've got all the pertinent information on my credit cards, right?"

"Yes."

"I gave Lee Ann that spare Wachovia Mastercard. It has a ten-thousand-dollar max out limit. How about you monitor it daily for me? Will be curious to see what she does with it. And when it gets a hair close to the bottom, cancel it, please."

"Ah, paying a little after the collapse tribute going out the door, eh? Understandable. Greases the skids some."

"Yeah, I suppose. Okay, that's it. Thank you. I'll be talking to you soon."

"Over and out." Click.

He felt a lot better after talking with Patty. She never preached or hollered at him. She knew he was a mess, but a damn fine lawyer mess and she helped keep him on the rails. He still had to get out of there for a while, but he didn't feel so lost anymore.

CHAPTER FOUR

OUTTA THE FRYING PAN

Meat Loaf

EDDIE HAD RUN away to the southwest corner of the Big Sky Country for his sagging, confused mental well-being and had initiated a process of recuperation that was mostly comprised of riding around looking at big mountains and plains, while the clouds made shadows of purple and verdant green on the ever rising and folding slopes. He slept a lot of it off in his something-out-of-the-1950s motor court room, watching copious amounts of ESPN and Judge Judy and old movies but also hanging out in Chick's and another bar called The Sump six miles down the road in tiny Sheridan. The Sump had good bumper stickers: "Mini-Vans are Tangible Evidence of Evil," great burgers, and an intimacy of wandering conversations.

Chick's, four times as big as the Sump, did enough business all the time to warrant not one, but two ATMs. Chick's was but twenty steps across well-pressed dust from Eddie's utilitarian Unit 4 so its access was exemplary. Chick's, declaring it had been there since 1949, was so busy there was a big, hand-lettered sign prominently taped in the front of the wall of bottles that read, "All open bar tabs must be paid off in full at the end of the month. If they ain't, you ain't no more." Imagine such back in the Carolinas. Fat chance. There was no Bible Belt in this Big Sky Country. The Sump had a few shot glasses lined up behind the bar while Chick's had pyramids of 25. Sometimes size did count. The Sump was laid out like a sawed-off shotgun, long enough and tight between back wall and bar. It had its charms. Chick's was a glittering, big room with high ceilings where some dollar bills were marked and initialed and taped to the HVAC ducts. The bar spread out and out like the unfolding wings of a flying wedge, a big, wide U.

And it was fair to say too, considering the substance of the topography, The Sump had nothing like the hot pulchritude looks of a gal named Mikey basking under giant ruby red bar lamps, enormous moose and other game heads, and the piece de resistance: a 16-point elk glaring from behind the bar. She bested them all, all of it. Mikey evoked and evinced the longing gazes of so many dusted-up-with-a-shot-and-a-beer field workers and cowboys. She was an eye-popper.

Mikey was simply a hot ticket with sex appeal as her base coat with much more beneath. Sharp-angled high cheek bones and glowing black eyes dressed her thoroughly. She was beautiful bait, worthy of hotted-up dreams, just keep them to yourself. Her high black hair piled up and cowgirl heeled-up boots rendered her taller than she really was. Her jeans, tight enough to show her religion, were torn and tattered in enough places to show plenty of her flesh, the rents working almost jaggedly up near her thighs and then up to her big, crowning, oval belt buckle which gleamed above what surely had to be her wonderland of a cinch bucket. She was dead solid perfect packaged heat.

They all wanted to be near her so bad. But she had a force field and wouldn't let them in so they could only circle her and listen to her laugh and talk and needle them and give them raucous shit. She had a couple of nice-enough gal pal buddies with her and she used them as pawns and screens as she worked around the bar, a flanker here, a pick or screen there. She was good and she knew it. Her confidence enhanced her desirability.

After a few days of reconnaissance and fieldwork, Eddie had come to realize that although Mikey was the Queen of the Ball at Chick's, she was approachable if she was approached right. So Eddie set to the task that late dusky afternoon to walk up straight to her and say, "I'd love to buy you a drink," and she answered, "I think that might be worth a nice idea," looking him over in his so-not-from-here blue blazer and pressed jeans and buckled loafers. The shield came down and off they went to the side to sit and talk. He was happy and she was intrigued. They were both having more than a few anyway as Conway Twitty and George Jones bemoaned loves gone in the dumper and hearts rented with sorrows.

"So what's this about 'getting away' from this Lee Ann squeeze? There's always another gal involved, isn't that right?" She gazed at him with an honest but patronizing smirk on her face. "C'mon, let's hear it, Mr. Eddie T."

Eddie instantly realized that she was interested in him and his mind cleared rapidly. He sat up, leaned in, and spoke clearly with a near-sense of urgency. This could be the path to a closing. "Okay, Miss Mikey, Here's the deal. I've been with a girl named Lee Ann Jepson for some years now. She real pretty, not quite like you but still real pretty. I met her working a murder case back in North Carolina. She worked up in the forensic pathology department, the coroner's office of the big medical school hospital back home. She was the receptionist. I was back and forth up there and we took a shine to one another and one thing led to another." He paused.

Mikey asked, "Uh, you married? And where'd the shine go? If there was a shine, I ain't seeing it in here. Batteries in that flashlight dead, huh?"

"Yes, good and dead and no, no, not married. No kids."

"But y'all living together for a while? Ain't that common law marriage?"

"No, thank God, North Carolina does not recognize common law marriage. If it did, I'd be up shit's creek without a paddle."

"Well, slick, Montana does recognize common law marriage so don't be coming around me calling me your momma and all that some such shit. Sounds like there's some trouble in paradise. Shiny ain't so shiny these days." It seemed she spoke it with a genuine interest.

"No, it isn't. Seems like over the last many times, a lot of things have happened and I feel like I'm in a hell of a pressure cooker and the lid's gonna blow. I had to get away. These days shiny to shit, it feels like. And I haven't been helping myself so much either." His voice trailed off as he realized she was smart and sharp too. She could work the angles and the corners. Impressive. Mikey looked at him, a genuine seriousness on her face. "So tell me."

"I will."

He looked for Val the bartender and caught her eye. He'd become a regular in just four days and she knew what her people wanted. A big gal with a bigger laugh with serving and pouring speed to burn, it was said she was fluent in three languages: English, profanity, and more profanity.

Happily, Val said to them, "Well, by damn you've been circling her pretty good now since you wandered in here. Good work so far but don't be a little bitch now, you hear?! Another bourbon? And, Mikey, he ain't a bad looking son of a bitch, is he? Y'all might be thinking about throwing a damn good one at each other sooner rather than damn later. I believe that's the goddamn truth! And another Bud Light, Mikey?"

They both nodded, grinning, acknowledging their simmering attractions. They were beyond being coy but not yet at crossing the river.

The place was filling up as the workday ended. It was a different world, folks open carrying, hard hats, cowboy hats that looked like cowboy hats, bandanas greased with dirt and sweat—these were gassed or ready to roll hard-ass people. Worn out old timers who just wanted to throw a few back and nurse a few more. Here and there, some spurs jangled. A few big women, a few larger. This was not the red carpet runway of pulchritude. A hot, red ball sun was going down, its red rays flashing through the front half-moon windows of the bar, coloring all in an erratic enticing siren song crimson glow.

Wherever she was in the big room, Mikey wore a Mona Lisa smile and turned heads like Scarlett O'Hara. Most of the men held lurid thoughts of lust and what-do-I-do next, and most of the women glowed with resentment and envy and the basic practical inventories of how I get from here to close to where she is.

The men felt a possessory, proprietary interest in her. She belonged to them; she was the primary adornment in their scabby, scraping hard world of cowboys and rig hands and welders and beef haulers. She was constantly in their presence and though they could not have her, they did have her. When she snapped off a knowing glance at one of them or laughed at something one of them said, they were each, to a man, proud and prideful and more deeply invested in her. Mikey was the coin of their realm, their Super Bowl trophy.

Val served them and stepped back, surveyed her perimeter, and began again to work her crescent of bar fly anesthesia, always with a twinkle, a big or small laugh as was warranted, a profane riposte and she was always, always watchful.

They took slow pulls on their drinks and looked off into a distant nowhere. Eddie said, while not looking at her, "So you really want me to tell you about it?"

"Yeah, I do. In case you hadn't noticed, I'm really am curious about you and also have a soft spot in my heart for high dressed rubes with town and country shoes who wander into this world of mine." She rolled her eyes and winked and sneered too, but just lightly. Turning toward him, she said, "Move over here and sit next to me, no need to be across from me on this corner; come sit next to me and talk to me."

He did and started, "Well..." and paused.

She said, "No false starts here. This is your chance. Let's see how straight and well you can do." And as she had asked, he told her about it.

"As you already know, I'm in a bad, rotting relationship with a gal back home, small city called Winston-Salem, tobacco and textiles and banks—lots of money there. She's a nice girl, a pretty girl, smart too but ever since we got together, got to living together it's just frayed and unraveled and she doesn't like me very much and I don't like her very much either."

Mikey asked, "Now, why is that?"

"I believe it's on both of us. She wants more than she's letting on and I want less of what she wants more of. Once it went from courting to keeping house, things started going south. I'm not sure, not at all sure, at this point in my ride, that I can be that interested. I know I sure do not want to be in this particular bucket at this particular time."

"What are you? What do you do? Are you a government cop, a private dick, some kind of company lawyer investigator? You said you met her while working a death case, hanging around a hospital. What's that all about?"

"I'm a lawyer, a trial lawyer, if we want to be fancy about it, we call ourselves 'litigators.'" He laughed, a genuine laugh. "You know a lot of people do not like lawyers at all. Some folks say that 'litigators' are actually 'licking gators,' always looking to finish the prey off but torturing it before they do."

She said, "Well, if the shoe fits."

"It was a murder case. I was representing the guy charged. They charged him with killing a guy but with the lift of a good autopsy, it turned out that three guys killed him and there were lots of different bullets in the stiff. So that's why I'm up in the forensic pathology-autopsy offices. Chill and drill we call it. Good times, but..." He switched directions back to the lighted way.

"Sure, sometimes people really put the stink on lawyers but not nearly as much as folks might spout as belief. There really is some renegade, some rebel in it for guys on my side of it, criminal and personal injury, and we do it to do two things: we do it to help people and we do it to make money or vice versa if you like. You know, the old which came first, the chicken or the egg."

"Fair enough. So you like your work and from the looks of you, you can cash a regular, good check. How'd you get in this line of work? And how in the hell did you get all the way out here in the southwest corner of nowhere?" He liked this girl. He knew she was a comet. He had no idea how long she'd carve a bright, hot path through the sky, but he was getting pretty sure he wanted to hitch a ride.

"Never had any intention of going to law school, never thought I'd graduate, damn near didn't, and never had any interest in practicing law but once I did, I never had any idea I'd end up in a courtroom, never imagined I'd be trying cases big, little, and in between before judges and juries, never thought for a minute I could be pretty good at it. But it all just happened and here I am." He shook his head considering the ridiculousness of it all. "And I love it and I'm good at it, really good at it and it frightens me."

Mikey nodded. "Well, seems to me you ought to stay scared."

"Right. That's the plan. But I'm working on something else too."

She looked at him curiously. "Well, if that ain't bait, I don't know what is. Before we go down that road, tell me, how did you end up in this tired-ass place?"

"Like I said, my gal pal deal turned into a nightmare. I know lots of success demands lots of attention and commitment, crowds out most everything else, which is fine. I had a law professor once tell all us greenhorns, 'The law is a jealous mistress.' We just sniggered and ignored him. Turns out he was right. She is a beautiful bitch and gets hold of you and will not let go. She comes first almost all the time."

"Why are you so interested in me, and you are, if you have problems being with a gal as opposed to a law book? I'm surely not looking to hang around here the rest of my life and I'm also not interested in playing one night stands this close to my current sandbox. You know, that old saying, 'Don't shit in your own mess kit.'"

"I sense you are cutting to the chase, at least one of them."

"You might be onto something."

The smoke and the noise and the babble and the voices and laughs and shrieks and hollers and gravel parking lot engines revving up and going low were continuous. It was the backdrop of a purple and red dusk.

"I'm interested in you because you're gorgeous. It's a good place to start. It surely is shallow but it's the best place to start. If I don't think you're physically good looking, then I have no interest to begin with. Make sense?"

"Yeah, but what if I ain't interested in return?"

"Fair. It takes two to tango. I think you're interested. Am I right?"

"Yeah, so far but let's not get carried away."

They both grinned. Val swept by, watching, nodding, and continued on her semi-circle circuit.

"Okay. Second. You seem to be interested in some, how might I say, adventure. No strings attached. No one is proposing, you know that old truth. When they started saying way back when 'till death do you part,' everyone was dead at forty-five." She laughed.

"I'm searching for a serious adventure, something with meat on the bone, something that calls for some risk as part of the investment. And so there's some scratch my back and I'll scratch yours."

"That might be true too." She looked away, then looked back, her eyes glowing just a bit. "Now hang on here a minute. How is it that you came to be out here and how deep is this going? What do you have in mind?"

They were leaning into each other now.

"Like I said, I've been getting stressed out and wound up and feeling like I would just blow up, blow out and I was getting bored too."

"With success, with money? Are you a little nuts?"

"Yes, I probably am, a little edgy, some high wire walking. Getting bored with the same old, same old, like eating rich food every day. But I'm a good guy. Really am." She nodded.

"Anyway, a few weeks ago I was taking a few drinks with some lawyer buddies to kick the end of the day off and we were all carping about how the work was closing in on us more than we liked, that we were getting uncomfortable and I knew I needed to get away and someone was talking about going out to Montana in the mountains and going trout fishing. I can promise you I don't care a lick about fishing. And that it was big and quiet and beautiful and there were not many folks around down near Wyoming and before Yellowstone and it started to gnaw on me that that kind of trip might help me clear my head.

"Last week I flew into Bozeman, rented a car, came this way southwest on the interstate, got off where it said this way to Twin Bridges, which reminded me of the weird old television show *Twin Peaks*, and drove along and found this place, the motor court, found this bar and here I sit and sometimes slump. I watch a lot of ESPN and old movies—I'm taking a multi-day pass on the news. Sick of the news. I like to drive around a lot, look at stuff. There's a lot of history here, gold, vigilantes, dinosaurs, spooky history of the orphanage down the road. Any of that make sense? I'm just a little addled these days. I haven't gone stupid or insane. I'm just trying to smooth out my flight pattern, maybe juice up the in-flight entertainment." He looked away, a little embarrassed, vulnerable.

She nodded slowly. He had just undressed his brain in front of her. Big time guy reduced to doubt and his confidence off the track.

"Makes sense enough." There was a hole of silence in the lively room.

"Now, hang on a second. I want to know about you. Please tell me."

She shook her head, not in dismissal but in that my-my-my way that signals, "This is unusual, strange and unusual, and engaging too." And so she told him about herself. She wanted to.

"I grew up all over the place. My daddy was an Air Force doc. We moved a lot. Have a younger brother and a sister. Brother I see every now and then. He lives in Nebraska. Not often. He does construction, I think. Sister is crazy as a mean loon, married to a doctor too. We aren't close. They're strange people. I really don't know where they are and don't care either. I don't want to be around them at all. My mom died when I was 19, cancer. I was just outta high school in Minot, up near the Canadian border in North Dakota. Big B-52 base. Tore my daddy up real bad. He loved her so big. I miss her too. Like I said, we were stationed all over the place. After my mom went, Daddy was transferred to Malmstrom AFB here in Montana next to Great Falls. It's about 200 miles north of here. Lots of missile silos..." she tailed off.

Eddie interrupted softly, "How old are you?"

She came back, laughed a little. "Now you Southern boys know better than to ask a lady her age. I've seen that in the movies!"

"Well, that's true but I mean no disrespect and think you're awfully pretty and sexy no matter your years. I'm just curious, not measuring, I promise."

She smiled, "I'm thirty-nine. You?"

"Fifty-one."

"Fair enough, neither one of us drawing Social Security. And we don't appear to be drooling on ourselves just yet." They both laughed.

"Well now, I don't know about that, fair to say, you could make a man drool! You do!"

She laughed and gave him a sweet shove. He rocked a foot away and rocked back to her. They were connecting. It just remained to be seen how far the extension cord would carry.

"Since we've established we're more rather than less age appropriate, please go on." He was serious. She understood.

"I stayed with him. No college for me. Wasn't interested in it to tell the truth. He maxed out there. I knew he was like an old sick dog, slipping out to the woods to lay down and die. He mustered out. I worked waitressing, dated guys here and there and found them all to be dull and duller, learned to do hair. He worked for a while in a free clinic but his heart wasn't in it. We had an apartment. I kept house, did a good job of it too, did it for him. He'd always been real good to Mom and me. He drank plenty but wasn't a drunk but it weakened him, softened him to where there was no starch left to him. I never fought him about it or scolded him. He finally just came on home and watched TV and drank and ate enough of my bad cooking to get by and had a heart attack in his chair one afternoon. Knew it, knew he was all gone when I heard his glass smash the floor."

Her pretty mouth wiggled in a sad corkscrew, and then he watched her eyes get wet. She sagged and then pulled her shoulders back. He reached to hold her hand. She let him for a few seconds, then squeezed and pulled hers back to her lap. She drew a deep breath, exhaled, then again. She shook her head, signaling she wasn't quite done with her story.

"Buried him up there. I drive up and see his grave from time to time. Mom's too but it's farther, you know. I get his military pension and got some life insurance too. He was generous enough with what little he gathered up. It occurred to me after the numb of his going that I thought I wanted some security, some companionship. I met a chopper jockey from the base. We got hitched. We were done in eight to nine months. He wanted a wife. I wanted a life.

"I wandered down this way about four years ago. Do hair over in Sheridan, like I said. Met some nice girls who don't bother me and a couple of them are good roommates in an apartment I've got over there and it helps with the money. I hang out over here a lot after work and on weekends. I know a lot of people good enough. It's enough fun and takes my mind off things. I walk a lot up in the hills. Keep myself in shape, keep myself looking as good as I can. For what it's worth, I'm really a nice person too.

"I've just been alone a long, long time. Probably gotten too used to it by now but what you gonna do?" She smiled gently, bravely. He was in awe. She had just pulled her deepest self out and showed it to him.

Val sallied by and eyed them, not as one but as a two. She nodded and watched their quiet. And then snapped them up with raucous, happy volume. "Okay, that's enough of this serious shit! It's a damn good night and it's a son of a bitchin' good night to take another drink! Y'all ready? Yes, you damn well are! So by God, let's get to it!"

They did and the jukebox got louder in their burning ears.

There was another pause, but it wasn't the "we are done here" gap. It was a prelude. Mikey asked, "Now what are you thinking about that's new and different and might make your boredom better?"

"You wanna dance?"

"Don't stall on me. Tell me. And I ain't kidding." Her face was happy and her eyes were steel serious. The needle on the jukebox laid down on Patsy Cline's "Crazy."

"I will. I promise. I will."

CHAPTER FIVE

RESCUE ME

Fontella Bass

FOUND ON THE front door of The Sump Bar in Sheridan, Montana:

> "Starting a fight or trying to cause trouble for someone in this bar will result in your being 86'd for a year. Bars in this town are becoming hard to find, so think about it!!!!"

They were tightly leaning on each other, feet hardly moving, imperceptibly swaying while all around them others truly did dance, step, slow twirl, step over as the dots of light from the silver moon ball spilled and cascaded all about them, all over them. If you watched the gleaming white spots swirling counterclockwise on the wooden, saw dusted floor, you would get dizzy even if you weren't drinking.

Neither spoke. Their eyes were closed and they were blind, blinded. A cocoon of silence had merged them into an obelisk of still. The twin lubricants of alcohol and hope had launched them up and over a very far away horizon. Moonshot to the heart. The place had gone reverentially quiet save for the music and the feet moving on their own.

The music stopped, the people stopped, some headed back to the bar, to their tables, and some stood in place waiting, a box 45 rpm was lifted away to its slot, a click, a whir encased in a blinking neon plastic shell, another click, the low grating of the needle going to work again, Johnny Cash loudly began to proclaim that he went down into a burning ring of fire. Some began to dance again, more vigorously, some with a hard edge to their shake.

Eddie and Mikey peeled back almost unstuck, awakened from the sweet drowsy, still holding hands. Eddie cleared his throat, Mikey coughed, looked down and back up. Time drifted by.

"Thank you for that nice dance. That was nice."

"No, thank you."

"Would you like to try another?" Eddie asked gently.

Mikey's eyes fluttered to alert, brightened.

"I've got an idea. Wanna hear it?" She looked at him bemused, inquisitive.

The music kept coming, now with some Waylon angry and sad. "Why, yes, sure, whatcha thinking?" He anticipated.

"First, why don't we go back over to the bar and finish our drinks."

"And then?"

"And visit a little more." He knew she was baiting him.

"And then say our goodnights and go on our way."

His face fell. "Oh, well, um, oh, okay, I was hoping."

She grinned, "Gotcha, silly! Let's go finish up. Get some to-gos. Pay up. You're paying, you know." And with a flourish, "Go on and get outta here. You okay with that?"

Eddie had swallowed the hook and was glad he was caught. "Sounds like a plan. Let's do it."

They went back to the bar, had some last sips and some desultory chit chat, knowing certain things. Val came by and said, "Another?" but there was no expectant oomph to her ask. She was, after all, the surveyor of all things at Chick's and had been for a long, long time.

She said, "Well, you two go have some fun and be safe out there. I'll get your ticket. Eddie T., you payin', right? You damn well better be!" Val laughed while she busied at the register. "You know, Mikey here ain't bought a drink for herself since the glaciers pulled back and also, just a thought, before y'all get going, I don't think it'd be such a bad idea if y'all didn't give each other a lockdown smooch before the door hits you both in the ass. It wouldn't hurt this bunch of want-her-to-be-theirs to see what a big finish looks like. You know they've all been watching and looking and dreaming, right? Seems like it's time for 'em to wake up and move on some." She pushed the ticket across the bar.

Mikey stared straight ahead, grinned softly, said, "Thank you, Val."

Eddie pulled out enough cash and then a good extra for Val, looked around to see who was watching them, discovered more than a few were, pursed his lips, processed and then thought, *Oh, what the hell! In for a penny, in for a pound.* Eddie reached over and put his arms around Mikey and said in his best Grade B romance movie husky voice, "Come here, baby." She did and tilted her beautiful no longer sad and lonely face up to his and they joined in a steaming, dripping, rolling lip-lock for the ages. If they had been engines, they would have redlined halfway through and seized up in the heat. They were having seizures all right, just the kind that kept twitching and surging. Then oxygen was required and they barely parted and just looked at each other.

Val started clapping and then Mikey's other gals joined in and then more of everybody kicked it up as happy hoots and hollers rose. Eddie took Mikey by the arm and turned to Val and bowed.

"Thank you, Val. I'll see you soon, hope tomorrow. Hope I'm here a little bit longer. You ready, Miss Mikey?" She happily nodded.

And then, as they were still turned toward Val, a big raw cowboy fellow with a yellowed mustache and jangling boots and a pistol on his hip grabbed Mikey's arm and jerked her hard away from Eddie.

She tried to pull back but he had a heavy hold on her upper arm. "Don! Don! What are you doing? Stop it, stop it, please!" Her eyes were filmed in fear.

People froze and gasped and mumbled out of the sides of their mouths. Eddie put his hands up in rapid calculation, watched and thought and decided quickly. Val was moving fast and low to the side bar back door as she slid her left hand under the counter.

The fellow Don violently swung Mikey around to face him, holding her ever tighter now with both big hands and exploded, his breath all beer and rye and bile, "Goddammit! What in the Sam Hill do you think you're doing? You think I ain't been watching this fuckin' cute little picture show? You leaving with this pussy boy? No, I don't think so. You ain't going nowhere, you whore bitch. I always knew it. Cheating on me, on us all! Leaving us, leaving here? What the fuck. Fuck that! I ought to knock the shit outta you." He raised his big right hand. "And I'm sure as shit gonna whip that city boy but good!" He turned and half-stepped toward Eddie while still glaring at Mikey, hanging onto his hostage who was mute with horrible fright.

He was red purple, shaking with rage. Gobs of drunk spittle followed his machine-gunned raging soliloquy. He indeed was a big, scary, imposing man. Things were going faster and faster.

But Eddie was not where he had been. He looked around and only saw Val marching down the curving edge of the bar toward him with a dead leveled over under sawed off 12-gauge scatter gun aimed at Don's crotch.

Val said without emotion, "Don, let her go. I ain't gonna say it again."

Don slowed to think this all through. Surely Val wasn't going to shoot her friend, her best customer.

And then Don must have heard very clearly a hard voice, "Pussy boy slick says fuck you!" He tried to turn to the voice but before Don could re-orient, Eddie full swung a bar stool hard into both of Don's back thighs and then clubbed him against his lower back. Don had just hung a fat curveball and Eddie powdered it. Don buckled and his knees slammed the floor. He involuntarily released Mikey who jumped back into the arms of her friends.

This wasn't going the way Don had figured it. He tried to rise, tried to find his holster, groped empty. Val was now on top of him, the gun an inch from Don's forehead. Don bent backwards, contorted like a failing gymnast on an Olympic beam. Don, his manhood and plan tattering, weakly kicked at Val. She crashed the barrel into his ear and kicked him hard in his shrinking balls with her big, square-toed boot. He groaned and curled fetal. Don decided it was in his best interest to stay still and listen to whatever was left of this night gone to shit.

"Don! Don! You dumb motherfucker! What in the damn hell fuck are you thinking?! Jesus Christ, she ain't your girlfriend much less your life, pard! Hell, I don't believe I've ever seen you say a word to her. What fucking fantasy land you been living in? You're done in here, done for motherfucking good. You fucking well understand me? Now, before I have your ass hauled out of here and hauled out for good, you are going to apologize to Mikey, you are going to tell her you are sorry for your very poor, very shitty conduct and then before you come up off the deck, you are also going to apologize to Mr. Eddie Terrell too. Do you understand me?"

The crowd was in a collective, stunned hush, still as dried paint save for the uncomfortable shuffling of feet. Understandably and weirdly, the jukebox kept on playing but it was muffled as though it had been pulled out into the parking lot.

Don at repose still retained a few last vestiges of anger, envy, jealousy, and combativeness. He shook his head in battered defiance.

"No, no, no I'm not."

Val tapped his nose with the barrel, then stepped on it grindingly hard and said, "Oh, yes you are and you are going to do it now or I'm calling the law and your ass is going to the jug for a long time. Miss Mikey has always acted like a by god lady in here and Mr. Eddie Terrell has always acted like a by damn gentleman. You have not. You get it?" Val was running steady hot, controlled but hot, and too Val had just hardmarked Mikey and Eddie as part of her nation. They were not to be messed with by anyone.

Don gave it up. He mumbled and drooled an insincere, "I'm sorry" in the vague general direction of his victims and his assailants and felt about for the sticky warm blood coming out of his nose and ear.

Val commanded, "Whoever of you stupid fuckers who still call this damn idiot your friend, get his sorry ass out of here and make sure he understands he is NEVER to come back in here again. He is damn sure fucking banned for life and if anyone in here ever tries to act like that in here again, it's just gonna be worse."

A couple of guys tentatively came forward. Val said, "Come on. Get to it. Now." And they hoisted him up and haul dragged Don out the door.

Val said, "Okay, everybody, that's it, fun's over, one round on the house, on me. Let's get back to what we do best." And the lights started to come back up.

CHAPTER SIX

ADVENTURE OF A LIFETIME

Coldplay

FOLKS WERE STARTING to mill about again. Someone turned up the jukebox and Charlie Daniels was sawing away on his fiddle belting out, "The Devil Went Down to Georgia." Some folks still looked at other folks in wonderment and curiosity, a few left, others started to dance, most headed to the bar where Val and her crew were pouring shots and cracking beers. It was a bazaar of swilling and hooking. The noise of the place was climbing back to normal.

Mikey stepped tentatively toward where Eddie stood, his chest heaving, sweating hard, his feet still batter's stance wide, still holding onto a lower leg of the bar stool, still sorting it out. It occurred to him that he had sure not choked up on that one. He'd taken a full cut. People were moving about and around him. It spun in his mind that she might simply be appalled and revulsed at this brawling, stupid mess. Don's blood stained the planks where he'd dripped and oozed.

He said, "You okay?"

She nodded, burrowed in under his shoulder and said, "Now, you really know how to show a girl something."

Relief was coming now, uncertainty dissipating and he replied, "Yeah?"

"Yeah." She looked up at him pleased.

"Damn, there still really is a Wild fucking West out here."

Eddie had her with him and they walked down to a far corner of the bar. Val saw them, came their way, wiping her arms and hands with a bar towel the size of a bath mat. Sweat was still pouring off her. She truly was a rock-solid tall block of a gal, grace under pressure, power in her sights.

Eddie said to Val, "Jesus. Damn! I want you in my foxhole every day. Thank you! Thank you a lot! That was some wild ass shit. Didn't know that was in the script. Thanks for having our backs." Mikey nodded vigorously, seconding the gratitude.

Val grinned, looked like business as usual for her. Eddie figured she had done this before. He wasn't wrong.

"Well, know y'all were trying to leave before and know you will before too long. But in the meantime how about one on the house from me?"

"Christ, Val, I ought to be buying this round in honor of you!"

"Nope, no way. Y'all are my guests in here and it's on me that that dumbshit got an off the wall case of the hot ass. I'm sorry. Should have seen something like that coming. Lot of these strong and silent types don't show much while the fuse burns down hidden under their hats and their boots. I just get used to them. Anyway, sorry all that went down. Glad everyone is okay. Now, a beer, a drink, a shot? What'll it be?"

"How about a shot of bourbon and a beer. Adrenaline still running up pretty good."

"Coming right up. Think double shot for you, Eddie. By the way, I may have helped put the hard bridle on him, but, damn, city slick pussy boy!" She winked wide. "You put his ass dirt down! Helluva strong move. You clobbered him! And by damn, the son of a bitch fucking had it coming! Good damn work!" She was a thesaurus of profane combinations. She was happy. She was just a great lady. The good guys had won.

It was obvious that Mikey was in a complete state of Eddie Thrall. Her new friend had just gone postal Sir Galahad all over that leering creep Don and he had done it for her. It had made TV and the movies look like ten cents waiting for change. Her cells were cascading to him, for him. If it had been visible to the eye, Eddie would have been drowning in fluttering little hearts. Her gaze was luscious.

Eddie tossed his big jigger back. "Y'all surely know. Don't you? I was scared shitless. I dunno. I knew I had to do something so whatever it was, I guess I did. I'm still pretty shaky. Val, you were the champ!"

Val said, "How about this? We all did just fine, just good and fine. Now, let's keep on keeping on."

"Val, I thank you again." He looked at Mikey, she nodded and he said, "Now I think we ought to be going. You know it's a long walk across the way to Unit 4." He winked.

Val said, stringing it out in good humor, "Oh yeaaaaah. That damn fleabag Unit 4 must be, what, twenty yards across that crappy dirt path out there." She laughed. "Come see me tomorrow. I know you're going on, going away soon. You're looking a little scruffed up, but a whole lot better now. Looks to me like your 'damn woe is me, I'm so unhappy' is lifted. Never, never ever buy into that bullshit! You're too damn good for all that crap. Hope you'll come give me a damn big hug and a damn good goodbye before you scram."

"I will. We will. Hope the rest of your night is okay. How about ya let me buy a bottle of Bulleit to go, please? Please keep the change." He quietly laid a fifty on the bar.

She handed the jug of bourbon to him. They were comrades at arms now. "Thanks. Good. I'll be looking for you two. Don't worry. It will be fine here. After what just happened, probably a whole lot better than fine for a good while to come."

They moved toward the door which opened up overlooking Highway 287, Sheridan and Twin Bridges to the north, Virginia City and Ennis to the south, all tiny in the string of pearls that rode along the way to Wyoming.

Eddie asked, "Where's your car?"

"Parked over there. Where you wanna go? I'd say my apartment, but my roommates are there." Her voice tailed off.

"I wasn't so much thinking that. As you have already heard, I'm the resident in charge at the moment of the just good enough Unit 4 here at Chick's Motor Court. I offer clean sheets, hot water, lots of towels, Direct TV, and thoughts and conversation about risks and rewards and about new ideas and adventure and a story of evolving identity. Might you please accept my offer?"

"Yes, I believe I will. Thank you. Which way do I go?"

As he took her arm, he whispered, "Which way do we go?" He saw her smile in the dark. She knew he had winked.

CHAPTER SEVEN

MOON RIVER

Jerry Butler

MIKEY WAS PERCHED up on the bed. The blankets were fresh, the sheets crisp, the room spotless, and there really was a TV set and a remote. It wasn't the Ritz but it was clean and plenty nice enough. Eddie came back with two motel glasses, each a third full of good bourbon and handed her one. They clinked a toast and drank a good swallow.

She said to him, "Jesus, Eddie, what a night! Thank you for laying that jerk out. You really are a brave and effective man. Don't think I'm not paying attention! I don't know what's come over me but my best guess is it's you. I've always been one to follow a good instinct, not always for the best I know." She grimaced and went on. "But something's going on here and as you can tell, I'd like to chase whatever it is. I think that's okay with you. I hope?"

"Yes, Miss Mikey, yes it is."

She smiled and her eyes were again sharp with the antennae up. "Well, before we fall into this bed and, if it's all right with you, wrestle a good bit, and I don't see you complaining, what's the new idea? What's the adventure?"

"I like the way you think and I think I know things, but please let me tell you two quick stories and then I want to talk to you about what I'm thinking and see if you'd like to come along."

"I'm all ears."

"Story Number One. And, by the way, so help me, they are both true. Not so many years ago, I went to the Kentucky Derby for three or four days of some of the best fun I've ever had. And among the many very interesting things I saw and did, there was one very specific moment that has stayed with me, something that I have thought about a lot and more and more these days."

"Excuse me. May I ask a few questions along the way?"

"Sure. Of course."

"Don't get me wrong. Not trying to mess up your story. Just trying to get, what do they call it, a perspective, a context?"

"I do. I understand. Now, it was at the end of the third day, ever bigger days as they came along like in a great, wonderful parade, Derby Day, the famous and incredible Kentucky Derby had just been run, 150,000 folks all dressed up and hatted up, men and women shouting and screaming at the top of their lungs, drinking and partying and betting and betting some more. Millions of dollars. And of course, in the rain and the mud and thunderous noise, a horse had won.

"And then that horse, the damn winner of the biggest horse race of all, got disqualified. Punted to the curb. All the betting tickets on him went 'poof!' Up in smoke. They weren't worth anything now, zip zilch zed nada—nothing! People were confused, mad, dismayed. You name it. It hadn't happened in almost a hundred and fifty years."

Mikey held up her hand. He paused. She asked, "Um, now who were you with? The Lee Ann gal or someone else? Just trying to get the picture."

"Sure, it was Lee Ann back in the better days. All she was into then was her looks, having a good time, and basically hitching a nice ride with me, which was fine."

"Did you have any money on the horse that got disqualified?"

"Yes, but it wasn't enough to cause me to have a sweat. And since that horse got disqualified, every other horse got moved up a notch and I did have a ticket on one that won me some third place money so it cut my loss."

"And then?"

"Anyway, we were leaving the track and the rain had stopped and we were in the shuttle bus line so we could be hauled back to where our driver was off the track premises. We were next to this nice, well-dressed couple and started shooting the breeze with them and noticed that she was happy, real happy, almost giddy and trying to keep it under wraps and he was pretty glum, pleasant but glum. And so we asked them what the deal was." He paused to set the lure.

"Well, go on now."

"He told us that they had been there for the last three days of racing, that they had not made any bets until it was time for the eleventh race on that Saturday, that they had decided before they got there they would just enjoy the racing and the food and drink and the spectacle of it all, but then they were betting the Derby. He had just put $5,000 on Maximum Security, the big favorite in the field of 15 horses. Maximum Security was the winner that was DQ'd. He had planned it for weeks and it all went up in smoke. He was downcast."

"What about her, his wife?" Eddie watched her carefully as she listened intently to him.

"The wife had bet her kitty of a thousand dollars on a big longshot, a horse nobody thought could win it even if he ran alone. And it was that horse that ended up second and then became the winner when Maximum Security got tossed out. You know why she bet him?"

"No."

She said she had always wanted to have a home in the country. So, she bet on a horse named 'Country Home.' And, man, did she hit it big. He paid 66 to one so her thousand grand turned into 66 grand."

Her eyes got big and she squealed in delight and exclaimed, "Now that's a great story and a great bet! I guess they can go get a good start on that house in the country! Wouldn't that be a fun thing to pull off!!"

"Mikey, that lady took quite a risk, didn't she?"

"Sure. Sure she did, but she was willing to take it so more credit to her. It would be fun to chase that kind of bet down."

"You don't mind taking some risk sometimes?"

"I guess not." She was happy with that story.

"You know, some risks don't work out, right?"

"Sure, yes, but if you don't sit down at the table, you never get a chance to play. My dad taught me that. Might have something to do with me tumbleweeding here and there."

"Fair enough."

"Why did you tell me that cool story?

"I wanted to see your reaction to a big, blind risk taking. I wanted to see if it worried you or if you thought it was improbable or if you dismissed it. And you didn't, which pleases me."

"Why?"

"I'm getting a sense of your comfort level for risk. Looks pretty good to me."

She was pleased. "Does this have something to do with your new idea, new adventure?"

"Yes. Hang on. Now, here's another story, just one more." She was attentive.

"Once, a long time ago, when I was in law school, I went to a local night club, a juke joint, met some friends, had some beers, and listened to the band play. It was called The Bitter End, which is funny because the real deal is up in New York City and is legendary and has been around since the 1960s and this place was just a wing and a prayer joint. The band was pretty good and had a very cute girl singer. The girl singer and I chatted during the breaks and decided to meet up out in the parking lot around midnight after her last set was done. And we did. Turned out she had a boyfriend who didn't like that so much who took a swing at me and missed."

"Hmmmm...seems like that kind of crap is always going around...huh? No answer necessary."

"My friends were right behind me. Then the guy pulled a knife and slashed at me. Got me a little above my wrist. I was pissed. The girl was screaming. I was standing outside my car with the driver's side door open. I stepped outside the door-car gap, grabbed him, and put him in the gap and then slammed the door on him. School was out and he was lying on the ground moaning. One of my friends said to the guy, "You shouldn't mess with Ed."

The guy mumbled, "Ed who?"

My friend said, "Ed Podolak. You know he plays for the Kansas City Chiefs."

The guy said, "No shit?"

My friend said, "No shit."

"Jesus, I just got smoked by an NFL star. Oh shit, I cut you too. Oh man, I'm sorry!"

"No problem, son. It's just a scratch. But I think you might be moving on now. I'll get the young lady on home."

Mikey asked, "Did you even know her name?"

"Nope. She did think I was a pro football player, but I told her that wasn't me. She was cool with that. She did tell me her name. I've long since forgotten it."

"Then what happened?"

"Guy took off. Thing was bleeding pretty good. Wrapped it with my shirt. She drove me to the emergency room in my car. Got some stitches. Drove me home. She spent the night. Nothing happened. I didn't feel so swell. I took her home. She not only sang in that band whatever it was, but she was also a teller at the main branch of Wachovia bank in my hometown of Winston-Salem. Know what's funny?"

"No, what? And then you gonna tell me what the lesson is here?"

"Yep. Here's what's funny. It was to me, maybe not so much to her. I remember this happened on a Friday night. I went down to the bank on Monday morning to see her, see if we could renew our acquaintance, if you know what I mean."

"Oh, yeah, I bet."

"Got down there and asked for her. They told me she'd been fired that morning. She's gotten caught with her fingers in her teller drawer. End of story. Decided right quick she was a bad bet, leave that one alone."

"Okay, lots of betting going on here. Do you think I'm a good bet and what's the point of this one?"

"I guess it's kind of silly but do you think you can pretend to be someone else sometimes, maybe for just a little while, maybe sometimes longer?"

Without hesitation, she answered. "Sure. I do it all the time. Been doing it for years and years. Been doing it as long as I've been going into Chick's. When I need to be Plain Jane, I am plain as can be. When I need to be Queen of the Ball, it's like throwing a light switch. I can be quiet, loud, chatty, silent, strong, weak, rube, brainy—you name it. I'm a chameleon. It's an excellent survival skill and it's fun too. Lots of time you get to watch yourself from the outside looking in and measure how you're doing. Sometimes I just get lost in doing it. Why are you asking me this one?"

"If we're going to undertake an adventure, using a new idea or two, I may, let me repeat, I may need you to do some role playing, some being somebody else."

She had been still on the bed, listening to him attentively and now, she leaned across and got up real near him and in a low voice, and said, "It's getting late now and I think it's time you told me what you've got in mind." She tilted her head and waited.

"Yes, I think you aren't afraid of risk, sometimes, maybe big risk. I think you're smart. I think you're an actress and I think you're up for something new, like we've said, an adventure. You want to help us and some others, as of right now not sure who all of them might be, but maybe make some good money? It'll have to be a one shot, one-time deal."

She leaned back from him, narrowed her thinking eyes and said, "Yes! This is something illegal, isn't it?"

"Yes, that's why it's gotta be a one-shot play."

"Are we stealing something? And why do you, an obviously successful and well-off lawyer, want to do something like this whatever it is? What about your law license? You could lose it, right? I guess at this level we're sneaking up on, what about prison? That worry you?"

"Sure, I've thought about getting busted but I've got a few things that might help soften the blow. Not that it's coming. So please don't dwell. Please don't. I've been a good boy for many years, I am well-respected and have lots of high-ranking lawyers and many, many judges who would say, "This is an aberration, this is out of character, this is a one-time mistake and this is not who he is." I have many wealthy, influential friends who would stand up for me. Besides, I know some things about them too." He winked.

"I hold the highest ratings for legal skills and ethics that can be given. They call it an A/V rating and have for a very long time. I have been very, very generous to so many local charities for years and years and I have never been an ugly, screeching political partisan. I have a many good friends on both sides of the political aisles. And I suppose it's fair to consider that if I get my ass in a crack, I've got plenty of resources to hire and retain the very best lawyers who will fight and motion and attrition and stall the prosecutors out and finally, if push comes to shove and I need to draw an ace or two, there will be folks I can roll over on and buy myself more leniency. Remember, even on a temporary basis, there is damn little honor among thieves.

"And no, we're not stealing anything. We, if we can get the few right pieces in place, are going into sales. And why? Honey, I'm bored. I want to see if I can do it. I want to see if I can organize it and pull it off. I want to see if I can score. The potential of it excites me. I want to make a good pile of money and then tuck it away, just to tuck it away. It's just a lot of stuff and it's been bubbling in my head for a good while now. It's become an itch I want to try and scratch."

"So what is it? Don't worry. And sounds to me based upon your game plan, you're hunting a cushy probation at worse. I'm in. Remember, I know how to play dumb too. And I ain't got any law license to lose either."

"Cocaine."

"White line fever, eh? Wow! Did not see that one coming. How you gonna try to do this?"

"I'll tell you tomorrow. I promise. Now, just between you and me, let's cook on it over the night. I'm doing it this way so we will have some thinking time. I have ideas. You are the only person I have ever said anything about this to."

She was quiet for a minute or so. He did nothing to interrupt her or query her. "So now, I need to do some role playing here."

"What do you mean? How so?" Eddie was a little puzzled.

"You see, I now have to turn off my curious, now criminally, oriented brain and turn on my I-am-going-to-vamp-and-hump-and-rump-you into next week brain and I only have a few hours to open the bidding!"

Eddie was excited. He said, "How are you going to do that?"

"First, go over there and turn those two lights off. Then, lose your clothes. Then get in this bed, not on it, in it."

"What about you?"

"Honey, you got a little work left to do." She happily leered at him.

He did as he was told.

CHAPTER EIGHT

JET AIRLINER

Steve Miller Band

THEY CAME OUT of their sound sleep to one-eye watch the other for a little while and then sat up, all tousled and disarrayed, and started playing pinch and play and got back after it one more good time and then both looked at the ceiling. It was almost 9 a.m.

Mikey laughed, "It's 'tell the plan time!'"

"Yes, it is. You think you still good to go?"

"Yes, I am. Don't worry. Yes, I am. It's gonna be an adventure, right?" She was cheerful.

"Yes, if I can get this thing wired together right, it is gonna be an adventure but you gotta remember, it's gonna be a serious adventure and you have to keep that in mind at all times and be aware, be careful, be cautious. Okay?"

"Yes, okay."

"I got a good working model in my head but as you hear what comes out of my mouth, you'll see it needs work. One of the most important pieces is I want to involve as few people as possible but I'm gonna have to involve some folks, that is, if they want to play. And some are gonna have to pay to play. So that entails money commitments and some folks still always want something for nothing. An old friend of mine once taught me a great lesson. Back home, he owns a wonderful sort-of general store for fine fashion and gifts. He's always been an independent. No Belk's or Nordstrom's for him."

"What's Belk's?"

"Family department stores back in the Carolinas and Virginia, run by the Belk family. A southeastern sort of Nordstrom's."

"Oh."

"My friend told me this once. Think about it. 'You cannot sell off an empty cart.' It's an old Armenian proverb."

"Makes sense, you gotta have something to sell. So you gotta have coke or solid and quick access to coke, right?"

"Right. So arrangements as to that need to be made. And as importantly as the little bit of thinking is that I've just touched on, whoever is involved has got to be able to keep his mouth shut and I mean all the time, all the time."

"Sure, secrecy, mum's the word. Got that."

"I want to put this together pretty quickly and execute it pretty quickly, keep loose ends and finish lines from dangling about out there. No need to make a trail that is long enough to follow. Now, are you really ready to roll?"

"Yes, sir! But first a question, please."

"Shoot."

"Where is the Lee Ann gal in all of this?"

"She's not. We parted company before I came this way."

"You sure?"

"Yes, Yes. I promise. Okay, let's make a little plan that will hopefully take us to the bigger plan. Let's get cleaned up and go find coffee. Then maybe drive around and just look at stuff and think and then over to Ennis and grab a good lunch at the Gravel Bar. We'll keep working on the plan. Talking it through. Let me make a few phone calls back home way before we set off today. You'll need to go to your place and grab some jeans and clothes and your lady stuff. Don't worry if you're short on something. I'll make sure you got what you need. Let's check outta here tomorrow first thing and I'll line up our plane tickets out of Bozeman so we're ready to go. I think we need to go see Val this evening and say our proper goodbyes and maybe grab a good steak and some drinks at the bar. God knows she saved our asses big time!"

"Sounds good. Let's find the coffee and then I'll head to my place to pack. That way, you can do your calls and I'll get right back on over here.

I'll leave my roomies a note saying I'm going on a trip and I'm not sure when I'll be back. I'm not on the lease. I'll tell them they ought to go right ahead and find my replacement. They'll be fine."

They began to move, to really wake up, fast loaded thick caffeine from Chick's breakfast bar and soon Mikey was on her way to pack a sack and leave a note for her roomies while Eddie was on his phone.

First call was to Delta. He rounded up two first class tickets to Atlanta for tomorrow and then onto Greensboro the next day. He called a friend who got him two good box seats to see the Braves play. It was a late afternoon tilt against the Dodgers. He loved baseball. A good baseball game had all the good angles of a good case. He made a late post-game reservation at Pano and Paul's—might as well get the pretty girl some wonderful fried lobster tails and a few glasses of champagne. He reserved a hotel room on the concierge level at the Ritz Carlton in Buckhead. He then called Patty back.

"Hey."

"You've been gone so long. What is it now, a week or so?"

"Yeah, yeah. I'm on the comeback trail. Feeling a lot better. Flying out of Bozeman in the morning. Going to Atlanta tomorrow to watch the Braves play. Staying at the Ritz, thought I'd give myself a cushy treat. Then home to get squared away and get back after it. How about get ahold of Rise and see if they can round up their friend Curt Minor and get the two of them to come see me in a couple of days? Let's do it on Thursday afternoon after lunch. No, let's make it lunch and beer. Find out from Rise what everybody likes."

"I can get that done, I think. What else? I want some serious sit-down time with you ASAP to go over these cases that are pressing."

"Of course." He knew that he needed to go ahead and get some heavy good money because if his plan flew and crashed, he was gonna need it bad. "How's Lee Ann been doing with that credit card by the way?"

"Not too bad. A good sign, I think. Made a deposit on an apartment over at College Village. Also, besides gas, food and such, she's been at The Village Tavern and Shobers every night. So she's moving on it looks like. She never struck me as the type who would let the grass grow under her feet. Her tabs aren't very high at all even though they're time stamped almost always around midnight. My guess is she got guys filling her glass regular. Looks like it didn't take her long to re-set her compass."

"Good. My feelings are hurt that she's moving on so quickly. Not really. How about drive by the house a couple of times tomorrow and make sure she's gone?"

"Will do. I understand. And what if she is there?"

"Go in and tell her I'm on the way back and her time is up."

"Got it."

"And, Patty, by the way, I'm bringing someone back with me." He waited.

"Oh, Christ! You are a fucking mess! This ought to be rich. Jesus! I can't wait to make her brief acquaintance. Bring her on and let's get back to work!"

"Yes, ma'am! I think you'll like her. I really do."

"Eddie, shut up, you always think I'll like her whoever her is. Get a move on! Goodbye." Click.

CHAPTER NINE

LEAVING HERE

Eddie Holland

MIKEY DROVE BACK to Chick's and tapped the door. She held a small bag and a light coat over her arm. "I'm ready."

"Me too. What you gonna do about your car?"

"Left the keys under the mat. Shannon or Debbie will come get it and take it back to the apartment."

"Good. Let's go spend a day and unwind it some more."

They drove around for a good while, looked at the incredible Montana scenery for a last time, maybe a last time, the mammoth mountains that surrounded them, the valleys that stretched out so very far and they talked and talked some more, dwarfs in a landscape that swallowed them. They were anonymous. They talked about politics, sex, religion, their lives, sports—of which she knew little, of which he knew a lot—books and reading which they both loved, his expansive love of his university in a little town called Chapel Hill, and her love of curiosity.

They drove into Ennis, a little town big on fishing. Neither of them liked to fish, but the place was picturesque and nice to visit with some good spots. She liked the Gravel Bar, so they grabbed two stools at the bar, ordered lunch and beers.

And they settled in. Mikey asked, "Anymore plan details?"

"Yes. Tell me what you think. Jesus, I am trusting you."

"Yes, you are. And I'm trusting you. Hell, I'm running off with you to God only knows where in Carolina to lay witness to a scheme that most folks wouldn't exactly be approving of."

They looked at each other and involuntarily grinned. They were in pretty good shape. "Fair enough. Well put. Here's what I'm thinking. Today is Tuesday. We're going to fly to Atlanta tomorrow and have a nice time there, do a few things, then on to Winston-Salem the next day. Gotta fly into Greensboro which is the regional airport. My car's there. We'll go back to the house, throw our stuff on the floor and head back to my office for a meeting we need to have."

The bartender brought their food, a cheeseburger for him and a taco salad for her. They got another round of beers. There were TV sets everywhere, all muted with sports and game shows and CNN blinking above them, moving bodies and squealing hopefuls and talking heads all running on silently. The jukebox played and the folks in the place just gave it a calm that Chick's could never have. She put down her fork. "Tell me about this meeting, please."

"Years ago, remember I told you I represented a gal, her name is Rise, on some federal charges, stealing people's Social Security checks. Yes, I know that's not a nice thing to do but she wasn't shooting or cutting anybody and I came to find out along the way that she was really smart, really nice, and I found I could trust her. Did all right by her. And because I did do pretty good for her, later on, when her little brother got charged with a serious crime, a homicide, she called me and I represented him too. His name is Kenny, and I did a really good job for him as well and I got to know him and liked him too. He's not anywhere near as smart as his sister, but he's a hard worker and gets things done when given straightforward instructions. He's also, from the for-what-it's-worth department, as big and broad as a house and I ain't kidding. He's a sweet fellow. And the guy Rise hangs with, dates, partners with—whatever the word of the day on being together is—he's a big, strong, sometimes mean, sometimes not a very good guy named Ben. Strong, silent type. He's smart and can be testy mean too.

She asked teasingly, "Now, what words would describe us, Eddie?"

"How about 'birds of a feather?' And then there's Curt Minor. Mr. Minor owns an indeterminate number of illegal places that sell illegal goods in illegal parts of the night, illegally pays no taxes, and has for many years, been really good at the illegal things in life. He has, I presume, many similarly situated illegally-oriented colleagues and acquaintances. If one were to think that Rise's Ben is the strong, silent type, then it would fair to say that Mr. Minor is a virtual mute most of the time."

"Are all these people coming to the meeting on Thursday?"

"Just Rise and Curt. Also, my legal assistant Patty will be there and you will too, if you want to be. I think everybody ought to be with everyone from the get-go."

"You sure?"

"Yeah. The plan kinda goes like this: Rise and Curt know a kid, well, Kenny does too, who helped Curt out with some stuff a while back. Curt was pleased with his work and so after the deeds were done and before the shit was going to hit the fan, to get him away from cop scrutiny and to get him better, higher-level trained up, Curt sent him to northwest Baltimore where he's been for a few years. From what little I know about him, I strongly suspect that he is very hooked up, has gained greater survival and effective business instincts and has been involved in all sorts of dealings that I am hoping will assist us in getting access to the inventory we need. That's why I need these people to come to the meeting. If that's the case, then we just gotta figure it out, how to get our hands on the stuff, how to get it from there to here, how to finance it and how to get it distributed, then get our money and call it a day. I'm thinking there is going to be some traveling up to Charm City soon."

Eddie turned and looked at Mikey who was still picking at her taco salad. "Uhm, you know this is pretty good...beer is good too...what's it called?"

"HayBag. Hey, you hay bag, you been listening to anything I been saying?"

She grinned at him. "Every fucking word. Sounds good, so far. What's next? And what's Charm City?"

"Good. Charm City is Baltimore. These days a very big irony as most of Charm City is anything but. Lots of drugs, corruption, incompetence, homicide, crookedness. That's where we find our dope, I hope. As the great bank robber Willie Sutton said when asked why he robbed banks, 'Well, sir, that's where the money is.' Let's go back, let me pile my stuff together, we got an early flight tomorrow. Let's go see Val—I think she's working at The Sump this evening and say our thank-yous and go get some sleep and get ready to hit the road."

As they walked out, Mikey said to no one in particular, "Jesus, this ought to be some kind of meeting."

The Sump was in nice, sweet little Sheridan, sequestered away in the basement of an old, fleabag hotel that was said by many to be haunted. One look at the place would not defy the theory. It seemed to lean drunkenly, almost swaying, though that was probably the result of the dip stick condition of her flat-eyed patrons. The window frames were crookedly off center, the paint peeled, gutters rusted. It wasn't just old; it was old and rotting away. The door to The Sump was bracketed by sand cans full of stinking cigarette butts where stacked and lined rows of glass and can empties spread across a cinderblock retaining wall. Its purpose and utility to the community was basic and consistent. People, mostly men, mostly hard-bitten, came there to drink fast and hard, heads bowed down in thought or blur, lingering only long enough to get the job done. It wasn't without its laughter and moments and times of jokes and good humor, but it was as though her patrons understood what the primary task at hand was. They firmly exercised that prerogative.

The bar was narrow, almost like a tight-squared edged submarine. Booze and bumper stickers ('If I wanted to listen to an asshole, I'd fart"; "I'm not a gynecologist but I'm happy to take a look") lived above the pool table mostly used for something to lean against. Twenty tattered, red Naugahyde stools lined the battered wooden bar where the patrons ate burgers of superior quality, always fresh Montana beef, alongside their beers. Coolers, a grill, and microwave were parked in the far back corner. Someone always fed the big play jukebox, an impressive piece of current technology considering the rest of its tired surroundings, dollar bill after dollar bill.

When Eddie and Mikey walked in, the place was half full with folks coming and going with Val in the center, leaning over in conversation with a nodding, slumping cowboy. She kindly patted his hatted head, looked around, saw her visitors and smiled, almost sweetly.

"Hey there. I'm figuring y'all are coming in to tell me goodbye?" She winked and made a funny face.

Eddie said, "Yeah, we gotta get moving. New adventures rising up back in Carolina and fair to say, don't want to be late for the train. We're flying out of Bozeman first thing in the morning. Just came by to tip our hats, thank you so much for everything."

Val nodded and asked, "Mikey, I take it you're on the train too?"

"Yes, I am. Yes, I am."

Val looked at them knowingly, "Well, by damn, good damn luck to you both! This is a helluva lot more interesting whatever it is than most of these old tired dogs in here and I can't wait to hear about it all."

A dusty brown head covered in a slouch hat sitting a couple of stools down slightly raised its hackles. "Tired old dogs? You're damn right. And, Val, you're running our tide toward old and tired and to the dogs. Fuck you." He spoke with the chuckle of experience.

"Fuck you back, Johnson."

"I know y'all don't want to linger, but how about one good big shot to finish us all off?"

Mikey said, "Absolutely, thank you." Eddie nodded.

Val laid out three good-sized jiggers, filling them full with Jameson. Val held up her big left hand for their benediction. "Well, hell, it's good Irish whiskey so let's finish these last few days off like this, 'May you have enough happiness to keep you sweet, enough trials to keep you strong, enough sorrow to keep you human, enough hope to keep you happy, enough failure to keep you humble, enough success to keep you eager, enough friends to give you comfort, enough faith and courage in yourself to banish sadness, enough wealth to meet your needs and one thing more: enough determination to make each day a more wonderful day than the one before.'"

Eddie and Mikey watched and listened in rapt attention. This was Val?

Val bowed her head slightly, muttered a quick "amen" and fired the whiskey down her gullet. Her communicants followed in fulsome appreciation.

"Surprised you, didn't it? It always surprises me, but I did go to a lot of church as a little girl and a lot of it stuck with me. I just cuss a lot." It was impossible not to laugh. "Okay, you two. Now, off with you!" She reached across the bar and they all bear hugged.

Eddie said, "Thank you again for everything! We'll be back."

Val winked and said, "Well, we'll see. It's been a trip. You be safe. Now, go!" They went on. Some of the bar flies watched them go. Most didn't bother.

Earlier that evening way across the country, Patty decided she'd go run a check at Eddie's house. If Lee Ann Jepson was still there, she'd have to run her off. It would be better to have a small shit show now as opposed to a later, larger one to finish this testy, heart string business.

Patty pulled out from downtown, ran out past the university campus and finally circled down a shaded street to pull into Eddie's drive. The weather was gray and gloomy. There was a black Pontiac Fiero, Lee Ann's car, in the drive and there were a few lights on toward the back of the house. Patty thought, *Damn, this ain't so good. But, what the hell. Let's get on with it.* She parked on the street.

She had a set of keys to the house but when she approached the front door, she found it to be cracked open. She went on in, switched on the overhead front hall light and called, "Hello? Lee Ann? You in here?" From the darkened living room just off the front hall, a quiet voice came out of the shadows.

"Hey, Patty. It's me. I'm here. I'm about to go on and leave for good. He's headed on back, isn't he? Otherwise, you wouldn't be checking over here. I just came by to get the rest of my things and to have a one last time look around and well, have a pity party too."

Patty walked in the room and turned on a table light. Lee Ann was sitting in a high-backed chair next to the fireplace, two large suitcases at her feet. She had on jeans and a western blouse. The irony of her wardrobe selection was not lost on Patty. She looked, as she always did, very pretty. Lee Ann's eyes were wet. She tried not to wipe at them.

"Lee Ann, I'm sorry it didn't work out between y'all." Patty knelt down in front of her. Patty was tough as dirt but she had a good heart and could see that Lee Ann was hurting. "You know, Lee Ann, he's a rascal and you can't change his stripes. I know you had hoped to make it, make something work, but obviously..."

Lee Ann exhaled and sighed and nodded. "Oh, he is a sorry son of a bitch at times but I'm gonna miss him and it's best that it's done while I've still got some time and I'm just gonna have to get over him, get over this and keep moving."

Patty nodded and stood up. It was a good time to end this meeting.

"Lee Ann, can I help you with your things?"

"Yes, thank you. I appreciate that. If you could carry one out, that would help. Wait, I need to turn a few lights off."

"Don't worry. I'll take care of those once you've gone."

Patty could see Lee Ann sagged just a little more inside. Patty held the door open and they trudged the big suitcases to the little sports car. There was no other way but to trudge. Lee Ann had packed for life and the detritus of those plans now weighed heavily in their reverse.

It took some wedging and hawing to cram the two bags in with the rest of whatever else: folding chairs, makeup bags, mini-coolers, empty Starbucks cups, beach towels in the alleged carry area behind the front buckets. Patty stood up and paused. Lee Ann came toward her cautiously with her hand extended.

"Patty, thank you for your help." Patty took her hand as Lee Ann continued to speak, measuring out her words.

"Please tell Eddie I really appreciate the credit card. Tell him I haven't been and won't be wasteful with it. It is helping me get back on with my life." She hesitated. "I need to find a man, you know what I mean. I've got to get settled. That's just how it is. I've thought about it a lot. I think I'd like to have some babies." She was wistful, looking away, nose twitching.

Patty just watched and slowly nodded and she did understand the universal stereotype because it was so for so many. Lee Ann, the Beautiful Drama Queen, morphing into an unsure, frightened little girl. It was touching. Patty was also not stupid enough to believe in the permanence of these temporal heartfelt moments.

"Patty, thank you for being so nice to me all this time. I'm sure my pain-in-the-ass moments were enough to make you pull your hair out. I suppose I've got a lot of growing up left to do. Anyway, thank you." And she squeezed her hands and turned to get into the tiny driver's side seat.

Patty called to her, "Thanks, kid. I expect we all still have plenty of growing up to do if we can just get there. Take care of yourself. Be safe."

Lee Ann shut the door, cranked the engine, waved as she backed out of the drive and was gone in a little, rushed roar.

Patty watched her taillights disappear over the rise and then reappear as the car climbed up out to Polo Road and turned on out. She assembled a couple of her thoughts, reassembled them. Having babies wouldn't make life all better. Patty walked into the house and started turning lights off in the dark quiet of the night coming on.

CHAPTER TEN

KING OF WISHFUL THINKING

Go West

VAL WAS WORKING the lunch-to-six shift at The Sump with Mr. Ford on hand to be ready when the traffic would start to pick up later. He actually didn't have to come on to work until 4 p.m. but he liked the place better than his crapped-out mobile home. The Direct TV was a whole lot better than his ancient roof antennae and like all true connoisseurs of bar caves, he was more comfortable, more at home at The Sump than anywhere else. Val was flipping burgers, frying rings, popping caps, pouring shots, giving advice, and shooting the breeze, only if they wanted to, with whoever was on the line. From time to time, it got nice and slow so Val could slide outside and grab a smoke and then could slip back inside and have a drink of something mellowing like an ice cubed Sambuca or a simple shot of J.

Her old friend Minnie slow sauntered in, crisp burgundy pantsuit, hair done to fried bleach, cigarettes in a leatherette holder with an outside notch for her Bic. She hoisted her erect, petite frailty up on a stool and sighed with the effort. She was gnarled old, ribald, and dignified. Never without her perfectly manicured nails and as good a pair of shoes as she could claw out the confusion of her closet, Minnie was legendary for her staying power, her longevity, and her constancy, all of which battered her but good every next day but never dissuaded her to relent. She had been run hard and hung up wet decades ago but it mattered not. Everyone knew as did she that only when she achieved room temperature would she give it up and then, so what, as she was then someone else's problem.

Val came around and took the stool across the corner of the bar from Minnie.

"Hey, honey, how you doing today?"

"Not worth a shit. Feel like I got run down by the 806 to Denver and then the goddamn thing backed up and hammered me again."

"Oh, I'm sorry. Can I get you some aspirins?"

This snippet of dialogue between the two had been repeated almost verbatim for seemingly the last quarter of a century.

Long ago discarded was any suggestion or advice as to slowing down, cutting back or laying off. Such was as best could be told Minnie's only boundary.

"Naw, honey, but thank you. These days it seems the only thing that much helps is a big bucket of the hair of the dog that bit me and I can promise you it was surely a big dog! So how about some of that good Smirnoff in a cold beer mug over ice."

"Absolutely, will get right away." And Val did.

She flopped a coaster in front of Minnie and set the frosty chalice down. "So what's going on? Whatcha been doing?" If the exchange had been a script on paper, it would be yellowed and greasy and tattered long before now. Minnie took a delicate sip. She needed to take this slow and let it drip life back into her slowed and punched drunk metabolism.

"Ah, that's better. Yes. Well, I went over to the Blue Anchor last night. You know how I like to spread myself around. Same place all the time gets boring for me and for them too. You know, it's how I keep my support group together." She chuckled. "Hell, I'm an old rummy. It's my entertainment. You know that. Had a few. Visited with folks."

"Guess because it was Twin Bridges and someone said something about how liberal CBS News had become and somehow that Charles Kuralt guy's name came up and we got to talking about him and all that mess. What was that double life wife's name? Pat something. They shacked up over there on the Big Hole. Guess that was part of the charm, right?" She sniggered.

"Pat Shannon. She was pretty nice, really. The two of them dropped in here and in Chick's, usually pretty late at night, every couple of months.

He was a bourbon guy. Very much a gentleman. They acted like they liked each other."

Minnie said, "You know, I suppose that might well be so. I never saw them, never met them, didn't know much about it at all. Just listening to it being talked about really made me wonder. How in the hell did he keep it all so secret and closed off for all those years? One wife there, one wife here. Hell, and keeping up with two and keeping it all apart. I couldn't keep up with one and was glad as hell when that was done. That son of a bitch I was married to." Minnie rolled her eyes.

Val said, "Yup. You know these relationship things are messy enough when it's just one on one but keeping up with two? I sure couldn't do it and God knows I screwed plenty of them up."

Minnie sipped again and looked off into the distance. Val noticed and told her if she needed anything to just wave.

The door opened and Don walked in. He was a couple of halting steps inside, his eyes adjusting from bright sunlight to bar dark. He saw Val and alarmed, reflexively threw his hands up. "Look, I'm sorry. Didn't know. I'll go. I'm going right now." Val had her hands on her hips, bar rag at her side.

"No, don't go. No. You're eighty-sixed up the road. As long as you behave, you can come in here. I want to talk with you anyway." Don lowered his hands and thought about it. There was a good-sized blossoming gray-blue welt running from his fat right ear down his jaw from where Val had barrel brushed him.

"Okay."

"Come over here and sit with me at the end of the bar and let's talk." She nodded to Ford and Ford understood. Everybody around these small parts knew about most everything most of the time. Ford stopped his leaning on the beer box and stepped forward to the knot of four or five guys drinking and talking quietly and said, "All right. You people need to keep me busy. Who wants what? Every third one is on the house."

Don limped down toward Val, the stool beat down on his back and legs still fresh. A few of the drinkers watched him; most weren't interested. A ruckus in a bar, even if they knew about it, wasn't exactly a world news flash. Generally speaking, someone would have to kill someone for such to resonate.

Don passed Minnie. "Hey, Minnie. How you doing?"

"I'm okay, Don, thank you. You? You don't look so good. Heard about it last night. Heard you got your ass good and whipped. And at that by some city boy and then got finished off by some badass barkeep." Minnie winked and nodded her head at Val.

Don grunted in assent. He was in no mood for humiliation but for now his smart-ass tongue had caused him more than a little trouble. Minnie took another satisfied sip, the burn beginning to warm her. He slowly eased into a seat across from Val. They looked at each other in silence and then both murmured the other's name in a quiet, colliding start to their talking.

Don held up his hand and Val told him to go on ahead. "Look, Val, I'm really sorry about all that. It's all on me. I was drunk and stupid and I just busted loose. Tried to write a check I couldn't cash. Just stupid. I never knew I had that kind of crazy feelings in me. I feel right low, real low about it. And I don't blame that fellow for clocking me and I don't blame you for finishing my mess up. It's all on me, all on me." He looked down at the door, pursing his lips. His words were halting, staggering out of him. He shook his head, despairing of himself, knowing that he had broken big rules and marked himself, of course with many others and now, even further deeply with Val.

Val just watched him, part in pity, part in regret, part in memory and in greatest part, in a nightmare bad lesson writ hard that wasn't going to go away. Long ago, they had tried to start a thing with one another which confused them, faltered, and scattered in irretrievable pieces and thus failed, only over a course of a few weeks.

For all his cowboy strop-tough taciturnity and hard strong physicality, Don held deep fears of inadequacy and papered them over with his silence, his heavy drinking, his never-neverland of fantastical thoughts of remote, glittered up impossible romances and his ever-present chronic cloying need to be always looked after. He had quickly driven Val half-crazy with his whining and his being suddenly always under foot like a passive old cat. Val now knew him to be weak and self-absorbed and knew this all had something to do with mommy issues which she just didn't have time to think about. He clung as a barnacle. He was a head case and a sad one at that.

Val just shook her head. "Look, Don. Apology accepted but that don't get you a ticket for readmission to Chick's. Most places ban folks for a year which is a long time enough, but you went way over the line with that one trick pony, way over. Now, before I say anything else, I want you to look me in the eye and tell me, clear and steady and loud enough for me and you to both hear, that you understand me and then say it again."

Don pulled his head up out of his neck, looked at Val and said it. "I understand, Val. I understand you."

"Fine. Good. Now, you need to know this too. You need to start moving on. It's called growing up. Whether you stay around here or go someplace else, if you don't get on with getting a bunch of those snakes out of your head, you're sooner rather than later going to beaten worse or killed or sent to jail or even prison. You tried to take possession of Mikey! What in the fuck were you thinking?! No, don't even try to answer that! For Christ's sake, that's just twisted sick."

Val's voice had come up like storm clouds cutting out the mountains across the valley. Minnie was blatantly eavesdropping and enjoying the show, sipping away more frequently now. Val knew it, didn't really care, but she pulled it back a gear or two.

"Remember we've got some sorry ass history between us and I'm not talking to you from out of dreamland. I know you good and while I can tolerate you now and too, you are basically the customer and the customer is almost always right—not always but close—and I do feel sometimes sorry for you, but you get the picture."

Val was winding down. She finished with, "You need to know this. Whatever game you ever thought you might have with Mikey needs to disappear and now. She's gone off with that fellow back South. They have left the building. And he seems like a pretty good, smart fellow with a set of brass balls to boot." Don winced slightly.

"Now, she may come back one of these days, when or if, who knows... and if she does, and you see her, you are to get as far away from her as you can as fast as you can. You are not to speak one word to her, not even tip your hat to her. If I hear otherwise, I'm coming for you. What you did was just horrible and scared her bad."

"Yes, I understand. I promise. I'm sorry." Don did now look properly sorrowful and alert.

"End of sermonette. You stay out of Chick's but you can come in here as long as you act right. I don't know how other places like Blue Anchor or the Stockman and others will handle it and handle you. Remember, it's a small place and word does get around."

Minnie looked at them and added her bit of unsolicited two cents. “Yes, that is surely right.”

Don sighed. He could say nothing, just looked straight ahead.

Val stood up. “Don, what you drinking?”

“Uh...you sure?”

Val gave him a tight smile and a wink, wiped her hands on her towel. “Yeah. You came in here to drink, didn’t you? You just thought I was up the road at Chick’s and you could wander on in, right?”

“Uhm...yeah...okay...how about a HayBag and a shot of Knob.” He put a ten-dollar bill on the bar. “Thank you, Val. I appreciate it.”

Val set him up and wandered down the bar to check on the others and the new ones who had come in. Don picked up the shot, looked around, saw Minnie right there and held the jigger up to her in toast and drank it back and then took the cold glass of beer and drained it away. He stood up.

“See you later, Minnie. Hope your days are better than mine.” He walked down the bar back to the door. “Thanks, Val. See you later.” Val nodded and he was gone on.

She walked back down to Minnie.

“You need anything, honey?”

“Yeah, another would be nice. Please. I’ll be right back. Need to go grab a smoke.”

“Right.”

As Minnie stood to go out, she said, “Val.”

“Yes?”

“You already know this, but Don has always been a pussy.”

Val nodded. “Yup. And so it goes.”

CHAPTER ELEVEN

WORKIN' FOR A LIVIN'

Huey Lewis and the News

EDDIE AND MIKEY arrived early at the regional airport in Greensboro, a saggy tribute to big ideas and bigger egos which never panned out. Half the gates were shuttered, and the place just moaned big void. It was not an entertaining place to walk through. Charlotte had just kicked its ass. More often than not, folks just drove to Charlotte and got better ticket prices to wherever, a good deal for the expenditure of but ninety minutes. Eddie usually did that but his most recent departure, spurred by the swelling tension and unhappiness in his life, kicked in as a directive that commanded to get the nearest airport and go now.

Their quick in and out trip to Atlanta had been fantasyland. A fun baseball game, a swell hotel with towels so thick and soft you couldn't stuff one in your suitcase even if you wanted to, a dreamy, fancy, romantic meal finished off by dancing in the bar at the hotel. They had met nice people and then went right back to airport, back to the harder cut reality of a different lifestyle. Eddie lightly warned Mikey that they were parachuting back into a new, far less glamorous place. He instantly saw that she understood and that pleased him.

He decided that they should go straight to the office. The mood was a bit tauter now, anticipations rising. They walked in the back door, straight into Patty's sunny office which spread across three desks in what used to be a Florida room before Eddie bought the place some years ago and turned it into Patty's smoking and get-things-done room. It was still just a few minutes before 1 p.m.

"Hey, Patty. Let's get some work done! And, Patty, this is Mikey. Mikey Riewey."

"Hey, Eddie, what took you so long?" She grinned with a cigarette slotted into the corner of her lips. "And, Mikey, nice to meet you." Patty looked Mikey over, appraising, sizing her up.

"I'll have to say this, Eddie. This is as good-looking a woman as you have ever brought around here." She turned to Mikey and said, "Yes, you are. It isn't even close. Do you need glasses or a hearing aid? What in the hell are you doing hanging out with this fool and bringing it all the way from Montana to boot?" Patty was laughing. Eddie was too. Mikey wasn't sure at first, then quickly realized it was going to be okay.

"I got Minor and Rise lined up. Rise coming by herself. Minor ought to be here soon. What's all of this about?"

"Mikey already knows. Come in my office, please, before Minor and Rise get here. Gonna explain. Mikey, please wait out here."

Mikey nodded, started holding her breath, sat down in a chair and blinked. "Well, this ought to be interesting."

In a couple of minutes, she could hear Patty's raised voice, "Jesus Christ! This is crazy shit! Are you serious!?"

Mikey's mind flashed, "Stand up, sit down, fight, fight, fight!" or was it, "flight, flight, flight?" Hell, no, she was in. She waited.

While being grilled by Patty, Eddie's mind randomly turned to his mother. Eddie Terrell's mother never failed to have an opinion about just about everything under the sun. Whether she knew what anything was about or not made not a whit of difference to her. She was a dire hose of thoughts, observations, and critiques. Smart and tart-tongued, she fired at will and sometimes, even at the target. She was known to many as Momma R, her lawful name of Rose early on being found wanting as too gentle and thus was supplanted early in her days by a more powerful moniker which she wore like a cop's badge. Eddie called her Mutha, because that's what she called herself, and also for reasons that probably are not lost on even the most amateurish of lexicographers.

She knew Eddie was a lawyer. She just was not sure what he actually did day to day. Well, she really did but preferred to stay above that unseemly pig sty of wrongdoing and venality. "I am often appalled by his behavior and manner and even more delighted by his successes, God only knows whatever they might be."

She had hoped he would go down the corporate, business, tax, and transactional roads to professional glory because the idea of criminals and wreck cases and suing doctors disconcerted her and initiated within her a dismissal of facts, a disconnect. She gorged on television, hours, and hours each day and was never without a good murder mystery or whodunit or doctor show. But to put Eddie, her Eddie into the nasty mix of bad guys and crooks and killers and incompetent doctors just did not sit well with her worldview, so she feigned and forged a puzzled ignorance. Eddie always wore a nice suit, had nice shoes and manners. It would be impossible for him to consort with such trashy people!

She was a practicing and skillful hypochondriac, so adept at the reception of any interesting illness that long ago Eddie regularly gave her current copies of Harrison's *Principles of Internal Medicine* and the *Cecil Textbook of Medicine* for birthdays and holidays. She did not like to dive too deep, but a good, symptom-laden, simple synopsis of ringworm or cellulitis brought her great pleasure. As she got older and her circle of friends began to narrow by virtue of stare-off-into-space-it-is or a final visit to ten-toes-up-room-temperature land, she was said to complain that all of her friends were dying. "What shall we do? What shall we do?" she would lament to her husband. The reply was always the same.

"Momma R, it's a simple solution. We need younger or healthier friends." This never satisfied her. She liked to wrap herself in disguises and illness along with all forms of martyrdom.

Eddie and his mother sparred often. She was a good talker and by way of the gene pool and example had taught him to talk and so he did effectively and hopefully, far more on point. She did not like any of his girlfriends, not a one. None of them were good enough for her boy. The impending arrival of Mikey within the confines of her world, albeit indirectly, was surely to portend more invective, punch, and counterpunch.

Her sense of self was one of highest esteem, often so ridiculously funny in its revealing that despite the obviousness of it all, she could never see it or understand it.

Once, on a late gray cold gloomy afternoon, she called Eddie at his office. No one else was there. Eddie answered his own phone as he often did.

"Eddie, is that you?"

"No, Mother, it is my well-hidden, evil twin brother. What may I do for you this crummy, dreary afternoon?"

"Son, you don't sound good. You sound blue. What is it?"

She was right. Eddie felt flat and down. Mutha-dar had again, as almost always, picked it up. Eddie was blue.

"Well, Mother, as you well know, my dear friend Books Bascomb, who I grew up with and was fraternity brothers with finally gave it up just a few days ago to the Big C that had stalked him for so long. I'm pretty sad about that."

"Yes, I know. Go on."

"And I just found out a little while ago this afternoon that another great friend and fraternity brother, Frank Carter down in Charlotte, has been found dead in his apartment."

"Frank Carter from Charlotte?"

"Yes, you knew him well. He was a guest in our home many, many times."

"Oh, yes, I recall him." Silence followed.

"So if you don't mind, I'll tell you I am blue, very blue. I've lost two good ones in less than a week and it makes me sad, very sad. Now, why have you called?"

More silence ensued and then, "Well, you know, son, I don't feel very well myself these days." This was but another matter that called for addition by subtraction.

Eddie quietly put the receiver down, got his coat, and walked down the hall to go to his car. He could hear Mutha's fading voice expostulating on and on, about what God only knew.

He closed the office door and she was gone. Even in moments like these of sadness, there was bliss in that silence. And if she ever got wind of this scheme, there most probably would never again be any silence.

In his familiar world, his office, Eddie stayed steady and calm despite Patty glaring at him. His desk was good-sized with a normal straight-backed chair behind it. He did not like those high-padded, over cushioned Queen Mary-on-rollers types. In front of his desk sat a small coffee table and three leather captain's chairs fanned out beyond it. It was a comfortable office, nicely decorated in grasscloth and a thick rug with handsome lamps and the usual assortment of hanging diplomas, prints, achievements, items that would one day be obituary fodder. There was a large television set for viewing tapes and recordings, but also it was hooked to local cable so sports and news could be watched as well.

"Patty, you ain't gonna be in it. You don't know shit and won't have your fingerprints on anything. I just need you to know about it so if I need help, need some cavalry, you'll get the call. You won't have to lie for me or about it even though you are one of the world's great liars."

She bridled a bit. Eddie held his hand up to continue and to stop the charade. "Hell, you know you are and you only do it when it is good for the cause. And if I pull it off, you'll get some green. As you know, I'll share with you. Always have."

Patty, calming, nodded. "You've done some crazy ass shit in the time I've been with you. I am curious about what motivates this but am not inclined to ask. As long as I ain't in it, I'll take you at your word. The less I know, the happier I am. But I will ask this: did the girl out there start the whole thing? I think it's important that I know that part. Fair enough?"

"Fair enough and the answer is a solid 'no.' I've been thinking on it for a while now and just need to see if I can pull it off. I need an adventure. When I was out in Montana, it started coming together about same time I met her and she does know about it and will be in it just a little. I trust her, she trusts me. She's smart and like all the best people, knows how to keep her mouth shut."

"You don't need a damn adventure; you need your damn head examined. But, what the hell, this ought to be something else. Wait a minute, I'll be right back. We're supposed to have company coming, right?"

Patty opened the door to go down the hall to check on the arrivals of Curt and Rise.

Mikey looked at Patty. Patty said, "I guess you heard most if not all of that."

Mikey slowly shook her head up and down.

"I've got a vague idea as to what's up but that amount of vague is vaporizing right now, I can promise you. You ever see the movie, *Men in Black*?" Patty asked.

"No, I haven't, I don't think."

"A classic. Check it out sometime. Will Smith and Tommy Lee Jones. Space detectives. They carry ball point pens so when they press the clicker, there's a flash and whoever is getting flashed suddenly and completely forgets everything about what's going on."

"Sounds interesting."

"It is. Now I'm going to round up, I hope, our company and y'all can go off and have a meeting. He trusts you so I trust you. But I do pay attention too so don't fuck it up. He's my meal ticket. Do you and I understand one another?"

"Yes. Absolutely."

Patty stuck her hand out, Mikey shook it and stood up. Then Patty hustled down the hallway. Eddie came to his office door.

"A little excitement which I expected. But not too bad. You hear it? I figured you would. I think we are all square."

"Yes."

"You okay?"

"Yes."

Patty came back down the hall and behind her walked two of the largest people Mikey had ever seen. One was a tall black man with broad shoulders and roped forearms. His movement was purposefully forward and he rolled his walk with every step. He was handsome and graceful with alert eyes. Behind him came an enormous black woman who did not so much walk as plow ahead. Her giant bosom carved the way. She was not graceful, just forceful. She huffed and hummed as she came along. She paid attention too and there was humor in her eyes. The man appeared to be waiting for the humor to appear. The black woman curved around the fellow and went up to Eddie and gave him a big hug.

"Haven't seen you in a while, lawyer boy! Glad to see you! Now why are we having this visit and who is this pretty young thing?"

"Glad to see you too, Rise. Hang on. Curt, Curt Minor. Thanks for coming. Been a while. This is my friend Mikey. She's straight cool."

Minor replied, "Good. Hey. More than a while. Haven't seen you since all that shit piled up on Kenny Peak. Isn't that right?"

Eddie said, "That's right but it's fair to say I try to keep smart people in my sight, even if they're a good ways away."

"Don't bother with greasing us. What's this all about? With Rise here, bound to be some business, right?"

"Right. Y'all come on in. Have a seat. Anyone want anything to drink or eat? We can get it done. And again, this is my friend Mikey. She's from Montana. You can trust her. I do. I promise."

Mikey looked at her shoes while the two newcomers looked Mikey over.

Rise said, "Y'all two be making nookie? That shit can color your mind. Honey, how is your mind?" Curt nodded in agreement.

Mikey levelheaded up with a happy, tight smile. "I promise you my mind is right. I see things straight. I didn't come along with Eddie out this way to go on a suicide mission. Remember, I'm from Montana. Not exactly The Land of Pussies."

Rise nodded. Minor grunted in an assent that mostly said, "We will see about that." Patty backed out of the office and shut the door tight.

Eddie started. "Here's what I've been thinking. I'd like to see us all make some heavier money. Does that idea appeal to y'all?"

"I'm down with that as long as my fat ass don't have to go back to that damn lady jug in Kentucky or someplace worse." Rise was being droll and giggling at herself as she flatlined it.

"Go on." Curt was attentive.

"Curt, you still in contact with the kid Pee Wee up in Baltimore? I heard through the grapevine he was still doing some pretty solid work for some folks you might know up that way, working up on the northwest side. Barksdale bunch?"

"Yeah. That's right. I sent him up there for seasoning. What's he gotta do with this? He's a pretty sharp little cat."

"I think he could be a resource for us, a trusted resource."

"For what?"

"To help us get, oh say, a few kilos of coke. Make some good money, one shot, one time deal."

"Man, you're jumping in the deep end with no life jacket on, but just for the hell of it, tell me more."

Rise was just watching and rocking back and forth.

"First, we get him to get us a couple of 8 Balls so we can check quality; we need good quality. That'll be about twenty-five hundred. I'll put that money up. If you'll put me in touch with him, I'll go get them too, bring them back. Curt, you can do the quality check, can't you?"

"Hang on, John Law, you're adding layers of make-work that don't need to be added. Pee Wee will get us good stuff. We can just go up and get it."

Eddie was no longer hesitant. He was thrilled. Obviously, Curt was interested and if Curt was interested, then the course was clearing.

"Curt, tell us how to do this."

"Here's the way I see it. I like the idea but it has got to get executed the right way. Clean, no slip ups. No mouthing off. That kind of shit can get a person killed. The kilos gotta be paid for, transported, and distributed, parceled out. How we gonna turn the blow into decent dollars? So Mr. Lawyer Terrell, whatcha say?"

"I can speak to a lot of it. Just need your help refining the plan. I expect y'all saw, or most of you saw, in the news the other day where the Feds picked what they said was a couple of hundred-thousand kilos off some Turkish transport ship in Philly. Starting value on that big dish kinda ride is well north of lots of commas. That's the kind of shit the Feds are looking for, the big bust stuff. Compared to them, we are small fry. You know, it's that old thing about a pig gets fat and a hog gets slaughtered. A kilo is about twenty-five thousand inland so I'll go in for little about one-hundred-fifty thousand. I've made enough over the years to have some serious set-aside money. Say we go for six Ks.

"Curt Minor, I respectfully propose you go in for one at about twenty-five grand. Unless you want more. You know a whole lot more contacts there and all about and which can be relied on. I know there really is honor in this."

Curt nodded in agreement. "There damn well better be."

"You and I both know you been serious drink housing and Mary Jane dealing for a long time now and as you are not a man of flash, you are a man of discretion and careful so I expect you have a good stash or two and can carry that ball. And I have a group of investors I'm going to approach, who I feel pretty good about. Most, if not all of them, going in on the deal so we can total up at one-hundred-fifty grand, maybe one-hundred and seventy-five. Will just have to see.

"And I think it's fair to say that once we assemble whatever we can acquire with our budget, you need to be the boss in charge of collecting and distributing the proceeds."

Minor nodded, "Fine. The basic cut is sixty-forty but I expect will need some adjustments, like 60 percent to us for working the deal, 40 percent to non-active investors based on who's putting what up—that's industry standard so I've heard. And by the way, what if these others don't go in?"

"I guess we'll have to see what their interest level is and go from there. And I think Pee Wee should get a big extra tip for his silence. I'll need you to go see him when the time comes to make the set up. And how about this? I'll go in for two units and Curt, you get what you make off that one, just you."

Minor thought for a moment and then nodded his assent.

Rise inquired, "This all sounds like a lotta fun, but where do I fit in and how do I get paid?"

Eddie turned and looked at Rise with true genial affection in his face. "You're gonna be the bus driver and your brother Kenny's gonna help you. And you're going to take me to see some people who may well just want to play."

"Bus driver? Say what?"

"Don't worry. All will be revealed. I promise. And Kenny will not, cannot, know anything about this right now. It will be up to you, and with Curt's advice and input, to share a little with Kenny when the day is done. The same goes for my friend Mikey here. I will be responsible for her receiving a proper emolument."

Rise said, "Okay, I'm in with Eddie. Curt, you in?"

"Yeah, but I gotta hear how we getting it here so count me mostly in. Fair enough? And what's this shit about a bus?"

Rise asked, "Does Patty know anything?"

"She did know for just a little bit that I was planning on doing something outside my lawyer world but she doesn't know anything at all now."

Mikey just looked at the floor.

Curt said, "Tell me about a bus, the bus."

Eddie said, "How does this sound? We'll go buy a small, in good shape, used school bus, probably over in High Point from Thomas. They got lots of inventory. A small one and we'll get Rise or Curt to take it over to one of their chop shop buddies on the east side who also does paint and body work and we are gonna turn it out to be nice looking, cleaned-up bus, so it won't draw attention to itself Need a good church name and city, all that." Eddie laughed. "How about 'Apostolic AME Church of The Highest Clouds?'"

There was a crack of silence and then everyone laughed, laughed good, and loud. "And doesn't it make sense to have the handsome, dignified right Reverend Curt Minor make the selection and purchase? I'll provide the cash, of course."

Curt said, "I have these thoughts too. But let's keep it a school bus. All the kids are in school these days and school buses are just a dime a dozen. People pay attention to them but at the same time, they really don't. If anything, they just make just about everybody be more careful, more cautious. If we make it a church bus and it's gonna have to carry some identifying name, some such shit and even if bogus, which it surely will be, could make some folks wonder or suspicious.

"Next, those chop shop boys are gonna need to do some undercarriage hidden compartment work, maximum sealed, airtight. We need to make this ride over a long holiday weekend when the cops and all are mostly busy with the main roads and interstates. This is a back roads trip all the way. No way we're getting this deal out on I-95 or some such. A few black folks driving a plain old school bus out in the sticks doesn't draw much attention. Basically no one gives a shit."

Eddie chimed in, "I think the bus has to spend one night hidden, covered up somewhere. It just might draw attention if it were wandering down some country road in the middle of the night."

Curt agreed. "Lawyer boy, you been doing some good thinking. This might be a lifestyle that suits you...hmmmm. Now, where you gonna put it overnight?"

Eddie replied, "I've got an old friend, great person, real fine lady who I used to go out with."

He looked at Mikey with that "no worry" glance. "She's a wonderful horsewoman, a helluva fox hunter, still flies over fences, has a few big barns. I think I'll make an inquiry of her."

Mikey said, "You still in touch with her?"

"From time to time. Nothing to it. All done long time ago."

"Okay."

"Let me go to work on our prospective syndicate of investors. I'll need to see two, maybe three of them here locally and will need to go down to Florida for a day visit as well. And once I have that information and hopefully commitments, Patty will be in touch."

Rise asked, "Whatcha think I ought to tell Ben?"

"I suggest that you tell him we were discussing matters involving Kenny and possible getting his probation shortened or terminated. It's strictly a family matter."

"Right."

"We all on the same page? *Omerta*, please, and for those of you not familiar with that word, it's Mafioso, the mafia word for an unbreakable total silence. Because if we all ain't, this deal is stillborn and graveyard dead and I think it'd be a damn shame for that to happen."

Curt uttered a warning benediction. "Remember what Mike Tyson always said. Everybody's always got a plan until I hit 'em in the face. So no fucking up the plan at all."

There was total assent by voice, nod, and gesture. The meeting was adjourned and the guests left the building.

Mikey looked at Eddie. "You have been planning, haven't you? Impressive. Your friends are impressive too. Eddie, this is a little scary but it's exciting too. Do you understand?"

"Oh, yes, baby, I do, I promise I do." And he pulled her to him and embraced her and kissed the top of her head just as Patty came into the emptied room.

"Jesus! Knock off the PDA. Get a room." She was chuckling. "Well, come to think of it, guess y'all already have. Eddie, we got to do some case review now, please."

"Good, yes, you mind if Mikey sits in?"

"Hell, no, I could use some help around here if she can pick it up. Mikey, whadaya say, wanna give suing folks and wrestling with insurance companies a run?

Eddie added, "You never struck me as idle. The alternative is to go to the club, lay around in the sun, drink, eat, get bored, fat, that sort of thing. I hope you'll join us here."

"I am very complimented and, yes, I will. I hope I can help somehow. Though that club thing sounds nice too, can save it till later."

Patty said, "Good! Now come on with us into the conference room. And, Eddie, just one question. How did your meeting go just now?"

"Fine, Patty. Just fine."

"I'm glad. Let's go to work."

CHAPTER TWELVE

LAWYERS, GUNS AND MONEY

Warren Zevon

EDDIE SAT AT the head of the long table with Patty and Mikey flanking him. They were surrounded by three walls of mahogany bookcases, all laden with law books, legal tomes, general and legal encyclopedias, the North Carolina General Statutes, the Federal codes, various and sundry magazines and newspapers and journals, plus enough medical texts and treatises to shame most any physician's collections.

Toss in works dealing with aviation crashes, accident reconstruction, train derailments, engineering, electricity, safe cracking, how to cook crack, and just about anything that warranted study because someone or something had gone wrong and gotten somebody or a lot of somebodies hurt or killed and that was the standard outfitting of any good trial lawyer's office.

It also helped immensely that there was also in town the fine Wake Forest University School of Law and its immense law library and treasure trove of professorial expertise. And, too, the Bowman Gray Hospital and Center for Medical Education had its own prodigious assemblies of texts and brains, so access to smart writing and thinking was always nearby if not immediately accessible.

Eddie, as all who recalled his formative days knew, was not much of a law student. Actually he was a pretty lousy disinterested one, save in his last semester when the light bulb illuminated and he began to learn to "think like a lawyer" and thus ground out some very high marks which elevated him in class rank to about five notches above the anchor. Once he passed the bar by the skin of his teeth, got out into the real world and the streets of that real world, what had before been to him mostly theoretical blah blah blah now became an urgent and desirable hands-on practice which it was up to him to handle and serve and repair, fix or claim with Patty as his right arm and often his commander-in-chief.

On the conference room table, Patty had laid out a stack of legal pads and pens and two thick black notebooks. In the notebooks were alphabetical listings of each case file in the office and included all pertinent information which included case title, jurisdiction, state or federal court, defense counsel information, insurance adjuster information, case designation (medical malpractice, legal malpractice, insurance fraud, murder and so forth), a synopsis of the facts of the case, statute of limitation and other important action dates and deadlines, directions to pertinent law, cases and articles, directions to what pattern jury instructions and causes of actions applied, lists of exhibits and always notes and more notes and observations. These meetings were held usually every two to three weeks and there was never more than four weeks to pass without this gathering.

It had come to be named "The Black Book Tickle" or BBT and it was a constant prodding reminder of what needed to be done. An extra, always updated copy was kept at Eddie's home, so if a horrible event such as fire, flood or Lord knows whatever else destroyed these in-office masters, reassembly and marching on could take place efficiently.

All of this was explained to Mikey by Patty and Eddie weaving with each other the whys and the ins and outs of it all. Mikey would ask a question here and there but mostly just listened.

"Are you basically comfortable with this?"

"I think so but of course I gotta crawl before I walk, right?"

"Yup, of course. We'll get you started on your training wheels for now."

Patty said, "Let's get to it. Eddie, why don't you open the bidding. But first, Mikey, come sit next to me so you can see my book rather than flying blind over there. In a few weeks, God willing and the creeks don't rise, you'll have your very own volume of torment."

Patty winked at them both. Mikey thanked Patty and came to her side and Eddie said, "Here we go. We will be talking about a lot of stuff now, but there are two cases that are just up in our wheelhouses so let's start there."

"They are the Pussy Preacher."

Mikey involuntarily blurted, "What the fuck?"

"Then let's start with our dear and good friend, the Pussy Preacher, also known in polite circles as P-Squared."

Mikey did not hesitate, "I cannot wait!"

Patty started, "We represent three young fellows, who played varsity lacrosse at our venerated flagship University of North Carolina down the road from here in Chapel Hill. Their families were referred to us by other lacrosse players from Eddie's old fraternity. Lot of Laxers, as they are called, in the DKE House. And Laxers do know how to party and have a big time. Part of their standing reputation.

"After concluding play in some sort of round-robin tournament down in Myrtle Beach, South Carolina, their spring break began and the players all went their vacationing ways. Our three decided to hang around down there and have some fun. A couple of them had a few of their daddies' credit and bank ATM cards and that's gonna be an important part of the story in just a little bit. They went to a strip club, Thee Doll House (TDH, for short), in the middle of one afternoon and got bombed, dog drunk as they say. As dark came on, they staggered up the street a few blocks to a spot called the Blockhouse and drank even more and were then so drunk, they got thrown out by foolish, foolish management that offered them no assistance, no taxi, no nothing. As they staggered about in a clot of confusion in the parking lot, they were all three run down by a speeding truck carrying four, no I'm not kidding, evangelical, Bible-thumping golfers from Indiana and all three got hurt—bad injuries, wrecked knees, shoulders, one of them lost a hand. Bad stuff."

Eddie asked Mikey, "Who all do we sue? This is sort of a quiz. Learning on the fly."

Mikey said, "Jeez. This happened down in South Carolina. How did you two work down there? I thought you were a North Carolina lawyer. And where's Mr. P Squared in all this? Sure you sue the truck driver. The rest of them I don't think so. Hell, in Montana people get drunker than horseshit and get tossed all the time and of course some of them get hurt and sometimes killed. Car wrecks and such."

Eddie smiled. "Nice start but it needs a little more. First, I'm also licensed in South Carolina so that's why I can work cases down there. It's another story for another time. Nice place to visit too. Charleston and Aiken are real special places to enjoy. We have indeed sued the driver of the truck and we have also sued both the strip club and the other bar. That's three big, fat liability insurance policies to chase down instead of just one."

"How can you sue the bar and the club? The boys just got real drunk. Y'all said they were torn up."

"Well, I don't know what the rule is in Montana—we could look it up real quick but maybe later but in South Carolina, it's against the law to serve alcohol to someone you know to be intoxicated, under the influence of spirituous liquors."

"How can you prove they were drunk and looked drunk in the first place?" Mikey countered. "Wouldn't the first bar say they were fine in here and they got hammered at the second place?"

Patty leaned in. "Here is where our good friend, the Pussy Preacher comes in. Who by the way, we have never met or even talked with. But he has helped us screw Thee Doll House. And this is why Eddie does almost all of his leg work himself. If almost always pays off to go and look and see for yourself and often go look and see more than once."

"One of the injured boys remembered there was a guy doing a comedy act and they were filming it to sell at the club, sort of that takeaway momento of bad taste and worse judgment while they were in there that afternoon. The comedian, oddly enough, is from right here in Winston-Salem. He is one crude, nasty bastard. Eddie went down to Myrtle Beach, walked into Thee Doll House to take a look-see. And lo and behold, in the glass case below the register is a VHS of the guy doing his act just as the boys had said and Eddie buys it and brings it back and we watch it and the three drunks on the rail right in front of Mr. Pussy Preacher are our three clients. And they are all drunk as Cooter Brown. And they keep getting served while the P Preacher rails on to the rolling camera. And it's about an hour-long show and you also see on a couple of occasions one of our guys and then another leave and then come back in a few minutes with a fistful of cash."

Mikey said, "Let me guess. Getting money from the money machine. Bet they had one in the lobby."

"Very good! Fast learner! That's exactly right."

"Have the folks you have sued paid up yet?"

"Not yet. We're gonna have a mediation in a few weeks where all parties and their lawyers and insurance carriers are there and I feel confident with the mediator's good help, we are going to achieve a very nice resolution."

"What's a mediator? What does he do?"

Eddie responded. "The mediator is a highly trained person, almost always a good lawyer or a former judge who helps bring parties in conflict together, to a conclusion, to a settlement, often a compromise. And keep in mind there are good compromises and some that are not so good. He is a respected officer of the court. The best ones really don't do anything except mediate cases and you can often tell the seriousness of the other side to get something resolved when they agree to let certain ones take the ball and run with it. A good mediator is always neutral and he only pushes for the case to settle. The courts have come to love the process. It helps them clear their dockets.

"In many states, South and North Carolina included, mediation in almost all 'serious' cases is mandatory. And happily, more often than not, the mediation is effective in either flat out getting the case done or moving the case closer and closer to being done. It's good stuff and it works to knock out lots of expense and time that would otherwise get burned through on the way to trial." Eddie paused.

"Now here's another fun angle that was real helpful as to getting ready to knock Thee Doll House over the head. Finding the damning goodies of the Pussy Preacher was the goal of my second recon trip down. By then I was hired and knew I already had them by the short hairs on the basis of what I had already dug up. The other sides bitched and moaned and complained that I had performed a premises examination and inspection without mutual agreement or court permission.

"I responded by saying I tampered with nothing, altered nothing to my advantage, that they had no proof or evidence to show that I did anything of the sort, and they didn't, and if anything, I enhanced the club's coffers by making a modest purchase. They were just, as usual, billing hours."

"What's that?" asked Mikey.

Patty said, "Typical defense lawyers. They love to pad their bills by charging for both real work and lame work. Lame work is unnecessary, just being charged, make-up work. Complaining that opposing counsel had the audacity to breathe their client's air, walk on his sidewalk. Pumps up their billings so their firms think they are 'more productive' and thus their positions in the firm hierarchy are kept stable if not downright enhanced. So much bullshit."

Mikey grinned and nodded. "Whores do come in so many shapes and sizes, don't they?

Eddie continued. "First trip was soon after I was getting ready to be hired. I held that consummation of the deal up—it was ultimately gonna get done and of course it did—but I wanted to avoid any recriminations or accusations that I had played unfair early by sliding into the place that I wanted to see, the insides of the place, just get a feel for it, how it was run, maybe see some of the fleshy offerings." He winked. Patty rolled her eyes. Mikey sneered and looked sideways. "Remember, it is often easier to ask for forgiveness rather than permission."

"I called a real estate lawyer friend of mine down in the Charleston area, had gone to Chapel Hill with him, good guy, smart guy, real Adonis handsome named Truck Tinker. Great name by the way. Doesn't know shit from Shinola about tort law. I said, 'Hey I'm coming to Charleston, will buy you a drink but to get it, I need you to ride with me one afternoon for a few days up to Myrtle Beach to check a place out that I've got in my gunsights. You're gonna like the view I think.' So he's in."

Patty said, "Y'all mind if I smoke? I'm dying for a cig hit."

"Naw, just go open those doors, please."

"Anyway, I go down to South Carolina, spend the night, pickup Truck at his office and drive North up Highway 17 to Sodom and Gomorrah. Truck asks what's all this about. He looks nice, I look nice. Dark suits, red striped ties, laced-up shoes, high shined. We look like we're two mannequins that have escaped from a Brooks Brothers front window. Two stiff, innocuous businessmen. It's a gray, gloomy, foggy mid-weekday up there. We walk in. No crowd at all. Pretty deserted. Just one or two other stiffs sitting around at a couple of low round tops with weak drinks and each has a pretty girl with him, dressed in orange or pink or blue negligees, gorgeous bosoms just riding in the wind, just wide out in the open. Nice stuff. These girls were put together very nicely. And that's an understatement! And sorry, sports fans, you cannot help but look and look and stare some more. No pasties either. They know it and it pleases them too."

Eddie is plowing a fine furrow in the field of tort.

"A hostess takes us to a table. Then the two same sort of really pretty girls come and sit down with us. Same garb. Now, I'm thinking this is where my boy Truck is gonna be some damn good bait. They ask us what we'd like to drink. A couple of beers, please. A waved signal is given to some coolie off behind a curtain and he appears with the frosties and some glasses. I say, 'Ladies, y'all going to have a drink with us?' There's a light suppressed tee-hee. She tells us she can't since she's on the job. We introduce ourselves and say we're in town doing some business. One of the girls is a brunette, the other a frosted blonde as curvy as a high mountain road reminding me of a glorious encounter I had a long, long time ago with Tinkerbelle."

"Huh?" asked Mikey.

Patty said, "It's an oldie but goodie. He'll get to it one of these days. It's so old, it's got dust on it."

"Shush, Patty!" Eddie smirked.

"Anyway, so the brunette said in such a soft voice, she was Carrie and the blonde was Carol. She asked what kind of business we did. I responded we're real estate guys, looking over some properties up this way, seeing if there's enough money in them for investment.

"We watched them look us over, sizing us up thinking if we're morals cops or shakedown artists or tax collectors. I suppose they couldn't be sure because we looked pretty, almost too straight but Truck was so ridiculously handsome, he could never been any of those things. He really did have real blond, real wavy hair and he had plenty of it, brushed back down over his collar like a movie star. Carrie was the bubblier of the two and after I asked her how she came to be at this establishment she said she hailed from Valdosta, Georgia and was ready for an adventure. She said the money's good and the place is clean and comfortable. She liked having people say nice things about her, look at her but not touch her, well, not too much. She asked if we wanted another beer and if they could dance for us. I said we were working too. Gotta keep our heads about us, right?"

Patty just shook her head. Mikey just groaned a "so pitiful, so lame" sigh.

Eddie continued, "I asked both girls, 'Don't y'all have this kind of conversation with customers all the time? Doesn't it get boring?' Carol said, 'Yes and no. It's our job. We're lucky. We got good work. We get good money. By the way, I like talking with you guys. You're nice, not trashy like a lot of them that come in here. Thanks for being nice.' I asked her if people come in here all the time and just fall head over heels in love them want to run off and marry them? She said, 'Sure, happens all the time. Management gives them one warning and if it happens again, they're barred. I guess you haven't noticed but there are a couple of really big men sort of over there in the corner shadows who keep watch over us.'

"We see the bouncers and then I ask what if a girl falls for a customer? Carrie replied, 'It happens sometimes. Most always, once word gets out or their relationship gets observed, the gal gets quick shipped off to another of our sister clubs, sort of traded out for a new face, if they want to keep working for this outfit. If not, they are just let go to go off and chase Mr. Right who usually turns out to be Mr. Anything But. We are warned about this.'

"Carol then offered in a whispered addendum, 'It's the coke heads who usually go down that road. Guys will feed them powder, not here of course, but they get together and the guys always come back to see their girl. It's pretty twisted on both ends. The guy gets jealous, the girl gets hooked. We're not like that. Most of us aren't.' Both girls were angelic.

"Truck had finished his first beer and was starting on his second and was starting to make low, deep, silent inhales, followed by low, involuntary, aching groans. We all looked at him. I need him to behave and be my investigative witness. Then Truck blurts out, 'I'm fine, but you both are just so beautiful. Oh, God! I'd be honored to marry either one or both of you. Just go off with you. On a beer and a half, I have fallen in the ditch. Oh, my God, my wife would kill me! I need to not be any trouble to y'all and I sure don't need to have her on my ass for the rest of my life which probably isn't going to be that much longer if she finds out anything about this. I apologize for my candor. Probably need to finish this and let's get going, Eddie.' So he drained his beer and expelled a little boy burp.

"Both the girls cooed and then I plunged, 'Ladies, I'm glad we haven't been awful. I worry that we are not much for y'all in the way of generating income. I don't think Truck here is feeling too good. So how do y'all make the good money, the kind of money I'm afraid y'all ain't gonna make off of us?'

In unison, Carol tipped her empty hand as if it was a glass to her beautiful mouth and Carrie shimmied her stunning chest within an inch of my face. Carol said, 'The playbook is a real simple one. Get them to drink too much and show 'em as much of the goods as you can and keep at it with a smile and some winks and you'll do fine, honey!' I then paid the bill, which amounted to sixty dollars: ten per beer, we had two each, and then the cover charge.

"After we're pulling out onto Kings Highway, I said to Truck, 'Pick up that legal pad and write down that the playbook is a real simple one: 'get them to drink too much and show them as much of the goods as you can and keep at it with some smiles and some winks and you'll do just fine, honey.' I told him those were Carol's exact words and told him that she opened the vault doors for us. 'Get them to drink too much,' which is very much frowned on by our solons here in South Carolina. Thee Doll House's policy is to get their patrons to drink too much, to lose their senses of control and comprehension. Thus, the customer can be, along with the seductions of the proffered and closely shown flesh, encouraged by such things as lap dances and back room shenanigans to empty their pockets.

"Then Truck countered, 'Hmmmm, but Eddie, I didn't drink too much and they didn't get me to drink too much and I was still, well, almost overcome by it all. Jumping Jehosaphat! They were just so great looking and so nice!' I told him it was okay and then he was known as a high dollar sucker. I then said, 'Don't get your feelings hurt. You, for all your good looks are a very sensitive, vulnerable guy. Some men, even strong men like you, just fall to pieces when put into that situation. I didn't know you would, didn't for a minute suspect it but you did and it's going to really help the case. I will have an affidavit prepared for your review and signature. You may need to give a deposition but I doubt it. This case is not going to a trial. I'll bet you a dime to a G.' Then I told him how Carol looked just like Tinkerbelle."

Patty said, "Eddie, you might as well tell Mikey the story, which I've endured about fifty times. But it's nice because in the end, it shows what an idiot Eddie can be. Keeps him humble. Go ahead, Mr. Cock of the Walk. Give it up!" Eddie and Patty were laughing and Mikey was fascinated.

CHAPTER THIRTEEN

SHAKE A TAIL FEATHER

The Five Du-Tones

EDDIE TOOK A deep breath, steadied himself, braced his chest and shoulders up and back, lowered his eyes and then raised them in a glazed look of faraway pleasure and then just as quick refocused and was off and running with a seminal tale of his long-ago days. "It's like this. When I was fourteen, I was in boarding school up in Connecticut. Five-hundred-and-fifty boys in four classes in a strict, supervised environment. Of course, we all always just as horny as rabbits on Spanish Fly. Any magazine that made its way into campus, like Playboy, was always quickly in tatters as its utilizations were early and often. Same for the old classics like Candy and Lady Chatterley's Lover. Sex wasn't just on our brains; we were self-soaked in it unto the core of our bones. Saturated except when it was time for sports and food. We ate like horses, a lot and fast. It was always said that they put lots of saltpeter in our food to knock the urges down real good but if they did, my little old peter, sorry, couldn't resist, never knew it or was immune."

Patty said to Mikey, "See, I told you he was an idiot." Mikey agreed, shaking her head.

"Anyway, those two things surely helped. Hard to think about the golden fleece when you were out on the football field or hockey rink trying to knock the crap outta somebody. And of course, there was hitting the books. The place wasn't stingy or thin when it came to our studies. It was as if it was a college or university for high school kids. It had a beautiful campus and an enormous library, and we were pushed hard with college level courses, pushed all the time. So your mind could wander only so much. You had to pull your oars. But the horns were always there, always there.

"There were these two sixth formers, that's what we called seniors. Herb was from South Carolina, a banking and textiles family, and Bennett was from Long Island, whose family was in the heating and air conditioning business in a big way. They'd talk to us rube underformers. Somewhere along the line, they asked me if I'd ever gotten laid. I stammered, blushed, and replied in the negative. The school year was wrapping up and they said, 'Well, sport, now's your time to fly.' Then they asked if I could round up a hundred bucks? I said I could and then they told me about a lady in New York City that they could line me up with. To say I was intrigued and excited was the understatement of the year. But then the certain sense that I was headed down the road to hell, fire, and brimstone surged to the fore.

"I asked them if she was a nasty ass street whore and they said, 'No, dummy! The lady is called a madame and she has call girls she can line you up with. These are respectable, good-looking gals who dress nice, are not stupid, have good jobs they work. They just do this on the side to make some nice extra money. They're clean too!' I had no idea and, yeah, I was in, in deep.

"They gave me the madame's name and her phone number in the city. They told me to call her soon and get lined up. It was the end of the school year and lots of appointments were being made from all over the northeast. Didn't want to miss my shot. The next night I went down to the basement of our school's main building. There were banks of old wooden pay telephone booths that had the folding doors that caused the overhead light to come on when you pulled them shut. I was furtive as could be, acting nonchalant even as I was jumping my motorcycle over the Grand Canyon. This was where everyone called their parents, their grandmothers, their girlfriends. Almost always the charges were reversed, collect calls to expectant parents. I was emboldened and scared all at the same time and of course, my little old fourteen-year-old preppy heart was gasping, pounding, and racing. It was in these old, beautiful pieces of telephonic architecture that nice things were said and done to loved ones and dear ones and here I was getting ready to make a call about pussy! Jesus!"

Mikey and Patty laughed out loud. Patty said, "Goddammit! I have heard this thing like fifty times and it still cracks me up."

Mikey said, "Unbelievable. I can't wait to hear how this all goes down."

"I knew school was out on June 12th. I was supposed to go into the city and stay with a friend and a cousin that night, both of whom were at a nice hotel suite that was owned by one of their daddy's companies. We were all supposed to take what we all called the Carolina Creeper train home the next day. My window of opportunity was set for me. It was all or nothing. I dialed the operator and gave her the number. She said to please insert one dollar and fifty cents. I did, listening to the quarters rattle like a shaken skeleton down the slot into the change box. I had brought five dollars in quarters. I did not want my call ended because I did not have enough change.

"It did vividly occur to me that you could buy two rubbers for a simple quarter in just about any crummy gas station bathroom in the South. I knew this because I had on a few occasions done just that, bought, and shoved them in my puny billfold, always in the hope that somewhere, sometime I would get to use them. They always dried to dust just like the dream. The line was ringing and a man answered, a fellow with a deep, warning voice. 'Who is calling please?' The 'please' was unnecessary. I was on the way to perdition. I was thrilled."

Mikey said, "You were even a little terror back then...you stinker!" Patty just shook her head and smoked some more and motioned for him to get on with it.

"I told the voice my fake name as it appeared on the military registration card, Bill Jackson, a friend had swiped for me and that I was referred to Miss Cindy James by two mutual friends at my school, Herb and Bennett who had used Miss James's services before. There was a pause and I could hear muffled speaking and then a woman came on the line. She was terse. 'Tell me what Herb and Bennett look like and where they are from.' And so I described Herb as a roly-poly, rumpled, receding hairline fellow from South Carolina and sure speaks and sounds like it. I described Bennett as a shorter guy who looks like Haskell from *Leave It to Beaver* (the irony of that description wasn't lost on me either) from Long Island. Talks like a Yankee blueblood. I then told her the name of our school and then she asked me my age and where I was from. I told her Winston-Salem and that I was eighteen. I was big and strong for my age, played football, had hair on my chest and a Selective Service card that friends had gotten from their older brothers for me. Back in those days, there was no photograph on them.

"Then she said, "Okay, you pass. What may I do for you?' Her tone was now accommodatingly gentle and genial. I then said I'd like to have a visit with a nice, pretty girl. She told me it would cost me a hundred dollars for one hour. 'What sort of girl are you looking for?' I thought this was like ordering off the menu at a Chinese restaurant. One from Column A, one from Column B, extra fortune cookies please. I said, 'I'd like a blonde with a great figure. Normal boobs. She doesn't have to be too tall but not too short either.' Then the madame asked me if I was looking for Barbie. She said, 'Wait just a minute and let me get my book.' I was nervous and happy. This was promising. She came back on the line and asked me what day I wanted my appointment. Then she said, 'I want you at this address at six o'clock sharp: 352 East 85th Street here in Manhattan. Your new friend will be Nikki. You will pay her a hundred dollars in cash. No checks. No credit cards. She won't have a last name and neither will you, Bill. If you no-show at the last minute, there is nothing I can do about it but you'll be cutting her out of earnings and me too and I will blacklist you and your buddies, Herb and Bennett. I hope you won't have to tell them that if it happens. Do you understand? This is a business and I run a tight ship.' I agreed to her terms and then she said, 'I hope you enjoy yourself. If you cannot make it, please call in timely fashion so we can make other arrangements for the efficient use of our resources. Again, no last-minute bail outs. Thank you for calling. Good luck and goodbye.' I hung up and just sat still in the booth, brain on hold, brain racing. I was in a warm brain bath. I was mentally salivating and wondering what I had done and what I was in for. Anticipation became my watchword. I had to go study.

"A few weeks later, June 12th had arrived. School was out, final grades were in, the basic mishmash of Bs and Cs with an A thrown in in Honors English. I was good at English. I had cashed my grandmother's gift checks, which were being pruriently diverted to assist in my deflowering, and had emptied my school bank account. I had about a hundred-and-fifty bucks on me. That was plenty.

"I took the New Haven railroad commuter train into the city and got a cab to take me to the St. Geneva Hotel where I was spending the night with a friend and a cousin. They both went to a place called Deerfield, another prep school. It was my cousin whose Daddy's company kept the suite at the hotel. We drank some beers and I was pacing all around. They teased me about having ants in my pants. Little did they know. It got around toward 5:30. It was real hot in the city. I said I've gotta get out of here for a while, go burn off some of this energy that's working on me. I'll be back by 7:30 and we can all go do something then. They said okay. They looked at me like I had rocks in my head. I bet I looked plenty wrought up to them. I was wound up tighter than a cheap watch that was gonna run never on time, just early or late, all over the place. But I damn well knew I was not gonna be late.

"I took the elevator down to the lobby and asked the doorman to hail me a taxi. He did. I remember I tipped him a dollar. I had the hundred folded in five twenties. I gave him the address. It didn't take long to get there. I paid, got out, looked at the address written on a notecard for the thousandth time and looked up at the door. It was almost the middle of June in a big city being baked by summer and there was a gigantic Christmas wreath on the door, hanging beneath the brass numbers 3 5 2. I couldn't decide whether that was weird or funny. It was vaguely unsettling, as though I was going into a time warp which now that I look back on it, I sure was. I was a few minutes early so I walked across the street and sat on a bench and just looked at the door. I was determined to be right on time, not early and anxious. Hell, I was already anxious.

A few minutes before six, the door opened and this beautiful blonde, perfect I thought, heart racing, looked out and looked around. It was quiet on the street then. She spotted me and then mouthed, 'Bill' with the accompanying question mark look. I nodded and she waved her 'come on in' arm and did it with a big, beautiful smile. I headed straight across, headed for the Promised Land.

"She opened the door all the way and stood there with her hands on her hips. My God! She was perfect. She was Tinkerbelle! I was already in love! I was booted from my little-head-now-driving-the-big-head coma, also known as taken from a great song that was out there somewhere: 'There's an angel on my shoulder but the devil's got the wheel' reverie by the blaring horn and swerving screeching of the tires of a long black Caddy limousine whose big, bald driver blessed me as he zoomed by with, 'Get outta da road, you stoopid motherfuckah!' as he fired out his left middle finger salute for punctuation. I paused. I looked at her. Her hands were over her mouth and she was laughing. She called, 'Come on now!' More carefully, I made it up the front stoop steps. She really was something. I didn't know what to do, didn't know the protocol of buying sexual congress from a real, live, honest-to-God call girl, so I shook her hand and said, 'Hi, Nikki.' That made her giggle. We sat down in her little front room in two plastic kitchen chairs. She asked me if I wanted something to drink. I declined. She had an obvious southern lilt to her voice. She said, 'Let's take a few minutes and just visit. I'll tell you a little about me and you can do the same. I'm guessing this is your first rodeo?" I came within a gnat's ass of saying, 'Yes, ma'am,' but killed that thought as it rose in my mind. I just nodded.

"She told me she was from Atlanta. 'All my people are still down there. Got a wild hair thing after going to school in Athens and came up here with a few other girls to get a job and well, see the sights and have some fun. Got a job in a steno pool at IBM, make good money. Met all sorts of interesting people. Miss Cindy came up to me in a bar a couple of years ago, we talked, I signed on. Truth is I like to fuck and am good at it so I figured why not. Her customers are the nicest and best. Never had any trouble. Why, just look at you. You're Exhibit A! Now, tell me, how old exactly are you? I'm twenty-six. Don't worry, just tell me, it's okay. 'Cause I don't think you're exactly eighteen. We are going to do some good work no matter what...you understand?' She talked like a Georgia Bulldog Tri-Delt at a rush party. It was a honeyed zero to a hundred in six seconds.

"I thought for a few seconds and spoke, 'Would it be okay if I was sixteen?' She laughed and asked that I tell her about myself. I tried, haltingly. It all sounded so boyish. 'I like sports. I really like football. I love to read. I go to a real good, real hard prep school over near Hartford. All my family are back in Winston-Salem. It's tobacco town.' She said, 'Sure I know Winston, know lots of good folks up here who went to Chapel Hill and Wake and Duke and all over. Would you like to have some fun now?' Then I remembered the five twenties. I pulled the little roll out and proffered it. It was awkward but she was smooth and gracious. I was enchanted. She pointed to the bedroom and told me, 'Get your things off and I'll be right on in in a minute. I know we have an hour and I think we've got plenty of time to have at it with each other.' She disappeared into the bathroom and I dutifully went into the bedroom, shucked off my Weejun loafers and dull khaki pants and Brooks Brothers striped shirt and just stood there. I realized that she was watching me, just tiny peeking around the corner of the door jamb. She had a playful glint in her eye. 'Go on now. Take off those boxers too. Go on and get in the bed under the covers. I'll be right there in a jiffy.'

"So I did and waited and sure enough, I was already pitching a pup tent in expectation. She came in wearing a little pink teddy. My heart was pounding. My God, this really is going to happen! She said, 'Close your eyes. No peeking. I'll tell you when to look. No cheating now.'"

The girls were just staring at Eddie who had gone on to another place. The conference room was still and quiet, eerily so. He was almost in a trance and they felt it was almost like a seance.

"I had squeezed my eyes tightly shut. I would follow her every instruction exactly as given. She said, 'Now, take a look. Take a good look!' I opened my eyes and as I did, she untied a string at the back of her neck and the whole thing slid softly to the floor. I had never seen anything like that. Ever. From head to toe, she was a gorgeous knockout. A dream. The only thing I could compare it to and I did so instantly was when I was about twelve when we all went out to my uncle and aunt's farm outside town on the river for a big fancy family Thanksgiving luncheon. My brother and I were all decked and knotted up out in coats and ties. It was a beautiful, very sunny cold day.

"We were the first to arrive and the grownups started the Bloody Mary Screwdriver phase upstairs in the living room and the young ones, us, were sent down to the playroom. It was just me and Freddie. He was about ten then. None of our cousins were there yet. There was a little bar in a tucked off alcove and while Freddie messed around at the pool table, I went into the bar, just casually snooping around. There was a wicker basket on top of a small refrigerator. It had magazines in it. They were *Playboys*! I remember looking around to see if Freddie or anyone or the Thought Police was watching me. No one. I picked one up and folded out the centerfold. I gazed at a lovely, sexy, leggy blonde, naked as a jaybird. I became instantly tumescent, swelling like a balloon. I had put my hand on a hot stove and I liked the burn very much. It made me very dizzy and totally focused and mentally lost all at once. I closed the cover and instantly put the magazine back and hand shifted my package to the straight upright position to lessen any curious eye attention until deflation came along. Now that centerfold blonde was Nikki and my dream come true. She asked me if I liked what I was seeing. I gulped out a breathy 'yes.' She came in beside me and asked, 'Don't you want to turn off that light?' I said, 'No, I want to be able to see everything real good.' She laughed and began to touch and caress and rub me. 'How about your glasses? You want to take them off?' and I said, 'Oh no, I have really bad vision and now I really want to see everything.'

"She laughed a little more and then directly she really began to touch me and she took me and took me some more and did things and showed me things and slowed me down and speeded me up and took us on a *National Geographic* exploration of her and me that I can never forget, and it was one of the most wonderful experiences of my life. And then it was all over and she said, 'Well, that was a lot of fun. Hope you liked it.'

"I had been struck dumb and then she said, 'Thanks for coming and come back and see me again sometime. I've got to go ahead and get ready for my next date, so...' I thanked her and soon I was back on the sidewalk as if nothing had ever happened but of course it had. I was deflated and deflowered."

Mikey asked, "Did you ever go back?"

"No. Two main reasons, I guess. First, it would never be the same, no matter how great it might have been. I just have always held that particular memory as a very special one."

"And what's the other reason?"

"I figured if I ever did go back I'd really fall for her and that would just never work out. That would have been a damn mess."

"Uh-huh, I think you're right."

Eddie paused and shook his head. "It was just incredible," he said to no one in particular. He was floating alone in outer space.

Patty said to Mikey, "This is why he says he likes sex so much, that he got trained right, right out of the box, so to speak, pardon my bad pun!"

Mikey blushed a little, swallowed and replied, "Yes, looks like he sure did. I'll leave that there."

Patty nodded and said, "Okay, Eddie, let's get to the punch line. We got work to do."

Mikey said, "You mean that's not it?"

"Nope, come on, give it up."

"Okay, we come home. I keep my mouth shut but obviously I'm so happily mind fucked. A few days later, I start my regular summer job working construction, heavy work building gas stations, running jackhammers, big tamps, digging ditches, rough finishing concrete, hauling 60-pound stacks of the stuff. It was a great way to get ready for football season. I'd been doing it since I was eleven.

"Anyway, a bunch of us are on jackhammers, ripping out old concrete and rebar, getting ready to help clear enough space to sink a 100,000-gallon gasoline tank. It's hot. Sun beating down. In heavy hot work boots, working without shirts, in shorts. I just remember feeling lightheaded and the next thing I knew, I'm laid out in the back of Mr. White's big work van and everyone's standing over me and Robert Brown is putting a cold rag on my head. He puts his hand on my forehead and high squeaks, 'Shit! The boy is burning up!' Mr. John White, our foreman who hated malingers and screw-offs and said sourly about a hundred times a day, 'Boys, shoot the shit or go home. Don't make a fuck to me,' was standing back of the bumper looking worried. I was scared.

"They closed down the job site quick and hauled me back to the corner in front of my house where they picked me up every morning. I was still a year and a half away from the liberation of a driver's license. Robert and this big fellow held me up and walked me to the kitchen door where our family cook Betty stood. 'Lawd! What is the devil has happened here?' They told her they didn't know and that I had just fallen out on the job. Thank God my parents were away traveling. They put me in Betty's car and she took off for the Emergency Room at Baptist Hospital. They rolled me in and asked who our family doctor was. I felt like a blast furnace was working on me from the inside. Dr. Henry Valk was paged and was soon there. They had given me some aspirin and cold water. He examined me and told me he wanted me sent upstairs and seen by a specialist, Dr. Bill Boyce, the head of urology and like Dr. Valk, a close family friend. In a few minutes, Dr. Boyce was examining my nutsack and its accompanying apparatus which now leaking some goopy stuff. He asked me where and with who I had been lately, and I mumbled something about New York City and a nice girl. He eyed me sideways and then told me that he needed to do something that wasn't going to be very pleasant. Said it had to be done. And then took what looked like a four-foot-long aluminum rod and ran it down my pecker to wherever the basement of my world was. It hurt so bad!

"He then pulled it out, backin' out which wasn't all that great either and flatly pronounced, 'Eddie, no need to have a discussion about this other than to tell you, you have a raging case of—"

Mikey interrupted, holding her hand up to halt Eddie's further remembrance, started to laugh and laugh, tears springing from her eyes. "Serves you right, you little prick. I'll bet you a dime to a doughnut you caught a big old case of the clap from your precious Tinkerbelle!"

Patty snorted, "Bingo!"

"Sure did. I was a stupid fourteen-year-old with a case of the clap. Jesus. They sent me home to go to bed with a couple of bottles of horse pill antibiotics. Knocked it out in a week."

Mikey asked, "Looking back, knowing what you know now, would you still have taken that chance?"

"Yup."

"You're an idiot." She was still laughing.

Patty added, "Remember men are just rocks with eyes." And rolled her eyes.

Eddie said, "That's the story of Tinkerbelle. I guess that's enough of that."

"Yeah, that's helluva good story but I need to be learned up some more. Eddie, glad I didn't know you back then. I would have knocked the shit out of you."

"Understood and agreed."

Patty readily segued them back the last piece of the Pussy Preacher.

"Okay, Eddie, how 'bout get us all up to speed on the Bible beaters at the Blockhouse Club."

"Well, we got the good Christian driving the truck. They'd been drinking and to boot at another club where flesh was being pressed. The driver didn't get charged but it was a close call according to the investigating officer. That is going to settle for the policy limits no matter what. If word got back to any of their wives, there would be in short order a mass castration in Terre Haute, Indiana, or wherever out there they all live.

"The tougher nut to crack was going to be the club itself. Their lawyers claimed the place to be a private club, had lots of signs and notices posted about that said so, so they are not subject to such a lawsuit under the laws of South Carolina. Said the boys were not members. Said they had not admitted the boys to begin with, that the boys just wandered in and used fake identification to buy alcohol. Said they ushered them out quickly. No violence and once they were outside, they seemed fine. Said it was all on the driver and they didn't care what happened at Thee Doll House."

"So what have you done to fight that?" asked Mikey.

"All that sounds nice but here's the deal. We got both smart and lucky. Three main things are going to pull their lying house of cards down. First, remember we've got ATM and credit card receipts and on those are dates and times of use and withdrawal. Our clients were sucking money out and making charges like sailors on leave in Tokyo which gives us a solid timeline and money trail which is irrefutable. It all also shows that they were in the Blockhouse for at least 45 minutes which sets up that timeline up with the first call to EMS and when the responders arrive, plus the EMS real-time chartings as to victims' conditions. Think, 'Reeking of Alcohol.' They were in there for more than a brief time and to boot, were doing multiple Jagerbomb shots. They were already good and drunk when they were being served.

"Second, to stiffen the proof on how loaded across the board they were on that afternoon and evening, we have retained the services of the most pre-eminent forensic pathologist in the state and one of the best in the country. Dr. Janice Haynie from out of Columbia. She has worked for defense firms, plaintiffs' lawyers, public and private sector companies, government agencies, hospitals, insurance companies, you name it. She's smart, meticulous and as a plus, she's a really nice, funny lady. Her husband is a psychiatrist of high reputation and as a fun fact, she is very well and broadly read. Fair to say we have become friends over the years. Have worked with her many times. If she has a conflict or someone has beat me to her, she always plays fair and says, 'No can do.' She has taken all the scraps and pieces of paper I just mentioned just a minute ago and has done a retrograde extrapolation and analysis of the boys' ETOH levels."

"What's ETOH?"

"Alcohol."

"Ah. Figured something like that. Figured you weren't talking ice cream."

"It's a working backwards analysis. It's a rigid, scientific, and mathematical process used by chemists and toxicologists to estimate to a most probable degree of certainty—that's the bar we must clear—what the individual's metabolic alcohol levels were at various times along the course and path of their frolic. And in summary, Dr. Haynie says these three were drunk as staggering dogs from about midway through their time at Thee Doll House until their ejections from the Blockhouse. So, we have clear and convincing evidence of both clubs serving booze to these blockheads when they are obviously and seriously under the influence of intoxicating spirits.

"Good, but what are you going to do about this 'private club' protection the Blockhouse has tossed up against you?" Mikey asked.

Patty said, "Now this is rich! Talk about damn, dumb luck!"

Eddie nodded in amused assent. "Well, true, we couldn't have gotten much luckier if an angel had shoved a golden horseshoe up my ass! Here's the deal. Truck and me rode over to the Patricia Manor. It's an old timey pretty seaside hotel, been there way before I was even a kid. Has a really nice dining room that overlooks the ocean. It's not Sea Island or Jekyll but it's very nice and comfortable in its own inimitable way. Went there all the time as a child. Still has real, honest-to-God waiters, gentlemen of color, black pin-striped trousers, white waistcoats, gold trim. It was early, the place wasn't crowded, we'd been given menus and left alone, and Truck was having a nerve-soothing pop. I messed with some notes and a cup of coffee and this very nicely dressed kid, maybe fourteen or so, came up to our table and he had on seersucker pants, a blue blazer, a crisp white shirt, a clip-on bow tie. A slicked shock of real blond hair. We looked at him. He looked at us. He looked like someone whose family were guests at the Patricia. He blended in. But he didn't fit.

"His name was Tommy Davis and without invitation just looked us over and began to speak. In a flat monotone, he said, 'I work for a very fine private club here in Myrtle Beach called the Blockhouse. It has fine food and drink and lovely hostesses and comfortable surroundings and privacy as well. It's just up the highway here.' The kid had rehearsed his patter and pitch down to a pleasant monotone. He didn't miss a speck of his script. I said, 'Really. How about that? Now, why would you be letting us know about all this?' and he responded, 'Well, I was wondering would you gentlemen have any interest in receiving complimentary passes to go to the Blockhouse.' Truck was looking at me with eyes wide. I returned his gaze lovingly and with only the thinnest of smiles. I said, 'I think we just might. Yes, we surely will visit. Thank you. Your offer is a very kind one. May I please see one of the passes?' The kid reached into his pants and pulled out a wad of what looked like business cards, at least a hundred or more, wrapped with a big, thick rubber band. Carefully he slides one out and handed it respectfully to me. It was on fine stock paper, good weight. I took it and looked around. If the wait staff was aware of this kind of thing going on, they showed no notice or awareness."

Mikey said, "Isn't this supposed to be a private club and here there's a kid handing out passes to strangers?"

"Girl, you are good." Patty nodded. pleased.

Eddie reached into his desk to show the Blockhouse pass to everyone.

WELCOME TO THE BLOCKHOUSE
MYRTLE BEACH'S FINEST PRIVATE CLUB
FINE FOOD, DRINK, AND LOVELIES
Admit One Guest, Good For Repeat Admissions
Up to 30 days from Issue
All Major Credit Cards Accepted
Please have time-stamped upon First Entry
Have a Great Time and Thank You!
s/ The Management
Date:_______________________________________

"We find out from Tommy that he gave out these free passes to guests. But I wanted to buy all of his passes. I said, 'I do want to pay you for them. For each one you hand out, let me guess, I bet the folks up at the Blockhouse pay you what, a couple of dollars for each one you move? Is that close? I'm going to give them out to friends as little gifts. How many do you think you have there?'

"He then told us he was given a hundred of them three evenings a week and made some two dollars and fifty cent commission on each. I said, 'Tommy, how about a hundred from me? And I'll bet my friend here would like to help out the same. We'll take the passes for free and just give you a gift cause you're such a nice, well-mannered, impressive young man. Now, when you go back, tell them there was a big convention here at the Patricia, real estate guys, all revved up, drinking a little too much, played golf all day; you've seen that sort of group before, haven't you?'

Tommy folded the money into his pocket and handed me the passes. No bribe was paid, there was no quid pro quo, no one was forced to transact business, no change was made to the evidence, no tampering, no nothing. We had no friends to reward, no enemies to punish. Remember, little Tommy there said they were free. By the time mediation was over in a few weeks, the cases would be settled and no one would have anything to say about anything. I'd send the other side a copy of the pass and that would be all it took with a Request To Admit Authenticity and we would also send Motions to Produce all bills and charges received and as charged to defendant from any and all entities for production and printing of said same complimentary passes created over the past five years. I'd bet they have ginned up and handed out tens of thousands over the years. Their liquor and operating licenses are getting ready to be in high, hard wind. This gets out and the guys that own that place will be running a shitbag Skee Ball palace down near the Pavilion wondering what the number of the truck was that just ran them down. They are no more a private club than I'm fucking Abraham Lincoln."

CHAPTER FOURTEEN

A HARD DAY'S NIGHT

The Beatles

MIKEY SAID, "DAMN. And this is just one case?"

Patty said with pride and admiration looking at Eddie, "Yeah, he's pretty damn good. He really is. Now, we got a few hours left so let's talk about a whole lot of others, maybe not so long on each, okay?"

"Cut the crap, Patty." Eddie was laughing. "She's seen me get my ass handed to me so many times, it's got calluses deeper than leather knobs on it. The only guy in this mess who is undefeated is either a liar or a rookie who lucked out on his first case. We have to fail to win. Took me a long time to realize that fact."

He smiled, tilted his head, clapped his hands lightly and said, "Oh yeah, I do love it so. Let's hit it again, Patty!"

And so they reviewed, more efficiently than anecdotally, a gamut of cases and matters. There were criminal cases, from the minor world of misdemeanors to the daunting vortex of serious, ugly, nasty felonies, murders, rapes, beatings, extortions, and assaults. There were always traffic tickets, DUIs, speeding, improper equipment, and more speeding and DUIs. There were automobile accidents and truck wrecks by the handfuls, degrees of damages of all types and varieties, soft tissue chiropractic to amputations and closed-head injuries.

There were plane crashes, burning injuries, and deaths, literary and copyright theft, misuse and misappropriation of individual identities, libel, slander, alienation of affections, dram shop cases, insurance fraud, theft of corporate secrets, premises liability, suits against government, boating deaths and injuries, products liability cases involving defective products and disingenuously labeled pharmaceuticals, electrocutions, broken necks in swimming pools, shattered limbs from neglect of basis security and safety issues in parking lots and outdoor dining restaurants, and it just went on and on.

And then there were the medical malpractice cases, reserved for a special high shelf in the firmament of Eddie Terrell's universe of practice. They were set aside for a few days down the road. Eddie had some traveling to do.

Eddie had been lured and enticed into dueling with these most difficult of legal beasts by chance and by his ego that was flattered by another fine lawyer's misunderstanding of how these devils coiled and uncoiled, struck and evaded while being struck. Eddie had done some good work many years ago in a criminal case that ultimately relied upon precise medical forensic analysis to help save the skin of one Homer "Kenny" Peak, the enormously large, sweet brother of one of his closest helpers, the inimitable Rise.

Mikey said, "Huh? The lady Rise I just met a little while ago? Her brother?"

"Yeah, the one and the same."

"Tell me about it, okay, just tell me a little about it."

Patty said, "Let me put a clock on it," and lit another cigarette.

Eddie laughed and started, "Watch this little Miss Know-It-All. And by the way, Mikey, I repped Rise a couple of times for stealing Social Security checks before Kenny ever came along. Kenny got accused of murder. We got him a much better deal—six years is of course way better than life—when we were able to prove that the victim, who was a rat shit little pimp and hustler named Bo Diddley, got shot multiple times with multiple calibers of bullets, any one of which could have been the kill shot and to boot, Kenny had no gun on him when he got picked up. Plus, it didn't hurt that the investigating detectives got caught talking ugly about 'niggers' and had to admit calling the killing 'a public service shooting for the great benefit of the citizens of Winston-Salem.' The trial judge went ballistic and jammed a deal down everyone's throats. We swallowed gratefully. The DA's office gagged but had to take it. How's that, Patty?" He stuck his tongue out at his Gal Friday. She blew a smoke ring at him.

"Anyway, there was a lawyer in the courtroom that day by the name of Birdsong, helluva guy, smart and funny and wise enough to keep a good read on himself. I got to be great friends with Birdie who watched my patched together but ultimately effective medical forensic legerdemain and asked me a few days later if I'd take a look at a case for him. He thought it might be a medical malpractice case and he reasoned with me that I seemed to be attuned to that sort of thing. I was a young pup back then and hungry for work and attention too and was just dumb enough to say, 'Sure, I'll take a look,' as if I knew anything, which I didn't.

"A nice lady named Meggie Lee Shorter, a very modest woman in her mid-forties who had a very early stage vaginal cancer, easily removable which they did. Very early catch. Her treatment followed on with radiation therapy which is where the horrible fuck up happened. Her radiotherapy docs gave her about eight to ten times the appropriate curative covering dose, did not follow or monitor her carefully—obviously—and they ended up burning a hole that could never be repaired between her vagina and her colon. The tissue margins in this type of radiation injury cannot be stitched or sewed back together. There are motility and physical pressure issues as well. The tissue is de-oxygenated and thus the cells cannot replicate for repair and they are friable and the knitting won't hold. This was pretty gross. When she needed to go to the bathroom to defecate, she'd give it a good push and one day shit started coming out of her vagina."

"My God! That's just awful!" said Mikey.

"Yeah, she was given a permanent colostomy and a bag for life. And it hurt and she was humiliated, and it was a great big, unnecessary mess."

"What did you do? How did it turn out?"

"I had no idea what to do but I called a good friend Perry Locke who was sort of one of the favored OB-GYNs here in town. I asked him if he'd take a look at it for me, just confidentially of course. A week later, he called me and we met for lunch at a club we both belonged to. More than a little irony to that as the radiation docs whose work was being assessed were also members of that club. I'll never forget it. We sat in a corner booth downstairs and talked golf and sports and Carolina stuff. The case never came up until at the end of our meal when he reached into his inside coat pocket and slipped me a thick envelope with the records and his note in it. All he said was in a very rapid, truly conspiratorial whisper, 'It's a case, a real bad case. You know I cannot touch it. It's local. Read my note in there.' And honest to God, he was gone. Like a spy movie. It was about then that I began to realize and appreciate that it seemed there was a conspiracy of silence among a lot of doctors. I could understand why too.

"I didn't dare read the note until I was back in my car in the parking lot. I remember before I unsealed the envelope, I rolled my windows up and locked my car doors. The note read, 'Call Dr. F. W. Wesley at the med school in Chapel Hill. He taught me. Tell him I have asked you to call him. I think he can help you. I hope so.' I did just that and he asked when I could come immediately with the records.

"I was in my car in ten minutes on the way to Chapel Hill, about east, taking me about ninety minutes to get there. He was the Chief of Gynecologic Oncology at the med school and his offices were in a real rabbit warren of a place. I straightened my tie and shoved my forever flapping shirttail back into my baggy suit pants. I buttoned my coat, pushed my hair back, and opened the frosted glass door to the department. I introduced myself to the receptionist. There were a number of people, four or five, sitting in the waiting area. That intimidated me. Everything was intimidating me. Truth be told, I was a little on the south side of frightened. This whole thing was taking on a sense of pressing gravity. I was ushered into his office. Dr. Wesley was dark haired, very handsome, set jaw, dark eyes, of medium height and serious mien. He motioned for me to sit and I did so quickly. He never looked up from the records and then said, 'Thank you for coming. I'll be in touch.' I was dismissed in less than five minutes. I found my way out and drove home in a state of hopeful and also inexplicable bewilderment. I remember being downright confused."

Mikey asked, "Then what happened?"

Patty said, "About a week later, his office called and said he'd like to see Eddie as soon as possible. I had Eddie on the move within a half hour. I knew this thing had really been chewing on him. Had started to chew on me too. I didn't know much at all about med mal cases but the idea that we might be starting to go down that kind of road was pretty heavy, almost ominous. I had asked some of my buddies from other offices about them, what they were like, were they complicated...that sort of stuff. Most didn't know anything and the consensus was 'stay away from them.' The few that did said they were bears and not very nice bears either. So, you know, I wondered."

Eddie went on. "I got down there to Dr. Wesley's office. Same drill. Quick flatlined efficiency. Put me in his office in the same chair. Felt like I had been sent to the principal's office in elementary school and boy, did I know that feeling. Guilty as charged, over and over again. He came in, shut the door, and stood behind me. It occurred to me that I was afraid that I had wasted this man's time and brought him a pig in a poke and that he was gonna be none too happy about it. I was afraid to turn around. Waiting for the guillotine to fall.

"And he said, 'I've reviewed the records, spoken to Perry about you and he vouches for you 100 percent. I have also conferred with one of my colleagues here, a very fine radiation oncologist. We have decided that we are both going to help you. What happened to Ms. Shorter should never have happened. This is a very unfortunate and sad case. Now, listen very carefully to me. Dr. Perry Locke must be kept out of this matter, these communications, no matter what. If it were to come out that you found me at his guidance, it would not be long before that segment of his medical community over there in Winton-Salem and too regionally as well would make him a pariah, would begin to blacklist him, hurt his professional reputation, his practice, his source of income. When I am asked how it came to be that you contacted me, and that will be asked, I will answer that I have no idea, that as I understood it, apparently you did enough reading and research to realize you needed to speak with a gynecologic oncologist and you started at the medical school at your alma mater and thus identified and contacted me. Do you understand?' I said I did and then Dr. Wesley said I could not thank Perry Locke for his help and must avoid social contact with him until this matter was long over.

"I felt a great sense of relief and also a strong sense of foreboding. I had brought this smart doctor something that was worthy and by virtue of that act of offering, he had taken it and I was now headed into the belly of a beast. And then the damndest thing happened. He walked around his desk, much more informal now, with what could only be described as a sly grin on his face. Behind his desk, there was one of those closed-door whiteboards that could be opened up and drawn and diagrammed and written on. With a quick flourish, he opened the doors wide open and said, 'Perry says you are a very serious Heels fan!' And behind those doors was a huge iconic cartoon, well known to all Atlantic Coast Conference basketball fans, of the great

Coach Dean Smith dressed up as a little Carolina Tar Heel Blue Riding Hood while his dressed all in red, Wolf Pack rival coach Stormin' Norman Sloan reeled from a big mallet which Blue had smote Red on the head.

"It was really funny and kind of surreal too. In a matter of minutes, we had gone from professor and pupil to fellow travelers in cahoots over our love of our Heels. Silly, I guess, but man oh man, it sure didn't hurt as we went down a lot of hard road later on. I got back to Winston-Salem and told Birdie the news. I remember he said, 'Now you gotta show me what to do.' Then I said that I didn't know shit about med mal cases but we were gonna learn together. And we did and months later, we won, not as much as we had hoped for but it was a good lick and it was an amazing experience."

Patty said, "You forgot to tell her how you and the lead defense lawyer, one of the real big bad boys of the bar, a senior kind of guy almost beat up one another in his office one day because he wouldn't give you the discovery you had been asking for over and over. That was a hoot. Eddie tried to turn the guy's desk over on him. The two of them were in there screaming cuss words at each other, 'you son of a bitch,' 'you motherfucker,' you get the picture. In this wood-paneled dignified, quiet-as-death, fancy partner's corner office. The great senior partner, Robinson Norwood had to come down those glorified halls of dignity and break it up and get this, Norwood was the guy that sponsored Eddie at his swearing in for the granting of his law license and Eddie's great-uncle was one of the founding members and partners of the defense firm when it first started. Eddie...Eddie...Eddie. Always a rebellious sort, weren't you?" Patty laughed. Mikey laughed too.

Eddie said, "How about let's let this be enough for the day? We've covered a lot of ground here."

Patty seconded. "I'll say."

Eddie looked at the two. "Thank y'all for staying with it today. Can I buy anyone a drink?"

Patty shook her head, said, "Thanks, but no. I'm heading home where it's quiet and I got my very own jug just for myself." She winked.

Eddie followed on with, "I've decided to go on down to Naples day after tomorrow to see my brother, just a quick down and back day trip. Patty, would you please get me a ticket lined up from Dick Anderson's Travel Palace or whatever the hell it's now called?"

"Sure, will have it here by lunch. You coming in?"

"Just to pick it up but that's it. I'm going to go on now and take Mikey to find a drink and food and then home. Tomorrow, think I'll spend some time showing her around, go by and say hey to Mother, and Mikey's got to get some clothes and gal things together too. We sort of just blew out here on the fast fly, didn't we?" Mikey cast her eyes demurely downward then back up with the light of the ending day in them.

"You got it," Patty said. "Have fun at your mother's! Mikey, just breathe and it'll go by quick enough."

"Yeah, keep it covered and don't let the bastards get you down."

"Good plan."

They had all stood up and Patty headed back to her office and Eddie took Mikey's arm and said, "C'mon, kid, let's go home."

Mikey said, "Home. That sounds nice. And what's all this about your mother?"

"Well, we're not gonna find out until we look, right? And, don't worry, my mother has never liked any woman I have ever gone out with, never, none, nada, zero, zilch, zed, so she'll be curious, chilly, and distant, and more I expect. You just need to be inoculated."

"Sounds fabulous. Eddie, you know you are exhausting..."

"Yeah, I know. I know. But as the smart fellow said, 'If you always keep moving, they can't get a clean shot at you.'"

CHAPTER FIFTEEN

HOMEWARD BOUND

Simon & Garfunkel

"YOU WANNA EAT out or want me to cook for you? Actually, I'm a pretty good cook. Aren't you pretty tired? Been a long couple of days I think."

"True. How about you cook for us? That would be nice." She squeezed his arm. "And, you know I'm curious to see your place."

"Fair enough. Now, you understand it isn't gonna be anything like Montana, well, look like Montana. It's a pretty nice but simple spot. I've been there a good while now. We need to go to the grocery store and the liquor store and get some provisions because I'm sure I have nothing at home that isn't spoiled or frozen. I should have asked Patty to stock me up but it just didn't cross my mind. Well, that's not all bad. It'll help with starting to get you to finding your way a little bit."

They drove out of downtown, way out Country Club Road to the ABC Store. The state had a monopoly on liquor sales and it was the typical Bible Belt chastity belt for the evils of booze used to allegedly control and temper the morality and the temptations of its herded sheep. The system was corrupt and wasteful and just pissed everybody off. God forbid that places that sold beer and wine like grocery and convenience stores might be allowed to also sell distilled spirits. It was just more inefficient blue law-hold over crap from those saving days of Prohibition.

Interesting, the Prohibition champion way back then when Raleigh was the saloon capital was big, fat Governor Robert B. Glenn. He was a whore lawyer for the railroads, a penny-pinching bastard who cared not a whit for the great unwashed of farmers and mill workers who well deserved a good stiff drink when they wanted it. He was a hard-preaching teetotaler and all the sinners would surely be sent straight to the devil.

At their destination Eddie grabbed some big bottles of good bourbon and vodka and tequila and rum. "Might as well stock up a little."

Mikey looked around and saw mini bottles. "These are cute. Don't see these much out West."

Eddie said, "Yeah, it's like the old days on airplanes. Fly the friendly skies of Carolina. They're pretty useless and too damn expensive, but if you want to sneak a few drinks into a ball game or the movies or some dry event, they're the way to go. Another example of government hypocrisy. We'll legally sell you this for our tax dollars so you can most probably use what we have sold you to break some laws here and there." He shrugged.

Back in the car, Mikey said, "That just looked and felt, well, weird."

"I know. Not at all like back out West where there is, at least as to booze, a whole lot more common sense."

Next stop was the grocery store, a place with the reassuring, comfortable name of Harris Teeter.

"Is that the name of the man that founded it?"

"No, honey, it's just a made-up name. There is no Harris, no Teeter. Just like there is no Aunt Jemimah and no Betty Crocker. They're made up names too. We all call it the Teet. It's owned by an outfit called the Ruddick Corporation out of Charlotte. They also make thread for sewing mills. Weird combo but it works for them, I guess. Come on and help me grab some vittles."

They got a cart and gathered some red and white wine, some beer and better than decent already chilled champagne, as well as steaks, lemons, limes, and Stouffers creamed spinach and mac and cheese along with a bag of charcoal and lighter fluid.

It was getting dark. Eddie paid and they headed on. After a few miles, they were winding down a forest-enclosed road with small, neat houses winking their lights. There were no big or grandiose homes, just nice houses and little yards carved out of gaps in the heavy woods. They rounded a curve and now up a short hill and Eddie nosed his car into a sloping driveway.

"Well, here we are. This is it. It's not fancy but it's home. I like it, been here fifteen years, maybe a little more." Eddie gestured to his right. Mikey peered out in the gathering dusk to a little brick house with gray shutters. There was a grove of tall, hardwood trees at the end of the drive and a good-sized lake behind them.

"Come on. Let's haul this stuff inside and make a drink and you can have the ten-cent tour.

Eddie unlocked the front door. Patty had left a small front hall lamp on, set on a little table in the corner. Its light was golden and small but illuminated the outlines of the rooms in the front of the house, a living room to the left, a small dining room to the right. The dining room had daffodil-patterned wallpaper above handsome white wainscoting. Mikey followed Eddie into the kitchen. He clicked a light on. The supplies were put down. Eddie asked, "What's your pleasure?"

Mikey said, "You know, I've gotten kind of used to a little champagne here and there. You've spoiled me, I think."

"Good." He quickly popped the cork and reached into a cabinet with a collection of plastic cups, all of which bore the imprimatur of the University of North Carolina in one fashion or another, poured her a hefty dose into one and handed it to her. "Now, here you go. Hang on now. Let me slosh a good one for myself." He cracked the seal of a big bottle of Virginia Gentleman and poured four fingers into a cup, added ice from the freezer tray and turned to her and with something more than mock formality, bowed toward her lovely self and spoke quietly and reverentially, his cup crowning above his shoulder.

"Cheers, my dear girl. I am very glad you are here. I truly am. Thank you for coming along on this obviously kinda crazy adventure. Thank you so much." He felt himself becoming unusually emotional, touched.

She held her cup out to him. She looked him in the eye steady, with a great gaze of head-tilted affection. "Cheers back to you, Eddie. I'm very glad I'm here with you. I've learned more in the past few days than I could ever have imagined." She paused. Now hesitant, she haltingly took her chance. "Eddie, I think you know I really like you, really care about you. I hope I can do a good job by you. You're a different kind of man, Eddie, I think you are a helluva guy and a helluva good man. I hope that came out right." Her voice tailed off.

Eddie could feel tears welling up in his eyes. He raised his sleeve to blot them.

She just watched him. Tears were coming to her now too.

They were tired. Tired can make a lot of folks a little weepy.

Eddie's voice was now a bit blocked up but he managed to croak out as he blinked fast. "Mikey, thank you. I hope you know I care about you, care about you a lot. I mean it. I truly do." And he regained his equilibrium. "Now, how about some big swills and let's take a quick look-see around and then I'll grill us some steaks. What do you say to that?"

Mikey nodded a sweet smile in the quiet realization that a long-distance fling, a criminal and legal and God-knows-what-else lark had begun to blossom further into some very uncertain paths. They both took deep, slow swallows.

"Come on."

Off the kitchen was a big, screened porch. Beyond it, the yard gently rolled down to the lake and there was a little dock too. He took her hand and walked her out on the porch.

"Do you come out here much? Do you use that dock down there?"

"Oh, a little bit. Not a fisherman. Bores me to death. Like to sit up here on the porch and just read, relax, look around. Sometimes in the winter, the lake will really freeze over, really hard, and deep and we'll get a bunch of us together and play ice hockey with brooms and tennis balls. Sometimes we can do it at night when we turn the flood lights on from the back of the house. That's a lot of fun."

He turned and led her back to the front of the house. As they went, she saw a desk covered in papers and office things, bookcases crammed with volumes of every shape, size, and color and a big TV set in a large room off the other side of the kitchen. There was a full bath too.

"That's your bathroom so we don't have to be bumping into each other all the time. And that's my work and playroom. I love to work. I love sports. I love to read. Come on. Over here is the living room. The fireplace works. That's another good place to sit and read and think. And this is the dining room where I rarely eat but will lay out and plan a case on the table all the time." Up the stairs they went, Eddie turning on all the lights. "I'm not big on overhead lights. I have no idea why. Probably taught to dislike them as a kid. Mother's influence I guess. This is the guest room, over here is my room, and there's another full bath in between."

Mikey looked about. "Eddie, this place is really cozy. All your furniture and draperies are pretty nice. Did you put it together yourself?"

"Yeah, mostly. I had a little help here and there from my mother and some of her resources. But fair to say, I was taught and taught well to have good taste and it stuck with me. I like this place."

"Uhm, would it be all right if I give you a great big hug? I really want to do that."

"Mikey, you can give me anything you want. I'm more than a little crazy about you. You know that. Feel free to eat me up with a spoon."

She grabbed him and they hung on tight to each and they kissed and they were very happy.

They went back downstairs and fired up the grill and he cooked the steaks and she heated up some Stouffers and got the knives and forks and salt and pepper and glasses together and they ate and drank wine and talked, talked easily about the this and thats of their lives. And they were really very tired.

As they were cleaning up after dinner, Eddie laughed. "You know, that was our first real foray into the jungle of domesticity. We did pretty good, don't you think?"

"I thought it was outstanding. I liked it a lot."

"Let's stay with it but not get too carried away. In truth it scares me a little bit. I don't think I'm very good at it. We don't want to mess up a good thing by going over into Ozzie and Harriett land. Don't you think?" She nodded and put her down her empty cup. "What you want to do now?"

"I want to go wash my face, brush my teeth, brush my hair, get out of these clothes, put on a T-shirt, and get in that bed with you and see how you handle the end of this day. Everybody's got some sort of routine so I'm sure you do too."

"True. I'll hit the can, clean me up some and join you in the rack. I like to sometimes watch a little television, like to read in bed too, read a lot there. But tonight is shaping up special cause you're here so I expect, if you like, can divert me as you wish."

"I like your thinking and I'll see you upstairs in a minute."

They went off for their ablutions and joined each other in Eddie's big bed that was now becoming their bed. The sheets were crisp and wonderful cold, the air conditioning was chilling away. Eddie picked up a book on the Civil War he had been reading off and on for the past month. Mikey snuggled up to him, her warmth lush and tender, tucking herself into and almost under him, her long legs twining his like tendrils of ivy. Eddie put the book down and turned off the light. It was very dark and still. They could hear each breathing quietly, steady. Eddie rolled over into Mikey and they did indeed divert.

CHAPTER SIXTEEN

YOU DIDN'T LOOK AROUND

Lesley Gore

THEY SLEPT WELL and hard and rose and got after their day. Eddie wanted to show Mikey around, take her shopping, and also help her get better oriented to the city. They went to the old, venerable Thruway Shopping Center where there was a Talbots. She shopped and Eddie watched. They went to Montaldo's. She shopped and Eddie watched. They went to the Gazebo out at Reynolda. She shopped and Eddie watched. They ate lunch at the original Village Tavern, arguably with the best Texas Pete and buttered up hot Buffalo wings, this side of Buffalo. Next, to the rustic elegance of the Reynolds estate that was the pretty campus of the very well-respected Wake Forest University. They drove over and slowly cruised along, Eddie pointing things out here and there. The campus had matured and grown and seasoned nicely since it was moved from the little village of Wake Forest near Raleigh back in the mid-1950s.

"You don't know this, Mikey, but this is where I went to law school."

"Really? I thought you were a North Carolina guy all the way, through and through."

"I pretty much am but I have grown to have a pretty big affection for this place. Sort of my hometown university. It helped me, kicking and screaming, get my law degree. And the school has a big-time national reputation so that's a good thing to have on my resume though truth be told, when I came through here, I have no doubt more than a few folks, at the behest of my mother, pulled more than a few strings to get me in here. And I was truly a rotten, bottom-feeding law student. Today, even if I held a pistol on them, I couldn't get in here. This is top-shelf academic now, nationally recognized. When I was here, they prided themselves on being a 'North Carolina and pretty much North Carolina Only' law school. No more."

"Did you like going to law school?"

"Not really. I was no good at it and didn't get after it with my studies the way I should have. Knowing what all I know now and have learned along the way, I kinda think it would be fun to come back and go through it again. I expect I'd get so much more out of it. But that's just a pipe dream now. Too busy and making too much money and having too much fun to take a three-year break like that."

As they were exiting the campus, Eddie mused aloud, "You know, I grew up not too far from here and my mother still lives there. Our house is so close to the campus, when they were moving the dirt and building the new campus, my brother and I would ride our bikes over here and watch all the bulldozers and earth graders and heavy Caterpillar big boys that would grumble and growl and push and shove that red clay. It was awesome. My mother still lives in that house. I need to just see her and check in. I want her to meet you. Like I've said, she's never much liked any girl I've ever gone out with. Our story is from the get-go to a proper old lady like her is pretty twisty. Plus, you are bombshell and that'll touch off her here's-another-girl-trying-to-get-her-Eddie to go off away from here. Do you think you can handle the dose? It won't take too long. She's used to me not staying long. We butt heads a lot. I think it would be best to just go ahead and get it done, check it off the list. Whaddaya say?"

"It's okay. Your cranky mommy won't be the first old biddy to have looked me over and found me wanting. Sure, let's go for a visit. I know how to say 'please' and 'thank you' and 'yes' and 'no, ma'am.'"

"Now tomorrow, I'll get you to ride me over to the airport and then you can take the car and I'll give you a card and you can go all over and explore and do whatever you like and round up things that you need. I'll call you so you can pick me up and we can later have dinner together. Just a quick day trip down and back."

"Who are you going to see down there again?"

"My brother. He's sort of a retired but not really, a money manager, kind of a stockbroker. Handles all of our family accounts and his own stuff. He's a very smart money and business guy. Can break down a balance sheet with great skill. Really good at reading between the lines. He's made me a lot of money over the years. He's made a whole lot of people a whole lot of money over the years. He plays a lot of golf and cards. Moved to Naples a few years ago. He likes the weather and it's pretty low key. He used to be a wild man but over the years he's destarched himself. He's a very good guy. His wife is a doll and a hoot. He can be cranky but usually funny cranky. A cheerful, self-deprecating curmudgeon."

"What's his name?"

"Frederick Ball Terrell, but we all call him Pablo the Grasshopper. Don't ask me why. I have no idea how that name came to be hung on him but it happened at our old fraternity house in Chapel Hill. I suspect our good friend Ernie Eldridge from Louisiana had a hand in it. He was always giving people nicknames. Pablo was a varsity wrestler at Chapel Hill. Ran a bunch of marathons afterwards too. A real bull of a guy. Little below medium height, big muscles that work, squeaky voice. Holds a 10th degree black belt in Korean Special Forces karate. As loyal to his friends as anyone I have ever known. A true gentleman. I've never saw him start a fight but I have seen him finish a few and how. Dropped the idiots like they'd been shot.

"When Fred and I were kids we'd fight each other all the time. We were so rotten, Daddy would clear all the furniture out of the front hall at home and we'd be just in our tighty whities and he'd lace us up in great big 18-ounce Everlast boxing gloves. They were like swollen feather pillows on our hands. No way you really hurt someone with those and we each had a corner and he'd time us out in three two-minute rounds. We'd just swing and flail away at each other. He was smart about it. Wore us out. And he'd boxed some in school and in the army so we learned something about fighting too.

"Fights? Ha. Back at Chick's a few days ago, you handled yourself pretty damn strong. And you and your brother did some tag-teaming? That sounds like something to see. Wham bam and pow." Mikey threw a couple of girl punches into the air.

"Okay, Cassius Clay, let's go see my mother."

Mikey set her jaw and her face forward. "Hit it, big boy."

They went down to the office to get Eddie's plane ticket to Fort Myers and Naples for tomorrow's travels. Mikey shot the breeze with Patty while Eddie went through some mail and grabbed his ticket. He started to go and then paused.

"Patty, let's talk a minute to talk about the Reynolds case before I get going."

CHAPTER SEVENTEEN

GONNA GET BURNED

Rachel Potter

"HERE WE GO. Zach Reynolds, a fairly young fellow in his early forties was one of a few direct inheritors of the massive R.J. Reynolds tobacco fortune. In their heydays, Mr. R. J. Reynolds of these Winston and Salem parts and Mr. Buck Duke of Durham were tobacco barons of giant fortunes, among the richest men in the country if not the world. Reynolds Tobacco and American Tobacco were filthy rich, I mean rich with a capital R. Zach was Mr. R.J.'s grandson and was said to be self-employed. That employment meant he collected lots of cars and motorcycles, played with his ham radios, was a champion shooter of skeet and clays, and also was an award-winning stunt pilot and aviator with a good-sized collection of airplanes that zoomed and zipped and climbed and dove. His conduct was always sweet and kind, often perplexed. Young kids adored him. He was sort of a Pied Piper to them. He always reminded me of an even goofier Gomer Pyle from the Andy Griffith Show days. He had a lisp which contributed to his childish charm. Not a bad looking young man, had a hank of black hair that always hung in his face and had to always be pushed away. He was not stupid but often acted like he was and maybe too he wasn't the sharpest knife in the drawer."

"You knew him?" Mikey asked.

"Oh, yes, just in passing but we knew one another. Our families knew one another. My mother and my uncle Ed knew him well. Here's a great story which tells a lot about him. One day I went with my mother to my uncle's real estate office here in downtown Winston. She had him helping her on something or other. I really don't recall. Zach came in. He was wearing a bright red Hawaiian shirt and a pair of the worst looking double knit pants that were so picked and fuzzy, it looked like he'd run back and forth in the briar patch for hours. I remember they were just this god-awful green and gold color. It hurt to look at them but I couldn't help myself. Anyway, after everybody said their hellos, my mother asked Zach, "What is that huge bulge in your pants pocket?" One look showed something wrinkled and heavy tugging downward, about the size of a big softball.

"He replied, his lisp prominent. He said, 'That's thuh Cursth of Wealth.' She didn't understand and asked him to repeat it. Then she asked, 'You mean the Curse of Wealth? What in the world are you talking about?' Zach grinned and pulled, really extracted the largest, roundest ring of keys I'd ever seen. 'This is thuh cursth of wealth. I've got so mutch twhit locked up and buried all over the place, I can harfly rethember which key unlocks what twhit, much less where the damn thang is.' We all hooted and hollered. It was well-known by many, many people that Zach distrusted banks and was constantly burying cash and gold all over the place up at the family's farm, place called Devotion. He was so pleased with himself with that joke. He was a smart dumb guy or a dumb smart guy. Never could be sure.

"Anyhow, there were a bunch of neighborhood kids, teenagers who always hung around him at his big house and bigger garage just off Buena Vista Road, right near my mother's. Like I said, he liked to have the kids around, ham radioing it up, checking the cars and bikes out and he'd take some of them every now and then for an airplane ride. He was a thrilling guy to them. He impressed them. A couple of them, because of Zach, wanted to get their pilot's licenses.

"One day they did get them and were so happy and excited and they went directly to Zach to show him what they'd accomplished. Once he found out, he took everybody out to Smith Reynolds Airport here in town which is also base to Piedmont Airlines and yes, more Reynolds family. They all piled into one of his planes, a souped up Cessna Skyhawk, and off they went speeding up toward Pilot Mountain, up northwest of the city. Many witnesses recalled seeing the little plane heading up that way flying above Highway 52, wings waggling and dipping.

"Zach was a many times over awarded acrobatic stunt pilot. And then the plane took a steep climb up and on up further and turned over, flattened out and slowed noticeably in what to many looked like a hammer head stall maneuver and then began to fall, curve back down toward the earth and gracefully level out. It was a pretty day, a sunny, nice day. But just one big problem. The plane never leveled out. It just flew at top speed crashing into the heavy forest beside Highway 52 and, of course, all of them were killed instantly. The plane's nose was buried almost six feet deep into the ground. Zach's strapped in body was in the pilot's seat, the captain's seat, the left side.

"It's a shock, a mess, a sad, huge tragedy. The FAA comes in to investigate and determines Zach is at the captain's stick and furthermore, his pilot's license had expired and he had discernible amounts of opioids in his system at the time of death. They find no mechanical or engineering or maintenance problems with the plane. And obviously, he had not kept his airplane under proper and safe control. And, oh by the way, he's rich so the families seek out the help of lawyers."

"Were you hired to help in this sad thing, Eddie?" asked Mikey. "Gee, all this stuff y'all deal with is pretty rough."

Patty said, "Eddie, how about let me take a swing at it here and get us tuned up a little better."

Eddie nodded. "The two boys killed were passengers so their families had wrongful death claims on behalf of their estates. Though the boys were buddies, the families weren't close at all so there was never any coordination between the two families. The Stirrup family hired someone over in Greensboro I recall and got their end of the matter wrapped up pretty quick, don't think they ever filed papers, never saw or heard anything about it."

"What about y'all?" asked Mikey. "Obviously at some point, y'all got in it. Otherwise, why would we be talking about it?"

Patty continued, "At the time of the crash and for months and months after, all we knew was there had been a bad airplane crash. Over time, like a lot of things it had faded from memory. We were working on our own stuff. The Wilson family, their boy was Steve, we later came to learn had hired a lawyer who was a nice neighbor to them and who was in a perfectly good, kind of old and stogy, solid but no flash firm here in town. Lots of prominent, respected names that marched across their letterhead. We learned a lot of all this after the fact. After a year, the boy's daddy, Mr. Wilson, went to their lawyer, a fellow named Whiteside who had initially cautioned patience and said something to the effect, 'When we gonna get started here?' The Whiteside guy, who was a partner in the firm said, 'In one year we're gonna make 'em sweat. They know we are out here. We are a threat. The statute of limitations for bringing a wrongful death suit in North Carolina is two years. We are well within that framework.' Mr. Wilson agreed and then time marched on.

"At the one year mark, Mr. Whiteside sent a letter of claim and notice and demand to Zach Reynolds' personal representative and also a representative counsel of many of Zach's significant business interests and investments around here. A few days passed and a reply was received. It read kind of like this. It's not verbatim or word for word but you'll get the drift. 'Dear Mr. Whiteside: I am in receipt of your letter dated whatever date. As the General Statutes of the State of North Carolina mandate all claims on behalf of a decedent's estate must be properly and timely presented to the estate's personal representative within six months, and your letter of claim and demand is dated well beyond the allotted time for such a claim. On behalf of the estate of Mr. Zach Reynolds, I must decline to address the asserted claim and further do reject it in its totality. Most Sincerely Yours, etc.'

"Now, imagine this picture. The Reynolds' estate lawyer had just completely destroyed and blown to all hell and pieces a 100-percent slam dunk multi-million-dollar case settlement which has cost Whiteside probably a fee in excess of a million smackeroos and now this attorney has now set his firm up for a mega-big, wincingly embarrassing, reputation-wrecking legal malpractice suit. Other than that, just another day in paradise. I bet you a dime to a doughnut that Whiteside guy and then all of his horrified partners, once he went to tell them what he had done, were puking their guts out in their trash baskets that afternoon.

"That's when the family came to see Eddie. It turns out the family has a daughter who is married to a smart lawyer, an immigration specialist, who lives up in Chicago, and she was close enough to her family, but when this terrible thing happened to her brother, she just sort of emotionally walled everything off and stayed out of it, stayed away from it. But then her mother called and told her the remarkable news that their claim for her brother had been thrown in the ditch, she moved into action. This now had become a lawyer fuck-up.

"The husband went to the Martindale Hubbell indexes, grabbed up and canvassed five or six lawyers around these parts of North Carolina, got a list of recommended names, called them, wrote them down and went to his wife and asked, 'Are any of these names familiar to you and if so, how? 'She looked at the list and said, 'Yes, Yes, Eddie Terrell. I know of some of the others too but Eddie Terrell sticks out because we all went to the same elementary and middle school. His younger brother was in my class. They're from a real nice family. His brother was just a great athlete. Eddie was sort of a fat pushover as a young kid but once he started playing football, he turned into a real tiger. He would come and knock the ever-living shit outta those guys. He did not like losing.' So they hired me.

"Have you sued the law firm?"

Patty replied, "No, don't think we're going to have to but we will see. Eddie, please explain that part of our thinking."

"This is, as has been mentioned before, an old, white-shoe, silk stocking outfit which has a well-established, long-time good reputation. Propriety is a big deal to them. Understandably so. We think they are going to try and do the right thing. We expect that we will have to help them along in order to get them to do the 'right thing.' We, once retained, did our due diligence, and quickly got in hand the necessary records and information, newspaper articles, FAA report and summaries, photographs, and of course, a copy of the original demand letter and subsequent denial letter, humbling and horrible. Can you imagine the pain which their presentation caused when presented to both the bearer and the recipients? We got a hold of an outstanding lawyer down in Charlotte whose primary expertise is in air crash torts. He's an aviation lawyer. He reported back in a few weeks. Said this was a case that most probably, to a reasonable degree of legal certainty was going to be won at trial and on any appeal as well and that the missing of the six months' notice for claims of creditors was not just negligence but really bad gross negligence which opens the door for a jury charge on punitive damages if the matter ever goes to trial.

"Now that we are in the game with big ammunition in our elephant gun, I sent our letter of representation to their managing senior partner, a haughty, grizzled old guy named Webster. Had met him some years before at a bar cocktail party. Nice enough but he did look down on me. Always like it when they do that. Always be nice when you're climbing up the ladder.

"A few days later, I got a phone call from one of the local, hell, one of the state bar's big cheeses, who's the managing partner at a very big and powerful law firm here in town. He's an old family friend and actually a very nice guy with a good sense of humor. He wants to meet, smooth things over. I am certainly amenable to that but smoothing here is an expensive, not a cheap thing. He knows that but he'll still diddle me. His name is Alphonse J. Baron. He's a past president of the state bar. Most everyone calls him Alph to his face and Chirpy behind his back. He speaks in a higher tone of voice, machine-gun style, and it's as though he has a case of the yips in his mouth, like a golfer who can't make a short putt, nervous, sort of an anxiety in his voice when he's agitated. It's a dead giveaway. That worry was in his voice when we first spoke on the phone.

"Obviously, the firm has not yet reported the claim to their malpractice carrier. Otherwise, we would have already heard from their professional liability insurance carrier. They would like to avoid doing that for many reasons, the biggest being that if they do, while the thing drags on, their professional liability rates will soar and eventually, they'll be dumped by that carrier and then they will have to flail around for new coverage that will be far more expensive with many more and bigger exceptions to the carrier, and that will pretty much drive us to file the suit and then will come the shitty end of the stick to them: press coverage and nasty adverse publicity and public stoning, which could very well mean the breakup and end to the firm's very being.

"But first, there will be plenty of inside the clubhouse name calling and backbiting. I can just about guarantee you that the Whiteside fellow held this case on his hip, never logged it in as is always proper procedure, waiting to whip it out as his surprise, big win piece de resistance, his 'look how great I am' big moment of glory in those dull, drudgery-assed halls of scriveners. And now, it is an Irish car bomb alarm that cannot be shut off and a stink bomb of nuclear proportion. And too, I can promise you many of their other clients would not like to be associated with the odor and taint this sort of screw-up throws off. A bunch of them will leave so fast, the door won't have time to hit them in the ass. And some lawyers too will get out. So there is systemic breakdown for them on the horizon.

"And just for our record, I could give a shit. Hurt feelings, burned up reputations, ruined histories, all scattered before the fiery winds of a self-created hell. Make no mistake. If it was me on that side of it, they'd have my balls barbecued before breakfast and that would be just for starters. So, give no quarter, ask for none. I have not yet told him about our aviation expert's opinions. But he knows I've got one. What he doesn't know is how strong it is and how strong the expert is. When we meet, I'll learn him up. Always nice to do so, up close and personal of course. And then too, there is one other thing. Think of it as the short, hard shiv in between the ribs to finish off the recalcitrant and the reticent." Eddie grins devilishly and with some clear enjoyment too.

Patty asked, "What is this you're talking about? Something new? Spit it out. Not fair not to!"

Mikey said, "I'm getting most of this but wouldn't mind more and also, what's a shiv?"

"My dear, a shiv is a short-bladed, maybe three inches, homemade, usually made in prison, knife used to take down an opponent in short quarters fighting or without warning at all. It's fast, effective, and deadly. Can usually reach whatever vital organ needs to be reached. Front, back, side. It's also known as an SBD, Silent but Deadly, and we're not talking farting either."

"Tell us, dammit!" Patty stuck her chin out while Mikey nodded in agreement.

"Here's the deal. Once we have a meet set up with Alph, and that meeting needs to happen here, then I'm gonna show you the little, dazzling nugget I've come across. And I will. Patty, please call his office and get that on the calendar. Also, make a note. Want both of you sitting in on the meeting. Alph likes ladies and will gently flirt a bit to open the bidding."

"Now, come on, Mikey. Let's go see Mother. And then go grab a drink and some food. I've got an early flight tomorrow. Thanks, Patty. See you on the flip side."

CHAPTER EIGHTEEN

THE HAND THAT ROCKS THE CRADLE RULES THE WORLD

Just Ask Her

EDDIE REMINISCED AWAY as they rode out to Little John Road, to the house that Eddie and his brother grew up in, to the house built on land that was given to Eddie's daddy and mother by Eddie's granddaddy when they got married, way back when, a long time ago. Eddie's first daddy, Daddy Joe, died when he was a little kid. He was supposed to have been quite a good guy and a smart businessman. And a few years later, Eddie's mother remarried and hit the jackpot again. Big Doug was an amazing man, had been a tank commander in Korea, finished college in Chapel Hill, then went to work for Munsingwear in New York City, and soon got hired away from the "Little Penguin People" by another textile company that wanted him to come down to North Carolina and run and manage their operations in and around Winston-Salem. He was a very handsome man, a real Southern gentleman, smart, well-read, moderate, and kind with a great sense of humor and big laugh. Eddie hoped he was home from the office by the time they got there. His presence would temper Eddie's mother.

"Mikey, now I've already told you that the chances are slim to none, and slim just got up and left the room, that my mother is not going to cotton to you. She just has never liked any girl, woman, or lady I've ever spent any serious time with. Please don't get your feelings hurt."

Mikey asked, "Eddie, are we spending serious time with each other?" There was no complaint or squint in the question. She just wanted to know.

"Yes, we are. I'm crazy about you. Is that enough? Does that help?"

"Yes, it does." She smiled sweetly.

Eddie said, "Here's a great story about my mother that'll give you some idea about her. Some years ago she had gotten one of the gals in our extended family and it's fair to say, there are a bunch of us out there, a niece named Jean to make her debutante debut."

Mikey said, "Isn't that some sort of big deal social thing, dances and parties and such for girls in fancy dresses? I think I get the picture."

"Yeah, you're close. It's when all these young gals are 'coming of age,' eighteen and they 'come out' in the big main ballrooms of a country club one by one and they wear these long, flowing white dresses and they have young guys dressed in tails and red and pink ribbons across their chests who are their marshals, usually a chief marshal and two others who march behind and they escort them out as their full names are announced to the gathered friends and families and so are 'introduced to society' and everybody claps and once that is done, there is dancing and drinking.

"What it used to signify was these girls, these chosen girls are the cream of local society, their white dresses signifying their virginity and goodness, and once they are so 'introduced,' they are now eligible for and thus ready for marriage, all in due time of course. It's all very formal and staged up."

"That sounds like some pretty rigid tricked-up stuffy stuff to me." Mikey snorted a laugh.

"You're closer to close there, for sure. I was a marshal in one form or another for about five years and back then we did it because it was expected of us and there were always lots of parties with plenty of booze and bands for the girls all before the big, main Debutante Ball. And the big finish was always cardboard stiff cause we couldn't drink like fish cause all the adults were there. And there were always big embarrassments, screw-ups, and bad behavior. Girls would get drunk, hurl all over the ladies' room, guys too of course, and couples would get caught in closets or out on the putting green humping each other like rabbits, bad language would get blurted out, you name it. As long as it wasn't me, that stuff always cracked me up. 'Hello, Mrs. GotRocks. How the fuck are ya?'"

"Was it ever you?"

"A few times. Good and staggering drunk. Not too much trouble though."

"Well, what about the closet and golf course moves?" She leered at him, smiling, "Hmmmm...I can't imagine a stinker like you missing out on that action."

"Well, I never got caught. You look like you don't believe me." He snickered.

"You're right," Mickey said.

"Anyway, my mother has a hard-on to get her niece Jean in this glorified march of the vestal virgins and Jean is no dope cause Auntie is going to throw parties for her and Jean is gonna get lots of new, fancy clothes and it's all gonna be some high-toned fun and Jean is going along with it if it gets her beaucoups of green stamps as the favorite niece to the fawning, proud aunt. So the planning and lining things up begins and there's a lot of it and along the way there is a big family dinner around Thanksgiving at another uncle and aunt's home, and during the cocktail hour, one of Mother's smart ass fourteen-year-old nephews asked, 'Why does Jean need to be doing this anyway?' And Mother said, "Tyson, you just do not understand. It is absolutely the proper thing for a lovely young lady like Jean to be properly introduced to nice people, to polite society.'

"And you can just see this train wreck getting ready to happen. Tyson said back, 'But I don't understand. Jean's already got lots of nice friends, knows plenty of nice grownups, is in a great sorority in college with lots more nice friends there and gets along with people and loves to meet new people all the time. She's real popular already.' Then Mother said, 'Tyson, you just don't understand. This is the way the nice people here in Winston-Salem and well, all over the South and even up in the North do this. It is an important rite of passage for these fine young girls to be introduced into adulthood.' Mother was increasingly peeved and frustrated that her explanations of what should be were not gaining traction with her recalcitrant jackass of a nephew.

"Everyone at the party was beginning to lean in and listen to this mini-debate that had ignited in their midst. Mother was well known for concluding dustups such as this with great, definitive finality. These declarations are often the human illustration of using a cannon to kill an ant. Tyson eyed her skeptically. Her towering Kaiser Wilhelm helmeted coif of spun and lacquered silver hair prowled menacingly toward Tyson. Tyson eyes suddenly brightened. A new idea had popped into his febrile brain. He said, 'Auntie Momma R, are we just trying to keep up with the Joneses?' My mother's lips tightened and pursed, her eyes grew wide as they flattened to blanks, her chin began to come up in stages, a shake, a pause, a shake, a pause, her silver helmet tilting evermore backwards, her chin now jutting menacingly toward Tyson's now wary face. And then came the burst, almost an explosion, but leveled heavy in a low growl. She exclaimed for all to hear, 'Tyson Terrell, we are not keeping up with the Joneses. We ARE the Joneses!!'

"It was impossible not to laugh and so, everybody did. Daddy laughed and laughed and laughed. He held his sides and laughed. We all followed suit. We thought Daddy was going to fall out of his chair. It was so ridiculous, so funny, so theatrical. And as our laughter subsided into gasping for air and our wiping delighted tears from our cheeks, my mother leaned forward toward Tyson and said squarely and really very sweetly to him, 'Now, son, now you understand, don't you?'

"Tyson was no fool. He simply responded 'Yes, ma'am.' She didn't think she was royalty. She knew she was. It was the portrait of her complete and total world view and she carried it as well as the real deal over the ocean there in Buckingham Palace. And so now, here we are." Eddie wheeled the car into the brick driveway and put it in park.

"Showtime, Mikey, showtime. And, honey, you look beautiful. You really do."

"Thanks, Eddie. Let's get this done."

The front door of the white brick house was opened and held by Man Friday Gunga Din Chuckles.

"Hey, Chuckles. How ya doin'? This is my friend Mikey from Montana. Mikey, this is Chuckles. He does it all around here and I ain't kidding."

"I'm good, Mr. E. Nice to meet you, Miss Mikey. Y'all come on in. I told your momma you were pulling in and she's in the back in her bed watching a movie and she said for y'all to just to come on back."

Eddie led the way down the long hall, holding Mikey's trailing hand. He got to his mother's bedroom door which was slightly ajar and leaned around the jamb to see who all and what all awaited them. There was Mother, lying in bed and Daddy sitting next to her in a chair watching an old Edward G. Robinson movie, now retouched up to a silvery black and white.

"Knock," Eddie began the proceedings.

"Oh, hello, son. Look, Daddy, it's Eddie. Where have you been, son? I've called you a number of times at home and nobody answers." She knew better than to call the office. That miserable tough-as-nails Patty would take one look at the Caller ID and just ignore the ringing. His stepfather said an enthusiastic "Hey boy!" and just grinned and then grinned a little bigger when Eddie slightly tugged and pulled pretty Mikey into the room.

"Hey, y'all. This is my friend Mikey from Montana."

"How do you do? Nice to meet you. Eddie, come over here and give your old parents a hug." Mikey did a slight, involuntary mini curtsey. Eddie did as he was instructed.

Big Doug laughed and said with a wink, "Oh, I bet! Very pleased to meet you, Mikey. Now, where in Montana are you from?"

Before Mikey could hit that softball, Momma R interjected. "I'm sorry. Mikey, is it? Not Michael or Michelle? What do you do? Where did you come from?" It was her way of setting her table of inquiry and inquisition, repeating the already obviously stated, freezing the intended victim with her repeated name and the implication that Mikey had just climbed out from under a rock or its sleazy roadhouse card table equivalent.

Eddie tried to provide some flanking cover but also knew at some point soon, Mikey was going to have to handle the ball herself without his protection.

"Mother, I've been out in Montana, taking it easy, doing some hiking and some fishing. Needed a little vacation. That's where I met Mikey. I invited her to come out this way for a while. She's been helping me and Patty at the office on some things. She's got a good aptitude and is a fast learner."

His daddy said as he leaned back admiringly, "Well, that sounds very good."

Momma R rolled in with, "Montana? I didn't think you could find that place with the map stapled to your backside. I know you know how to walk but hiking and fishing? You hate fishing! And whatever happened to that, what was her name, Flea Ann Jackson? She still over at your place or has she now gone down that rabbit hole of burned out love like all the others? And Miss Mikey, tell me about yourself. You are certainly very pretty and it does appear that someone has taught you a modicum of good manners, but this is my boy and he is often so confused. Of course, because of him, I stay confused too! What do you think about that awful shaved, bald head? Isn't it just awful? It's just so common! Don't you think?"

Mikey said, "Yes, ma'am, yes, sir. Though I do think, with all respect, that I kinda like his head." She was sturdy and faced Eddie's parents with composure. Eddie's mother put the movie on mute and motioned for Mikey to pull a desk chair over toward her.

Eddie laughed internally. "What about me? Where's my invitation to sit?" *No, Mikey gets to be ground zero so here we go...*Eddie found another chair and settled into the cheap seats.

Mikey got the chair, sat down, and told them about herself. She was polite and straightforward, complete without embellishment. Eddie's parents listened attentively, and Eddie could see his Daddy appreciating this girl's willingness to talk and not be intimidated by his Big Momma R. And furthermore, he could see in his mother's eyes growing flickers of understanding that were accompanied by nod after nod of concurrence.

His mother asked, "So where did you meet Eddie?"

Mikey replied, "This won't sound so good, but in a bar in a little place, no more than a crossroads really called Alder, Montana. That's down in the southwest corner of the state, near the Wyoming line. And no, I didn't have a boyfriend, haven't for a long, long time now. Eddie has been a real gentleman with me. He's very protective. And, I'd just do have to say, it is a very nice bar and they have good food, good steaks. And I am not a bar fly. I do go there a few times a week with my girlfriends. It's about the only place we have to go."

Momma R, filling in the blanks, asked, "So how did you get here?"

"Eddie asked me to come with him. I've never been this way so I accepted his invitation. We flew out of Bozeman to Atlanta. Eddie took me to see a baseball game. Then we came here. I've learned and seen so much in the last many days. It's very nice here."

"How long will you be staying?"

She answered decisively. "As long as Eddie would like me to." Her voice trailed off softly and she glanced at Eddie.

"I see." Momma R contemplated the totality of the moment. She had figured she was going to flail this girl from the get-go and yet, she discovered she thought the child was nice, nice enough anyway.

"Young lady, uh, Mikey, would you like something to drink, a Coca-Cola, a glass of wine? Let me call Camara." And before Mikey could answer, a bullhorn of a voice erupted from Momma R and she shouted, "Camara! Camara! Come in here!"

The call could be heard from one end of the house to the other. Momma R, also well-raised in her day, nevertheless usually forgot or intentionally neglected the basic niceties, such as using her inside voice as opposed to braying like an angry moose, and the words "please" and "thank you" are rarely to be heard trilling from her imperious lips and that was not just with her help. That was with everyone.

Camara, a tall, thin, trim dignified lady outfitted in a long-sleeved white shirt and long, black pants and black Nikes came into the room and said, "Here I am, Mrs. T. Oh, hey, Eddie. How you doing? Who's your friend?"

Eddie made the introductions and Momma R swept her hand like magic wand out in front of her.

"All right, everyone, what would you like?" The late afternoon had settled into a truce, a declaration of camaraderie.

Eddie's daddy said, "An Old Fashioned, please, Camara."

Momma R declared, "Camara, I want some cranberry juice with one jigger of vodka, no more, no less, you make sure now, and bring some of those good cheese straws Mrs. Margaret Taylor brought by the other day. Now, Eddie, Mikey, what will you have?"

Mikey stared at Eddie with one of those "This isn't turning out the way you said it would" looks. Eddie shrugged his shoulders and said, "How about a big, cold glass of white wine, please, Camara."

Camara turned to Mikey with the same question.

Mikey paused and then said, "Well, if you have any champagne, that would be very nice, please, and if not, a beer would be great too." She gazed at Eddie's parents and explained simply, "Eddie has been teaching me to like champagne."

Eddie closed his eyes and then looked up. His mother was shaking her head and smiling in great amusement.

"Camara, go find some champagne. If need be, put a couple of ice cubes in it. Don't worry, Mikey, it'll be fine." They all then commenced the continuance of a very nice, lively visit.

CHAPTER NINETEEN

I'M MAKING BREAKFAST

Parachute Express

"THANKS FOR THE ride. I'll be back tonight. I'll call you just before I leave Fort Myers. Think you can find your way back to get me okay?"

"Eddie, did you know they have signs out there on the highway that point you where to go? Duh...I'll see you this evening. Be safe out there."

"Thanks, kid." He kissed her cheek and squeezed her hand. His mind was already on the way to west Florida. He rolled out of the car, jumped the curb, and got his boarding pass, then headed for security and the gate. The sun's rays were beginning to glint through the terminal's tall windows.

After a normal, short flight under two hours in the half-empty plane, the wheels extended and he was in Fort Myers. He had no luggage, not even a carry-on or briefcase. He got a taxi at the cab stand and the car moved out toward the wide concrete expanse of Interstate 75 toward Naples. Florida is so flat. The sun now harshly reflected on the ribbons of concrete. He told his driver, "How about let's head up to the Another Broken Egg on Tamiami Trail." The fellow nodded and swung south.

His brother, Pablo the Grasshopper, almost always shortened to Grass, was a creature of comfortable habit. A lack of variety in his partaking has never troubled him from early childhood forward. Grape bubblegum always suited him as did cherry snowballs and ice-cold Coca-Colas. Grilled cheese with ketchup, a dark blue Chevy SUV, a gray suit, a blue blazer, always from Brooks Brothers, Snappies (a crunchy cheesy salty snack) little nubs of fried dough in a blue and yellow can made by an outfit in Indiana. Titleist # 1 golf balls, Bicycle playing cards, golf clothing from Maus and Hoffman, loafers from Gucci, a persistent and almost always chronic aversion to travel save for a few very sporadic golf outings to Pinehurst or Fishers Island or Ireland, always with a bunch of fellow gentlemen. Grass was not a misogynist but most women did not appeal to him. The exception to that rule was his amazing, gorgeous, funny wife Sharon, know to all as Shay.

He just found most women useful only to a limited degree and after that simply bothersome. And pretty much every morning, at a few minutes after 10 a.m., Grass could usually be found wandering into the Broken Egg with his *Wall Street Journal* and *Financial Times* tucked under his arm. And this morning when he went to his usual booth in the front corner, there he found his brother Eddie, stirring milk into his coffee, reading the *St. Petersburg Times* Sports Section.

"Eddie! Hey! Eddie! What brings you down this way? Where'd you come from? No call? No heads-up? Mother said the other day on the phone that you seemed to have dropped out of sight. She was a little worried. Not too bad. Anyway, a nice surprise! Glad to see you! What's up?"

"Hey, Grass. Came to see you. How you doing? Glad to see you too!"

They were very close. They always had been. Grass slid into the booth and they shook hands and hugged and looked out over the snappy little restaurant and its patrons with bright Gulf coast sunlight bathing the place.

"You know what this reminds me of, Grassy?"

Grass replied, "No," and waited in refreshed good humor.

"Remember that Mafia don up in New York City? Guy always ate in some made joint in Little Italy. Always, always sat facing the door so he could see who or what was coming. Then, one day, he relaxed. Wasn't careful. Sat with his back facing the door. And some of his enemies came in and shot him in the back and killed him. What was that guy's name? Hmmmm...it'll come to me. Yes! Joey Gallo. Joey Gallo at Umberto's Clam House!"

"Is that why you always sit facing the door?"

"No, but come to think of it, seems like a good idea these days." Eddie put his paper aside.

"You're a pretty hot shit lawyer. You got enemies I'm sure. Is that what you do? Should you?"

"I don't think so but times do change. Maybe I should incorporate that into my regular routine."

"Why not? These days, you can't ever be too careful. How about let's order and eat and go back to my office and see what's going on. That okay with you? I notice you have no bag, not even a little one so I now presume that this is a quick in and out visit, and so I further presume that even though you love your big brother so much, you've got something on your mind and you've come to talk to me about it and keep moving. Am I getting warm?"

"Yes, you are."

"Fine by me." Grass motioned at the sweet young thing with a Florida Gator inked on her right forearm. "Miss Jenny, may we please order now? My baby brother has joined me and after his travel this morning, he surely is very hungry. And, by the way, my ticket please."

"Sure, Mr. Terrell. Will you have your usual?"

"Yes, dear."

"Good. You know if you didn't I'd be kind of worried." She smiled gently at him, almost maternally. "And for you, Mr. Terrell too? Did I get that right?"

"You sure did. I'll have whatever he's having, plus some more coffee please."

"Coming up." And off she went, soon to return with bowls of hot oatmeal and sliced fruit.

"Yum," murmured Eddie. "Not exactly stick to your ribs bacon, eggs, and pancakes."

Grass noted, "It's damn good for your bowels. Gotta keep them moving. They are key in the maintenance of good health."

Eddie nodded his grudging assent as Miss Jenny chimed in with, "That's what Mr. Terrell here says every day!"

CHAPTER TWENTY

THE OFFICE OF THE GRASS

GRASS PLOWED QUICKLY through his breakfast with gusto, making sure not one jot nor tittle remained. He was an eminently thorough man and inspected his bowls as he finished to ensure that no remnant worthy of savoring was left behind. Satisfied, he stopped peering at the containers and looked up and peered at his brother.

Eddie was not as enthusiastic in this particular culinary effort as Grass and so he had been pushing blueberries and raspberries and steel cut oatmeal here and there across the curves of his bowls with at best a desultory scoop, taste, and chew. He of course knew that his brother was right about these healthful ways but he too was a creature of some habit and was resistant. He also knew that his focus was on the upcoming visit with Grass, not any meal, and suspected too that Grass knew he was coming to ask for something. So it followed that Grass would make him wait a bit before that conversation. It all made good sense.

They made pleasant small talk as close knit brothers would, about family, friends, business, projects, cases, the sick, the dead, the dying but nothing about personal relationships, Grass's wife, or Eddie's most recent romance. Finally, Grass waved Miss Jenny down for the check, studied it quickly, mumbled, "Yes, times two," and carefully left two crisp twenties under his water glass and waved a thank-you to the young lady.

They went out into the parking lot, got in Grass's sort of a truck, sort of a station wagon, and headed out onto the service road. Grass asked, "Is this visit a 'go by the house and visit with the Missus too' visit or is it an 'across the desk face to face office visit?'"

"I think the latter is best, please."

Grass lived in a very attractive three-bedroom condo, with his so very much fun wife, overlooking an enormous boat harbor and marina right off the cusp of Tin City that nestled close by the run of the Golden River. He was mildly sorry they would miss that visit between the three of them. It was always fun and funny. But this smelled like pure business and private business at that. Eddie's coming had not been preceded by a phone call. And it was true usually that from time to time, when either of them had an "ask" in mind, they would just address it on a phone call.

While Eddie seemed unhurried, this had a lurking sense of hurried to it. Grass was not one to hurry so any degree above that resonated.

"You got it."

They headed down toward now newly luxe Naples, once jeered as but the repository of flocks of drooling, doddering elders, caning and walker wheeling slowly down her sidewalks and beach walks. Now, Phoenix-like, newly emergent Naples not only held her goodly share of wealthy, mostly unpretentious AARPs, but also the young and the youthfully active middle-agers who all came to mesh with chic shopping, glittering and enticing restaurants, resplendent yacht harbors and fine golf and tennis clubs, and swell bell-and-whistle hotels and condominiums and apartments. Her beaches were still as beautiful as ever. The difference was that people now were on those beaches often in skimpy au courant swimwear and were in the water doing more than just standing there, flapping their arms about listlessly.

In Naples, a high society order would come soon enough but it would take a while for her to show her ass. In the meantime, Naples was just pleasant and better than the surging nouveau money Palm Beach. Grass drove down 3rd Street South and pulled down a narrow alley to the side of a very nice Italian restaurant called Campiello. It was an excellent eatery for both lunch and sometimes dinner and did not ever act bigger than its britches. Its people and product acted like they had been in the end zone before. Grass had, over the years, come to know its management and lots of its ever coming and going staff and he appreciated what they accomplished and they in turn appreciated his appreciation.

Grass parked the car behind Campiello's parking lot where a couple of bicycles were chained to a hold post. Broken chairs and random table legs skewed in a Jenga pile. They walked to a gun metal steel door at the back of the building. Grass unlocked it and they stepped inside to a small foyer with an elevator door. Grass pushed the button and the shaft hummed with the car's short arrival. They got in and went up and the doors opened onto a shotgun suite of a waiting room and two offices, all beautifully done in gnarled cypress, handsome bookcases, comfortable furniture, and good art. The back two offices had surrounding windows that all opened toward the sun and the water.

There was no one in the waiting room. The first of the two offices seemed considerably smaller than the one behind it but that was because the last office was where the Grass did his business. In the first office was his assistant, a pleasant middle-aged lady named Martha.

Grass offered, "Martha, you remember my brother Eddie from North Carolina, don't you?"

"Why, of course, yes, indeed. Hello, Eddie. How are you? It has been a while. I hope you are well."

"Yes, ma'am, all good, thank you. Hope you are too."

Grass opened the door to his office and motioned for Eddie to come in and take a client's seat at the front of his desk. Grass went around and sat in his hard-backed swivel desk chair. "Notice how she never asked you, never asks anyone, 'What brings you here or Why have you come to visit us today'? Such a nice, smart lady. Plus, what the hell; she doesn't need to. Whenever there are transactions, she sees them on her screen. She knows as much as me all the time, probably more." Grass grinned. "It's that sort of little touch that makes the clients feel safe, feel private."

Grass paused and focused on the kaleidoscopes on his desk. With furrowed brow and finger to his lips, his eyes hooded and darting, scanning back and forth and up and down, he watched the hundreds of lines and colors and symbols and numbers blink and dance on three big screens and from time to time, he would stroke a key or two or three and something would happen to make money move about, sometimes to the fore, sometimes down a rabbit hole, sometimes to South America or Europe or Asia, sometimes to God knows where. His desk was large, thick, and long. The three screens all facing Grass were pulled forward and stationed sentry-like, one at each corner and one in the center. Grass had four hearts, his own and his three messengers. Folks that knew Grass, knew his business, said numbers were his porn and he was more often than not, addicted. To him, they were beautiful, erotic, naughty and docile, that is if the application of good judgment and analysis fell his way. It usually did. Of course, he'd been jilted many times but never enough to keep him from the dance floor or the boudoir.

Eddie just watched. He had always admired Grass's skills and understood very little of it. Grass had made Eddie lots of money over the years and continued to do so. Eddie stayed the hell out of the way, never ever ventured a suggestion as to buy this or sell that, never pushed a cocktail party or drunk tip. Then again, Grass never offered a path of cross-examination or a thought as to a motion to be filled. They respected their skills and their individual niches.

Grass, satisfied for the moment that his hand was firmly in control of the boat as the breezes of filthy lucre buffeted it, came around and sat easily in the captain's chair next to his brother. He had shrunk over the years but he was still big and wide and his height mattered not. He moved on the balls of his feet lithely as a gymnast. Though his voice was high-pitched, from whence it came made it powerful and pointed.

He turned to Eddie and tilted his head and simply said, "Now, my dear baby brother. Let's get down to it. To what do I owe the honor of this visit?"

"Grass, you remember some years ago, well, really, not so long ago, I'd get in a fix and you'd take some of my money you'd made me and sometimes, some of yours too, and you'd help me get things squared up?"

"Yes, I recall those few times. You've been good, hell, no, great now, in real good shape now for a good while time it seems. Is something the matter?"

"No, everything is fine, better than fine. Thank you. But please let me go on a little bit now."

"Okay."

"And do you remember how you would always say, always say 'If you need something, if there is a problem, you have got to come talk to me about it, come ask me for what you need before everything gets worse?"

"Yes, sure. I remember. But you've just said nothing's wrong. But you're here to ask for something, right? And you wanted to meet here in my office so this ain't no family social?"

"Yes, that's right. I want to put you in an investment. I'm putting together a small syndicate, just five or six very trusted folks, all of whom have strong balance sheets. I'm putting a good lick of my money in too."

"What's the investment?"

"Well, here's the rub. I don't want to tell you that. I don't think you need to know that. It's better that you not know that."

"Huh? What in the devil are you talking about?"

"Let me put it this way. You've been really good to me over these years about money and well, about everything. I'm trying to do something for myself and for you too, of course. I want to see if I can do it; if I can pull it off. You've made me plenty of money as an investor over time and now, I want to see I can at least in part, repay the favor. I want to see if I can do it. Does that make sense?"

"I think I get it. I appreciate that. But why don't you just get me to get together some money, whatever the number is, out of your accounts and just do this for yourself? I don't need to be messing up your deal."

"No, that's not the point of the deal. I need to ask you for some of your money so I can try to make some money for you. And, I'll tell you what. I will repay you at least your full investment and hopefully a good sum more within a year."

Grass was looking at his brother, searching his face for some clue as to what was going on but there was none other than total sincerity.

"Are you in trouble? Are you gonna get in trouble?"

"No and I don't think so. Of course, as you well know, with all investments, there are elements of risk." Eddie intoned the mantra of all the banks and brokerage houses and couldn't help but grin. "But basically here, there ain't none to you, so long as you just let me go to work. I know you like to know every angle and you know I respect that to the max. But this time, I'm hoping you'll let me fly you a little blind. It would mean a lot to me."

Grass couldn't help but mirror his brother's smile. He was silent, thoughtful for a few seconds, then stood up and asked, "What's the number?"

"Twenty-five thousand."

"Just twenty-five Gs? Now, you and I know that's pretty much chump change. That's all you want? Really?"

"Really. That's it."

Grass looked at his brother, shook his head and said, "I suppose I could dream up all sorts of scenarios...wait a minute. Does this involve a broad? Jesus, you've always had a mess of a time with broads. Do you have to pay someone something about a broad?"

"Nope, I've got a nice gal pal but that's a story for another time. She's not an investor. That's it."

Grass shrugged his shoulders, murmured, "What the hell," not in resignation but in assignation, went back around to his desk, pulled a checkbook out of a bottom drawer, uncapped his Scripto loaded blue ink pen and leaned to the next check.

"How do you want this made out?"

"Just to me. And remember, no matter what, it's just a gift to me until I can get square with you within the year."

"Fair. You know I'm intrigued. You haven't asked for the sun, moon, and stars. Hell, you've barely asked for the down payment on a new car. You know why I'm doing this in the dark?"

"Because I asked." Eddie bowed his head enough to show respect.

Grass stroked the check and said, "Yes, you did. Thank you."

They shook hands and Eddie put the check in his wallet.

Grass asked, "Well now that that's taken care of, whatever 'that' is, how about lunch? The place downstairs is knockout good. What time is your flight back?"

"Thanks, Grass, thanks very much but I'll take a rain check if that's okay. You've never chewed in a place down here that wasn't. But if we went and ate a good meal now, we'd probably have some wine and you'd be like Mother used to always say to our dates, 'Be careful, young ladies. Those boys are gonna try and ply you with spirituous liquors and loosen your tongues and a whole lot more!' and I don't want to keep ducking your now temporarily sublimated persistent curiosity."

Grass laughed good at that memory and agreed with that assessment of his intent.

"Please tell that lovely Shay of yours I send my love and my best and I'll be back soon enough. And I will." Then Eddie headed for the elevator. "Again, nice to have seen you, Miss Martha. Martha, would you please call me a cab. I'd appreciate that."

He was quick stepping as she was dialing. "Hey, Eddie, you know I can give you a ride back to the airport?" Grass winked big at him.

"Not this time but thanks just the same." Eddie big winked back.

In a few minutes, a big, yellow Plymouth with moon disc hubs and bounced out creaking shocks and a cabbie who was Rochester's twin from the old Jack Benny show, replete with leatherette chauffeur's brimmed cap, pulled to the curb and cheerfully asked out the window, "Where to, boss? Think dispatch said Fort M airport but never hurts to be sure."

"You got it. I'm ready if you are."

"Well then, hop in and let's ride, Clyde." And so it was game on.

CHAPTER TWENTY-ONE

LEAVING ON A JET PLANE

Peter, Paul and Mary

HE WAS SUPPOSED to leave later that afternoon but his meet with Grass had gone much quicker than he'd imagined. He'd thought there would be lots more to it but like so many things in life, they got to the essence of it efficiently.

He got hooked up for an earlier flight and had an hour to kill. He whipped out his Nokia to call Patty after trying his house. Mikey didn't have a cell phone. "Hey."

"Hey yourself. How's it going with whatever it is you're doing down there?"

"Went fine, really did."

"Good. Now, you coming back today?"

"Yeah. Have gotten an earlier flight and should be in by about 5 or 5:30. I tried the house to get Mikey but no answer. Any chance you've seen her today?"

"Nope. Not yet anyway. Give me your flight information so I'll have it if she does swing by and if not, I'll run by your place and tell her or leave a note."

"Good deal. Thanks. Here it is. Piedmont 1995, arriving Greensboro 5:24 p.m. Now, a couple of things, please. Would you please call Gigi Faye Erin and set up a lunch with her for me tomorrow, say meet me at Old Town about 12:30? We need to follow through on those jewelry gals we met a few weeks ago over at The Alley. And, how about get Rise and Curt to come by the office tomorrow afternoon about 3? Just want to get everyone an update."

"Sure. Will get on it right now. Anything else?"

"Naw, nothing for now but we know, don't we, sure as shit some more mess will come floating along, sooner rather than later."

Eddie found the Aero Tavern next to a newsstand. He bought a local paper for fifty cents and pushed through the joint's swinging door. It was not exactly well lit but it appeared that a couple of suits nursing drinks heads down at the bar sure were, their conversation sporadic and mumbled.

There were a couple more uprights and some uniformed flight attendants and a pilot doing the same over on a couple of chipped Formica tables a few feet away.

He bought a double bourbon rocks, went over to the tables and dropped down into a rickety, folding chair. He loosened his tie and shirt's top button, got up and draped his coat over the back of the chair and sat down again and opened the paper to the sports section. He felt suddenly very tired.

Not a bad thing, just an earned weariness. He had a sense that a lot of things were coming together. He shook the thought as it made him more tired. There was plenty to tumble over and tie together soon enough. He was almost blank but not quite. He watched the pilot and the two female attendants. They were lively, animated. The women were giggling at something the pilot just said. They all had glasses with ice and fruit in them.

They saw him watching them. No one was staring but it was obvious all were paying attention. The pilot's uniform looked good on him. He was a good-looking man. The flight attendants were young, leggy, and pretty.

The pilot asked Eddie, "Where you headed, traveler?"

"Greensboro, I hope."

"Why you say, 'I hope?'"

"Well, I'm wondering if you're my pilot?"

"Sorry to disappoint you but we're all off duty now. Just got in from last leg outta Charlotte."

"Ah...good...good. Looks like y'all are having a nice time. That's good."

"Yeah, we think so."

"Lemme ask you something."

"Sure."

"Just hypothetically of course, if you had to, could you fly one of those big planes from back here to Charlotte if you'd had a few drinks?"

One of the girls laughed and made her eyes real big and hooted, "Captain Dave can do anything!"

Captain Dave shook his head, amused and replied, "Lemme ask you something? What do you do for a living?"

"Me? I'm a trial lawyer."

"So, do you think you could try a case in front of a jury after you'd had few drinks?"

"Uhm, I suppose I could but my screw-up chances would increase. I get it. Right." Eddie nodded.

Captain Dave said, "Remember, it's okay to be dumb but stupid can get you killed."

"Thanks. I needed that."

"Why? You seem pretty bright to me."

"Gotta lot of irons in the fire right now. Can't afford to be stupid."

"Fair enough. Looks to me like your glass has a hole in the bottom. Since you're not flying the plane this afternoon, why not go grab another and visit with us a while before your plane takes you safely to GSO?"

"Thank you. I think I will."

CHAPTER TWENTY-TWO

YOU CAN GO HOME AGAIN AND SOMETIMES YOU JUST GOTTA KEEP GOING HOME

UPON LANDING, EDDIE tried to reach Mikey, but again no dice. He hoped Patty had been able to get word to Mikey. He walked out to the curb to sit on a bench and wait. As he began to sit, a car horn blared twice. He looked up and there was Mikey.

"Hey, honey. How were your travels?"

"Hey. Good, real good. Very glad to see you. Thank you for coming to get me. Did Patty get word to you?"

"Yes, she left me a note. I had to hustle to get on over here. I've been out all over town sort of sightseeing and had gone by the house to wait for your call and there was her note. Anyway, how did things go? How is your brother?"

"I guess no way to get you word that I had caught an earlier flight. Things went real well. It wasn't a long visit but Pablo the Grasshopper is great. We had a nice breakfast together. He's a health food advocate now so a good dinner out tonight would have also been bark and fruit."

"Sounds less than appealing."

"True but when in Rome, do as the Romans do and to boot, as I was going to make a request of him, no way I was gonna buck the current trend."

"Are you gonna tell me what the request was?"

"Sure, we went over to his office and talked a little bit and we now have our third investor in the syndicate, such as it is."

"Oh that's great! Who are the first two?"

"Me and Curt. And remember, you know nothing. Grasshopper doesn't either. It's just an investment or a gift right now. You understand that, don't you?"

"Yes, I promise I do. Is that enough for you to get started?"

"Close but no cigar. Got some more prospecting to do, which I'll take a swing at over the next few days. I know it's barely 6 p.m. but I'm starving. Could you tolerate it if we went some place fun and good and had a few and ate this early?"

"Love to. I've been exploring all day and haven't had anything except for some coffee and toast this morning. By the way, this is a pretty interesting town."

"Great. Thank you. And, yes, it is in spite of us all." Eddie grinned.

They went to a little spot over in the old Reynolds estate, the Village Tavern, which featured the best chicken wings in town. They perched up at the bar and ordered drinks and wings and he asked her about her day. She was excited. She had retraced, with only some minor difficulty, the way to his office, to his mother's, to the campus at Wake Forest. She had discovered downtown, the big bank buildings, the tobacco factories, the East Side and Salem College, and the very moving and lovely Moravian Graveyard in Old Salem. She had driven up Highway 52 to Pilot Mountain. She told she'd also checked out a few car dealerships—Mikey was ready to acquire her own wheels.

"That's near where that Reynolds fellow crashed, isn't it?"

"You are right, young lady, right as rain."

She was smart, curious, and enthusiastic. He admired her.

They went home and read and were asleep before the sun was even barely down.

The next afternoon at about 12:30 p.m., Eddie was sitting on the red silk brocade couch in the lobby of Old Town Club. Gigi Faye bounced up the brick steps and Eddie popped up to open the glass door for her.

"Hey there, stranger. Where have you gotten yourself off to these last many weeks?"

"Well, that's a long story," Eddie remarked, "I'll get to it in a little bit." She eyed him curiously.

They walked down the stairs to the club room for lunch. This was good taste, old money land. White-coated waiters moved seamlessly about the many who were dining, the conversation was subdued, the clinks of glasses and the tap of silverware were more pronounced than the voices. He held her chair for her, and the maître d' Frank Cuthrell brought them menus.

"Hey, Frank, how you doing? This is my friend Gigi Faye Erin. She's a crackerjack insurance investigator."

"How do you do, Miss Erin? So far I think I'm in the clear if that's all right with you. Now, this Eddie here, this is a whole 'nother story." Frank smiled. Gigi Faye did too.

Eddie said, "You don't know the half of it." He winked and made a face at the same time. Gigi Faye gave Eddie a sideways look. She sensed a pattern.

"Y'all take a look at the menus and I'll be back in just a little bit to get your order." And he was on the move to the other side of the room.

Gigi Faye asked, "I was sort of under the impression that we were gonna get after it and press those gals about that ice. Go see that Mama Rabbit gal. See if we couldn't wrap this up pretty quickly. Push hard and be done. I went ahead and got everybody's addresses and have been waiting to hear from you. And what do I get? Radio silence. What's the deal?"

Eddie said, "Hang on. He's coming for our order."

Frank Cuthrell swept back by and asked, "Have y'all decided yet? No rush now."

Gigi Faye order the chopped salad with vinaigrette on the side. Eddie got a cup of tomato bisque and half a tuna fish sandwich. Frank went off to put their orders in.

All of a sudden, Eddie knew he wasn't very hungry but he needed to be straight with Gigi Faye. He again noticed how really gorgeous she was. It made him lonely and a little sad but he knew where he was and business is business. There was no need to dance around this because the cabin doors were getting ready to close and this was the only thing that could happen, at least for the time being. In truth, probably for all time.

Eddie said, "You're right. I went off the rails at a bad time. But I'm back now and want to go on and get after this thing now. I think we should go see Mama Bunny as soon as we can line up going together."

"I agree. What about this afternoon?"

"I've got a three o'clock that won't last more than an hour. Why don't I pick you up at your place about 4:30 or so and let's go a 'calling?'"

"Now, tell me more. Tell me about why you dropped off the face of the earth for a pretty good while. You're a little anxious. I'm glad to see you. I think I enjoy you on a number of levels and now I'm wondering."

Eddie grimaced and said, "Okay, here you go. Do you remember over the course of our work on this jewel project that I was going out with a gal?"

"Yeah. I remember."

"Well, she'd been living with me for a while and at first it was pretty good but then it just went downhill. She just started pounding on me and pounding on me."

"Oh that happens all the time I've heard." There was deadpan in her voice.

"And then you and I end up spending the night together and when I got home the next day, she went bat shit."

"Sounds reasonable." She smiled.

"And I was just getting to the end of my rope and things just kept jarring me over the next few days, so I went home and told the gal school was out and she had to move on and quickly."

"Inhospitable but understandable."

"And I knew I had to get away for a while and clear my head."

"Panic does come in so many different forms, doesn't it?"

"Some friends had told me how beautiful southwest Montana was so I went out there."

"I've always heard that was pretty country out there. So how did you do? How was it?"

"Well, it helped and I met a gal out there and we liked each other, so I asked her to come back here with me and she did."

"Jesus, there's one born every minute. Eddie, I never thought you were a dope but maybe you're just a chump."

"I'm sorry. I didn't mean to just take off and leave you hanging but I didn't think there was a whole lot of tail on what we did the other night." His voice washed off and he looked away.

"Nice pun." She sighed. "It was a one-night stand. That's all. Fair to say, I was hoping for a few more but such is life. No more. The wager window is now closed. Got it?"

"Yes, I got it. I'm real sorry if I misled you."

"Of course you are. Now, I'm gonna shake this off pretty quick and we have work to do. I'm not your fairy godmother and you sure as hell ain't my Prince Charming. You get paid by the hour. I get paid when the job is done. So you understand that while you may have winged my heart, you haven't done shit for my pocketbook. I want to make my money. Do you understand?"

"Yes, I do."

"Now here comes our lunch. Let's eat and go and I'll see you around 4:30 at my place."

They quickly ate in silence and Gigi Faye, finishing first, stood and said, "Your check I presume, and by the way, do they really let lightweight scum like you belong to a place like this?" She arched her eyes inquiringly and turned and walked out. She knew she could cut him. It was business. He understood.

Eddie had taken only a few rueful bites. His stomach hurt.

He signed his check, put his member number on it and stared at the ticket. He was ashamed and didn't know why.

He drove to the office for his next meeting.

He was sitting there, looking vacantly out the windows behind his desk, feeling sorry for himself. Patty knocked, peeked around the corner of his door and said, "Curt and Rise are here. And, uhm, Rise don't look so good. Just an FYI so you won't act surprised, okay? And Mikey's here and I'm working with her on a bunch of stuff. You know, Eddie, she's gonna be good. I'd appreciate it if you hung on to her for a while. Big help to me. If you get my drift."

Suddenly very alert, Eddie said, "I hear you." And he stood and told Patty to bring them in.

Curt came in first, his face tight, and behind him walked Rise. She came in tentatively with her face turned away and down. The left side of her face was swollen like a large gourd and there was a visible cut along her eyebrow. The blood vessels in her left eye were abundantly visible with a swelling trauma. Neither had the purposeful, forward way they usually carried themselves. Curt was distant and Rise was shamed and humiliated.

"Hey, y'all. Thanks for coming. Please grab a seat." Eddie's voice was flat, modulated, perfunctory. There was a dirge in the room. He shut the door.

They sat in silence for some seconds. Curt's jaw was hard set. Rise just looked away, though the sadness in her eyes was impossible to miss. Eddie looked at them, one, then another, then back again. No one spoke or even seemed inclined to.

Then Eddie asked quietly, "Rise, what happened to you? How did this happen?"

"Ben. This isn't the first time. He usually goes with body shots. Been going on last year or so. Ben been drinking a lot lately. He's angry."

"At what?"

"Me. Us. At first seemed like it was all cooked up by the drinking, just feeding a mean streak, now, he feels like he's being cut out of something. Feels like he's being cheated."

"Go on, please."

Curt interjected, his head whipping around to speak to Eddie. "He smells a deal that we're working on which doesn't include him. And the dumb motherfucker shouldn't be in it anyway because he's a dumb motherfucker to begin with. He's been drinking way too much anyway these last many months. Gets angry, gets mad, gets all agitated up. He heard Rise talking on the phone to Kenny about something about going to Baltimore and that got his vibe to shaking and he grabbed Rise and started hollering at her and she said, 'what are you talking about?' and he just hauled off and smacked her hard across the face. I was standing there, had come to pick her up. There it is. It does look bad, don't it? Then he took off. This was this morning. We ain't seen him since. I do know Kenny heard it over the phone. I expect Kenny's out looking for him now."

Curt inhaled. "Some bad shit...some bad shit."

Eddie agreed. "Where's Kenny now?" Kenny was a sweet, docile Ferdinand the Bull almost all the time but when stung by any serious mistreatment of his sister and of course, himself, he could and would go blind with rage.

"Who knows?" said Rise with a sigh. She and Curt knew what Eddie was thinking. They were all thinking the same thing. Again, everyone was silent for a bit.

"Let's make this quick. Ben could really fuck up our deal. We all know that. So could Kenny unless we get control of this quick. So, let me fill you in where I think we are and then here's what I think we need to do. We now have a good chunk of thousands in hand and I'm going hunting for more over the next few days. I feel pretty good about getting together at least another seventy five thousand so that gives us enough working money for the buy. Curt, because you are gonna be the air traffic controller on this deal and will distribute and collect accordingly, you will get one extra kilo courtesy of me as I earlier said to profit off of as you see fit."

Curt nodded, "Cool. Again. Thanks."

"Rise, you and Kenny will be taken care of by me. Don't worry. You know I'll be fair." Rise nodded.

"The rest of our investors, there will either be three or four, will simply be investors and will not know how or in what their money will be placed. They are or will be flying blind which is to their obvious benefit. Curt, I'd ask that as soon as possible you get in touch with Pee Wee and just ask for a meet and then once that's set up, go to Baltimore, and make the ask for the buy in person, nothing over a phone. And while I'm thinking on this, how about let's all get a bunch of one call, no trace disposables? I'm presuming that Pee Wee will be able to provide that which we are asking for.

"Once that's decided and agreed upon and we are almost ready to go, I need both of you to go buy a used, not too beat up, regular issue short school bus and take it over to Leon's Body and Paint up off Upper Meeting Street for a schooled-up, not-too-flashy paint job. Also, have Leon make a couple of ready seal compartments that will fit inside the inner walls of the engine compartment, enough size to hold our cargo. I'll get your five grand in cash. That ought to cover a used bus and paint job and upfitting. If not, let me know and I'll tend to the rest. Once we have that ready, Rise and Kenny are going to Baltimore for the pickup and then will take a longer way home. I'll make arrangements for an overnight cover stop in Virginia.

"Then, Curt will take possession and go do his thing and we will stand by for hopefully some good results."

Curt nodded, "Sounds good. I guess we're going with the school bus plan. What's next?"

Rise had been paying close attention now. "Ben. Ben is what's next. Ain't that right?"

"Yes, that's right." Eddie cupped his chin in his hands. "So what to do?"

Curt said, "I think we need to run him off and get rid of him."

Eddie asked, "Rise, is he your man? Really your man?"

"He was. Not now. I ain't gonna put up with that shit. No way no how no more. I want to be rid of him. He's gotten to be a mean drunk and he ain't gonna get any better. He's got poison in him and it ain't coming out and now I'm worried he's gonna get to fucking with our deal, get us all in deep shit."

"Can we run him off, buy him off?"

Curt offered, "We can do either, do both, but with the hard drinking, there's no guarantee that he won't be back later to bite us all in the ass."

"Rise, what do you think?"

"I agree with Curt. I'm with y'all, not him. He's out. Things change."

"Well." Eddie paused. "If we think running him off and/or buying him off will not be conclusively effective, then we either ignore him at our risk or we do something about him that is conclusively effective."

They all looked at each other. They all, again, knew what their collective thought was.

Curt said, "I'll say it. He needs to go. He needs to go away for good."

Rise followed on, "Kill him. Yeah, get rid of him."

Eddie steepled his fingers and said, "Well, things sure have gotten deep today, haven't they? I guess it was inevitable that something like this would come up. Shit. Let's get moving. Rise, please go find Kenny, calm him down and bring him to me as soon as you can tomorrow. I have a 4 o'clock this afternoon that's going to eat up the rest of my day, so how about 9:30 or 10 in the morning?"

"Yes, sure. By the way, where's that nice lady friend of yours?"

"Oh, she's in the back working with Patty on some cases. She's been a big help and learns a little more each day. I'm glad she's around. So is Patty."

"She sure enough is a good-looking thing. You gonna hang on to her?" Rise grinned and grimaced through her knotted-up cheek. Eddie ducked the question. "Go on now. Go find Kenny and calm him down, please. Let me know. Look forward to seeing y'all in the morning. Thank you!"

Curt started to get up too. Eddie asked him to stay a little longer. "Curt, let's talk this over a bit more. I want the further benefit of your thinking."

Curt nodded. "Okay. You start."

"How we gonna do this? Christ. The thought passed my mind that we send or take Ben up to Baltimore and let your boy Pee Wee's bunch clean his clock, sort of get it, get him out of our hands."

"I'm not seeing that one. Let's walk through it. If we just send him by himself, how do we know he won't get drunk, wander off, not get to where we want him to be? And also, how do we know Pee Wee wants to do this? I'm pretty sure Pee Wee is no virgin when it comes to taking fools out but that's on his turf. And if someone takes him up there, who takes him? Rise? Rise and Kenny? Kenny? Man, that's bad combinations across the board. And I ain't taking him up there and you ain't either. Seems to me we gonna have to do this on our home court, so to speak."

Curt continued. "Here's what I'm thinking. It'll be simple: give him more booze by his bed while he's sleeping off a bender and then all of us get there at night ready to drag him away after Kenny strangles him. Zip his ass up and get rid of him, wallet and all and any ID."

Eddie said, "Jesus, this is cold. So how do we get rid of him once all this fun and games is completed?"

"Burn him. By the way, you want him cold and done or warm and wiggling? Didn't think so."

"Where?"

"I'm working on that angle. I think it can be done neat and clean. But I gotta work on it first and then I'll get back to you, soon I hope." Eddie just sat there. The speed with which all this moved had jerked him up, had rattled him.

"Jesus, Curt, I'm impressed. I'm a little shook up too. You done anything like this before? You sure are a thorough thinker on this."

"Well, let's just say that I've been around. Now, as you lawyer boys know, there is no statute of limitations on killing, on murder so I'll leave it at that."

"Fair enough. Let's see what you can put together for the end game and let me know. Obviously, we both have things to do so let us keep on keeping on. Why don't you start getting in touch with Pee Wee? You need any money?"

"A G for working on things would be good."

"Good." Eddie picked up his phone and buzzed Patty.

"What's up, boss?"

"Hey. How about you pull a G outta ready cash and bring to me, please?"

"Sure. Gimme a minute."

Curt laughed. "That must be some petty cash box you got."

"We keep two, one for petty cash, one for ready cash, if you get my drift."

"I do. There's little money and then there's working money."

They sat in silence for a few minutes and then Patty opened the door, nodded at Curt, handed an envelope to Eddie and went back out.

Eddie handed it to Curt. "I've got another appointment now. Thanks for coming by. Stay in touch."

"Don't worry. I will."

Curt left. Eddie went to the back offices.

"Hey, y'all. I've got a four o'clock with Gigi Faye. I'm not sure when I'll be done. Patty, would you please give Mikey a ride home? I'll just head straight there once we're done if that's okay."

"Sure. No problem."

Mikey asked, "Who's Gigi Faye? What's this one about?"

"She's an insurance investigator. We're trying to track down some heavy-duty missing jewelry. She's a real pro. Nice lady too. We've got a pretty good lead, so we're going to take a shot at having a little visit with someone who might be able to fill in the gaps and lead us to the stuff."

Patty asked, "Who y'all going to see?"

"Madge Roberts."

"No shit?"

"Yeah. For real. We were at The Alley a few weeks ago. Met these two glammed-up gals who were sporting what appeared to be big hunks of missing ice. We think they may well work for Madge. We took a bunch of photos with Gigi Faye's new digital camera. The stuff shows up good in them. Thought we'd go and politely ask Miss Roberts if there is a connection. If so, then good. If not, then we go see the girls. While I was gone, Gigi Faye dug up all the necessary addresses."

"Damn." Patty lit another.

"Now, who is this Madge Roberts lady?" Mikey wondered.

"A real fine seamstress, very skilled and talented. And, oh by the way, she runs a string of the finest poontang housewives in these parts. She is the Queen Madame in this town."

"How do you get involved in all this stuff? Geez."

Eddie grinned and winked. "It's an acquired skill and another long story. See y'all later."

Patty hollered after him, "Eddie, you are so full of it!" and both girls laughed and laughed some more.

CHAPTER TWENTY-THREE

THE FAMILY JEWELS

HE DROVE AIMLESSLY going to pick up Gigi Faye. It was an obvious act of temporary avoidance.

Eddie swung through random neighborhoods, wheeling about, playing the radio loud, windows rolled down, air breezing through, washing over him, looking at houses, their yards, some nice, some trashy and unkempt, looking at their trash cans lined up on curbs, looking at their discards, old furniture, mattresses, kids' busted up toys, weird collections of lumber and paint cans and never completed do-it-yourself jobs. It all reminded him of him, discombobulated, erratic, waiting to be picked up and sorted. Jesus Christ. In a matter of minutes his conversation with his co-conspirator low-level amateur drug dealers had escalated into the planning for a premeditated killing. And in order to get to that low-level deal and make it work, it did appear that the more heinous deed would have to be committed.

He finally got around to making his way over to the Regency, and as he eased his car into a parking space, there she came down the steps, all business and buttoned down and as always, stunningly beautiful. He ached involuntarily and let it pass. She had chewed him a new one at lunch which he felt he deserved, though he could not exactly explain why, and he now waited for the next hard slap. She opened the passenger's door, hopped in, did not look at him, slipped down the sun visor, looked into the compact mirror on the reverse side, tilted her head, wet a few of her fingers with her luscious tongue, patted a few loose ends into satisfactory organization and slipped the visor back up. Then she looked at him and he watched and thought, *Please, sir, may I have another?*

There was a pause and then she spoke. "Look, I'm sorry. I really am. I've been thinking about it a lot these last few hours. I was way off in the wrong. I had no right to say those things to you at lunch today. We are all big boys and big girls and, well, fucking doesn't much rise to commitment these days. We had a good romper room moment and I'd hoped we might have a few more along the way, but right now you're in it deep with your new friend and I have no right to expect you're gonna show up and ask me to go steady. So, please accept my apology and let's work on being friends and now get about our today's business. I hope you'll forgive me. I was an ass. I hate it."

Her mouth snapped softly shut and she looked at Eddie imploringly. Eddie was surprised. It all made him want to take her in his arms and kiss her forehead and soothe her. He was feeling like shaky jelly. She wasn't mad. She was hurt. He steadied himself. He knew now was not the time for running the comfort train. That would only make matters messier and worse. Women made him crazy and here was yet another Exhibit A. He was not confused. He understood.

He leaned back against his driver's door not in retreat but in the surety of a little more distance from her while his mind composed. "Gigi Faye, I'm not mad at you and your apology is not necessary. You're a great gal. I appreciate it. I really do. I think you are wonderful. I like working with you and I sure do enjoy your company. I never meant to upset you and since it's pretty obvious I did, I need to apologize to you. I am very sorry for giving you any incorrect impression. When I took off a few weeks ago, I had no idea all this other stuff would happen. And, yes, she's here now and she's learning from Patty, learning a lot, and we do get along pretty good. But you're special too, really special. I don't know what's gonna happen. Hell, I'm not sure what's gonna happen in the next five minutes. But I sure need your help on this deal. Is it okay if you and me just concentrate on Madge and the glitter girls for now?"

"I'd like that to happen and I appreciate what you just said. We'll be okay. You ready to go now?"

She sat up very straight, almost primly in her seat and instantly reminded him of his old fourth grade schoolteacher, with her long tan legs and blonde sparkling sun-lit hair. Miss Millie Brown, who'd tutored him in math one summer while she sunned herself beside the pool that belong to the folks she rented from. Jesus, she took his breath away and stirred him up like crazy. And that was happening now. His pencil, both then and now, was erratically scribbling way outside the lines. He pressed his hands to his temples, exhaled mightily and said, "Where to, my dear?"

With a funny, goofy grin, she said, "Eddie, my very interesting friend, we are going over to 1895 Norman Street. It's on the Thruway Shopping Center side of Country Club, over near Knollwood Baptist Church. I'll show you. I did some site-specific scouting while you were away."

"Is this Madge Roberts' place?"

"Yes, neat little house, neat little yard, late model Chevrolet in the driveway, nothing flashy, nothing signaling anything; very much in keeping with the precision of a fine and careful seamstress."

"Do you have the photos of the goods and the gals?"

"Of course."

"Well then, let's go see if we can scratch up something worth a damn."

Eddie had on a coat and tie and between him and Gigi Faye, they made a nice looking, not very threatening couple. They pulled up in front of the house and looked around. There was an old guy across the street struggling to trim a raggedy hedge, quietly mumbling grumpily as he chopped away and there were some kids riding bikes around in circles and loops down the street.

Otherwise, it was just a quiet afternoon in middle-class America. No sign of disorder here. That was all behind the closed doors and curtained windows. No one ever escaped trouble. It just depended on what that trouble might be. They got out and went up the walk. On the porch was a closed umbrella, a brushy floor mat, and a decorative gnome. There was a wreath of dried flowers laced on the door. They buzzed the doorbell.

In a minute or so, the door cracked open and then further, and a diminutive, middle-aged woman with a henna beehive asked, "May I help you?"

She was just as plain as could be. Attractive enough, but the plain was draped on her. Not a hint of her notoriety shown through. In her neat drabness, she was not worthy of notice. It was her camouflage.

"Miss Roberts?"

"Yes, that's me. Who are you? What do you want?"

"Miss Roberts, hello, I'm Eddie Terrell and this is Miss Gigi Faye Erin. We are not here, let me emphasize, not here to cause you any difficulty. I promise that. I'm a lawyer here in town and Miss Erin here is an insurance agent. We just would like to show you a few pictures and see if you can point us in the right direction."

Roberts looked mildly skeptical. "I've heard of you, Mr. Terrell, but I don't think we've ever made each other's acquaintance."

Gigi Faye chipped in, "Miss Roberts, obviously we don't know each other, but what Eddie is saying is the absolute truth. I promise. We are not in any way associated with any law enforcement or government agencies. We are trying to solve a mystery. Some very expensive jewelry which my company insured has gone missing and expensive loss claims have been paid, and now, we believe these pieces have resurfaced and we are just trying to recover them. Basically, this is an investigation of insurance fraud and it does not involve you in any way."

It seemed that the girl-to-girl assurance slaked the edginess off Madge Roberts. "Insurance fraud? But why have you come to me?" She was opening up with a specific curiosity.

Eddie said, "We want to see if you can simply identify some people in a few photographs and if you can, point us in their direction." The three of them standing in the doorway knew the undercurrent of Madge Robert's primary mission on earth need not be spoken of.

"Uhm, please come in and let's shut the door."

"Thank you. I assure you under all circumstances we will not be here long. And we again promise we are not interested in you save for a bit of information you might be able to give us. And, if you have no such information, we'll be on our way promptly. And we thank you very much for allowing us this bit of time with you."

"What you got to show me?" It was get-down-to-business time.

Gigi Faye said, "Here's a little background. Eddie is my moustache if you will. This is my primary job. I'm an insurance fraud investigator. From time to time, I need a nice-looking fellow on my arm when I dive into places where we think perps might be hanging out. Gives me the look of attached, make me a little more harmless, keeps the antennae from raising up."

"I understand. Go on."

"A couple of weeks ago, Eddie and I went downtown to The Alley to scout about. We'd gotten a tip we might run into some of the lifted goods."

"Yes, I know The Alley. High-end joint. Might well be a good place to go hunting. Now, go on, please."

"There were two gals there, nice looking and nicely turned out. They each had some very fine baubles on their persons which looked like what we are looking for. We bought them some drinks and introduced them to some well-to-do fellows that Eddie knows who were down there hanging out, looking for whatever."

"Yes, okay, I get that picture."

"And along the way, we took a few photos of the gals with my point-and-shoot here. So, we'd just like to show you those and see what you might have to say about them. That's it."

"All right, let's see what you've got."

Gigi Faye pulled out her pink Canon and tapped the album of five photos to life. She handed the camera to Madge Roberts.

Roberts scrolled through them, did so again and said, "Wait here. I'll be back in a minute." She went down a hall and returned in a few minutes, carrying two ten-dollar bills and a small address book.

She said, "Y'all know what I do to make a living?"

"Yes, ma'am. You're a very valuable and skilled and talented seamstress down at Montaldo's and Nita's."

"Seems you've done your homework. So, I'll put it this way. Do you know what my other work is? I think you do."

"Yes, ma'am. We do."

"Here, take this ten-dollar bill." She handed it to Eddie. "Please hand it to Miss Erin." He did so.

"Miss Erin, Mr. Terrell has just hired you for $10 and other valuable consideration to act as his employed legal assistant. Do you understand that and do you accede to it?"

"Yes, ma'am, I do."

She then turned to Eddie. "Mr. Terrell, I am now retaining your services for $10 and other valuable considerations and now you and I share the attorney-client privilege, correct?"

"Yes, ma'am."

"Now, Miss Erin. I believe you to be Mr. Terrell's legal assistant by extension in this particular setting and thus the privilege between us all also extends to you and me by virtue of your employee relationship with him as your employing lawyer. Is that correct?"

Gigi Faye said, "Yes, ma'am. That's fair and correct. I appreciate your thoroughness."

"Now, do you know the names of these two gals in the photographs?"

"They told us they were Tina and Mitchell." Eddie pointed at the pictures.

"Yes. That's them. And they were stupid enough to use their real names. I know them. Let's leave it at that. I've never seen the jewelry before. It does appear to be substantial. Foolish, foolish girls. And to think they let you all take their pictures. Indiscreet and dangerous."

Roberts pursed her lips and shook her head. She had the look of a very disappointed and put out boarding school headmistress.

"You might want to write this little bit of information down."

Eddie pulled out his pen and a couple of business cards.

Roberts continued as she looked into the black book. "Mitchell is Mitchell Scott. She resides at 5467 Old Clemmonsville Road here in town. Her phone number is 336-725-3877. Tina is Tina Andrews. She lives at 308 Burke Street, also here in Winston-Salem. Her number is 336-768-9752. I am going to call them as soon as you leave here and am going to tell them to meet the two of you at 7 p.m. at the Quiet Pint Pub which is at the foot of the hill down from Wake Forest Medical Center at First Street, just off Hawthorne. I am not going to tell them who you are. I want to scare the bejesus out of them as they finally put two and two together, though I am forced to recall that old, true saying, "You can't coach stupid." I am going to tell them to bring all of that jewelry with them, have it in a shoe box so it is not visible to any other patrons there and give it, return it to you two people. And then I will arrange to meet with them later and provide them with, shall we say, further guidance. You needn't trouble yourselves with that.

"Now, it's about 6 p.m. I suggest you two go down to the Pint and get a booth in the back and wait for these two idiots. I will tell them to look for two people in the back of the place. They'll be there on time, I promise you. Now, I believe our visit is concluded. Thank you for bringing this to my attention. I don't know if our paths will ever cross again but I wish you both good luck. Mr. Terrell, if I ever feel the need for your services, I will be in touch. I have heard you are accomplished. Miss Erin, I cannot imagine I will ever need your services but you surely are one polished, smart, fine looking lady and I expect whatever you are up to in the days to come, you'll do just fine."

Eddie and Gigi Faye each shook hands with Madge Roberts and thanked her for her time. They let themselves out.

As they walked to the car, the old man was still wrestling with his recalcitrant shrubbery and the children on bicycles were still wheeling about and laughing and calling to one another. Eddie held Gigi Faye's door open for her and then got behind the wheel. They looked at each other with wide-eyed amazement. Eddie blurted out, "That's the damnedest thing I've seen in a real long time and I am just floored. We got the whole nine yards!"

"Yep, paydirt baby, paydirt. And you know what—Madge Roberts is one smart, sharp, and nice older broad."

"You got that right. Jesus. Never expected all that. No wonder she is a successful businesswoman!" He was chuckling to himself and Gigi Faye was shaking her head. "What the hell. Let's get on down to the Quiet Pint and wait for our pair of pretties. I guess they're getting their calls right now and shitting bricks as they get their instructions. Nice work, kiddo. You had the perfect touch in there. She gave it all up to us because of your good way."

"Thanks. I don't know about all that but thank you just the same."

"Well, we aren't quite finished. Let's go get the stuff and see what the count up looks like."

As Eddie drove, Gigi Faye fished about in her bag and pulled out the list of items they had been searching for. She scanned it up and down, then folded it and set it in her lap.

Eddie was suddenly curious and asked, "Have you...er...talked to your principals in any way about what we were thinking we were about going to do, what we just ended up doing?"

"No, I just told them generally we had some leads we thought we were going to run down and I'd let them know when we did. They're not hot to trot on this kind of stuff. Remember, this isn't my only file and sure isn't like that with them. There's always plenty of cases to work on. Pick one up. Put one down. They'd paid the loss claims many months ago, booked them out for accounting purposes, and just sent me bird dogging. And even when you vamoosed, you damn idiot, I figured you'd be back around sooner rather than later. Knew you weren't gonna walk away from a practice as good as yours." She smiled. It was genuine. "Again, Eddie, I'm sorry I ripped you. I think you got scared and I got scared and we were both scared and worried for different reasons and I just reacted badly. I feel like a dope."

"Hey, let it go. It's okay. Like I've said, we're all grownups but even grownups get a little out of kilter from time to time. Hell, look at me, allegedly a grown man and I just ran away as far as I could go like a frightened kid. But, we're back at it now and making progress, so let's go reclaim some of these hot rocks for fun and profit."

He pulled his car into the parking lot and edged up into a space around the back. Cars and trucks were whooshing by above them on the Interstate.

The Quiet Pint was crowded this early evening and deservedly so. It was a good-looking, rustic, warm, long room, great bar, good food, many cuts above the so-called bar fare, had an excellent wine and beer list and lots of televisions. The clientele was expansively varied. Doctors, nurses, businesspeople, hippies, purple and green hairs, art school types, cops, EMS workers, college kids, with lots of good ink on them too. It was a live and let live kind of place. And it was clean. That, in these days of perpetual grimy and greasy, was a huge plus. Eddie loved the place.

"You ever been here before?" he asked Gigi Faye as they walked in.

"Nope. Driven past it many times. Looks nice. Looks interesting too."

"I think, in addition to what we're getting ready to accomplish in a little bit, you'll enjoy it. Let's aim for that booth over in the very back." They wandered down that way. There were two young couples in their early twenties cozied up there, finishing their drinks.

Eddie grinned at them and leaned over and quietly said, "Hey, y'all. How y'all doing?"

The four looked at him quizzically. "We're good," one of them replied. "What's up?"

Eddie said, "Please let me ask y'all something. My partner here and I have a really big deal business meeting set for 7 o'clock here. We've got to meet two others about a serious money deal. Y'all look like y'all are about close to done and I was wondering if I picked up y'all's checks and also threw a crisp Ben Franklin in for y'all's further pleasure, could we just go ahead and have the booth now?"

"Mister, we ain't gonna be here but another ten minutes. You can have the thing then and you don't have to do anything for us. That's a nice offer though."

One the girls looked at the young man and said, "Are you nuts? We can't beat that with a stick. Let's take him up on his nice offer and just go over to the bar and keep on with whatever we're doing. Come on y'all. Let's go." She stood up. The others did too, the one fellow who spoke first was a little sheepish. Eddie handed the girl a brand new hundred-dollar bill right out of the ATM and asked her to get their server so he could take care of their tickets as promised.

"Thank y'all so much. This is a big help for us. We just need to get settled before the others get here. Sort of correctly positioned. Call it the Feng Shui of a business deal."

The other fellow simply noted, "Whatever works, dude. We appreciate it. Hope it all works out for y'all."

They all moved off and Eddie stood aside so Gigi Faye could slip into the booth. He'd noticed the restaurant's patrons giving her strong, steady admiring looks at she rustled in. She was one good-looking thing. She could be distracting and that often was a good thing. Eddie sat next to her. They were looking out a big picture window and could see well and broadly out, but folks coming across the parking lot could not see them as the top of the booth's backing was curved and so covered their faces from view. This is exactly what Eddie had gamed the spot for.

Gigi Faye giggled. "You just feel better when you got every thread tied down, don't you?"

"Leave as little as possible to chance and always position yourself in a more dominant than not way when transacting business. It oftentimes really does pay off. Same thing in a courtroom. I was trained and it really did stick with me to create a powerful picture that I own the courtroom. It is mine, my territory. Now, you don't do it arrogantly or rudely. That's of course counterproductive. Just be the benevolent owner and let others come along here and there and use it as they should.

"When these two gals get here I want them coming through that door and turning right and looking for us and then seeing us, as they've been told to look in this very back corner and that will be the first time they've seen us since The Alley. I promise you there is some good effective confusion and shock value to that."

"You fascinate me. I like working with you too. How about a drink while we wait?"

"Absolutely a fine idea."

The waitress came over. Eddie started with, "I'm taking care of the checks for those two couples who were here and are now over there down toward the end of the bar. Here's my card. Please add a 25-percent tip to it when you bring it back for me to sign. And, my friend here, Gigi Faye will have a...?"

She said, "I would really like an ice-cold Bell's Two Hearted Ale. Do you have that?"

"Yes, ma'am, we sure do and that's nice of you to pick up those other people's checks. Any particular reason or just being nice? I'm just wondering. By the way, my name is Mary P. for what it's worth." She was cheerful, playful. "The P's for Parrish. Sort of like Parrish the thought." She giggled with a throaty voice. She was blonde, very pretty, had a gorgeous figure and energy just busted out of her. Her step was just shy of a skip. There was a determination about her that was simply charming.

"I'd like a double Bulleit on the rocks and we're here doing a little business this evening and thought this was the best spot to get as much done as we can. There will be two women coming to meet us here in about a quarter of an hour. They will be carrying a shoebox. I'd ask you to be on the alert. When you see them sit down, please come right on over and ask them what they'd like to have to drink. Would you do that for us, please?"

"Sure. Happy to. I'll be right back with your drinks." She turned toward the bar and then turned back toward Eddie and leaned to his ear. In a whisper she asked, "Hey, just out of curiosity, what's going to be in the shoebox? Is this a drug deal? She made a funny "yikes" sort of face.

Eddie said, "Sorry dear, there is no *French Connection* angle to this. Something far more boring and still expensive enough."

"What's *The French Connection*?"

"Ah, yes, you are a bit young. *The French Connection* is a great old movie about drugs and cops and crooks in New York City. Starred a couple of great actors, Gene Hackman, and Roy Scheider. Absolute thriller. Bet you can get it at Blockbuster. Came out in the early seventies."

"Thanks for the tip. Now, I'll go get your drinks. But I'm still gonna be curious about that shoebox." She winked.

"If you're really a good girl, maybe we'll let you have a peek before we go."

As they waited for their drinks, Eddie and Gigi Faye sat quietly, watching the crowd. Their drinks came. Night was coming on in and the neon lights in the windows and on the rooftop signage and the strings of outdoor lights over the covered terrace glowed and glittered with color. It all made the place shine. People were visiting, joking, laughing, paying attention, wandering around, putting money in the jukebox, looking at one another, looking all around. There was a hum to the place. Traffic passed by on the street beyond the parking lot, cars would pull in, cars would pull out, the traffic lights at the near intersection would flash red and yellow and green, taillights on cars would go red, then white as they pulled away. Gigi Faye and Eddie just took it all in. It was a few minutes of exhaling respite before they could focus and be back at it.

Eddie looked at his watch. "Shouldn't be too much longer now." Gigi Faye nodded, both moving their eyes into the parking lot and at the entrance door.

"Well, well, here they come," Gigi Faye murmured, gesturing with her head out toward the terrace. They spotted Tina and Mitchell, hurrying, each carrying a shoebox.

Eddie asked, "How much candy did these broads hustle? Is your count a good one?"

"You know, I thought it was pretty solid but it's possible we've missed stuff or there could also be other pieces that weren't in our loss inventories."

Eddie said, "When they see us, wave happy, wave them over."

The two women came through the door, into the small vestibule, paused, turned, looked to the back corner of the restaurant. Eddie and Gigi Faye motioned to them. Upon seeing the couple the women showed visible confusion. "Why look, there are our fun friends from The Alley" and "What a coincidence" and then the much larger basic sensation looming, "Uh-oh, why are those people sitting where Madge Roberts has told us to go?" The two walked tentatively to the corner. Tina frowned and Mitchell bit her lower lip.

Eddie said, "Hey y'all! Come on, grab a seat."

Gigi Faye said, "Yes, please do."

They did and they slid in the booth. They were wordless save for, "Hey, what are y'all doing here?"

Mary P. right on the money, arrived and told the two newcomers, "Hey. My name is Mary P. I'm your server this evening, here to get you whatever you'd like to drink or eat. I've already helped your friends with their drinks. What would y'all like?"

More confusion. The two looked at each other, trying to unravel this little mystery that was raveled up before them and it just was not computing.

Eddie said, "Y'all go ahead and get something. Don't be bashful. It's on us." He was absolutely gregarious and Gigi Faye, pretty as ever, nodded him on.

Tina said, "Well, okay. I'll have a Cosmopolitan. What are y'all doing here? We're supposed to meet some people. Maybe we're in the wrong corner." She looked around, trying to orient.

Mitchell followed with, "I'll have the same. Thanks. Are you two who we are supposed to be getting up with?"

Mary P. left to quickly fill their orders and was efficiently back with the glasses. She eyed the shoeboxes and eyed Eddie as well. She stepped back just a bit but was obviously hanging around, her curiosity up.

Gigi Faye said, "Let me help y'all out a little now. We are who you are supposed to be meeting. We met with your boss lady earlier today. In fact, she helped us arrange this gathering. Do you have in those shoeboxes what you are supposed to have?"

There were collective gulps and nods from one side of the table, accompanied by widened eyes and the recognition that they were in the center of some sort of scamming bullseye and obviously, they both would be investing soon.

"Who are you anyway?"

Eddie's tone went from friendly to flat.

"Well, just as we told you a few weeks ago, I'm Eddie Tyrell. I'm a lawyer here in town just like I told y'all back at The Alley. Gigi Faye here is my friend and just like we also told you a few weeks ago, she's in the insurance business and she is. Here's what we didn't tell you. She was on my arm to make us look like just another couple out to have a good time and y'all bought into that easy enough. We had a good time, didn't we? And the other thing, the most important thing is that my buddy Gigi Faye here is also a top-notch, tough-as-nails insurance fraud investigator and we got a tip that night that a lot of missing jewelry, very valuable missing jewelry was gonna be seen down at The Alley and we appreciate that you helped us validate that information we received. Now, as you have been instructed, please hand both boxes to Gigi Faye here and she's going to see if you have brought us what you were supposed to have brought."

Dumbstruck and ashen, Tina and Mitchell slid the boxes across the booth's table to Gigi Faye. She took one, put it in her lap, took the top off and gently and slowly moved her hands and fingers through its contents, feeling and touching and looking and assessing. She then did the same with the other box. She pulled out her list and looked it over, then looked back in the two boxes and folded up the list and put it in one of the boxes. Then she looked up at Eddie and said, "Okay, we're good." Eddie just watched.

She said to the two girls, "You understand all this is going with us now. False insurance claims for the loss of these pieces have been filed many months ago by a number of individuals. The claims were paid then as we had no proof of the falsity of them. But there was significant suspicion that these were made-up losses. So my employers, a couple of insurance companies, put me on it and I asked for Eddie to accompany me to make me and us look legit and we started inquiring and hunting and scouting about and we got a tip, and so, here we are."

The two girls nodded. All their light bulbs had just come on. Mitchell worriedly asked, "Are we in trouble?"

Gigi Faye shook her head. "No, not with us now. Now, if you hadn't done what Miss Roberts had told you to, if you hadn't brought us these items as you had been instructed, there would have been all sorts of problems. We would have been forced to go to the police, the authorities, and you would have been charged with receiving stolen goods and probably a few other felonies as well such as being accomplices to felony insurance fraud, felony secreting of evidence, and obstruction of justice are some that come quickly to mind. And, you would have pulled Miss Roberts and her business operations into the open as well. Don't y'all see what a huge mess this could have become? And we know y'all didn't think about that, didn't think that anything like that might fall on your pretty heads, now did you?"

The two girls nodded their rueful understanding. Tina asked if she could ask another question.

"Certainly. Ask away."

"What about the men that gave us these things? What will happen to them?"

"In some instances, but not many, nothing will happen other than their fine arts and special valuables policies will be canceled and the word will go out over a national network of information that they will be marked as cheats and blackballed, so that no such policies should ever be written for their benefit again. That's going to probably happen to all of them. You can well imagine their spouses' curiosity and we'll leave it at that. Some of them will be quietly contacted to return the insurance money they earlier received, depending upon the level and amount of claims made. These are all well-to-do people and they don't want any trouble either so they'll cough it up. And no need to let the police in on their stupidity. Everything gets handled quietly and confidentially. And truth be told, y'all picked your marks well. You understand now, they were taking their wives' jewels, helping them 'disappear' and then filing claims for their insured value. And then for whatever service y'all rendered, you got paid with all this ice.

We understand y'all help Miss Roberts out, are in her string, but this looks like y'all were working outside the lines. We have a strong idea that she is going to be speaking with both of you about this pretty soon."

Both girls nodded glumly. Tina wiped tears from her eyes. Mitchell burned a thousand-foot hole in the table and then turned and looked out the window.

Eddie followed on. "We cannot imagine y'all didn't know something was more than a little fishy with all of this. Only a fool would be able to not get a handle on the high quality and value of all these goodies. And, girls, y'all ain't fools. We've spent time with you, remember. So, we know you are complicit in it good and deep. No need to respond. So that wraps this up. Go on and finish your drinks now. I'll take care of the tab. I'll say this as well. You both are attractive, pretty, smart, and fun. This is a bad moment for you. But, you'll get over it after a while and move on. We truly and sincerely wish you both the best with hopes for lots of good luck in the future. Now, y'all go on now."

They slid out of their seats and stood in frozen unison. Tina hesitantly raised her hand, as a third grader would do when seeking affirmation. Gigi Faye nodded at her in assent to the coming inquiry. "No cops? Really, no cops?"

"That's exactly right. No cops. No cops at all. I expect you've got more than a little trouble coming with Miss Roberts, but that's private, that's between the three of you. And, as it appears your services with Miss Roberts were both skilled and appreciated and obviously worthy of the receipt of good value, you'll not be wanting for more business opportunities in the future. Not sure how she's gonna handle y'all but in my opinion, it wouldn't be wise to throw the baby out with the bath water. I'd think she's gonna put y'all on a strict cash and carry-only basis. You are both excellent and active fucks, but girls, when you work in the employ of a pro like Miss Roberts, you just cannot work off the books. You'll get your asses in a crack every time. Now, go on and get out of here."

Tina and Mitchell departed, holding their heads up in false dignity, knowing too that they had caught a big break in the act of their being broken.

Mary P. sidled over. "Y'all just read those two the riot act. I couldn't hear it all but got enough of the meat of it. Jesus, y'all are big time, aren't y'all?" She was grinning big, an ear-to-ear job.

"Since they're gone now, can I see what's in those shoe boxes? I won't tell nobody but I am about to die of curiosity. Please, pretty please?" She held her hands up in prayerful solicitation.

Eddie looked at Gigi Faye for her response. He said to young Mary P., "This is her gig. I'm her second. This is her call. Whatever she says is the rule and nothing gonna change that. Do you understand, Maid Marion?" Mary P. nodded and looked on imploringly.

"Well, Miss Gigi Faye Erin, what say you to this young supplicant?"

Gigi Faye looked out the window vacantly for a few moments, turned her face to Mary P., grinned and said, "Sure. Why not. But listen, kid, we are not gonna spread all this stuff all over the table. You got that? This is to be a quiet look see and that's it. You understand?"

"Yes, ma'am."

"Then, sit down over there across from us, where those two gals were earlier. Do you understand what this is about from your eavesdropping?"

"I think I got some of it. Looks to me like some sugar daddy men took their wives' nice jewelry pieces and such and gave it to these two hookers who were just here in return for some fast and furious humpadiddy action and also, those sleazy men called the folks that insured that jewelry and made claims for their losses and got a bunch of money back. So kind of some double cheat 'em up action it seems. And end of story, y'all caught 'em but good. That's my take." She then folded her arms in self-affirmation and looked at Gigi Faye and Eddie and leaned back.

Gigi Faye and Eddie looked at each other as Mary P. was finishing up her *Reader's Digest* version of the affair and when she was finished, there was a brief, pregnant pause and then they both busted out laughing. "Couldn't have said it any better or more concisely myself. Honey, you've earned a look. But take it easy. Go gentle, please. This is some heavy stuff."

Gigi Faye carefully pushed the two boxes across to Mary P. She carefully lifted one lid off and then the other. She did not look down until both were clear. And then she looked and began making that click-click, cheeky giddy-up sound that people moving horses around make and then she hiss-whispered to them.

"Holy shit. Look at all this stuff! Rings, bracelets, necklaces, earrings, pins. Good Lord! How did I get in my shitty cheap line of work? And my cheap-ass no-good boyfriend wouldn't, no couldn't give me anything like this. Sorry, stream of consciousness. How much is all this worth? It must be a fucking fortune! Excuse my French but they got a fortune for fucking! Actually, if I don't say so myself, that's pretty good!" She was dazzled and awed and also pleased with her clever turn of a phrase.

Gigi Faye said, "It really is a lot of valuable jewelry. Our companies paid out in excess of six-hundred-thousand dollars on all of these pieces. There were so many in such a short time from a very short list of men. You can understand how our suspicions got raised."

"Jesus, that's most expensive pussy I've ever heard of! This is heavy-duty impressive."

Mary P. slowly put the tops back on the boxes and shaking her head in wonder, pushed them back across to Gigi Faye and Eddie. "Thanks y'all for letting me see. You know, that's about as exciting a thing as I can ever think I've seen. I appreciate that. I really do. I think that was a whole lot better than drugs. No, I know it is."

"A whole lot prettier too," Eddie added on.

Mary P. looked up. "Well, back to work." She hopped up from her seat and asked, "What else can I get you?" Eddie looked at Gigi Faye who nodded and then asked Mary P. for two more of the same and the check. Mary P. scooted away.

Gigi Faye observed, "That's one smart and pretty girl. Funny too. Maybe you ought to spring for her law school tuition. She's a pistol."

"Agreed. She got fun and trouble written all over her. She'd probably make a hell of a courtroom lawyer. Great personality. But no time for apprenticeships these days."

Then Eddie asked, "Is that most of it?"

"It's actually more than all of it. There are four or five pieces, no, six in there, a couple of rings and some bracelets that are not on our list. We got extra. What do you think?"

"Easy answer is that some of these bedroom jewelry box thieves may not have filed any claims. And can't you just hear Madge Roberts snapping each word off like a hot cracking whip to our two maybe not the sharpest-knives-in-the-drawer gals."

"But I'm not inclined to turn it in with all the rest. You know how tight-assed bean counting these insurance companies are. To do that will just raise a lot of questions and all."

"I've got an idea. Let's get out of here and go match up the boxes' content with the list. Cull out the odd ones. How about your place?" Gigi Faye looked at him with her most serious skeptical spectacles on.

"And, no, funny business, I promise. But we can be private there. I'm not crazy about going over to my place unless now is when you'd like to meet my new friend Mikey. And I don't want to go down to the office. It's too far for right now and your offices are even farther out."

"I understand. I'll trust you on this one. You damn well better keep your nose clean and your hands to yourself. And now's not the time for a meet and greet for me."

Eddie started laughing. "Hey, gorgeous. Unless my memory fails me, you were the one that started the fun and games of the other evening."

Gigi Faye grinned back of him. "Fuck you," she cooed. "And let's get going."

"Well, yes, you did." And he stuck his tongue out at her strutting back as she marched away.

Ten minutes later, they were back at Gigi Faye's place. She unlocked the door, turned on some lights, gestured for him to sit in the alcove at her tucked, small dining room table. She went into the kitchen, brought back two tall glasses with a couple of ice cubes, a bottle of bourbon, and a tall boy beer to crack. She then went and grabbed a pen and a pad. She then sat. Eddie poured himself a good one. She tilted her glass so the pouring beer would not get a big head on it.

She said, "Okay, let's get to it."

She flattened the typed list out on the table, untopped the shoeboxes, and began to match the descriptions of the pieces with the piece itself. Her searches were careful and precise. She had a good eye.

Eddie said, "You know what, Gigi Faye?"

Gigi Faye, pen clinched in her teeth while she rolled a piece around with both hands. "No, uhm, know what?"

"You are impressive with this stuff. You really seem to know your business."

"I'd better be or I'm not in this saddle. I've been at this a long time and have learned a lot along with way. It is a learned skill."

He continued to watch and the time drifted by.

She said, "Interesting. There are a few pieces of paste in here but most of it is legit. Some paste would have to be expected, I suppose."

Eddie noted, "I think it's fair to presume that our two pigeons were none the wiser. They should have had it all appraised but that could get dicey too. Some credible jeweler might well check the missing claim lists and then another unhappy game on. I bet they were told by their marks not to do that. Keep it to yourself for a good long while before you do something like that. Insurance claims offices can forget plenty over time and they do."

"So for these extra pieces, no one knows we have them except for you, me, and Tweedledum and Tweedledee and the latter two ain't gonna peep a word. So, now, what do we do? How about lay the extras out and let's get a look? And, am I correct in presuming that you have a pretty good feel for values, retail and street?" He eyed Gigi Faye with an amused smile.

"Yes, that's fair to say. There are six. Eddie, I think I kinda know where you're going." She eyed him back.

"I bet you don't. What do you think about this? First, let's get a feel for values, please."

There were three rings, two diamond, one emerald. There were two bracelets, both heavy gold, neither engraved or marked, and there was one gold and diamond necklace, almost a choker but not quite. He pulled a piece of paper out of his pocket, got a pen and said, "This emerald ring is what, retail and street?"

Gigi Faye held it up to look at it, reached into her pocket, got her jeweler's loupe out and pressed it to her left eye and peered and squinted at the piece, her lips knotted up in thought.

"Damn! Girl Scouts come prepared. I love it!"

She looked up, the loupe still in place. "Retail twenty-five thousand, street seventy-five hundred."

They repeated the process. When they were done, before them lay the six pieces, total estimated retail value of $82,000 and total estimated street value of $25,000.

"What do you want to do?"

Eddie asked, "Find out if there's anything unusual or unique that would assist in identifying them. I presume they could be reset or melted down?"

"No, they are all of good quality. But none is a 'special' or signature piece. And, yes, they certainly can be taken apart, reassembled, or rendered down."

Eddie said, "Let me have the six in here. I'm going, as a present to you, to make up for my bad behavior and my immaturity and foolishness, make you an investor in a small syndicate I'm putting together. You do not have any need to know what the investments are. Like all deals, there might be a nice return, might lose it all too. This is, I emphasize, a 'please don't ask cause I ain't gonna tell' situation. Each of my stakeholders put in 25K and lookee here, that's your expert street valuation figure on these few random extras."

"What in the hell are you up to?" She looked at him with eyes arched in curiosity. He was grinning.

"I'm now going to take possession of these six pieces and put them away. You do not know anything about their existence. They no longer exist. They have never existed. Do you understand? And then they will soon reappear far, far away in scurrilous, private circumstances where they will be revalued and reused in new forms. At the end of that process, your stake is made and goes into the pot. And then we'll see what happens with that and the others."

"I think I get it. Eddie, I've never dipped my quill in the company ink but this is fascinating. I've gotta ask this. How many investors are there and would any of them know about this, any of this?"

'That is a fair question. There will be five total, I believe. One investor is putting up a double share so the total amount available will be 150,000K. And, no, none of the investors will ever know about this except you and me, and since you seem positive about this, you don't know anything about it either, which leaves just little old me."

She leaned across the table, her face but inches from his. She was silent and then spoke quickly, pushed it out in a burst of wanting. "I think the framework of what you have laid out as I have pieced it together from your questions and my answers is brilliant. Damn, I am happy to have these baubles go away, which means less explaining for me. I appreciate your thoughtfulness in including me and so I'm glad to be an investor. I accept not because you were bad or a jerk but because you have offered it and it would be bad manners to decline. It isn't necessary, not at all, but it cleans up a lot of loose ends. And it's kind of exciting and daring. I've never been much like that. Sort of buttoned up all the time. I can't help but thinking when I unbuttoned with you the other night, that has loosened my leash a bit, well, more than a little." She smiled a guilty-as-charged, wide-eyed smile and her cheeks reddened just a little. Eddie's pulse quickened but he pushed that opening door back.

He looked at her for a moment, considered her, nodded at her.

She nodded back. "I'm in."

He cleared the six pieces from the table, wrapped them carefully in some paper towels from the kitchen, and put them in his pocket.

He sat back down and cleared his throat. "Okay, good. How about one more good drink and then I'm off?"

"Are you?" Her voice was gravelly soft and her eyes studying.

"I think so. I think that's better. As you know, I have a new friend waiting for me at home. I need to work on my reliability issues. You know that. Our business, you and me, is complicated enough. I think it's the better idea to hold that line, certainly for now as tempting as the alternative surely is."

She paused before speaking further. "My God, Eddie, are you trying to grow up? You are a...a...an enigma. You're as all over the lot as they get. But I understand. And you're right for now. But if something changes?" She was not mad. She was not plaintive.

"Honey, you'll be the first to know, I promise. Now, let's drink to a good business plan. Let's see if we can roll this ball."

So they sat at the kitchen table in silence, clinking their glasses, drinking a tall whiskey and a cold beer, mostly staring off into space, glancing at one another and then away. The lamp light glowed soft golden yellow. Eddie drained his last. He took her hand and kissed it and squeezed it.

"Thank you for trusting me, for trusting us. It counts."

He stood up, kissed her on the cheek, said, "I'll be in touch. Take good care of yourself. Good luck with your reports. If you need me, just holler. I'll submit my final billing hours to you efficiently. I've loved working with you. We're not done yet. I'll keep you posted."

"I've loved working with you, Eddie. Hope we can some more."

"Oh, honey, we are. We are. Have a good night." He shut the door quietly. He was gone.

Gigi Faye just looked the door and thought she was a little sad and a little happy too. She noticed her heart beating. She went on to bed, suddenly exhausted, suddenly agitated. She sighed herself to sleep.

Eddie drove slowly and carefully home, thoughts ping-ponging between his ears. It was after midnight. He'd had a few and wanted another. He was restless. They'd gotten it done. But they hadn't.

He let himself quietly in the house, took his shoes off and went softly to their bedroom. Mikey was asleep, the bedside lamp still on, a book slumped on her chest. He went to her and kissed her forehead. She stirred. She started to sit up. He gently held her down and gave her a big hug.

"No. No. No getting up. Go back to sleep. It's late. I'm here."

"Hey. Uhm, but one thing. How'd y'all do? You were with that Gigi Faye gal, right?"

"We did good. It's finished. Case closed and there are some extra benefits I'll tell you about in the morning. Now, go on back to sleep. I'll be back in here in a little bit."

She smiled, yawned, and rolled over on her side, settling back into her slumber, slow burrowing into the linens. He admired her contours. He picked up her book and set it on the table. He turned off the light. He went out and back to the kitchen.

Eddie poured himself a good, straight, stiff one and dropped a couple of ice cubes in. Then he sat down at the kitchen table in the dark and looked out across the porch at the lake. There was a three-quarter moon and its light silvered the little lake and it glimmered tiny lapping waves as the breeze would come along and then die down. It was peaceful, quiet. He could hear the clock ticking in the living room. It had been a family gift from long ago. Usually it comforted him.

He took a big slug. He spoke to himself in a soft, thinking voice.

"Okay, Eddie, me laddie, what's next? Well, son, you've got a lot going on. Let's see..." He began to count with his fingers. "Court cases, lots of them, some really big. A crazy ass drug deal. Gotta raise a little more money and get it organized. And there's the Ben problem. Inconvenient. Need to minimize the nasty."

He took another swallow and closed his eyes. "And there's Mikey and there's Gigi Faye. Maybe I should just go back to Montana and rewind this reel." He chuckled. "Too late for that now."

He drank down the rest of his nightcap and went to bed. He quietly dropped his clothes in the hall and found his way to Mikey. He held her close and as he did, he thought how beautiful she was. And as he slipped away, Gigi Faye kept peeking around the corner at him.

CHAPTER TWENTY-FOUR

BAD PLANS

Spaceuntravel

THEY SLEPT LATER than usual, almost until 9 a.m. After some coffee and toast and getting gussied up, they finally headed out. When they got to the office the next morning a little after 10:30, Patty said with pursed, impatient lips, "Curt Minor is in your office. He's upset." Eddie quickly informed Patty that they had sealed up the jewel fraud case the night before, and that he would tell her all about it later and then asked Mikey to wait with Patty and went to his office.

Curt stood up when Eddie entered. "Eddie, I'm sorry to show up like this but Ben's done it again. He beat Rise bad last night. Real bad. We gotta do something and get it done damn soon. Rise wants something done like yesterday."

Eddie shook Curt's hand and motioned for him to sit down. "Where's Rise now?"

"I've got her hidden out over at Robert Peddyford's place. Robert's an ex-cop, tough as dirt. Ben doesn't know him or where he lives, but if he did find out and come over there, he'd sure as shit wish he hadn't come round. One of Robert's hands is the size of Ben's motherfucking head. Robert's wife is a part-time floor nurse over at Katie B. and is looking after Rise now."

Eddie nodded. "Where's Ben now?"

"At their place. Sleeping his drunk off. Like I said, it was a big one. They're getting bigger and bigger all the time. You still in on the take-him-out thing?" There was no hesitation.

"Yes. Let's do it tonight. Can you round Kenny up for us? How long before you can get him over here to meet with us?"

"Probably a couple of hours, I can have him here by one or two. You gonna let Kenny do the honors?"

"Yes, indeed. You and I both know he'll need no encouragement to snap that sorry son of a bitch's neck."

"Let's do this," Curt said. "How about go buy two or three bottles of whatever rotgut shit Ben drinks and take them by there so they are right there ready to use by him when he grogs up. Let's keep him good and drunk. I've got something to make his pain go away too. Go buy a big tarp to wrap his ass in. With a zipper, rubber is best. We're gonna need a junked-out car to put him in and then take him where he needs to be. How 'bout go buy one over at Leon's Used..."

Eddie called Patty on the phone and said, "Please bring me a couple of thousand, no, twenty-five hundred. Thanks." Then Eddie turned back to Curt. "I've got a client out on Bailey Road who owes me a favor or two. I've gotten his ass out of a crack more than a few times. He's got the tool we need to finish this right and quick. Just as soon as we finish here, I'm going to see him and get an appointment lined up for tonight. Is two grand enough to get one that runs okay?"

"Yeah. What kind of tool?"

"Car crusher. We're gonna turn Ben into a cube that will then go to a shredding plant for industrial recycling. In the regular course of business. Ben's gonna disappear."

"I like it. I'm going to run my errands. How 'bout I take Kenny with me to buy the car?"

"Sure but don't tell him nothing yet. How about go buy the booze first and take it over to Ben's? Then go get the tarp, one that seals up, please, then go get Kenny and y'all go buy a decent clunker and let Kenny follow you over here to the office. In that order, please." Patty came in and handed Eddie an envelope. She eyed Eddie. He counted out the hundred-dollar bills and handed the envelope to Curt.

"Right. Got it. I'm outta here."

"Me too."

Curt paused and looked at Eddie.

"Thanks, man."

"My pleasure. Oh, one more thought. How about get some ganja for Kenny? I think it will help keep him calmer before we get this done tonight. I think that'll be another helping babysitter so to speak. Oh, lemme see your hands. Hold one up." Eddie paired his palm with Curt's.

"You and me are standard, so how about get two pair of regular rubber gloves and one extra-large? I think they'll come in handy. Will be good thing to grab when you get the rubber zip bag, don't you think?"

"Sure, like those ideas. Will help calm the raging bull. And minimize the marks when the time comes. So, three pair. You going with us tonight?"

"Yes, I am."

"Good. Appreciate that."

"It's like what the fellow said a long time ago when all those men signed the Declaration of Independence."

"What's that?"

"We all better hang together or for sure if we don't, we will all hang separately."

Curt laughed. "Independence, my ass. We already slaved up again. You too, you crazy motherfucker. In up to our shit-ass, crimed-up necks." Eddie shrugged his shoulders.

Curt went out the front door. Eddie walked through Patty's office. Patty and Mikey looked at him, curious, questioning. He saw their eyes.

"I'll be back in a little while. No big deal. I've gotta go see a man about a car. Y'all got plenty to do, I'll bet. Curt Minor's gonna bring Kenny over to see me this afternoon. Patty, how about in a little while y'all go over to the deli on Liberty and get a bunch of turkey roast beef sandwiches and chips and a couple of six packs of cold Bud?"

"Okay, uhm, what's going on?"

"Nothing much. Don't be worrying about stuff. I'll be back in an hour or so."

"So now, you're talking in code, are you?" She smelled the rat but couldn't see it.

"Now, come on. It ain't no biggie. Now, I gotta go." And he did.

CHAPTER TWENTY-FIVE

BIRDS OF A FEATHER

Joe South

IT WAS A cooler day with a lowering sun. Eddie drove north out of town up Highway 52 and then swung off at the College Park Road exit. The name "College Park" had always amused him. There was no college out there, not even the hint of anything so modest as a correspondence diploma mill mail drop and if there was a park, it was well disguised by industrial suburban blight, heavy machinery outfits, trash piles, spectacular litter, molding, rusting mobile home clusters and overgrown, graying mutant plant growth that sprouted and spread in spite of the throes of soon-to-visit death by pollution and suffocation. Heavy films of dirt dust and smoke dust were prevalent on everything, streaked by rain and wind. It was a desolate place, mostly broke, mostly unhappy. There were no schools, no neat yards, no bright, straight standing mailboxes, no signs of organized governmental order. There were more than a few Confederate battle flags. This was a doughnut hole of rebellion in the sea of municipal order.

Eddie sat up straight and tried to pay attention. There were many things on his mind. He knew they had to get this one right. Failure was not an option.

He drove about three miles and then turned left onto Black Ankle Road, a wide dirt and gravel packed avenue, bumpy and rutted by a constant back and forth flow of heavy trucks, tractors and trailers and rolling equipment, much of it loaded with tons of loose metal, construction site detritus, disassembled buildings, wrecked cars, trucks, limousines, even eighteen wheelers. The dust was always high and trapped in the roadway by high overgrowth on the edges that had not been trimmed or cut back in years. It created the driving-down-a-blind-barrel effect. Eddie turned on his windshield wipers to sweep the dry grit away and popped out his headlights as well.

He pulled into the front parking lot of a low cinder block building, where plenty of cars and pickups were crammed together. Customers, dealers, contractors, metal thieves, amateurs, professionals, all gathered to buy and sell in good order.

Whatever illegality embedded in the commerce had long since been ignored and neglected by local law enforcement. The place just hummed, rattled, slammed, and banged along. The county had no noise ordinances out this way so any such complaints would be per force muted. The tall, brightly lit signage of the place ran across the entire length of the sagging overhang front piece ledge of the roof. The background was bright yellow, the lettering was all a foot high in a brighter red.

R and R Car Crushing
We Buy and Sell Metal-Fair Weight Scales-Top Prices Paid
Highest Grade Industrial Stripping, Shredding, Shipping
Proprietor: Reavis Rakestraw. We been here for years and years.

As Eddie got out of his car, a huge trash loader truck pulled up behind his dust-encrusted Mercedes. The driver rolled down his window and looked Eddie over, resting his bulky, inked left bicep on the frayed weatherstripping. He grinned.

"Son, the last time we seen a fellow as pretty as you out here, white shirt, suit and tie and some such, was when the coroner had to come do an ID on some schlub who got too familiar with a big Cat's tracks when he weren't paying attention. Busted him open like a water balloon. You ain't carrying no doc bag, so why is a handsome fellow like you out this way?"

Eddie said, "Well, thanks for the compliment, I guess, and I'm here to see Reavis. We go way back. After I'm through visiting with him, you want me to stick around for a while? Can help make the place look good, right?"

The garbage man liked the banter.

He laughed. "Hell, no! First, you'll just get filthy as a mud-swimming goat standing out here in this shit storm and also, as long as you're here, you just make the rest of us look even shittier than we usually are. Now, I gotta go save the environment. Later, dude!" And he shifted his big roll into gear and gunned it, so the stinking juices in his hauling pan sluiced out in a small tsunami of sour rotten green poison. Eddie waved and hustled into the office.

It was but a few steps to the service counter where he was greeted by a see-through black bustier struggling to encase a set of bulging, seam-popping titties. Attached by slim shoulders to a tiny head and neck inked in tribute to Jesus and Satan and God Bless America and some random horoscopic symbols, her name tag read "Candy." The height of the counter kept the rest of her out of view. Eddie was grateful. Behind her sat four battered desks, each with two dial-up telephones and the basic chaos of paper and parts, soda cans and candy and sandwich wrappers. At each desk, men were on their phones, taking notes and orders and cracking jokes. Two of the men were white. Two were black. They were all big men. All the conversations were loud. Flowing profanity was a helpful thread. There was an egalitarianism to the place. Window unit air conditioners hummed. It was cold in there.

"Hi, Candy." She fluttered back.

"Hi, Mr. What's Your Name? What can I do for you?"

"Hey. I'm Eddie Terrell. I'm an old friend of Mr. Rakestraw's from a ways back. I'd like to grab a quick visit with him if he's around."

"Oh, he's here. That's him. Over there on the phone in the corner with his back turned. Let me go over there and write down that you're here. How do I spell your last name?" She took a piece of scrap paper and leaned forward up over the counter to get writing leverage, thus forcing her gorgeous breasts to surge out and up like rising biscuits. Martha White Hot Rise had nothing on Candy. Eddie told Candy how to spell his name and she carefully block printed it all out and then showed it to Eddie.

"Did I get that right, Mr. Eddie Terrell?"

"You certainly did, Candy, and I appreciate it very much."

"Good. I'll be right back." She was pleased with herself.

She maneuvered around the office's little maze, peeked back over her shoulder toward Eddie, tossed her hair. As she was moving more into the complete field of Eddie's vision, it was apparent that Candy was blessed with anatomical gifts rarely found in a car crushing shop. Eddie casually wondered if Rakestraw was banging her. Always nice to have a shared employee-employer compensation plan, he supposed.

He watched her tap on his bent over shoulder and hand him the little note. He nodded, gave Candy a thumbs up, held up a "one minute" finger and ground through his call and hung up. He swung around, saw Eddie, and jumped up, calling a welcoming, "Counselor!"

Like all of them he was a big man, strong, bull-necked. He had, at some point, completely shaved his head to a waxed sheen. He had a diamond stud earring and a perfectly groomed and managed silver-gray moustache and goatee, better known in these parts as a "prison pussy." He had gotten thicker in the middle with the passage of time but was still a very handsome man with dark hazel eyes that paid attention all the time.

"How the hell are you, Eddie? Long time no see. What's up? How can I be of help to you? Really glad to see you! Wait. Wait...you wanna talk about anything in particular? But first, we gotta take a pull!" Reavis Rakestraw was a genuinely affable man, a gregarious man in a rough and rugged business.

He pulled a bottle of Ancient Age out and pulled its cork out. Eddie knew this drill well and was amenable to it. It would help with the forthcoming ask.

Eddie had helped Reavis a few times, both times successfully. There had been that matter of the underage farm girl many years ago that had been found to be potentially inebriated by spirituous liquors provided by Mr. Rakestraw. They were able to dance away from that one by virtue of the girl's leering assistant DA assigned to the case who almost drooled as he signed the dismissals. Eddie did not feel that was a time to get the morals on. So instead he encouraged the replacement of one lecher with another.

There had also been some strong suspicions on the part of the local authorities that Mr. Rakestraw had been dealing in some pretty high-priced stolen auto parts, but some timely and gently placed cash had greased and teased a tip from a deputy who needed the down payment for an above ground pool, and by time the po-pos arrived with search warrants in hand, everything had just "gone away," actually into the mammoth shredder where it evolved into unidentifiable strips of thin metal. It was this memory in particular that Eddie hoped to replicate just a little later as day went on into night.

"Straw, I'm glad to see you too. Delighted to put a bubble or two in your hootch." It was offered and the bottle was taken and lifted. Eddie's two big swallows were appreciatively appraised by Rakestraw and then it was the big man's turn and he accommodated the tradition. The lawyer-client relationship endured. The office folks grinned and nodded in approval.

"So, Eddie, glad to see you haven't lost your touch. Now, what's on your mind. I know you didn't come out here to get dirt on your shoes." Rakestraw grinned.

Eddie asked quietly, "Straw, can we go outside and talk for a minute?"

"Sure. Come on." And they stepped back out into the cacophony on the yard, around the entry gate to where the whole place opened up before them.

"Eddie, does this have something to do with this place? My empire?" Rakestraw winked and waved his arm widely at the few thousand wrecked and battered cars and trucks and the huge tractors and lifters and spikers and tracked bucket cranes that smashed them into useless submission before they were taken to the shredder.

It was all set on twenty acres, give or take, and in actuality was an international operation. Vehicles were first prepared for oblivion. Gasoline and oil were drained as was antifreeze. Those fluids were recycled. Batteries were removed as were catalytic converters. Then they were crushed or cubed, assaulted and attacked and flattened or compressed with 150 tons of piston driven pressure, after which they were stacked on flatbeds and hauled about half a mile to the shredder where they were dropped or pushed into giant whirring blades and hammers that screechingly, slammingly turned them quickly into strands and bits and clumps of metal of varying sizes and thicknesses depending on the dimension sets of the operator, all the while being cooled by jets of water that firehosed the remnants and the tools that tore at them and broke them down.

Conveyor belts lifted the results up and over into piles. Then large compression pushers shoved and spread the piles onto cooling platforms where they were claw-grabbed and crammed into big barrel-like containers, sealed, and marked for transport overseas. Larger trucks were in and out of the yard all during the day and night, the finished products being repeatedly hoisted and stacked onto their flatbeds for transport away, almost all of it going overseas.

There were always at least fifteen hundred to two thousand objects of destruction awaiting transformative disposal. More came in all the time six days a week. For years and years it had been like this and had never slackened. It started each morning by seven and though the front office was usually closed by 5:30 or 6 p.m., often times it was not unusual to have the ballet go on until 9 or 10 at night.

"Well, Straw, yes it does. I need a favor. I'd like to have a car done in tonight and sent on its way quickly."

Rakestraw eyed Eddie just for a moment, and staring off toward the dust and noise of the yard, replied, "Eddie, I'm happy to get that done for you this evening. I suppose I need not know about whatever that car is about. It's fine. We will get it done."

"Thanks, Straw. It's important. Might I give you a touch for your trouble?"

"Hell, no. You never charged me enough way back when I was on the way to shit city and you pulled my ass back to safe. Wouldn't think of it! It's on the house, as they say. What time will you be here?"

"About 8:30 if that works. After dark. I'll be in one car. Two black guys, trustworthy, will be in the subject vehicle. Great big one's name is Kenny, the other is Curt."

"Good. I'll be here to oversee. I'll get Coitus to get it done and will let the few boys down the line know that it's an expedite priority."

"Coitus?" Eddie laughed.

"Oh yeah. He's actually Curtis but he's so fucked up, we all call him Coitus. Dumber than a box of rocks and about half nuts, walks around mumbling to himself all the time, greasy hair spikes out like he's stuck his dick in a light socket and he dresses and smells like Joe Shit The Ragman, but he can flat drive a crane and moves the levers and lifts like an idiot savant genius. He's all-pro at machinery, cubing and crushing. Been here well over five, six years. Don't think he's ever missed a day and has a 100-percent clean employee record. In truth, he's an amazing employee. By the way, he don't know shit and don't say shit."

"Might I give Coitus a touch then?"

"No. No. That'd be out of the ordinary and I expect we want nothing out of the ordinary tonight, right?"

"Good point. Thanks."

Straw said, "Go on now. Get outta here and I'll be looking for you about 8:30. Unless there's anything else."

"No, there isn't. I appreciate it. Will see you in a while."

They shook hands, nodded at one another, and Eddie headed back to his office but only after sliding through a quick car wash. When he got there, Patty and Mikey had the food and beer on the conference room table.

Patty asked, "Okay. What's next?"

"We wait. I'm going in my office to do some reading and thinking on the Reynolds case and the upcoming Pussy Preacher mediation. I suppose I ought to be scanning our case lists too. Mikey, how about come see me for a minute, please?" Eddie held the door for her and then closed it gently behind them. They stood face to face. Her eyes implored him.

"Honey, I can tell by the looks on both your faces that you're concerned, worried a little bit about whatever might be going on. Please don't be. Patty knows this drill better than you do. She's been through the tough-it-out mill a million times. You, you're a little more of a rookie. Sometimes, we've all just got to stay calm and keep moving and it'll all be all right. And it's gonna be. I promise." She bit her lip and looked down.

"Eddie, are you okay? Are you all right? I feel like I ought to be worrying about something but I have no idea what that should be. Does all this have something to do with the big plan that we all already know about?"

"Well, I'll say this. I've got an appointment this evening that will be a big help to the big plan. Once Curt and Kenny get here, we're all gonna eat and have a few beers and then I'm going to go off with them. I should be home ready to hug and kiss you by 10 p.m. Now, please go help Patty, keep learning this crazy business and rest your mind. Please and pretty please." He kissed her cheek and her lips and held her close.

She sighed. "Oh, Eddie. Be safe. Please be safe."

He let her go, looked at her and said with a big smile, "Damn good plan, girl!"

And he opened the door and asked for some files and they all worked and waited.

CHAPTER TWENTY-SIX

SHOP AROUND

The Miracles

CURT DROVE OVER to the ABC store on Northwest Boulevard and bought two fifths of Canada Dry bourbon. He paid cash. That stuff was so rotgut, even the salesclerk asked, "You really want to drink that shit?"

"Sure. Why not? After a few pulls, you just go numb anyway, right?" He winked as he quick stepped out the door.

The clerk just shook his head and turned back to his counter and register.

Curt then made his way over to Phillips Smith hardware where he bought three pairs of tight fit rubber gloves and a large, zippered, rubber all-weather duffle bag, paying cash for those items as well. The salesclerk cheerfully noted, "Good sturdy stuff. Expect you got a honey-do list in your future." Curt nodded and smiled stiffly.

He put them in the trunk of his car, a bland, plain-looking, dark blue Chevy Impala. Curt hated to call attention to himself. Most of the time, when folks saw him, they really didn't see him or didn't remember. He approached his life as a silent cipher. Next, he went to one of his drink houses and pulled a couple of small doobies out from under the bar and wrapped them in some tin foil and carefully put them in his breast pocket.

Curt made his way over to the rent house on Cromartie where Rise and Ben had been staying. It was at the dead end of the street, the last of five rent houses on that side of the street and well above it on a good-sized hill was the forested perimeter of Winston-Salem State. Behind it was a weedy bank and culvert.

He drove up into the graveled, grass-sprouted drive that ran around to a trashy backyard and a slumping back porch. He climbed the tilting short steps carrying the two bottles of hooch and knocked softly on the back door. There was no answer. He waited and then knocked again, this time a little louder. Again, nothing.

Curt jiggled the doorknob, then tried a turn and the back door opened easily. He slipped in and crept toward the back of the house. He could hear the splattering, snorting snores. They either were those of a dying man or a drunk man. Sooner rather than later, the entire description would fit.

The bedroom door stood wide open and on the bed, which faced the door, there lay Ben on his back, mouth open, a pool of drool beside his cheek and ear. His breathing was labored but even. His eyes were closed and he was still. He was oblivious.

Curt crept in, surveyed Ben more closely, satisfied himself that his target was out cold and carefully put the two bottles on the bedside table without clinking or sounding. Ben's breath was sour and stunk to high hell. Curt breathed through his mouth to lessen the stench. He quietly backed out of the room, watching Ben's rumpled corpus closely as he withdrew.

Curt silently mouthed, "Sleep good and tight, big boy. We'll be back for last call real soon." Curt went on back out, softly closing the door as he went.

And then he arrived at Kenny's place. He banged on the screen door and Kenny came along and saw him and let him in.

"Hey, Curt, how you doing? What's up?"

"Hey, Kenny, I'm square. How about you?"

"I'm good. Kinda bored. Watching too much TV. Need to make a little money, you know what's I mean?

"I think we can work on that. Mr. Eddie and I have a job for you. You up for something like that?"

"Sure. What's the deal?"

"Come on with me and you'll get learned up soon enough. Put on your shoes and first we got to do some shopping."

"Shopping, huh? What we shopping for? Hope you got the shopping money 'cause I ain't got jack shit."

"No worries, my brother. I got the cash."

"What we hunting?"

"We are going to go buy an old used car."

"Why that kind?"

"Come on and you will see what this is all about soon enough. We need your help. Mr. Eddie Terrell has asked for you to help us."

"He has? Wow! That's pretty sweet!" Kenny seemed oblivious to Ben's latest ass whipping of his sister.

They went out to Curt's car. Kenny asked, "Where we going?"

"To Leon's Paint and Body. He's always got some old stuff that still runs pretty good lying about on his back lot."

"Square by me."

Leon's, out over near the airport, was a big cinderblock building and lot surrounded by chain link fence topped with barbed wire and signed with, "Keep Out, No Trespassing ,Guard Dog On Premises," and so forth, but the classic was "Yes, we have guns and no, we don't call 911."

They pulled up and went in. Leon, an older and dignified man with the look of a gentleman who also could go crooked with the best of them, was leaning on the counter, yacking with a gas station guy from next door.

They were discussing the effects of putting high test in an engine that wasn't made for it and bullshitting about the local Minor League Baseball team, the Winston-Salem Red Sox, a loaded group which included a couple of guys who were surely on their way to the big leagues sooner rather than later.

Curt heard the tail end of that and volunteered, "Hey, Leon. You're exactly right. George Scott can flat slam those taters and Joe Foy is slick as shit at the hot corner."

"Hey, Curt. How you doing? Yeah, will be fun to watch those two and a few others as they rise on up. What brings you here to visit? What can I do for you? And, aren't you Kenny? Rise's baby brother?"

"Yessir, I am," Kenny answered deferentially.

Curt asked, "Leon, we are looking for a very old, very used car that still has some steam, not so much but enough, tires better than bald, still has some zip in the engine. You got anything like that out back?"

"Naw, just thirty or so. Hell, most of what's out back fits that description 'cept the few that are worse off than that." They all laughed. The gas station guy said his goodbyes and headed down the street to rotate some tires.

Leon said, "Come on. Let's go out back and see what we can root out."

The three went out on the back lot and nosed around, wandering up and down the rows. Leon explained, "Now a lot of these are waiting for body work or paint jobs but the ones with the soaped Xs on their windshields, those are your prospects. Now, how about this here not too bad Oldsmobile Eighty-Eight?"

They looked at the tires. They still had some decent tread. The car's paint job was dimmed by sun and time but was still a nice emerald green. One could tell it had a big trunk as well. They checked the odometer which read well north of 125,000 miles. She was an aged-out junker that Curt hoped had a little more juice left in her.

Curt said, "Let's crank her up. Can I take her around the block?"

"Sure. Lemme go to the office and grab the keys."

Kenny said to Curt, "That's a pretty nice ride. Wonder what he wants for her?"

"Not as much as you'd think. High miles. Let's see how she handles. Wonder about the shocks and transmission."

Leon returned and handed the keys to Curt and told them he'd be back in the office when they returned.

Curt asked, "How much you looking for on this one, Leon?"

"Oh, I suppose three grand but let's see what you think once you run her a bit."

Curt nodded and he and Kenny got in. He turned the keys and the engine came nicely to life with some sputter but no gag. It backfired once.

They pulled away and headed down past the airport on the Liberty Street extension. Kenny reached to turn the radio on, but Curt shook his head and Kenny pulled his hand back. "We need to listen to this car. We need to feel this car."

They headed out to Highway 52 and moved north climbing the hills toward Sauratown Mountain and Pilot Mountain. Curt punched the accelerator. The car gasped, then caught and surged. It had a big engine, loads of tired horsepower. There was some exhaust trail and the car rocked noticeably. The shocks squeaked. The muffler was about gone as the car rode noisy. It was mushy in the curves but that was of little interest for Curt, save for his points when making the offer on it. The car was serviceable for the purposes intended for it.

They went back to Leon's, parked in front and went in.

"Well, boys, what you think? How'd she do?"

Curt replied pleasantly, "Not bad but not so good either." He started the count off on his fingers. "Engine is catchy. Rides real soft, bouncy. Gonna use a lot of gas. Needs a new muffler and shocks."

Leon laughed, "Hold on. Now hold on a second. I know she's a pretty beat up old thing. I take no offense. What you wanna do if anything? Maybe go back out there and look at another?"

"Leon, I'll offer you two grand cash for her right now. That's it. That's all I got and all I'm gonna have on this one. Now, I do want to come back in a week or so and talk to you about a nice, decent condition short school bus that will need one of your nice paint jobs. Hopefully, that'll help you a little to get to yes on this one."

"Oh, well then, she's all yours. No reason to haggle on it. I like the idea of another sale too. Let's see your money and I'll fill out the paperwork and hang a thirty-day tag on her and y'all can be on your way. Who is the buyer? You?"

"No, let's say the Church of the Heights is the buyer and put the address for Gilmore's Funeral home on it, please." He handed Leon twenty crisp Bens. Leon arched his eyebrows and then giggled and sing-songed.

"Something going down around in this town." He followed with, "Fine by me. Am I to presume by time the paperwork comes back from Raleigh, this old Olds gonna be moving along?"

Curt just looked out the window and hummed Leon's sing-song. Kenny just watched, wondering what all this had to do with the job Curt and Mr. Eddie wanted him to do.

Pulling into Eddie's parking lot, Curt waited for Kenny to lumber the Olds in next to him, its double jet chrome rocket hood ornament gleaming in the daylight that was slowly leaving, a reminder of the car's better days. They got out.

Curt asked, "Now that you've driven from there to here, what you think?"

Kenny was quietly pleased that a man as sharp as Curt would ask his opinion on anything, much less anything as important as the condition and driving quality of a dubious used car.

"Not bad. Not bad at all. Compared to the piece of shit I drive, it's pretty classy. Problem is mine's tougher than dirt and keeps on keeping on no matter how crummy it looks. This thing was a big deal in its day. Now, its time is almost up. Curt, you gonna have to spend a bunch of money on these wheels just to keep it barely in decent shape."

"Kenny, you are exactly right. Your car, I guess, is a mule that will just haul and haul some more. This thing was like a thoroughbred racehorse, a Kentucky Derby kind of horse, could just fly and looked good doing it. Now, she's broke down and headed for the glue factory. But she's got a little leg left in her and we're gonna use her to a good end."

Kenny was now doubly thrilled that he had given a real opinion to Curt whom he regarded as his boss now and that his opinion was affirmed and respected.

He ventured cautiously, "Uhm, when do I get to find out about my job? Not trying to be pushy or anything. I guess I'm just wondering." Kenny pulled back a little bit, concerned that he had stepped over a line.

"Don't worry. You'll get filled in soon enough. And I can tell you this. Mr. Eddie and I will be right there with you and we will all help you get it done. Won't be long now. Fair enough?"

"Yes, sir." Kenny was glowing inside.

Curt was no fool. Like the army drills its recruits, you only tell them what they're gonna do, then tell them what they're doing while they're doing it, then tell them what they've just done. Same thing with a respectful and timid self-esteem. Build them. Reinforcement, repetition. Get them ready to be sure, strong, and brave. Curt had no doubt about the latter and could see the first two legs of the three-legged stool steadying and standing.

"Come on, let's go on in and see your lawyer and mine, the one and only, Eddie Terrell!" Curt laughed and Kenny grinned and nodded and they walked up the path past the giant oak tree and up the steps of the old, latticed 1885 Rogers House that sat up on the hill and looked down on the courthouse. The place was an old classic, late 19th-century gingerbread house, turned into a powerhouse lawyer office.

Kenny spoke almost reverentially. "I haven't seen Mr. Terrell in a while. He's sure been good to me and Rise. I'm looking forward to seeing him again."

Curt said, "It's a good time to see him again." He opened the double wooden and glass doors and gestured to Kenny, "Come on. Age before beauty." And Kenny went in, wondering what that meant, and Curt went in and pulled the doors tight shut behind them.

CHAPTER TWENTY-SEVEN

PEOPLE GET READY

The Impressions

"HELLO, MISS PATTY. Hello, Miss Mikey. Good afternoon to y'all." Curt removed his ball cap and nodded in good manners toward them both.

Kenny stood by. They had come through the front and had walked into the back offices where Patty and now Mikey kept the seams of the jealous mistress of the law running steady and sealed efficiently tight.

"Good afternoon, gentlemen. Kenny. It's been awhile. How are you doing these days?" Patty had always like Kenny and thought him to be basically a sweet kid. Curt was edgier, had a sense of sharp razor in him. But Patty knew that Curt was decisively disciplined and could be more distant. Eddie heard them and walked in to greet them. "Hey, y'all. Let's all go in the big conference room. Patty and Mikey have rounded up some good sandwiches and chips and cold beer. Let's all go have a good lunch!"

Eddie was welcoming and cheerful, just to a few degrees north of what would have been perfectly comfortable. Both Mikey and Patty were not tone deaf and they glanced at each other, yet still in the dark as to what the play was. They were simply baffled.

As they all made their way into the big room and its impressive tapestries of law book spines, Eddie spread out his arms in beneficence and said,

"Y'all have at it. It's from the good Greek deli just down the street. And we've got water and soft drinks and some good cold Bud in the refrigerator too to help wash it down. Please help yourselves!" He gestured to the alcove in the back corner where the sink and coffee maker and fridge were. His mood was almost elated. It was as though he had been released from something.

The group began to put their food on the paper plates, and Eddie went to the back-side window, looked out into the parking lot and saw the big, old green Eighty-Eight snuggled up to Curt's plain jane Chevy. He looked back at Curt who caught the look and held up two quick fingers. Eddie smiled and turned back and filled his plate and sat down at the head of the table. They ate mostly in silence, drips and quips of innocuous conversation rattled out here and there.

"Curt, what have you been up to these days?" Patty asked.

"Oh, some of this and some of that, you know how it is." (Unspoken real answer: "Helping Eddie here rub out a bothersome fool tonight who threatens a big score for all of us.")

"Patty, how's your family?"

"Oh, everyone is fine, thanks." (Unspoken real answer: "Driving me fucking crazy every damn day of my life. SOSD2...same old shit, different day.")

"Mikey, how you liking it here so far?"

"Oh, I like it a lot. Learning new things and enjoying the place." (Unspoken real answer: "I do like it here but Eddie's scaring me with some kind of serious, mysterious shit going on.")

"Eddie, you working on anything good these days?"

"Lots of good stuff. We've been lucky." (Unspoken real answer: "Well, other than setting up a coke buy and plotting a premeditated murder, it's all good.")

"Kenny, how is Big Rise these days?"

"Fine I guess. Haven't seen her in over a week." (Unspoken real answer: "Fine I guess. Haven't seen her in over a week. Hope she's okay. She's still with that asshole Ben.")

The responses were standard, almost elliptical. They were all finishing up. It was after 3:30.

Eddie stood and said, "Guys, let's the three of us go over to Kenny's place and just hang out and watch some television and have a few beers. Would that be okay with y'all?"

Kenny shook his head in a sort of wondering agreement. "Sure, that's be fine with me." Curt nodded in assent.

Patty and Mikey gave each other the obvious, "Just what in the hell is going on here?!" look but by that time, knew to stay out of it. Whatever was going on, was going to go on and it was not going help anything if the two of them went into 20 questions mode. "Ladies, thank you so much for rounding all that up. That was delicious. Come on, guys. Let's get going. Mikey, honey, I'll see you later on tonight, not too late so don't be worrying." He put a six-pack up under his arm, and they went out.

Patty and Mikey, in silence, then went about the quick business of throwing the trash into the can and wiping down the table. Patty finally said, "Something is up but I don't know what. I'm concerned."

Mikey said, "Yup and I'm scared." Patty nodded and they went back to their work, distracted.

Out in the parking lot, Eddie instructed. "Curt, how 'bout you leave your car here and you and Kenny go together in our new car? Let Kenny drive and I will follow. I like the green ride. It's pretty nice."

Curt locked up his car after removing his purchases from earlier in the day and removing all tags and paper labels that were on them and put them carefully folded into the back seat of the new acquisition. He balled up the bits of paper and tossed them down the storm sewer at the far curb line and then they were on the way.

The sun was beginning its arc down to the west. The air was a little chillier and there was some wind picking up.

They arrived at Kenny's place a little after 4 p.m. Its buildings and grounds were timeless in their stripped down, trashed out, raw, scraped presence. It was typical brick and block public housing that had been neglected and ignored for years and its residents didn't give a shit about it either. It was just an unnamed stationary planet that stood outside the money line of the city's moon. Crisscrossed trails of red clay crosshatched the yards.

They went in. Kenny had a variety of rickety chairs, a Barcalounger with some padding poking out, a long threadbare couch and a scratched up, ring-covered coffee table. None of it had come from Scully and Scully.

There was a big box color TV with rabbit ears atop of it. The three sat, waiting for Eddie. Eddie pulled three beers from the plastic hang strip and handed them out. They cracked the tab and all drank.

Eddie asked Curt if he had brought "that additional stuff." Curt said he had.

Eddie leaned forward and looked at Kenny. Kenny was excited but knew to keep still and wait.

"Kenny, we're all here together to get a job done and we need your help. This is an important job, one that you will be rewarded nicely for if we get it done right and it is one which will need all three of us to be calm, cool, and collected. Do you understand? When I say "calm, cool and collected," we mean it. This is a job that none of us can afford to lose our shit while we go about it. Do you understand?" Eddie looked hard at Kenny, dead hard into his eyes.

Kenny now knew that he was going to be doing some serious work and simply and straightforwardly said, "Yes, sir, Mr. Eddie. I understand. I will stay calm, cool, and collected."

"Thank you. We appreciate your paying attention and your answer. Curt, would you please give Kenny one of those items you brought with you here?"

As Curt handed the joint and his lighter to Kenny, Eddie continued. "Let's enjoy our beer, watch a little TV, get calm, and in just a little while, I will go over our assignments about 6:30, after the six o'clock local news is over. First though, Kenny, please enjoy the Mary Jane Curt has been nice enough to provide to you to help us all out."

Kenny lit up and inhaled mightily, held it and then slowly let it go out. It sounded as a far wave coming in from the ocean. He hit it again smoothly.

Curt was thoughtful, a rhythmic, low guttural noise coming from his closed throat. It was a peaceful sound.

Eddie turned the TV on and said, "Cartoons? That suit?"

It did and they all settled back. They were not over the drop zone yet but they were in the air and on their way. Kenny had another beer. That was of no concern to Eddie or Curt. Two beers in a man the size of Kenny was akin to tossing a Dixie cup of water into a lake. The dope's effect was obvious. Kenny had been a longtime participant with weed and his system was well used to it effects and its comforts. Kenny was alert and calm and pleasant. They had laughed at different parts of the cartoons and now that the six o'clock local news had begun, they were aware that the time for a knowing was drawing close. They all were paying attention to Lee Kinard reading his copy on Channel 2, listening and hearing, their attention mechanisms tuning up.

As WFMY morphed into the CBS Evening News with Dan Rather, Eddie said, "Well, boys, it's time." He turned off the television, and in a soft but clearly audible voice, spoke to Kenny.

"Kenny. Thank you so much for coming along with us this evening. We do need your help and it is an important job. We have to give you some hard news first but everything is okay now. We just need to finish the job." Kenny found himself to be focusing just fine. He was calm.

"We hate to tell you this, but your big sister has recently been treated very badly by Ben. This has happened now on an increasingly regular basis and he's injured her but she's now getting better and is going to be just fine. I promise you she is in safe, strong hands now. This will never be allowed to happen again."

Kenny could feel his heart rate step up and his respirations increase but he was very conscious of his physiological steadiness and the importance of being cool, calm, and collected.

"He been beating her, hadn't he?" His voice was flat. His eyes were distant. "He's a mean son of a bitch. Someone ought to whip his ass good and run him off for good."

"Well, we think that's a very good idea, but we think we need to be a bit more thorough about this rotten situation."

Curt nodded and now too leaned forward to Kenny. "Kenny, please listen real carefully to Eddie here."

Eddie continued. "Now, you don't know about this part, but we have planned to make us all some very nice money, including you and Rise. You will learn more about this in just a few more days, but we need to address this Ben problem first and think we should do it in just a little while this evening. And we will all be together when we get this work done. And remember, everything we do now and later is absolutely a blood oath secret. Got it?"

Kenny nodded and said, "Yessir. I'm ready to do my work for y'all. Y'all have treated me with respect. Most folks over the years have not and that would include that asshole Ben. Beating on my sister. Shitass Ben. I'm grateful for y'all's kindness. What do you want me to do about Ben? That's it, right? Do something about Ben, right?"

"Yes, Kenny, that's right. Now here's what we think needs to happen..."

CHAPTER TWENTY-EIGHT

PSYCHO KILLER

Talking Heads

AT ABOUT 7:45 p.m., the sun was almost down and the sky to the west was a blazing palate of blood red. Two cars eased out of the parking lot, an older but still handsome, faded emerald green Oldsmobile Eighty-Eight followed by a sleek black Mercedes sedan. They headed for Ben's resting place on Cromartie. It had been decided that to avoid making any lasting impression on any passersby that Eddie would park at the top of the street in a small lot adjacent to a grove of trees. He would then walk down the short street to join Curt and Kenny.

Eddie was deep in thought as he followed the others. He was surprised at his calm, his sangfroid. He was not agitated in the least. He recognized the stealth amoral which hid within him. He supposed he had grown it so. In the Eighty-Eight, Curt was driving. Kenny had his window cracked and a little cool air whispered in.

Curt asked, "Kenny, you okay?"

"I'm good to go on this. Looking forward to this. Don't y'all be worried. I got this." Curt reached across and patted Kenny's shoulder and squeezed his neck in the dark.

"Thanks, Kenny." Brothers-in-arms, they drove on.

As Curt turned off of Stadium Drive onto Cromartie, he could see Eddie pull off to the right and kill his lights. Curt slowed and then parked on the curb one house above Ben. That particular house had a dim light on in the back somewhere but there were no signs of activity anywhere on the street. Curt turned his lights off as well. They waited. In just a few minutes, Eddie was at Curt's rear driver's side door and in the backseat. Curt slowly went down a little further and pulled into the drive and around to the back of the house. He did a tight three-point maneuver so the Olds' rear end was at the steps of the back stoop. The daylight was on the edge of dusk and darkness.

Curt was now in charge. He spoke tightly and calmly. "Now, Kenny, here we are. I'm going to open the trunk before we go in. We will all go in. Quiet. No speeches, no nothing. Just do it quick and hard. Snap him. We will all be right there. Now, this is important. Be quiet, be careful, and no talking about this. We do not want this to turn into a fucking Red Ball."

Kenny asked, "What's a Red Ball? I ain't never heard of that."

"A Red Ball is when something goes down and it's real ugly and high showing and stirs everyone up, like the killing of a kid or a police shooting and the cops' bosses and the mayor go crazy and they throw everything at it—cops, cars, detectives, lab techs, doctors; it's like a tidal wave of police and the law and all their helping peeps coming after the perps. Don't want that, now do we? Now, I don't think police land ever give half of a shit about a bum like Ben, but the way this is gonna go down might stir up some spooked-out Halloween shit and flip some switches so we gotta go slow and stay low. Got it? No Red Ball."

"Got it." Kenny nodded. Eddie smiled. He loved working with a pro. Curt resumed.

"Eddie, how about get those gloves out? They're underneath the duffle bag and everyone put them on. Kenny, we got you some extra-large. Eddie, you carry the rubber bag. Once he's gone, Eddie and I will get the tarp underneath him real quick and let's bag and zip him before he shits the bed. We must make sure his wallet is with him. I've brought a little flashlight so we can fast sweep the room to make sure we have not missed anything. My best bet is he's as drunk now as he was when I saw him earlier today."

Kenny looked at Curt. "You saw him today?"

"Yeah, we knew he was sleeping a big one off so since we wanted to keep him good and still, I bought more whiskey and left it by the bed. I expect he took the bait and kept on swilling."

Curt continued. "So, any questions? No? Okay. Let's go."

They quietly got out, followed Curt to the steps and Curt eased the back door open and they all stepped inside. There was little light left from the day but only just a little. The only sounds to be heard were a dog barking way off in the distance and the deep, rattling snoring of a man in the bedroom down at the end of the short hall. They went into the bedroom.

Curt snapped on a penlight and scanned the room. The room's contents were sparse. Of the two earlier delivered bottles, one was almost empty, the other unopened.

Ben was unconscious, still stinking and probably on the verge of fatal alcohol poisoning but they could not take the chance that his addiction would finish him off this night. Curt moved over to Ben and shone the penlight on Ben's bulging back pocket.

"Yes, there's his wallet. Good. Let's make sure both bottles go in the duffle too. Okay, Kenny. Eddie, go on and unfold and unzip the bag. Kenny, wait for Eddie to have her wide open and ready to go. Wait for my word."

Kenny nodded. The unzipping was soft. "Now, go on, Kenny."

Kenny's hands enveloped the entire circumference of Ben's neck. A massive, choking, crushing throttling began. Ben eyeballs bulged, rolled open but only in a growing void of rapid oxygen deprivation. His tongue waggled between his teeth and small, struggled grunts escaped his mouth. His body shivered but never fought. And then he was frozen limp and dead. It had taken one long minute. Ben Lewis was graveyard drunk, strangled dead. The sheet was clean save for the yellowing of age and old sweat stains.

Curt said, "Let's get him and his wallet and those bottles in now. Once he's in and it's closed almost but not quite all the way, strip gloves off and put them in bag too. Make sure your bare hands do not touch the body."

Kenny stood and the three hoisted the body into the bag and made sure they had his wallet in there too along with the liquor bottles. The gloves went in carefully. The bag was fully closed. Curt swung the little light about the room. There was nothing else.

The three then hoisted the body up, carried it out of the house and put it in the trunk. Before the trunk was closed, Kenny softly said, "I enjoyed doing that. Good fucking bye, you sorry son of a bitch."

Eddie said, "I'm going to get my car. Y'all come on now."

CHAPTER TWENTY-NINE

MY HUMPS

The Black Eyed Peas

STRAW AND COITUS walked out of the R and R offices as Eddie and Curt and Kenny pulled up. It was 8:45. Straw waved them to the side gate and led them through. Large arc lights lit up the yard. An eighteen-wheel flatbed loaded with a couple dozen auto pancakes rumbled by. The dust was again swirling. Down the way, a tractor was roaring and grinding away. Straw spoke to Eddie. Coitus stood by. Curt and Kenny stayed in the car.

"Is this green one the one you want done?"

"Yes, Straw, it is."

"Good. Now, question. Do you want it flattened or cubed? We're full service out here, you know." He grinned with a little wicked on his lips.

"What do you think is best?" Eddie asked back. There was the obvious presumption shared between the two that the car needed be done as completely and as quickly as possible. Straw was not going to look behind Door Number Three. He did not care. He did not know and he did not want to know.

"I think flattened, pancaked is best. Then to the shredder. Then shred into barrel to make faster pickup and haul off to make every little piece unrecognizable. In thirty minutes we're done and you're outta here. Coitus here will take her from soup to nuts. Cubed is nice and neater but they do sit for a while awaiting pickup and transfer."

"Okay, good, let's have at it."

Straw looked at Coitus and said, "Magic time, boy! Make it disappear! You gentlemen need to hop on out now. Leave keys in, leave it running. Coitus, be gentle with it, just thorough. We don't want any doors or the trunk to pop open until we're in good shape. Right, Eddie?"

"Yup. You're right."

Straw knew. Of course he knew but he sure wasn't letting on. Eddie guessed he had explained the operation in a sideways fashion to Coitus. Kenny and Curt got out. Coitus got in and drove the Eighty-Eight to the leak away pit, the place where the oil and gasoline were let free into the recycle drains. He turned it off and got down underneath her and cut her gas line and released the motor oil cock. As the fluids flowed out and then ebbed, Coitus scrambled back to level ground and climbed into his tractor, roared it to life and swung his tracks and huge hanging bucket and jaw claws toward the car and picked it up, swung it around and put it down carefully and lowered the bucket to the center of the roof, caving the middle of the car completely in.

All the windows exploded outward in a shower of glass beads. He again dropped his bucket through the center of the front engine hood which spread out and bulged as the engine block was broken and flattened.

Then Coitus began to ride up and over the car, front to back, back to front. He was precise and careful. The tires exploded and fast sagged, the rims destroyed. After four runs, the car was a pancake. Nothing had opened. All had just been crushed and flattened. What was once a vehicle of some impressive height and length, a great highway cruiser was now an unrecognizable wrecked, smashed, shrunk-down dwarf.

Coitus looked at Straw. He shouted over the roar of his giant yellow Komatsu, "Enough?"

"Yes, let's go to the shredder now," Straw hollered back over the noise.

Coitus lowered his jaw claws and enveloped the remnant, seized it up off the ground and carried it swinging toward the eastern part of the yard. There was some dripping of random liquids from the carcass but it was all unrecognizable save for the odor of petroleum.

They all walked behind the cortege as it tracked along, its prey locked in for its final moments. On all sides of them, layered well above their heads were wrecked cars, destroyed cars, flattened cars, stacked cubes, piles of engine parts. It was as though they were in the dinosaur extinction valley of Detroit. Coitus rumbled along.

Coitus arrived at the shredder, a giant steel box with huge hydraulic pneumatic hammers and blades. On the shredder was a badly scrawled sign duct-taped just beneath the control panel which read, "Let me run 5 min after use. Please don't try to adjust me. I'm as good as I get!" Eddie thought that could apply to just about all of us.

He placed the dead Olds in the center, released his claw grips and backed away from the box. The metaphor of car coffin flashed through Eddie's mind. Coitus turned off his engine, hopped down to the ground and went to the control panel for the shredder. He turned the master key and pressed two buttons that flashed green. The shredder burst to life and began to rock and shake as the hammers and blades began to process big pieces to small. The noise was hellishly loud. The screeches and shrieks of the metal being torn and broken apart careened through their ears. Then the box would stop and huge strong mechanical arms would reach over and grasp across the diminishing hulk, flip it over, and the destroying process would renew. The old car was coming apart quickly, rapidly vanishing into detritus.

Straw said to Eddie, "Hell, we could drop a full eighteen-wheeler in there and it would be gone in seven minutes. You know, I love this business. Get to just tear shit up. Loved to do that as a kid too." He grinned. Straw was happy. He loved his work. He patted his girth in pleasure.

Eddie murmured, "Impressive."

Kenny was fascinated. Curt implacable.

Coitus was pressing more buttons that lit up the board. The pieces were being spit out onto a wide conveyor belt and automated claw grips gathered them up in clumps, stuffing them into large metal canisters that were self-sealing. Coitus was the maestro. In about ten minutes, it was all over.

No parts of Ben Lewis were ever to be seen again. He had just disappeared from the face of the earth.

Straw said, "Nice work, Coitus. Thank you. Appreciate your help this evening. Now go on home and I'll see you in the morning."

Coitus said, “Happy to be of service. Evening, Straw. Evening, gentlemen.” And he rubbed his wild, greasy hair with a sweaty hand out of his face and walked back across the yard and got in his car and was gone.

Straw said, “Well, Eddie. I think we’re in good shape. Those containers will be shipped to Wilmington along with few hundred others in the morning and will be on the high seas within thirty-six hours. Anything else we need to be doing tonight?”

“No, Straw. Thank you so much. We’ll be on our way now. I’ll be seeing you around. Call me if you need me.”

“Of course I will. Glad I could be of help tonight. Take good care now.”

They all shook hands and Eddie and Kenny and Curt got in Eddie’s car.

CHAPTER THIRTY

YOU GOT IT (DONUT)

DJ Jazzy Jeff & The Fresh Prince

THEY RODE IN silence for a while and then suddenly Eddie laughed and said, "Kenny, did you know we and you just sent sorry old Ben on the biggest trip of his life?"

"Where? To hell?"

"I'm sure that's his last stop but on his way, but his ass is going to China and India first and all and both at the same time. That's a pretty good trick, don't you think?"

Curt started laughing. Kenny was puzzled. "How does that work?" he asked.

They explained it to him and he was delighted. The tension of the last hard moments was lifting. They were almost back to Eddie's office.

Curt asked, "Okay. What's next?"

Eddie pulled in and parked next to Curt's car.

"You got some paperwork on that Eighty-Eight? I expect you do. How about you go tell Leon tomorrow that someone stole the car last night and the paperwork went with it? And then go and burn all those papers. You never had any insurance on it, did you? And tomorrow morning when you go see Leon, let's see what he can do about putting a short school bus together for us."

Curt winked. “Nope, no insurance. And right on with all the paperwork. Got it. School bus too. God knows the children need their learning. Check.”

“Okay, guys. What happened tonight just did not happen, right? We agreed on that, understand that? We know nothing about Ben. As far as we know, he just moved on. Didn’t discuss nothing with us. Right?”

“Right.”

“Yessir.”

“Okay, now we gotta get back to work. First, Curt, how about you and Kenny go over to Robert Peddyford’s and have a private talk with Rise? Just y’all and her. Robert will understand the privacy. Only tell her that Ben seems to have left these parts and no one expects to see him back again. Tell her she, if asked by anyone, has no idea where he’s gone off to. Then, Curt, take Kenny home. Everyone go to bed. No drinking or doping tonight. Kenny, tomorrow meet her over at Cromartie and take that mattress and those nasty sheets and blankets and pillows to the city incinerator and burn them. First thing.”

Eddie pulled out his wallet, lifted $600 out of it and handed it to Kenny.

“Then go buy a new mattress and sheets and blankets and pillows. Don’t fuck this up. We are so close to the finish line and I’m not real interested in us getting fucked over. Then come back up here and tell me exactly what you did. Bring Rise with you. You got it?”

“Yes, sir!”

“Curt, I think after you have inspected our big finish from behind as we have just discussed, how about come see me tomorrow so I can juice you a bit? And then you’ll head to Baltimore and get up with Pee Wee and set up the buy. Do it quick and get on back. You think you can find him without a lot of trouble?”

“Oh, yeah. It’s at worst a two-question ask. I’ll find him and we’ll get it in place.”

“Boys, we will all touch base tomorrow. No going quietly into this deep dark night and do not rage, rage against the coming of the light.” Kenny and Curt looked at Eddie with curiosity.

“It’s a play on one of my favorite poets, Dylan Thomas. Lord, apparently he could drink a lot of scotch. And the stuff helped him write too. Tonight, the night has been good to us. And tomorrow when the sun comes up, tomorrow’s gonna be good to us too. Let’s keep our mouths shut and do our jobs and keep working and good things will happen. Now y'all go on. I'm going home."

The two got out of the Eddie's car, got into Curt's and pulled off into Cherry Street and hung a right onto Fourth headed east.

Eddie sat very still at the wheel, thought about the day and felt dead bone tired. There was a conscious physical effort to get moving again. He felt leaden. But he willed himself to move. He then pulled out, got on Business 40 and headed west.

Then it occurred to him. Mikey was waiting for him, surely worried. He needed to take her a tribute, a silly tribute.

He took the South Stratford exit and peered down the way. And there it was in glowing orange and red. He saw famous "Hot" and "Now" bookending the neon green "Doughnuts" of Krispy Kreme.

He pulled into the left. There was no traffic. There were no cars in the parking lot. He quietly walked in the door. To his right, the big doughnut machine was extruding soft dough and helping it wend its way to bubbling firmness to glorious glaze high calories and fat and bad-for-you morsels of goodness. A tall, nice looking skinny kid who needed to stand up straight was checking intently here and there behind the glass, bending over in the fashion of a praying mantis.

At the brightly lit counter in front of him stood two very pretty girls. They were deep in conversation and did not notice him. After what he had experienced in the last many hours, he just paused and slowly appraised them. He needed some sweet prettiness now and they delivered it.

One was a bit taller than the other and had long, blonde hair. She smiled easily. They were both nicely built, filled their tops up with laudable firmness. Both wore the white Krispy Kreme uniform, white lace-up rubber soled shoes, and the little white paper tri-corner KK hats. He did a double take on the other, the slightly shorter of the two. She was almost a dead ringer for his Tinkerbelle of long ago with piercing blue eyes and a short, blonde ponytail and a bright smile as well.

They talked with one another in a mutuality of gesture and movement, a sort of shared internal kabuki. It was as though they were twin sisters but they obviously were not. He dared not move. He was enjoying watching them and did not want to disturb them. He could get to the goodies soon enough. They were delightful.

They wore name tags. Tinkerbelle's said "Mel" and the other was "Andi." They reminded him of the old Lucy and Ethel tag team. All that was lacking was the comedic fiasco of the chocolate cascading down the line and actually, it was more fun this way.

Mel said grinning, "And then that little shit kicked me in the shin! I'm 'bout over some of my neighbors' kids." She rolled her eyes.

Andi responded empathetically, "Can you do anything about it?"

"Gonna talk with his parents but don't expect much but gonna try."

"Well, I'm sorry about all that ill-mannered crap and too, I do know this. We both need a vacation. We need to get to some place warm where there are little umbrellas in the drinks. We ain't getting any younger and we need to do some pampering. And I ain't talking about kiddie diapers. Hell, soon enough, grownup Depends...yuck!"

"Hell, yes!" said Mel.

Eddie spurred by the dialogue, chimed in from the shadows. "Well, sounds real good to me. Can I go too?"

They turned in unison as if on a turntable. Both mouthed, "Oh!" and Mel put her hand over her mouth in embarrassment but her laughing eyes belied her amusement at being caught in a little verbal naughtiness. Andi just grinned.

Andi said, "Sure, what the hell. Come on!"

Eddie said, "I'll come back another time and we can plan it out but good. Well, not really. Probably not really anyway. How about this? Would y'all help me with something? I've had a long, tough day and I've got a nice lady at home who I'm sure is worried about me cause I'm late so I want to take her something fun."

Mel said, "Sure. Sounds like a good idea to us. What can we do to help you out?" She looked at Andi who nodded affirmatively.

"Well, I've got a friend from Alabama who told me about this thing called 'The Whore's Breakfast.' Please, first let me explain." He held his hands up in supplicating patience and good humor. They both looked at him with increasing intrigue and they gladly waited.

"When she was just a little girl down in rural Alabama, she started worrying early on that on her birthday, she wouldn't get her cake. So she asked her momma to let her have her cake first thing in the morning of her birthday to make sure it was a sure thing. And her momma was fine with it and it has over the years become a family tradition. Along with her cake, she drenched herself in glitter and slathered on gobs of eye shadow to become the zenith of her celebratory day. My friend is now 53 and every year she tackily glams up and has birthday cake and a little bottle of Coca-Cola to start every one of her birthdays. Her very proper manners, up-tight grandmother took one look at her and enormously disapproved of it all and instantly called it 'A Whore's Breakfast,' but the family didn't care and ignored the old snooty biddy. So that's where that came from. I'm on my way home from working late and saw the 'Hot Now' sign and it just came to me so as a variation on that theme, which I think is wonderful. By the way, I'd like a dozen hot now glazed and two big Coca-Colas with crushed ice and a carry box to take home to my sweetie. Obviously I can't tell her the name for my inspiration. She might be confused or even offended but I sure can take her the goodies."

Mel laughed. "Gotta love that. That's a new one for me. No problem. Now that's what we are here for." And then she hollered toward the back in a good, fine screech, "Harry! Harry! Get twelve of our very best hot glazed together in a box and bring them up here pronto!" From the back came a muffled but very audible, "My pleasure!"

In but a few minutes, Harry, gangly, all arms and legs, the stubble of a sneaking shadow darkening his youthful chin, hustled with the box outstretched in his helping hands to Eddie.

Eddie said, "Thank you, Harry, right?"

Harry replied, "Yes, sir. My pleasure!"

Andi placed a carry box with the big lidded cups in it along with straws down next to the box of delicacies.

"Here you go. You need to get on home now to make a warm delivery, right? Y'all enjoy!"

Eddie reached for his billfold and pulled a couple of hundreds out and handed them to Andi.

"Y'all use what's left over for a couple of those tropical pops y'all are going after. And how about give Harry here a couple of twenties for his good help too? No change please. Y'all have fun. Thank you too. And it was my pleasure too!"

Harry beamed. The pretty girls slight curtsied in unison.

Eddie picked up the box and carry-on and winked and smiled in gratitude at them and was out the door and on his way home to Mikey. He missed her fiercely.

The smiling Krispy Kremers just looked at each other and watched his taillights slide down Stratford.

Mel and Andi nodded at Harry and then they all just went back to it after they made change, paid the ticket and handed Harry his forty. Harry as was his wont loved the scent of fresh money so he gave his windfall a good, big sniff and returned into the making room. Mel told Andi to hang onto the rest, that it was a sign from God that they needed to plan to travel and that maybe they ought to try a "Whore's Breakfast" when they did.

Andi said to Mel, " You're right. We'll go and we'll go soon. That was a pretty cute guy, wasn't he?"

Mel looked out the window. "Yes, he was. They're out there you know. I need to do a better job looking..."

Andi responded, "Don't worry. You will. We both will. You'll be fine. We'll both be fine."

CHAPTER THIRTY-ONE

CAN'T HELP FALLING IN LOVE

Elvis

EDDIE NOSED THE car down Stratford to the Five Points intersection and headed left toward Reynolda Road. The aroma from the hot glazed was marvelous. He could hear the quiet slosh of the Cokes and crushed ice in their Styrofoam cups. As the next light changed from yellow to red, he stopped and closed his eyes and thought for a few seconds. There was no one behind him. The road was empty. It was pushing on toward 11:30.

"Let's see. AV rated for the highest skills and ethics, accomplished, and successful trial lawyer, accomplice before, during, and after to a very premeditated first-degree murder, criminal creator of the methods for the disappearance of the corpus by very violent means, bantering with two adorable cute gals over doughnuts and Cokes and a funny, goofy kid too, taking donuts and Coca-Colas to his beautiful, lovely, smart sweetheart who probably by now at worst has run away or at best is so pissed at him, she'd cut him to soprano, now need to work on a cocaine deal and get some more good cases settled. Jesus. Just another day's work..."

The light turned green as he opened his eyes and pressed the accelerator. He went left on Reynolda, then left onto Polo and on and went on home. The porch light was on. He carried the treats to the door, bent over, and set them on the porch and started to fish for his house keys. The front door opened. There was Mikey in her robe, her hair askew, her beautiful entreating face lined with tears and the strain of not knowing. He silently held out his arms to her and she came folding into him. Her words flowed as from a fire hose.

"Oh, Eddie, Eddie. I've been so worried. Where have you been? I've been worried sick. Are you all right? Are you okay? Oh, God, I must look like a hot mess. Is everything ok? I've been sick with worry. Oh, God. Should I be mad at you?" He held her tightly and rubbed the back of her neck. Her tears were seeping through his shirt and she was sobbing, breathlessly heaving, letting her fear go.

He whispered to her, "It's all right. Everything is all right. I'm fine." He repeated it over and over again softly, nuzzled her neck and kissed her face in every place he could find. And began again and again. It was a hypnotic. She calmed and snuffled and sniffled. And she finally looked up at him and asked imploringly, "Should I be put out with you? Should I be mad at you?"

He pulled her back into him and quietly replied, "No, my darling girl, not at all. This night was just about business and it's all done and taken care of now. I promise."

She said, "I know you're not going to tell me about the business, not going to tell Patty either, and I understand that sometimes that's a part of your work but are things really okay?"

"Yes, honey, they are. It was an old case that needed to be resolved and we got the matters settled. It's over."

She nodded. "I was so worried."

"I know and I'm so sorry to have worried you but I had to go off and get the matter resolved."

She nodded and her composure and color were coming back.

"Now, I've brought you some treats." He gestured down at the box of doughnuts and the two Styrofoam cups in the carrier.

"You haven't been here all that long. I don't think you've ever had the pleasure of our local treasure which we call a Krispy Kreme hot glazed doughnut. Have you?" She shook her head in the negative.

He reached down and opened the box and pulled one out and held it before her lips. "Take a bite, please." She did and her eyes widened and brightened.

"Oh, Eddie, that's really good. Oh my!"

"Now how about a little crushed ice Coca-Cola to wash it down."

He put a straw in one of the cups and held to her lips.

She pulled on it and smiled. "Oh, yes, that's so good too!"

"Oh, yes, they both are. They all are. Come on. Let's get off this porch and turn off this light and go in the kitchen and have some special late dessert."

They pulled the door shut and went in the kitchen and sat at the kitchen table and ate three Krispy Kremes each and drank their Coca-Colas.

They just smiled and stared at each other. Eddie's eyes began to water. He was being overcome by the day, by her basic goodness and kindness, by everything. He wiped his eyes with his shirt sleeve.

Mikey solicited, "Eddie, what's wrong? Honey, what's wrong?"

He wiped his eyes again, this time with his fingers.

"Baby, I'm just real tired, really worn out and when I get like this, my emotions run hot and bubble up. I'm fine. I promise. I'm fine."

"Which emotions?"

And he blurted out, "Well, I think I'm beginning to fall in love with you."

"Oh, Lord, Eddie, I'm falling in love with you too. You know that, don't you?"

"I...well, yes...I sure do now."

"Well, what should we be doing about this?"

"As best as I can tell, I'm gonna just keep falling and I hope you will too." He took her hands in his.

Tears came back to her eyes. "Lovers' leap, I guess here we come."

They stood up and held one another tightly and kissed for a long time and then turned off the kitchen lights and went back into the dark and then joyously lit their worlds up.

CHAPTER THIRTY-TWO

BUSTED

Ray Charles

THEY WERE SHY the next morning, tentative and brief with their words, cautious, glancing at each other, more looking away than looking at each other. Then Mikey just came right at it. "Eddie, you falling in love with me?"

Eddie stood up straight and looked straight at her. "Yes, I believe that's what's going on. Yes, I'm falling in love with you. Hope that's okay."

She laughed sweetly. "And I'm coming right along with you too if that's okay." Mikey knew it was. They were smitten.

She continued, "So can we please stop all this Adam and Eve stuff in the Garden of Eden and stop hiding from each other in plain sight and acting like we're unsure about what we've done? There sure wasn't any doubt back in there last night." She smirked luridly at him. He replied in the same as the relief of confession had freed him to love her.

"Yes, you're right. Let's go on and get after our lives, whatever that might all lead to. Agreed?"

"Agreed."

Eddie was fully energized again, empowered with his and their future. "How about this? Let's go get some coffee and some newspapers and get on down to the office and get that all rolling again. Patty is, I bet, missing me and certainly you too. Curt is coming to see me and so is Rise. And, there's something, no, two other things to do as well."

"Sounds good. Let's get cleaned up and dressed and get to it. What are the other two things that we need to do?"

"Wait a minute." He went into the kitchen and came back quickly with two Krispy Kremes on a plate. "Here you go."

She took one and he the other and in seconds they were gone. He asked, "Still pretty good?"

She nodded happily.

Eddie said, "I don't know if we'll ever get to the altar, but don't you think those things are pretty good substitutes for engagement rings?"

She laughed and agreed. They were floating with their feet off the ground.

"Now, what's the other thing?"

"We need to go get you a car. We gonna have to quit this carpooling thing. I did graduate kindergarten a ways back and so did you. You need to have your own ride. And don't worry. It's going in your name. What do you think you would like? How about something snappy? But not a Rolls Royce."

"Oh, Eddie, are you serious?" He nodded in affection and pleasure.

"That's so nice. Well, how about let me think about this a little bit? Remember, I've got that old Plymouth back out in Alder. Maybe we should just go back and get it."

"Not a chance. Think on it. We could go shopping later this afternoon."

"Fair enough. Thank you!" And she hugged him and kissed his neck. He blushed. He had been reduced by her, been sent back into to his hormone-busting adolescence.

"Let's get rolling."

Her fears and his horrors from the night before had faded back to a distant horizon. Of course they were still there. They always would be there but starting a new slate assuaged them and gave them some relief, some protection.

They walked into the office where Patty, planted at her desk as though in her foxhole with a hot boxed one hanging from her lips, squint-eyed them both and closely at that.

Eddie clicked his heels and saluted Patty. "Eddie and Mikey, reporting for duty, Miss Patty. Ready for assignments, please and thank you!" They were holding hands.

She took a long drag, plumed the room and asked pointedly, “Are you two all right? Is there something I need to know? Anything?” Eddie leaned forward and anchored his hands on her desk, shook his head and said with a big, very real, grin, “No, nothing at all. Nothing.”

Patty looked at Mikey, questioning that flat response.

Mikey shook her head and shrugged her shoulders and had a look of complete placid happiness about her.

Patty conceded and said, “Now what do we need to be doing this beautiful, weird day?” and as she said that, it was suddenly obvious to her that these two idiots had fallen in love.

“Oh, brother,” she grumbled to herself.

Eddie asked, “By the way, any follow-up on with our old friend Miss Jepson?”

“Well, yes, to this extent. I checked last week with the nice folks at Wells Fargo. The card is maxed out at its ten thousand level. It’s useless to her now.”

“Good. Hope she got some value for it.”

“Want me to go find her and get it back or make sure she cuts it up or what?”

“Sure. That’d be the smart thing to do. How you gonna do that?”

“Make a few phone calls. Get a run sheet from the bank of all her charges. That’ll show me her spending patterns. I’ll find her. Just give me a little while, okay? We got a lotta shit going on around here that we need to get to. Don’t you just know that’s so!” Patty gestured to a stack of car and truck wreck files. “All of these need a call to the adjuster and then another. All of them have already received comprehensive packages with demand letters. They’re informed. How about I give you one or two a day and that’ll be your daily dose? Better yet, I’m gonna get Mikey to hand them to you. Now, you damn well better pay attention to that, right?”

Mikey had come to like Patty so much. She was a rock, smart, tough, funny, and loyal to them and to their office. She was gonna make the show run come hell or high water.

“Come over here please, Mikey. Here are two files. One is Sylvester, the other is McElheny. Please hand them to Mr. Terrell there and tell him to go in his office and call the adjusters and get some stuff settled. We need to pump up our cash.”

Mikey walked the three steps to Eddie and formally presented the files to him and said, "Okay, mister. You heard the lady. Now, please get to it."

"Fair enough. Y'all got me. I'm off to make these calls. I'm expecting Kenny and Rise and after them, expecting Curt. We're getting our big plan rolling now."

Patty nodded and asked Mikey to help her carry a couple of larger files into the big conference room. They needed to get the Pussy Preacher/ Blockhouse ready for its upcoming mediation and needed to get Zach Reynolds ready for a serious sit down with Alph Baron.

Eddie headed to his office, closed the door, and dutifully made his two calls. And then Rise and Kenny came in his office door as Patty showed the way.

CHAPTER THIRTY-THREE

FOR THE LOVE OF MONEY

The O'Jays

RISE'S FACE WAS still puffy on her right side and her right ear was still swollen, both conditions having been caused by Ben's slamming haymaker right fist which as it turns out to be was the last fight he ever won. Eddie stood watching them, appraising them. They sat down and looked at Eddie.

Rise asked, "So did it really get done, Eddie? Did it? Kenny won't say a word to me about anything. He just got me at the Peddyfords this morning in a friend's delivery truck and we went over to Cromartie, stripped the bed and took it all, sheets, blankets, pillows, mattress, and box springs, everything and took it all over to old city incinerator on Vargrave and burned it all up." Kenny looked away, out the window.

"Well, did it?" Rise was tilting into a hiss.

Eddie nodded his head imperceptibly, barely a half-inch of affirmation. "Rise, let us never speak of this again. I believe, we all believe, that he knew he was in a lot of trouble by virtue of the things he had done to you and I think he knew he'd just do it again and again because he could not control his drinking and we think he just hightailed it out of town. I think, I strongly suggest that become your thinking on the matter too, if you might ever be asked."

"Well, that old glide heap he drove is still over there in the far back. The keys are still in the front room. Why didn't he take that with him?"

"I think he's just gone to big city to get away while the getting was good. He won't need it in the big city. Kenny, how about get those keys and move the vehicle to Leon's? He can scrap it."

"Yes, sir." It was Rise's turn to look away.

"And, Kenny, thank you for looking after your sister like you have. Between the two of you and me, we've put a lot of miles on our roads together and I'm grateful to both of you for your trust and faith in me. Now it's time for a new project and we need your help. I believe you both will be rewarded nicely once this new project is completed. Curt will be here real soon and we will start putting all the pieces in place. Rise, in a little while I want you to go with me to see Mr. Harry Davis, to help introduce me to him. You're still helping out and cleaning up over there a few days a week, aren't you?"

"Yes, that's right. I had to take more days off than I liked to because of... well, because of...well, you know..." She drew a lame wave at her face. A couple of big tears dripped down.

"Good. You will, I think, be helpful to the cause."

Eddie got up and came over to Rise and gave her a big hug.

Curt stuck his head in the door. "Good time?"

"Hey, yes, come on in. Let's go over things."

Curt seated himself next to Rise and Kenny and murmured at Rise, "You okay?"

She sighed. "Coming along, I guess, coming along."

Eddie got the ball rolling. "Curt, you checked behind Kenny and Rise?"

"Yes, All good."

"Appears Ben neglected to take his car with him when he took off to wherever, so I've asked Kenny to go over there in a few minutes and take the car over to Leon's and ask him to scrap it. I'm gonna take Rise with me for a visit to Mr. Harry Davis down at City B and then take her home to wait for Kenny. They need to go do some shopping for bedding and sheets and such. Here, Rise, this is one of my credit cards. Use it nicely and please bring me the receipts. Get yourself some nice stuff, some comfortable stuff. Please. You deserve it after what all you have been through."

Rise nodded appreciatively and stuffed the card down into her ample bosom.

"Curt, how about you go down to Leon's and tell him Kenny gonna be bringing a junker in soon? And to just scrap it and keep tabs. Then tell him we need a short school bus, in used but okay condition with good tires and a sturdy engine. I think we can get something in total for about eight grand. I'd like it painted white with light blue striping and have the following name on the side: "County School System" and then below that "Chantilly, Virginia." Tell him to please grab some Virginia plates for it. And we'll need welded up underneath and next to the gas tank a tight-seal steel box that can carry about 12 to 15 pounds tight and wrapped in mylar. Put the title and registration in the glovebox. Ask him to have it ready in about three or four days.

"And, Curt, here is another of my credit cards and four grand toward the transport bus. Tell Leon he'll get the other four when the crate is ready. That should take care of it. Then, go out to the airport and get a round trip ticket for this afternoon to Baltimore. Come back tonight. Take a cab and go find your old buddy Pee Wee and tell him we want to buy six kilos of good, not highest quality, but good quality coke. Tell him we will send our friends Rise and Kenny in a regulation issue yellow school bus with the money to get it in a few days. Tell him they we will bring him one-hundred-fifty-thousand dollars, a hundred and a quarter in cash and the balance in some very fine jewelry that is now not very hot and is probably worth more than the remaining quarter. That should be about right, all being old friends and such. Pee Wee should be someplace in west Baltimore, probably working as a lieutenant to your old friend Nathan Barksdale or his crowd. Then how about come over here first thing in the morning and let's see if the pieces are coming together? How about all three of you come back in the morning? Hopefully it won't be but a few more days before we can send you in our new old bus."

Curt nodded. "I can make a call. By time I get there, I'll know where Pee Wee will be."

They all nodded. Kenny had been mystified before. He was no longer.

"Now everyone keep your mouths shut. Only communicate as need be. Now, let's get moving. Rise, how about you meet me out at my car?" They all dispersed and Eddie went out to Patty's office where she and Mikey were head-down working.

Patty looked up and said, "Well?"

Mikey looked up and said, "Well?"

"Kids, for better or worse and God knows I'm a big fan of better here, it's on the move now. I've got two more investors to call on today and I feel good about both. Rise is going with me now to see one of them. We'll have a good picture of where we are in the morning."

Mikey stood up and walked over to Eddie. She hugged him. She sighed and said, "Well, I signed on for this. Be good. Be safe. Be home soon."

"I will, kid. Later this afternoon, let's try to go get you some nice wheels. If we put this together right, I'll just be here in town with you waiting it out. We'll all be together. Now, let's get the finishing touches done on the P2-Blockhouse case for the mediation next week and I'll look it over with both of you when I get back later this afternoon. Also, time to get Alph over here for a come-to-Jesus talk that involves punctuation and profit. I'm hurrying on a lot of stuff now and getting impatient. Patty, please set that up." She popped one thumb up.

Eddie went out to the car and opened the door for Rise to get in. As they headed over to City Beverage, Eddie asked Rise, "You are sad? I know you are. I'm sorry. I really am."

"Sorta. A little bit. He was bad to me but we got along too. But I know he had to leave. I know he did."

"I hope you know I understand. I promise I do."

Rise just nodded her head. They pulled up on Burke Street and went in.

Bing was at the counter. "Hey, Rise. Ooooh. What happened? You okay?"

"Yeah, Bing, I'm okay, just ran into a door. Bing, this is my friend Eddie Terrell. We'd like to see your daddy. Is he in?"

"Hey, Mr. Terrell. Heard of you. Lawyer, right? Sure, Rise. Lemme go let him know."

Eddie nodded a thank you and they waited. Bing returned quickly and said, "Y'all just go in. Mr. Siddon's in there with him." They walked in.

When Harry Davis saw Rise and the remnants of her injuries, he uncharacteristically stood up in a respectful way toward her. Syd Siddon followed Harry's lead, looking on curiously. They had been sitting at Harry's battered old work desk playing gin rummy. They laid their cards down, face down. Obviously, they would continue on in a bit.

Harry said, "Rise, what in the hell happened? I've been wondering where you'd gotten off to... are you all right?"

"Yes, Mr. Harry, I'm gonna be fine. Thank you. My old friend Ben kept getting more and more bad drunk and beat me up a bunch and finally took off before my family and friends like Mr. Eddie here came for him." It was a bravura performance. Rise was a natural. Eddie marveled at her delivery of being a brave martyr and defiant victim.

"Well, he damn well should have. Surely he doesn't have the bad sense to come back here. Hell, I'll help your crowd thrash him but good if he does."

"Thank you, Mr. Harry. Mr. Harry, this is my friend Mr. Eddie Terrell. I think you might recall somewhere along the way these past years that Mr. Eddie here helped me out real good a couple of times when I got in some trouble with the post office and then he also helped out my brother Kenny when he was in real bad trouble over the shooting of a really sorry guy in a drink house. It was all a long time ago."

Harry nodded. "I remember, Rise. I do remember. Mr. Terrell, I've heard of you. You've got a fine reputation. I'm pleased to make your acquaintance. This is my business partner, Syd Siddon." The three men, three professionals, shook hands.

"Now, Rise, Mr. Terrell, what can I do for either of you, both of you, one of you?" He looked from one to the other.

Rise said, "Mr. Harry, I know I've been gone for a while and I'm gonna need to be gone some more for just a little while more, but I'd please like to come back again steady like things were before. Would that be all right, Mr. Harry?"

"Why, yes, of course, Rise. I'm so sorry you've had to go through all this. We've missed you." Syd Siddon nodded agreeably.

"Thank you, Mr. Harry. Thank you." She was genuinely grateful and relieved. "Now, Mr. Harry. I think Mr. Eddie here would like to ask you something." She stepped back. All four were still standing.

Harry Davis said, "How about we all go ahead and sit down again. This sounds...interesting." He grinned a crooked grin.

Eddie said, "Mr. Davis, please let me come straight to the point. I'm putting together a small group of investors, a little private syndicate if you will. I've heard Rise speak so highly of you over time and it would be fair to say that by virtue of some of my professional involvements, I am aware of your fine and successful efforts over the years. I'd like you to invest with us. We are a small group, five maybe six, all professionals. This is a very private matter."

Harry chuckled. "Obviously you know I sell alcohol in high volume and, with my friend Syd's good help, we are also high volume bookmakers which is, as you also know, a high cash volume business as well."

"That's one reason I've gotten my old friend Rise to bring me over here to you. Sort of like when they asked Willie Sutton why he robbed banks and said, 'well, that's where the money is.' And other reasons too. You keep your mouth shut, you don't call attention to yourself, you're smart, and you know a good deal when you see it."

Harry and Syd laughed and nodded.

Davis said, "I am complimented. We both are, I think. So, what is this good deal and how much are you looking for? What are the chances of being successful?"

"Let me go at it this way. I'm looking for twenty-five grand. It can certainly all be lost like any investment, but if successful, you can probably expect a return of times four maybe times five on your play. I feel pretty good that something like that can be accomplished. We are well-organized and a small outfit. And, in order to protect everyone, only a few of us know what the investment vehicles will be. I will make the selections. That way, folks like you know nothing one way or another. Ignorance is bliss and so forth."

"Hmmm, a blind twenty-five, eh? Rise, you in on this?"

"Not for the money. I gots no idea what gonna happen with that. I have owed Mr. Eddie here for a good long time. My brother Kenny has too. I'm just here to help."

Eddie said, "If this works, she'll be treated well. If not, she'll still be treated well."

"Twenty-five grand and we don't know what you're buying. Son, you got some brass balls on you."

"Well, for what's worth, Mr. Davis, it takes one to know one and there's no doubt you know where to find me if you are so inclined to do so."

"Syd, what do you think? Hell, I remember when we'd go on those junkets and get drunker than dogs and fifty, no seventy-five grand would just disappear in three days or less."

"Hell, Harry, it wasn't but a few days ago that both of us lost a couple of Gs apiece on that certain stupid bet we held thinking we had a sure winner and of course, everything that could go wrong with that game did go wrong. This sounds like something interesting, kinda fun really. I'll split it with you if you like. That way if it goes in the dumper, the sting ain't so bad. And the return sounds promising."

"This is a different kind of thing. Yes, we've got an obviously slick, smart lawyer here but he's here with one of your real good people, Miss Rise. That doesn't signal scam. This isn't a hustle. This is a play where we're being kept in the dark and I think it protects us too. Gee, sorry, officer, I can't help you. I don't know nothing." Syd looked at Harry.

Harry said, "What's a realistic turnaround time here?"

"Sixty to ninety days."

Harry Davis looked off in the distance. "Syd, you want half?"

"Yes, sure do."

"Then by God let's do it." Harry smiled. It reminded him of the good old days when he really did fly blind.

"Y'all hang on. I'll be right back."

Harry Davis shambled away from his desk and wandered off toward the back into the dark. They heard some keys jingle, a lock unlock, a door open, and the faint sounds of a safe's tumblers clicking. He could be heard making mumbling, counting sounds. He returned and put a fat, large number of bills in an envelope and handed them to Eddie.

"Syd, you can pay me back later. Mr. Eddie Terrell, you do accept cash, don't you?" Harry Davis winked. Eddie winked back.

"Thank you, gentlemen. We'll be in touch." They all shook hands and Eddie and Rise made their departures. Harry and Syd, intrigued in the future of their money and amused at their youth-like spontaneity, settled back to their card game.

CHAPTER THIRTY-FOUR

PICKING UP THE PIECES

Paloma Faith

EDDIE TOOK RISE back to Cromartie and took her in. Kenny was there. Eddie said, "Short and sweet. Kenny, you're doing a fine job. Now, you all know the plan. Help Rise, get this place niced up and everyone keep their lips zipped. Rise, you got the card. Y'all go out to Target or Belk's. I gotta go."

He had three tasks left to complete. He mumbled to himself, "Okay, one, two, three—one last investor, the kindness of Risty, and doesn't a new car cost more these days than most engagement rings? Damn more useful too, so let's see if you can hit the trifecta, dumb ass."

Curt went to see Leon, told him that the lawyer Eddie Tyrell was helping him with this, offered him eight grand for a short school bus with built-in, lined compartments and a simple yellow paint job and a full tank too. Leon nodded that deal would work, showed Curt out on the back lot what he had and a bus was chosen. It was an innocuous thing, a short, snub-nosed runt of the litter, and Curt gave Leon four Gs as a down payment, the rest due on delivery. The tires were fine. The color scheme was uniform in the United States and Canada with the simple lettering in black: "County School Bus" on each side and "Caution: School Bus" on the front hood and back escape door. Schools were in session now all over the country and this thing, carefully driven, would pretty much be invisible.

Leon mused, "Lawyer Terrell. Now, he's gots the big time, big name. Curt, my boy, you be moving on up."

Curt just grinned. "Hell, he will always help you now if you just call him."

Leon flipped through an old file of bogus temporary tags and found one that read "State/County Property" with a number that was more made up than Dolly Parton with a trough and a trowel. They also agreed that on the spare tire holder on the back "Caution: Students on the Way to Learn!" would be lettered along its circumference.

Leon promised to have it ready within a few days. Curt thanked him and drove the twelve miles over to the regional airport. He went to the USAir counter and bought a same-day round trip ticket into BWI. It left in two hours. Curt bought some newspapers and a sports magazine and went into another one of those ubiquitous Aero Taverns to nurse a few beers until departure at 2:15 p.m. The flight would take less than 90 minutes.

At 1:45 they loaded, took off on time and arrived in Baltimore on time. With no luggage to haul about, Curt walked straight to the cab stand line and hopped a Checker. The driver said, "Where to, mister?"

Curt said, "The Pit. Franklin Terrace. West Baltimore. Please."

The cabbie turned his head and said, "You really want to go there?"

Curt nodded out a low "Uh-huh."

"That ain't exactly a safe area, so if you don't mind, I'll drop you off at the Shell station about two blocks from there. It's on Mulberry Street. Well lighted. You know what I mean?"

"Yeah. Fine. Let's go." And they went.

Upon arrival under waves of fluorescent lights, Curt paid the fare and asked the cabbie for his call back card and also asked, "What direction?"

The cabbie handed Curt his card and pointed south. The cabbie asked, "You ever been there?" Curt shook his head "no."

The cabbie said, "You can't miss it. It's a high rise, kinda light colored with a big open space in front, kind of like a playground but not really anymore. It's all tore up and scuffed up with raggedy trees and old busted up furniture and chairs and couches all around. You know, there's a lot of drug trade down there."

Curt deadpanned. "You don't say. Then I'll watch my step and hopefully in about an hour, I'll call you back for a ride back to BWI. Fair deal?" He stepped out of the cab. Trash was everywhere in the gutters and he could hear loud, harsh rap music playing from countless boom boxes. Down the way, he heard people yelling and calling out to one another.

The cabbie said, "Fair enough but right here, you understand?"

"I understand." The cabbie pulled away quickly. Curt began walking toward the raucous cacophony.

This was when it helped that Curt looked like a stone-cold bad ass Shaft-like creature. Broad shouldered, a heavy jacket that bulked him up further with eyes that could cut a man, he was not someone to be fucked with. And he was not so stupid as to have carried a weapon. No need in signaling violence if he was found to be carrying.

As he moved down the crumbling sidewalk on West Fremont, he could see people ahead, moving in and out of alleyways, coming in and out of front stoop doors, leaning on walls in shadows near phone call boxes. They eyed him, often eye-fucked him, as he passed. He could hear a coin being slotted in the phones with whispered descriptions of a big, ominous stranger heading toward the project. Curt knew the game. These were the scouts, the wannabe boys, the outliers wanting to be useful up the line to the outside pit bosses and inside floor bosses and lieutenants and captains so even maybe they would be well reported to their Lord Overseer, Kingpin Barksdale. They were vigilant and skittish and did not want to make a mistake that might bring trouble to the operations and also much more trouble to themselves. They all carried handguns of varying calibers. It was a hard and cruel operation, and failure at this level was never tolerated.

As Curt passed on the second block, he could see the dingy and desolate towers raising over the dusty trees. They were bathed in a baleful yellow streetlight that made them looked jaundiced. The hanging interior stairwells had but a few lamps lit on their square exterior windows. That's where most of the better deals went down. A little light, if any. No cameras. A lot of dope, a lot of money as almost always. And if there was trouble, these small, dark spaces and corners were as good as any place to put enough slugs into a miscreant fool with a specific exacting of street justice and little chance of discovery. There was a terrible efficiency to it all.

Two larger boys sauntered up to Curt. "Hey, fool. Who you be coming around here? What you want?" It was a harsh challenge meant to intimidate. Curt coolly, calmly took their steam and evaporated it.

"Good evening, gentlemen. I'm Curt Minor. I'm from a little city in North Carolina by the name of Winston-Salem. I would like to see your boss, goes by the name of Pee Wee. We go way back. We're old friends. And if Mr. Barksdale is available, I'd like to pay my respects of friendship as well."

They stood silent for a few moments, hangdog by the hierarchy being calmly shoved in their false street arrogance.

Curt studied them and then quietly said, "Did you hear me? Did you understand me? You did, I believe. Now, go do as I say. Now. I'll wait right here. Make sure a couple of your boys watch over me until you get Pee Wee to me. "

Mumbling inaudibly, the two low-level gangstas faded away into the darkness of the shadows. Curt stepped off the sidewalk and found a spring busted chair to sit in.

A few more minutes passed. A black and white with only a driver cruised slowly by but swung no lights. The driver didn't bother to look at Curt. It was a cursory, slow night. It was a good day to be here on business. Curt sat facing the darkness and waited.

A voice whispered from the shadows. "Curt, Curt, is that really you?"

"It is. It's me."

"Walk toward the sound of my voice into the dark. I'm right here. I'm gonna be glad to see you!" There was unadorned happiness in those words. Curt rose and stepped into and beyond a tree line toward the sound.

"Over here."

He slightly corrected his angle of approach and then there was just enough light to make out the unmistakable form of Pee Wee. They quicked to one another and bear hugged with the enthusiasm of little boys.

"Damn, son, it's been a while. You've gotten wider, bigger, stronger, but we gonna need to be putting lifts in those shoes of yours!"

Pee Wee low laughed at his former boss. "Always been paying attention to me, haven't you? Why would I want to get any taller? Shit, just easier to spot. Hey, how'd you find me? It's not like I advertise my appearances. Damn, I'm glad to see you! How have you been? How is everybody? Why have you come up here?"

Curt smiled. He was glad to see his apprentice, proud of him too.

Behind Pee Wee stood the two not-so-now-surly, more curious messenger boys and another very young and robust fellow who just oozed competence and control.

"I have my resources," said Curt, "I can make a call every now and then. I know how to keep up. You look good, boy. You're a captain now, indoor, and outdoor, right?"

"Yessir, I am. When I got here, the Barksdale high guys hooked me up with guard and spy duty working the perimeters, on your recommendation. I've worked my way up. It's a good gig and I'm good at it and I like it. Money ain't too bad neither if you know what I mean." He beamed with real pride.

"I'm proud of you, Pee Wee. I really am. Now, as to your questions, let's see. Obviously, so far, I'm good. Everyone is good. As a matter of fact, I'm hoping you get to see Rise and Kenny soon. I'll explain quick enough. Who are your friends back there? Two of them were properly suspicious of me, nasty pushy, though they were. The other real big fellow was not with them. Introductions?"

"Sure. Get to see Rise and Kenny soon? That would be great. I'm surely down with that. And these two that met you first are Screw, short for Screwball, and the other is Lennie." The two briefly nodded and stepped forward ever so slightly. Their costume of challenge had melted to curiosity and respect.

"The third fellow here is my chief assistant. Goes by the name of Punch, short for Suffolk Punch. Not only does he pack a serious wallop, his daddy worked for years out at the Police Horse Stables up near Pamlico and they had a bunch of police horses up there that were the breed called Suffolk Punch. All muscle and bull chests and not a bit of fat on them. Big fuckers. Great on crowd control. So we call him Punch 'cause he looks like one of those horses was his momma."

Punch grinned amiably and said, "I'm just here if anybody needs anything."

Curt said, "Nice to meet you all. Now, Pee Wee, I'm not planning on being here long at all. Gotta fly back home in just a little while. I need to be brief and get to the point. Can you and me, and I guess Punch, have a sit-down?"

"Absolutely. Screw, you and Lennie go on back to the line now. Thank you for getting me up with Curt."

Wordlessly, they headed back up the block. Pee Wee watched them go and then turned to Curt.

"I'm really glad to see you. You helped me out so good. What might I be able to do for you? I'm guessing you didn't just drop by to chat."

"You're on the money. Here it is. I'd like to buy six kilos of good, not perfect quality, snow from you all. Don't want to kill anybody on the later buy. I'm working with a good, smart lawyer, you know that guy who saved Kenny's butt when he popped Bo Diddley? I don't think you know him and I don't think I should tell you his name. You understand, I think."

"I do."

"I've heard up here fair wholesale number is 25K a kilo."

"That's close enough."

"Can you round that up for me in a few days? Do you need to clear it with Mr. Barksdale? I'd love to see him, say hello."

"Yes, no problem. It's not so much blow that I've got to climb the ladder. I play straight with him and his generals and they play straight with me. Consider it done. They told me you'd like to see him. That won't happen tonight. He's not receiving just now. He's done at his strip club blowing off steam and getting blowed." They both laughed softly at that.

Curt said, "I understand. All work and no pleasure makes a man bark." They laughed at that too.

Pee Wee said, "How we gonna make the delivery? Punch will be on the assist and of course, I want to see my old peeps so I'll be there too. I know it'd gotta be quick. As you know, in this business, you just have to be."

"Yup, got that. Rise and Kenny will come in about a week, I'll get word to you, in a little short church bus with built-in sealed compartments for the kilos and stuffing. Just everyone say their hellos and goodbyes. I'll be back soon before they come. I'll bring you $125K in cash and the balance in some pretty pricey jewelry that I expect you can fence for something above the line. And off everyone goes. Should they come here?" Curt pointed at the street.

"Yes, we'll be waiting for them at the side street just down there where the streetlight is. Just have them pull halfway down to the blue door. They'll arrive in daytime? Daytime is better on a small deal like this."

"Yes, we'll arrange that."

"Curious. Why ain't you buying more? Y'all could play a much bigger score, you know."

"We just wanting to make some good money for a few of us. I'll distribute to my Carolina contacts. They'll get theirs. We'll get ours. Simple enough. You know the old line. A pig gets fat and a hog gets slaughtered. I ain't got no wish to be bacon. Just want to be a squeaky clean pig."

Pee Wee nodded and snickered.

"Okay, we good to go?"

"Good to go. You gone?"

"Yeah, gotta get the bird for back home."

They embraced.

Pee Wee asked, "Why don't you come on back with Kenny and Rise? Then it would really be old home week."

"Nah, too many cooks fuck up the soup. Isn't that how that goes?"

"Yeah, I suppose so. Now, go on. Be safe. I don't know how you're gonna get me the word but I know you will."

"It'll come from Barksdale."

"Cool. Punch, how about please walk Curt here back to Screw and Lennie? Tell him to take him back to his ride and wait with him until he goes."

"You got it, boss. Come on with me, Mr. Curt. Where we going?"

"Shell station two blocks down."

"Good choice. Lots of lights."

Curt and Pee Wee shook hands. "Be safe now."

"Thank you. You too."

Curt began the short walk with Punch. He was handed off to Lennie and Screw. They strolled briskly three abreast.

Screw asked Curt, "How you know Mr. Pee Wee?"

"Long story, boys. He did some really fine fast work for me down in Carolina many years ago. I knew then he knew his shit and was gonna be a pro with a future. I sent him up here to be trained. I think I was right. What do you guys think?"

The two escorts vigorously chorused, "Yes. Uh-huh. He's a good one. Good to us too. Treats us respectful."

"Good to hear."

They arrived at the station. Curt pulled some change out of his pocket along with the cabbie's card. He dialed the pay phone.

"Hey, remember me? I'm the drop off at the Shell station not so long ago. I'm through at the Franklin. How 'bout come get me and take me back to BWI. As you said, I'm at the Shell station now."

The cabbie said he'd be there in five minutes. Curt hung up.

Curt told his escorts they didn't have to wait around, that his ride would be there soon enough.

Screw shook his head. "No, we don't do like that. We're here until you gone."

Curt nodded and they waited. Soon enough the Checker wheeled in. Curt shook hands with both, thanked them and wished them luck. They nodded and stepped back and waved to each other as the cab drove off.

When Curt returned to Winston-Salem, it was mid-evening. He called Eddie's phone and told him the bus and the buy were in play and in place. Eddie thanked him and asked him to come by tomorrow and get an update on the school bus and mused out loud that he was going to get the buy money together and maybe it was a better idea for Curt to fly back up and prepay as a sign of goodwill for efficiency's sake. Curt agreed, noting it was fun flying on a jet airplane and then they hung up and Eddie went back to pleasantly getting Mikey to giggle and coo.

The next afternoon he headed to his mother's house. He had his own house key and let himself in and went down the hall toward her bedroom door. She was always watching one of those old black and white Turner Classic Movies, laid up in bed, awash in newspapers, two telephones (one worked well, the other not so much—guess which one she liked to talk on?) and mail and bills and heating pads and catalogues and God knows what else. He always wondered when a hanging shelf or miniature chest of drawers would collapse into her sea of detritus. As he walked down the hall, he saw a shape moving off to his left in one of the guest rooms. He paused and peered into the dark and realized it was Chuckles.

"Hey, Chuckles! How you doin'?"

"Just fine, Mr. E., and you?"

They shook hands. Chuckles was a small, wide man with a graying moustache and a ready grin. He'd worked for Eddie's mother for a hundred years. It was said he had 11 or 12 children by way of four or five or six women who clearly didn't give a damn or pay attention. He took a heavy drink on the regular and suffered from periodic bouts of "can't remember shit." Eddie's mother had fired him so many times, over and over again; he swore he'd never return, but she always relented and he always did. He was faithful, loyal, protective, and compliant. When Eddie's first daddy had died so many years ago, it was said that it was Chuckles, resplendent in one of his father's garish, feathered, fire-engine red hunting hats standing at salute with tears streaming down his cheeks that met the cortege of black Cadillac limousines that lined up in front of St. Paul's Church.

Eddie once asked Chuckles, "You get fired so many times. I'm curious. Like Green Stamps, when you get fired each tenth time, do you get a prize?"

Chuckles just laughed and said, "No, but she always gives me extra money when she does so I can have bus fare to get back here when she calls."

"Real good. Chuckles, what are you doing? It's almost pitch black in here. How can you see what you are up to?"

"Oh, Mr. E., I'm just dusting and such."

"Well, how can you see what to dust?"

"I'm just supposed to stay busy so I rattle around in the dark here and there and then go have a smoke break and start again. She gets mad at me all the time and cusses me out, but that's just because she's old and frustrated and not feeling so good. I don'ts mind. Just the way it is. You know I pretty much do's the same things all the time before. I can wear that vacuum cleaner out. We gonna have to get a new one soon enough."

Eddie grinned at him and said, "Good. Don't get too fancy with it. That ain't the style of this crib. Hang in. I'll see you around. She in there?"

"Oh yeah, you know it's movie time, right?" He turned back to his invisible rubbings.

Eddie moved on down the hall and stuck his head around the corner of her door and said "Hey!"

She looked away from the television and smiled. "Hey, son. Come in. Sit over here. This one is very good. Clear all that off that chair. This is Tyrone Power and Marlene Dietrich and Sir Charles Laughton in *Witness for the Prosecution*. How are you? And where's that cute girl you brought home from out West? She's interesting...what's her name? Ikey?" She tailed off and turned the volume up, settling back in her pillows.

He cleared the chair next to her bed. Her pocketbook weighed an easy five pounds and pads and paper fluttered onto the floor. The place was a high-end hoarder's dream.

"Yes, this is a great movie. I've seen it at least ten times. One of my all-time favorites. I'm fine. Mikey's at the office working with Patty. She's good too."

She shushed him and said, "Well, if you like it so much, be quiet and let's watch it together."

"Fair enough." And so they did.

Eddie was there for the last ask of the deal so it behooved him to be pleasant and amenable. Plus, it was a helluva good movie. As he watched and recalled so much of the dialogue, he remembered how all of his siblings from time to time had gotten sideways with her when she was often found to be a hard ass. She was always hidden in a basket and when you took the lid off, you did not know whether you were going to get a cobra or a bunny rabbit.

He laughed quietly to himself about one memorable exchange that summed everything up. Many years before, his brother Grass was on the phone with their mother and in truth, it was a pleasant and interesting conversation of some length. Suddenly, the line went dead. Their mother waited a few seconds and then called Grass back.

"What happened to our call? We were having such a nice visit. Did the telephone company have a break in their service?"

"No, Mother, I just hung up on you."

"Why did you do that? We were having a nice conversation!"

"Oh, I know. I just didn't want to get out of practice." She howled, as did he.

Along the way, the door opened and in walked Camara, her alert eyes taking in everything.

Camara was the great anticipator. She knew what her queen wanted before her queen knew it. And she was a tuned in sports fan. Always affable and calm, she was a keystone. She had also in recent years become his mother's lead travel companion. That was a big deal. His mother traveled in the style of an Indian raj, replete with many bulging bags, her own pillows and linens, coats and hats and scarves and shawls, small kitchen appliances and always a large replica of Big Ben. It took patience, a strong back, and military logistical skills to get her caravans on the move.

Camara whispered, "Hey, Eddie. How are you? Do you want something to drink? And Mrs. T., can I get you anything?"

Eddie shook his head and asked, "Did you see them play the other night? What did you think?"

"They're gonna be real good. Real good."

The movie was paused.

"Y'all stop all that sports mess. Stop being so familiar with one another. It's just not proper. Now, Camara, would you please go to the drug store and pick up my two prescriptions they've called about and said are ready?"

Camara and Eddie smirked and Camara complied with a sing-songy, "Yes, ma'am. Anything else?"

"Not right now but keep your phone on cause as you know, I might just think of something. I know that one of the prescriptions is my eye medicine, so if you miss on that one and I keep getting blind faster, just think how much more pleasant I just might be." She winked.

"Yes, that is so true." And off she went.

The movie resumed and finally, the mystery was solved and the television was clicked off. She turned her head toward her son and said, "Now, what are you up to? Why aren't you at your office?"

"Let's see... I've been mostly at the office and just dropped by here for a visit. I'm working very hard on many cases, just made a nice lick of money on one and have others ready to pop so my office finances are in good shape. As you know, being a plaintiff's lawyer is very much like walking a high wire without a net. Mikey and Patty get along real well and Mikey has been a fast and smart learner and is a help to Patty so obviously that's good. And right now, I'm concentrating on three real big cases, two of which I believe will resolve right soon and the last of the three will most certainly go to trial, so there's plenty of chance and doubt to go all around there."

It had taken a while, but finally his mother had come to the realization that the fact that Eddie had not become a corporate or real estate or tax lawyer was not a shameful or embarrassing thing (though the representing of those nasty criminals was simply not what a Terrell should ever be about, but alas, he had always had that rebellious streak), and that in representing people against doctors and hospitals and insurance companies, Eddie her eldest was skilled and respected and so importantly, was making plenty of honest money. Now, his personal life was always a mess but that was another story of greater length than space available.

"I wish you'd bring that girl back over for a visit. She is attractive. And interesting. I liked her."

"I promise I will soon enough. And too, the other thing is I've been working on a business plan of potential excellent return which does involve investment from investors."

He let that one hang as a fat, slow swinging bait for her eminently predictable lunge. She did not let him down. She came at it immediately.

"Now, that's interesting. What sort of business plan? Who are your investors? Tell me about this."

She peered at him, her glasses sliding slightly down her nose, thus amplifying her searching stare.

Eddie said, "Well, Mother, it's a nice group of people, lawyers, insurance folks, investment savvy people, that sort of types."

"Do I know any of them?"

"Yes. A few. I'm an investor as is your other son, my younger brother. I don't think you know any of the others."

"Pablo is a smart money man and he's putting his money in?"

"He already has as have I and all the others. It's not a big group. Just five or six. We'd like you to be in with us as well."

"How much has each investor put in?"

"It's twenty-five thousand for one share and we expect the return to be a good one."

"And you and your brother are in it together?"

"Yes, ma'am. We are and it's a good, experienced group. Do you remember that little mutual fund I put together so many years ago? Had uncles and aunts and cousins and about ten, twelve folks in it? I recall everyone put up twenty-five hundred and I picked the investments, and a year later gave everyone their money back, plus a tidy profit. That was a fun experience. Do you recall it?"

"Yes, I certainly do. Is that what you're going to do here? Assemble the money and then select the investments?"

"Yes, ma'am. That's about the size of it. Would you like to be an investor? I think we have some vehicles we are eyeing that are very attractive and hold great promise."

"So right now, you aren't sure what your targets are?"

"That is so, but it won't be long now, and we think we can get a good return back to everyone in a fairly short period of time. And it's for sure this isn't some half-baked crazy deal like that couple over in Thomasville that sold their kid for a car. I'm dealing with real professionals here."

"Well, if you and your brother are in it together, that's a good enough endorsement for me. I'm so glad you are trying to cultivate the innate businessman I've always known that was in you. Your father had it and your brother has it, and now maybe it's time for you to have it too."

"Well, I sure hope so."

"Hand me my checkbook, please, and let's get this business on the move."

Eddie did as he was instructed and she stroked the negotiable instrument for 25K solid and handed it to him. "Now, do well with this, son. I'll be interested to see how this evolves. Now, go see if Chuckles is still here and send him back to see me. I'm tired now and think I want some peanut butter crackers and buttermilk before I take my nap."

"Yes, ma'am. I'll track him down for you. Thank you. I'll be back to visit soon and will bring Mikey with me."

"Good. I'll look forward to that. Now, just crack that door a little bit as you go."

He headed down the hall and could hear the volume come up on yet another movie, a classic to be sure. He gave Chuckles his marching orders and went out to his car.

He sat for a few moments and thought about the time not so long ago that they were all at a family wedding up in the mountains of North Carolina. At the rehearsal dinner there were toasts after toasts after more toasts. It was clearly evident that much alcohol fueled these gushing adorations and proclamations. It did drag on and all the guys' toasts were all about "we all grew up together and you're such a great guy" and all of the gals' toasts were all about "We love you so much and if you do anything to hurt her, we will come and kill you." Finally, the parents of the groom had to call these meandering testimonials off for the sake of time, much to the teary, drunken dismay of a couple of young ladies who had thus had their last chance to slobber and emote.

Eddie's mother had been sitting at a table near all the merriment next to the minister who was to marry the couple the next day. As Eddie approached his mother to ask how her evening was going, the minister asked his mother if he could get her anything.

She replied, "Well, if they hadn't gotten that flood of toasts stopped, I would have asked you for a gun so I could shoot myself and you could administer the last rites to me as I made my escape. But for now, a glass of ice water would be nice. Thank you."

Eddie laughed to himself. She was a catbird all right. He just hoped he could pull off this deal so she wouldn't feel the need to shoot him. But he had made his nut and wanted to move things along now. He headed back to the office and told Mikey to get ready. They were going car shopping, but first he needed to make a quick phone call. He went in his office and closed the door. He needed a favor from an old friend up in Middleburg, Virginia, up in hunt country near the beautiful Blue Ridge mountains.

She was Risty Emiligia, a tall, blonde beauty of a crackerjack lawyer who could ride to hounds like a banshee and was a crack shot to boot. They had been real good friends a ways back and though the bloom was off that now, they had stayed in touch and truly were curious and cared about the other. They checked in randomly from time to time and that was nice.

It was late afternoon and growing dark and he figured she would be in at home after working her horses and running her errands and selling some real estate. He dialed her number and she answered after a few rings.

"Hello, you scoundrel. What are you up to?"

"Well, let's see. For openers, I'm calling you and as always I appreciate your taking my call."

"Don't be so sure, mister. My Caller ID isn't working that well today." Risty had placed him on speaker phone which he hated. Eddie could hear her clap dusting her hands, something she always did when a matter was, to her way of thinking, concluded.

But there was a deep and playful chortle to her voice so he felt she wasn't going to throw him in the ditch just yet.

He asked her, "Do you want to hear a good line? Might be able to put it to good use any time now."

"Fire away. I'm game."

"Here you go. The ex called his ex and asked, 'Do you still hate me?' She responded, 'Hell, yes!' He whined, 'After all this time?' and she said, 'Hell, yes! Listen, doofus, if I had a gun with two bullets in it and Hitler and the devil were in the room with you, I'd shoot you twice!'"

She howled and coughed out a laughing "If the shoe fits..."

"Thought you'd like that one."

"I sure do, you sorry so-and-so." The good humor stayed in her voice. "I've got a good one for you if you want it."

"You know I do. Shoot."

"Nurse Tracey worked at an assisted living place and one day saw that Mr. Johnson was at the end of the hall, slumped in a chair, very glum and gloomy. She went up to him and gently asked, 'Mr. Johnson, are you sad or upset about something? You look very down in the dumps.' Mr. Johnson just shrugged and Nurse Tracey knew that indeed there was something troubling Mr. Johnson in a very big and serious way. So she asked again, 'What is it, Mr. Johnson? I can tell there is something on your mind. You can tell me. I'm here to help.'

Mr. Johnson looked up, gazing off into an unknown far distance and said, 'I'll tell you, but I don't think you can do much of anything about it. My private part died last night.' Nurse Tracey, knowing how confused and addled some older folks got, patted him on the shoulder and told him, 'Well, Mr. Johnson, I'm very sorry to hear this news and I'm sure the days ahead will be better. Remember, you are of man of some age and with the passage of time, sometimes these things happen.' Mr. Johnson grunted, 'Yes, I know,' and he wandered back down the hall to his room.

"The next day, Nurse Tracey was doing paperwork at the nurses' station. She looked up and there came a shuffling Mr. Johnson with his private thing saluting very erectly out of his pajama pants. She rushed over to him and said, very quietly and breathlessly, 'Mr. Johnson, I thought you told me yesterday that your private thing had died?' Mr. Johnson sweetly smiled at her and replied, 'Oh I did. Today is the viewing.'"

Eddie screamed with laughter. "Big Johnson lives! Perfect! Great joke! Great telling too. You could always nail a good joke."

"True. Now, let's cut the fun and games bullshit. How are you and what's new?"

"Spoken like a true horsewoman. I'm good. Gotta new gal pal who I met in Montana and she's come back South to hang with me. She's working in the office with Patty. Fast learner and smart, almost as smart as you. Business is good. Am working on a few other projects too. So how about you? What's going on?"

"Hmmm, dating a nice new guy. You'll hate this part. He played football at Virginia. Still riding to hounds every chance I can. Still love it. Renovating another old house up this way. You know how I always like a new project as aggravating as they always are. Selling some real estate here and there. Staying busy. What are your new projects?"

"I can't really tell you about one of them just yet. But I will soon, I promise. The others are a couple of good-sized cases I've got to get ready to either settle or try. I think I can get two of the three wrapped up before courthouse time, but the third one is a bear and I have every expectation that we're going to try it. Involves the death of an infant."

"Whoa, that sounds grim. Good luck with all of it. So why can't you tell me about the one, the mystery project?"

"It's a secret. It's too early but I will eventually. You know I trust you and this one needs lots of good trust. So, I've got an ask for you."

"An ask?"

"Yeah, I need your help on a little something."

"How so?"

"In about ten days, two very nice folks who work for me are going to take the slow road from Baltimore back to Winston-Salem. They'll be in a nice, respectable little short school bus. I was wondering if you would let them park the bus in one of your barns for the night? I want to keep them off the road if you get my drift. They'll get there at dusk. They'll sleep in the bus. They'll have their own food. They will not bother or trouble you in the least and they'll be gone by dawn. Whaddaya say? Please, Miss Risty. I promise I will tell you all about it in-the-not-so-distant future and, of course, I'll let you know the day of their arrival."

"Eddie, why does this sound pretty shaky to me?"

"I know. I know it does but honest to God, you're not involved in anything and don't need to know anything and it's just a few hours. Please, Risty, I need your little bit of help here. These folks are not criminals. They're good people. I'm trying to do some good for them and some others too."

"You sound like fucking Robin Hood." She paused. Eddie dared not speak. "Yes, I'll have the first barn on the right up Sidehill Road open and waiting. Juan will make sure of it. Jesus, I have such a soft spot for you. No wonder I hate you from time to time. But, yes, sounds simple enough. Hey, what are their names?"

"Thank you, Risty. Thank you very much. Their names are Rise as in 'rise and shine' and Kenny."

"Should I go over and say hello, introduce myself to them when they get here?"

"No, not a good idea. No reason to be able to identify anyone, right?"

"Christ, now I know this is a shitty deal, but I've said yes, I don't know jackshit, am in the total dark and I can always say they just showed up and pulled in, and so, you better get 'em in and out fast and then you get your ass up here and take me out to a big ass fine dinner and tell me all about this story. You understand me, mister?!"

"I do and I will."

Risty sighed. "I'm holding you to it. Now, how's your family? Your mother, brother."

"All good. Cranking along. Your family?"

"The same. I sometimes wonder if I didn't get switched out at the hospital the day I showed up..."

They both laughed. Then they were both silent for a few moments.

Eddie finally spoke. "I really appreciate you, kid. I really do. I think of you all the time. You have become such a special friend." It was true.

"I miss you, Eddie. Come see me, please." He could hear just a little wistful for the old days in her deep, now soft voice, not too much, just a small trace of years' past.

"I will."

"Take care of yourself."

"I will. You too. I will see you soon, I promise." And they hung up. She was pure class in the best of ways. Regret, temporal he knew, rose up in him and slid away quickly.

He was such a bum. He created a bad taste in his own mouth. He had tried to play her for his stupid deal just because she was a dot on the way back, but at least she had figured him all the way out and had not busted him. She knew she was safe enough. She did not spit the bit. She was the unindictable co-conspirator. The remnants of old love and care remained. Eddie sat very still in his chair for many minutes and looked out into the parking lot and saw nothing but Risty and her farm and a horse she had had back way back when, an easy 18 hands high, long ago, named Charlie, a beautiful, huge chestnut. Some things just never go, never give back. *More things than some,* he thought.

And then he roused his reflective self and his good-in-this-moment humor back up and went out and got Mikey.

And his plaything, reckless drug deal was rolling and they were going to buy a car. Eddie skated from the criminal ridiculous to the retail sublime.

"Patty, please check in on Curt and if he's back and around, let's get him and Rise and Kenny on in tomorrow morning. Final game preparations and so forth. Come on, Mikey, let's go to the AutoMile and get you properly rigged up."

She grinned and off they went. As they rode along to the thicket of car dealerships, he asked her, "Well, have you thought about what you'd like to get? Have you done any studying on this looming decision?"

Mikey glanced slyly sideways at him with a sweet smile and said, "Honey, yes I have. I have thought and studied and think I know exactly what I'd like, if it's okay with you."

"Honey, I'm curious. Before you tell me what you want, how did you learn about it?"

"I looked at newspaper ads, I read *Consumer Reports* online. Drove to a few dealerships when you were in Fort Myers, remember? I knew you were serious about this and I wanted to be prepared to be serious too."

"Gee, baby, that's great! I'm impressed. You have really done your homework. That's a whole lot more than most people do. So what's it gonna be?"

She drew in a deep breath and held it for a couple of beats and then, rapidly said, "With your help and permission, Mr. Eddie Terrell, I would like a charcoal gray BMW X-5 with the basic package. I don't need a lot of bells and whistles. They're just pricey add-ons."

"No convertible?"

"No convertible. Don't use it that much. The tops fade. The mechanisms often get warpy and fail. Just one more thing to get fixed."

"No bright red?"

"Too flashy. This town doesn't need me lipsticking about here and there in a cop magnet. You've got a reputation to hold and I've got one to make so that's the last sort of thing either of us need."

"No next year's model?"

"Nope, this year's is just fine. And if they've got some of last year's left, that would be even better. Can save good value on that kind of buy."

Eddie whistled in admiration. He had a Mercedes which he liked a lot, but this was a fine pick and he was proud of her. She was gorgeous and smart and thorough. He reached over and squeezed her hand to affirm her. She nodded.

"Okay, baby, let's go see some folks at the Bavarian Motor Works shop." He wheeled off of Interstate 40 and headed down Peters Creek Parkway to a big chunk of the Flow Auto Empire.

They parked, walked in the showroom, briefly glanced at one gleaming car after another that had been arrayed to catch the eye. They all came with initials and numbers and all were shaped differently, all very geometric, very German. An attractive, tall young man with a big tousle of brown hair sprouting up like an unruly crown, displaying "Meyer Ritchie" on his name badge, approached them and affably stuck out his hand and asked if he could be of service to them.

"Mr. Ritchie. We'd like to buy a car. Specifically, we'd like to purchase a charcoal gray BMW X5, preferably one of last year's models. No bells and whistles. Just the basic car. It's, as you know, a fine piece of machinery."

"Please call me Meyer. Do you want to test drive one? Talk about things that could be good, helpful add-ons?"

Mikey interjected, "Meyer, I've already been out here and test driven one, and also, I'm from the sticks out in southwest Montana and am used to driving a beat up old hunk of junk, so just the basic car we're asking for will make me feel like Cinderella with a glass slipper that really fits. Now, do you think you can round up from this dealership here or from one not so far away one of last year's models? As you know that will save us some serious moohla."

"Yes, ma'am, yessir. Y'all clearly know what you want, so let me see what I can find out. Do you want to wait while I search around? It might take a bit."

Eddie said, "No, we would rather not. Here's my card. Call me when you have found something. I'll be back with a certified check for the bottom line amount when we come to get it. Please put the title in her name. Her name is Mikey Riewy, address 746 Lynn Dee Drive, WS NC 27106. She's got a Montana driver's license. Mikey, let's let him make a copy..." Mikey fished the license out and they handed it to him, smiling.

Ritchie had it copied and handed it back. "We'll be back when you call with a bank check for full total."

"You don't want to haggle or bargain, just a bit?" Ritchie was a little mystified.

"Nope, not at all. You be fair with us and we'll be back. You aren't fair with us and I'll make sure everyone I know knows it. I'll look to hear from you. Have a good day."

And off they went. Richie just stared at their backs, a little amazed, a little appreciative too.

They went home and changed and went out to dinner and enjoyed each other and then went back home and fell asleep like little puppies.

CHAPTER THIRTY-FIVE

THE DIRECTIONS SONG

Scratch Garden

WHEN EDDIE AND Mikey walked back in the office the next morning, Patty looked up from her cigarette and coffee and did a droll, throwaway, "Good morning, oh by the way..." They turned to her.

"Got the washed-out credit card back from Lee Ann last night. Popped into Diamond Back for a pop and there she was, all perked up with just guess who?" She grinned salaciously and Eddie knew it was going to be good.

"Okay, good job and spill it."

"None other than dear old and I do mean old Alph Baron, giggling and cooing at her every word and Lee Ann just batting those baby blues at him and giving him a wide-angle lens Grand Canyon shot of those big guavas she carries to market when she's working. She had him eating out of her hand like a chickadee at the park. I sat and watched for a while, saw them order and slosh back a couple of drinks and admire each other to the blue max and then thought it was a good time to wander over and say 'Hey.'

"Lee Ann seemed genuinely glad to see me and was very friendly and polite and without my asking, just reached into her purse and handed me the credit card. Alph stared at the transfer with puzzlement."

Patty reached into her top drawer and pulled the card out and handed it to Eddie. He glanced at it and simply said, "How about you just cut it up and throw it in the trash, please and thank you? Is that it? Gotta be a little more..."

"Oh, you bet there is. Old Alph didn't understand what the hand off was about and you could see he was trying to gin up some cute chit-chat to divine the mystery but he got cut off at the pass. Obviously, Lee Ann didn't want to talk about the card, so she introduced me to him real quick and breathy, 'Alph, this is Patty, Eddie Terrell's chief legal assistant.' He reflexively extended his hand to shake and as he did, the realization came over his face like a dark cloud as to who I was in his now not-so-much-fun universe. We did shake hands and then he stood up plenty quick and said something like, 'Please excuse me, ladies, but I've really got to be going,' and skedaddled out the door mumbling and shaking his head hanging low. Lee Ann called to him, more than a little mystified, 'Alph, I had a nice time with you. Call me again soon.' But he was gone.

"Lee Ann looked at me and asked, 'What was that about? We were having such a nice time. Strange...' and I just told her, 'We got a big case with him that ain't gonna go his way. Eddie's got him by the short hairs and gonna start yanking hard soon. Once he heard I was with Eddie, I expect that jolted him a little.' Lee Ann nodded thoughtfully and just said, 'That Eddie, he sure is a caution. Well, I guess I'll just have a nightcap.' And she asked me to join her, but I said I'd better call it a night and kept moving. Pretty good stuff, huh?"

"Oh my! That's a damn sight better than pretty good! That's great stuff. I love it when the good luck tide runs hard in our favor. Patty, please call his office now and ask for him. Oh, he'll take your call for sure. He knows this grenade with its pin out is now bouncing to the center of his desk and then off the ledge to lodge just ever so snugly between his legs. He is now officially in 'I'm so fucking fucked' land. Introduce yourself properly and pleasantly and ask him if he would please come over for a visit with us tomorrow afternoon, say about three o'clock, to talk about resolving the unfortunate air disaster case. He'll accept. Y'all be glammed up too cause y'all will be sitting in. He's such a mark when there are ladies around."

Patty picked up the phone, sing-songing with delight, "Oh, karma is a bitch, but if she's on your side, she can ditch your itch." Eddie and Mikey stood by and watched. Eddie was smirking with his hand over his mouth. Mikey was amused. "One Ringy Dingy, Two Ringy Dingies, Three Ringy..."

A muffled voice on the other end could be heard to say, "Baron, Prince and Otter. How may I help you?"

Patty asked for Mr. Alphonse Baron and told the receptionist who she was, adding a layer of stone-cold-bitch-get-outta-my-way presumption. "I'm quite certain Mr. Baron will be taking my call. Please connect me now." All very level and cool.

The disemboweled voice replied, "Well...um...let me see...well yes...I'm connecting you now..." and the first hurdle had been leapt. There was a pause and then, "Mr. Baron's office. This is Phyllis speaking. How may I help you?"

Now Patty pushed it into fourth gear, having fun with it as she continued knocking the pompous, self-important barriers aside. "Phyllis, how are you? I'm Patty Cherry, Chief Legal Assistant to Attorney Eddie Terrell. I'm sure you are familiar with the sad, sad case where Zach Reynolds killed those sweet boys when he pretty much crashed his plane almost into Pilot Mountain." She let the poison seep through her voice.

"Why, yes, yes I am. What may I do for you?"

"I want to speak with Mr. Baron, please."

"I'm, uh, not sure Mr. Baron is available. May I take your number for a call back later?"

"No, I'm sorry. That just won't do. I saw Alph Baron out at the Diamond Back tossing a few back last night with an old friend of mine and we were introduced so I am positive that he wants to take my call right quick. Please get him on the line."

"Uh, Wait just a minute." There was a pregnant hesitancy in her voice. She had just been told that her seigneur, the top of her pile, her lordship was seen last night in a raucous enough spot to have been possibly visiting with someone whom Mrs. Alph might well disapprove of and when Mrs. Alph disapproved, it was not a mild moment but rather the enraged claxon of torrential anger. Fair to say, Alph had spun this sort of waltz before. Phyllis, now defenseless, lamely relented her post at the gate. "Yes, Wait just a minute. I'll go get him on the line."

Patty mouthed at her bemused audience, "He's coming." Then, "Mr. Baron, Hello, this Patty from Eddie Terrell's office. We met last night when you were with Miss Jepson."

"Uh, yes, hello, I recall. What may I do for you, Patty?" His simple question was cringeworthy. What devils and demons lurked just beyond the words?

"Mr. Baron, Eddie would like to meet with you, just you tomorrow afternoon at 3 p.m. here at our offices. May I please mark that now in my book?"

Baron knew the noose was drawn, that it was time to mount the scaffold. The wait to save his foolish clients was rushing at him as a blow dart dipped in curare. A loud voice bounced inside his skull, "Yo time is up. Yo time is up." There was no sense in fighting it or ducking it. With a crisp resignation, Baron replied, "Of course, Patty, I'll be there at three o'clock sharp and as you have instructed, it will just be me. I assure you."

"Thank you, Mr. Baron. See you tomorrow."

"Yes, uh, Patty, one more thing. I presume that you told Eddie about seeing me visiting with my friend last evening?"

"Yes, that is so."

"Now, she's an awfully sweet girl and I wouldn't want anything embarrassing to get rumored around out there."

"Oh, I understand. Yes, I surely do. That old thing, 'The truth walks, the lie rides a motorcycle."

"Yes, that's exactly right. May I count on your and Eddie's discretion? I don't want to upset others, you understand?"

"Sure, why don't we say that we should ALL do the right thing here, right?"

"I agree." Baron understood the blade was poised.

"Good, we'll see you tomorrow. Oh, and Mr. Baron, one more thing. How long have you known your friend Lee Ann?"

"Oh just a few visits over last few weeks. Nothing serious to it." Baron could feel the hard roll of nickels wrapped up in a big, hard fist waiting out there in the ether.

"No, of course not. Just for your further information, Miss Lee Ann was Eddie's live-in girlfriend for a number of years until recently and though they have parted company, they remain good friends. Just thought you ought to know that. Have a nice afternoon."

Patty hung up and glowed the gleam of absolute domination.

Eddie hollered and jumped at her and hugged her and said, "Bravura! Just bravura! Great job, Patty! Thank you."

Mikey added, "Man, that was something, Patty! Learning from a master!"

"Great stuff, Patty! Back to aligning the stars in our interesting and reasonably fucked-up universe. I'm going to the bank to get the money together. It'll take a couple of stops, but my bankers are friends and good guys and they will service me as I have serviced them these many years. And the remaining $25K is the jewels locked in my safe. Curt is going to come by in a little while to get the money and all and take it to Baltimore. Might as well prepay the deal. Pee Wee and his folks may be into some shady shit, but he and they are honorable and old friends to so many of us. Barksdale does run a straight-up operation."

Patty asked, "You sure?"

"Yes, no doubt."

"Also Curt will give us a status report on the school bus. Let's get Kenny and Rise over. Mikey, would you please take them to get outfitted in khaki shirts and pants and black school bus driver shoes over at Belk's? They'll show you where. And also, go to the Halloween Hocus Pocus shop over off of Hawthorne and buy them each school bus driver hats, you know, black with shiny visors. Can they use your car, please? Mikey's will be delivered in a few days so it's not available yet."

Patty laughed and said, "Oh, what the hell, oh, Great Pumpkin, I don't know anything anyway so I'll just take 'em all over there. We'll get 'em looking sharp."

Mikey just shook her head and said, "Man, this shit just flies like rockets!" She laughed.

"Great! Thank you! I'll be back in about an hour and a half. Call Curt and tell him to come over in an hour. Oh, two other things. Let's lay out the Zach Reynolds file in the big conference room so we can all be familiar and good to go tomorrow when Alph comes over. When is the mediation set for in Pussy Preacher/Blockhouse?"

Patty looked at her calendar. "Next Wednesday. Need to get prepped on that one too. I suppose there'll be a school bus out there somewhere sometime winding its way back this way."

"Yes, you're probably right. Lots of irons in the fire. Let's get it all going."

Eddie ducked into his office, grabbed the checks and money and a little bag with the baubles from his desk safe and pulled a three sleeve of checks out of his checkbook. Then he plucked an innocuous, plain brown leather briefcase from his office closet for Pee Wee and waved as he scurried out the door just as the brother and sister duo arrived.

Rise and Kenny were given their money and told to go buy enough snacks and drinks for the trip. Eddie admonished them there was to be no alcohol on this ride, that they were to always stay at or just under the speed limit, that they could stop only at large truck stops for bathroom breaks and that their collective behaviors were to be polite and perfect. They understood. Eddie asked them to be at his office by 5:30 a.m. on the morning of departure. As today was Tuesday, the bus would be delivered Thursday and they would head to Charm City early Friday morning. And by the way, just to be on the safe side, if there was going to be any drinking by either of them, it had to be tonight and it had to be lowkey. No hangovers or blurry thinking. They both agreed they would abstain until they successfully returned.

Curt took the briefcase and headed to the airport.

Curt reappeared on the sidewalk just down from the heartbeat of Barksdale's "tower of power" late that afternoon. There was still a goodly amount of daylight. And in a moment of déjà vu, there just ahead of him, in the fringes of the trees, were Screw and Lennie walking the point as though they had never left their posts. Curt wondered, *Do these sharp-eyed fools ever sleep? Oh, they must want to move on up the big ladder bad.*

"Hello, Lennie. Hello, Screw. How are y'all today? I'd like to see Mr. Pee Wee and Punch too if you please." They blinked in unison.

Screw asked, "You're the Curt fellow that was just here a little while ago, right?"

"Yep, the one and the same. I have something for Pee Wee. Please go let him know."

"Yessir. Right away. Lennie, you and Mr. Curt walk over further into these trees, and, Lennie, you watch over him until I get back with the others."

Lennie nodded and motioned for Curt to follow him.

Standing in a grove of trees, Curt asked Lennie, "How they hanging these days?"

Lennie laughed and offered, "Pretty good these days. Pretty good."

"You any good with directions? I've got to get some of my people here in a few days right down that alley up there right next to the blue door on the right side. I'm gonna direct them in on Highway 85 north."

"Sure, I'm fine with that. Want me to write it out for you? You know, Mr. Curt, when you work for an outfit like this, you got to have skills. Mr. Barksdale won't hire no dumb people or people who can't read or write or think good. We're all pretty proud of that."

"That's impressive, Lennie. Yes, if you could do that for me, I'd appreciate it. Now, I'm not gonna be here long today, so if you could snap that out for me pretty quick, that would be fine."

"Yessir. As soon as Mr. Pee Wee and the others get here, I'll go do it fast."

They waited a few more minutes in silence and the Screw reappeared with Pee Wee and Punch. Pee Wee laughed and said, "Did you really miss me that much?" They all laughed as Lennie waved 'bye saying he'd be back with the directions.

Curt said, "Pee Wee, I didn't see any reason to wait to get this to you," and he held the briefcase up.

Pee Wee sent Screw back to his station and then noted, "A prepay? You are a pretty agreeable bunch."

Curt handed him the case and said, Please count it and check it out. There's a hundred and a quarter in cash and a bag of jewelry worth more than the last 25Gs...it's all there."

"No need. I trust you. What's that some fancy white folks say? Honor among thieves. Works for me."

"Thanks. Day after tomorrow a couple of your old friends, Rise and Kenny are going to come up this way to make the pickup. They'll be in a simple, short yellow school bus. They'll come right down the street here toward this Franklin Terrace. They'll get here about 3 p.m. Would you please have some of your sharp eyes out up the street to catch them and signal them into the alley so everyone can say hey and hug and make the pickup? They'll quickly be on their way back. Lennie is nice enough to go draw up some directions for me to get them here."

Pee Wee said, "You got it. I'll have Punch on it along with Screw and Lennie. It'll go smooth."

Curt concluded, "We're gonna send them the slow way home, over toward Frederick, and then down to a farm in Middleburg and then on home."

On cue, Lennie reappeared and handed Curt a piece of paper on which, in fine handwriting, laid out the way step by step and there was also a small, easily decipherable map.

"Thank you, Lennie. That's very nice. Okay, everybody, I've gotta go. See you around out there one of these days. Pee Wee, thanks for your help. Everyone take good care and be safe out there." They all shook hands. He turned to walk back up to the Shell station and Screw and Lennie fell in behind him.

"Fellows, you don't have to look out for me here. It's a nice day. I'm fine."

Lennie said, "No, sir. We got rules and you're one of them now. You are part of us and we look after our people."

"Well, thank you, gentlemen. I appreciate it."

They walked along, got to the station, Curt called for a cab and they waved at him as he went back to the airport.

As he rode, Curt thought of a backup direction plan for just in case. When he got to the airport, he made a collect call to Eddie's office. Patty answered and accepted the charges. Eddie picked up quickly.

"Hey, Curt. How'd it go?"

"Delivered. Smooth as a baby's ass. I'm on the way back. I got an idea."

"Good and what is it?"

"Are you a member of that AA outfit? I bet you are."

"What? Alcoholics Anonymous?" Eddie laughed. "I probably ought to be but not yet."

Curt laughed back and said, "No, man, no. I mean that car deal. American Automobile or something like that."

"Oh, you mean Triple AAA? Yeah, I'm a member."

"Yeah, not the radio station. The car help place that makes trip and travel maps. Can't they do a couple for us?"

"Hell, yes! Great idea. I'll go over there this afternoon and get them."

"Here's what we need. Get something to write on and a pad."

Curt waited. Eddie said, "Now, tell me."

"Get one from Winston to Franklin Terrace in Baltimore... get them to route it up from Winston up 158, then on to 29 all way up and then catch US 40 into Baltimore, going east onto Edmonson, onto West Mulberry. Turn right onto North Fremont, turn right onto West Lexington and that'll take them to the pickup alley on the left. Pee Wee will have his sentries on lookout for them and will wave them in."

Eddie now jumped in. "And the comeback route? I've got it lined up so they can park in a closed barn in Northern Virginia in a little crossroads place called The Plains. Curt, here's what I'm thinking. I've done a lot of driving all over that part of the countryside. I'm thinking route them back scenic roads west and then down 15 to The Plains Road, will take them through Middleburg, on down toward The Plains. Turn left off The Plains Road onto Sidehill Farm road. By the way, they'll go to the top of the gravel drive on Sidehill, then will pass a big lake to their right and at the top of the hill, there will be a big, dark brown barn first off the right. They go in there and pull the doors shut behind them, spend the night. Leave in the morning. Get them on 29 and that will take them all the way down through Virginia and into North Carolina to 158 and that will bring them back into Winston."

"Sounds good to me. Go get 'em. I'm on the way back soon."

"On the way now to round up. Come see me in the morning and bring Rise and Kenny and they're new school bus duds. Bus will be delivered Thursday."

"K. Later."

Patty and Mikey were in the conference room laying out and sifting the Reynolds file in anticipation of Alph Baron's visit tomorrow afternoon.

"Hey, y'all, I gotta go out to the Triple A and buy a couple of those flip maps that help get folks from one place to another."

Patty chuckled and said, "Eddie, sometimes you live in a bubble. You've got a Triple A membership. I got it for you years ago and I renew it every year. Your AAA card is in your wallet. What you are going to get is called a Trip-Tik. Got it?"

Eddie blushed that he understood and that once he was back, they'd break the case down into its most direct, simplest elements, the old 3x5 index flash cards approach, and then took his Curt notes on the planned travel and headed out the door. Patty looked at Mikey. "Lord, he can be such a goof!"

Mikey nodded in agreement and added, "And he's the most wonderful, gorgeous goof in the world." And then she stage-coughed in self-teasing deprecation.

Patty rolled her eyes and hack gagged in amusement and smoothly the two went right back to the distillation of tomorrow's instructions to Mr. Baron. And there was no doubt Mr. Baron was going to be instructed, and if he resisted or dissembled in the least, his ass was gonna be taken hard to the woodshed.

Once back at the office, he tossed the Triple A mappings on Patty's desk and joined the ladies in the conference room. He sat with Patty and Mikey and went through their file pull outs of what they thought was important and convincing. It was all good stuff. They had assembled the necessary essence. He asked himself how to bend and break Alph.

Eddie thanked them for their good and concise work, and also noted that Curt and Kenny and Rise would be over in the morning for pre-flight briefing before Alph Baron's arrival. He grabbed the phone beside the big table, looked up Leon's number and dialed. Leon answered, "Leon's. This is Leon. We got it if you want it. What can I do you for?"

"Leon, this is Eddie Terrell. Hope you're good."

"I am indeed. I believe it is you that done sent Mr. Curt Minor to get the little bus I'm finishing up this afternoon. Isn't that right?"

"Yes, sir you are correct. I'm calling to verify that you'll have the bus ready and to us by Thursday."

"Yes, that's right. Is 9:30 in the morning too early? I will bring it to your office."

"That time is just right. I'll be here with the balance of the payment due. Four thousand. I trust cash is acceptable."

Leon laughed. "Yes, that's just right too and that'll do just fine. I think we are agreed. I will see you the day after tomorrow with your new toy. I think you'll like the way she looks and goes."

"I look forward to it. Thank you." Eddie hung up. He was excited now too. It was all pulling together. He gathered himself now, refocusing on tomorrow afternoon's nut cutting.

He sat back in his chair with his arms folded tightly across his chest. He was hugging himself into self-containment. He was thinking intently, his eyes slitted, his brows knitted up. Mikey and Patty watched him. They both had come to know this mood. His hands and fingers then steepled, covering his mouth.

"Three million. No, three and a half million," he said in a whisper. "Yes, three and one-half million." His gaze was focused through the window across from him.

"Excuse me?" asked Patty. "Three and one half million what?"

Eddie was very still and then he shudder-shook himself like a dog coming out of a lake and became very alert, the cloud of vacuity over his face suddenly disappearing.

"That, my lovely ladies, is our demand. Now, may I please have some of those big, index cards, about thirty of them and a large point black Sharpie? I'd like red cards, please."

Mikey said, "That's a pretty big number."

"Well, yes. There's been a pretty big fuck up. I promise you I could make the number much larger and I may well have to if they decide they don't want to swallow soon." Patty brought him the notecards as he dialed his clients.

After an hour or so, the day was winding down. Eddie came out of the conference room with a bunch of the red cards and asked for a manila envelope. He slid them in it and told Patty to go on home, that she'd knocked herself out today, that he appreciated it very much. Patty lit one up and coughed and said, "Thanks, Eddie. Dress code for tomorrow?"

"Glad you asked. As you well know, after all, we are staging a sort of a play tomorrow, aren't we? I want you both very glammed up, not going to a church wedding so much as going to a damn good party after the church wedding. Nicely plunging necklines, shorter skirts, snappy heels, a little extra blush and lipstick and perfume, rather more fitted than baggy or shapeless and so forth. We want him distracted. Y'all play to him in the beginning before I read sternly to him from the Ten Commandments and more. Is that a can do?"

Both ladies grinned. "You bet! Later, kids!" said Patty and then she was gone, her smoke trailing her like the great locomotive she was.

And then Patty turned just as she was going out the door and looked back. "Eddie, I distinctly remember you said some time ago that you had a surprise in this case, something that was gonna blow their and old Alph's socks off and we begged for you to tell us and you said you would once a meet and greet was on. And now the meet and greet is on so, what gives?"

Eddie turned his jaw at her just a twitch and chortled. "What a fine memory you have, Miss Patty."

Mikey said quietly, almost plaintively, "Yes, you did say that. What's the story? Is this one of those 'gotcha' moments I've seen on TV shows? Time to tell us what it is as you said you would." She folded her arms in the manner of all good elementary school teachers who had their prey ensnared and looked at him with a combination of impatience and implore in the mix.

Eddie was silent, nodded his head in confirmation and thought and said, "Yes, you're right. I did make that promise to you both. But now I'm going to have to hold my promise back just a few more hours and I will explain after the timer on the bomb goes off. You will watch in real time the thing go up in his face. In a perverse way, I want to not only watch his reaction. I want to see yours as well."

"Jesus, you can be such a jerk sometimes, don't you know." Patty was frustrated but laughed too.

Mikey, exasperated, pursed her lips and shook her head and asked Patty, "He always like this?"

"Well, I'll put it like this. Not all the time. But when he's playing with loaded dice and they're his loaded dice, he does have a sense of pretty savvy timing that, shall we say, can often add value. Now, goodnight, you two. And don't keep each other up too late. I want both of you fresh, fresh, fresh!" She breezed out the door.

Eddie looked at Mikey. "You had enough for this long day?"

"Yeah, if you have."

"Let's go out for a choke and chew. You up?"

"Sure, where to? You pick."

"How about the Diamond Back. It's good, it's fun, it's near where we live, and it's where Patty spied old Alph Baron, but I doubt he'll be around. Place always has good people watching."

As they drove, Mikey turned to Eddie and asked in a serious voice, "Are you happy with me here? As they say on television, am I meeting or exceeding your expectations?"

"Oh, Lord, honey, yes and yes some more. I'm glad you're here, very glad. And remember, closed track, professional driver, do not attempt this at home."

He winked at her. "Now, are things okay with you and me?"

"Thank you. Yes, I adore you. You are fascinating. Talk about walk on the wild side. I'm glad to be here. I just wanted to take your temperature on that." She sat back and exhaled. "Well, this certainly is one helluva nutty high wire act. That's for sure."

"Oh, don't worry. It'll get crazier. It's the nature of the beast."

"Eddie, please just no trouble now. Please." She was looking straight forward, face frozen golden in the rays of the lowering sun. "Yes, ma'am. No trouble now. I promise. We're gonna smooth it, I promise."

Inside his gut, he grimaced. *Jesus, please God, no trouble now.* The days of fly high or crash and burn were upon them. *Would be a damn shame to fuck it all up now.* So he said to her, "No worries now. I got this." And leaned over and kissed her quick on the cheek.

When they parked at the Diamond Back, he took her in his arms and told her he loved her and that they were on the verge of some pretty good stuff. His determination was front and center.

CHAPTER THIRTY-SIX

LOOK BEFORE YOU LEAP

The Archies

WEDNESDAY MORNING, EDDIE and Mikey woke up and wrestled fiercely and only then straightened themselves up. Eddie chose a simple navy blue power suit and a shimmering navy tie with a simple white handkerchief in his suit's breast pocket. His black, lace-up lawyer kicks glistened high gloss as a black diamond would.

Mikey disappeared into the bathroom and then with her towel wrapped around her, eased coyly into her closet, shutting the door behind her with a quiet click. Eddie was sitting at the bedroom desk, going over his red flash cards and making notes and staring out the window, thinking. And the closet door opened. And out stepped the same beautiful creature he had first seen in Alder way back when. He tried to suppress his happy gasp but instead just let loose with, "Oh, my God! I don't want you to strike him deaf, dumb, and blind! And you just might, damn, you just might!"

Mikey had done the old office garb switcheroo. Cowboy boots to the top of her calves, glove-tight jeans, a turquoise and beaded belt that sealed the center of the hourglass with a silver buckle that signaled hormonal eruption on any male horizon; a gingham shirt tied in a knot at her navel with its sleeves rolled up, all of this made her beautiful chest imploringly taut; her hair up in ringlets and ribbons, one glaringly large silver bracelet on her left wrist. She was all "West" with no false feel at all. And then she giggled and slipped her plain, black-rimmed glasses over her nose and looked up in searing innocence.

"Mr. Terrell, will this be all right?"

"Uh, yes, yes, Mikey, that will be." He paused. "That will be just more than fine. That will be just exactly right, thank you."

"Oh, thank you, Mr. Terrell." She was little-bad-girling him. The thought occurred to him that he would just as soon not leave the house right now. She sensed his warming mood and kept working him.

"Now, Mr. Terrell. You seem to be wrestling with your thoughts. Let's remember that some of our co-workers are coming over to the office this morning and we don't want to be late, now do we?"

He longingly unchained his tumescent libido to regretfully shoo that old friend away. "Yes, Mikey, you are perceptive and also correct. I need to get my big head in its dead center slot. Ah well, so it goes."

As he held the door for her on the way to the car, he drew in some cool air and then some more and it helped staunch the fires. They were no longer a wall of inferno.

She said quietly as she walked before him, his eyes locked onto her swaying undercarriage, "Eddie, I know we've and especially you have a lot going on. Let's get this afternoon behind us, one way or another, and I promise later this evening we can have an exploring party. You can be Lewis. I'll be Clark." She did have her ways. It amused him. She was a sharpshooter all the way.

As they walked into the office, Patty bellowed out smoke and cried, "My God! Holy shit! Y'all look like *GQ* and *Town & Country* come to kill. Jesus, no one better try to touch you. They'll melt, no—burn! Eddie! Eddie you look smooth strong but Mikey, honey, you are the Montana mountains she-wolf! This is just great!"

"Thank you, Patty. You're looking, well, strong, and take no prisoners great too!"

Patty, who was very well proportioned and ample under all circumstances, grinned with pride. She wore black stiletto six-inch heels, a tight, short black skirt, a simple, snug white blouse which was on the cusp of a rupture that precipitously would open the other half of its buttons as might a sling shot and all accompanied jingle jangle jewelry, rings and bracelets, all of which glittered and were meant to be distracting, as if the décolletage alone wasn't enough in that department.

"Thanks, Mikey! This is kind of fun. Jesus, I hope I don't fall on my ass. I wobble in these things something fierce."

To top off her presentation, Patty had brought out her signature party piece, a large gold chain that dipped coyly into the crevasse of her straining bosom. It was a heavy gold chain with a tag that simply read, "BITCH."

Eddie loved it all. He surveyed his crew with admiration and pleasure and said, "It's like this, boys and girls. As the fantastic Reverend Ike used to always say, 'You can't lose with what I use!' Patty, kick those shoes off now. We don't need you crashing before the big show. I will place both of you in your places before Alph arrives. In the meantime, let's get some stuff done before our transport friends arrive. How about let's get Pussy Preacher Blockhouse laid out. I'll watch while y'all do and help where I can."

Patty said, "Good. It'll give me and Mikey a little bit of time to get Wilson/Reynolds/Law Firm packed back up in correct order. Mikey, before you come join me, give old slick here a couple of more car wreck files. Let's keep him busy. Idle hands and all that bullshit."

Mikey went to the file racks and pulled two at random and handed them to Eddie. He went one way. She went the other.

After a while, his office door opened and Mikey smiling beautifully said, "Eddie, they've called and said my car can be picked up Friday afternoon." She handed him a piece of paper with the final figure on it.

"That's great, honey! Looking forward to the acquisition!"

"And also, Curt and Rise and Kenny are here and they look so official!"

"I'll be right out."

She started to close his door, then pushed it back open and smiled at him. "Thank you. Thank you so much, Eddie. You just don't know..."

He waved her away with two thumbs up. "You're welcome and I love doing it. Now, go on. Scoot. I'll be out there in a second."

She blew him a kiss and pulled the door shut.

Eddie sat for a few moments in silence, trying to order his mind which he felt had become a blivet, a two-pound bag with three pounds of shit in it. He knew such was basically futile. The gerbil was running the wheel and the slots were tumbling and it was all going to fall out one way or another.

He surrendered. Then he mumbled, "Oh to hell with it," and marched out into the waiting room.

The three were right there. Curt was the game show host, slow arming the display of the tag team of Rise and Kenny who stood erect and confident next to their ringmaster.

"Check them out, Eddie. They look like pros. Seasoned for the reason!" Eddie easily admired them.

Rise and Kenny were the epitome of school bus drivers. Starched khaki shirts and pants, black Nikes, bus driver's frat hats with the faux leather sheeny plastic visors. They'd even gotten hold of some thick, brown leather Sam Brown belts which lent a martial, serious authority to their mien, and they wore clip-on name tags that read "Senior County School Bus Driver." Curt had given each three ballpoint pens and a small notepad each which peeked over the tops of their breast pocket protectors.

Finally, their parade-straight chests gave way and sagged as they began to giggle and glance at each other in amusement. Eddie clapped as did Patty and Mikey.

Eddie exclaimed, "Y'all just look great! Wonderful execution! Thank you all, especially Curt, for getting this all together. I'll tell you what. If we can pull this deal off, I'm buying the four of us one of those ice cream trucks that plays all those calliope tunes and you two will make us a fortune!" Rise and Kenny beamed.

"Eddie, you think me and baby brother looking good! Thank you! We're ready to go!" Kenny nodded enthusiastically.

Curt said appraisingly, "You know, Eddie. They really are. I reviewed routes and pick up instructions with them. You got those Triple A map guides?"

"Absolutely." Eddie took them from Patty's desk and handed them to Rise.

"Who's driving?"

"We both will."

"Who is the better driver?"

"We both are," they shot back and Eddie chuckled and relented.

"Okay, y'all, the bus will be delivered tomorrow morning at 9:30 a.m. Be here just before then to check it out and take a practice spin in it. Before you go study the map. Follow the designated route to Baltimore, make the pickup alley. Come back the way we have laid out for you, spend the night in the barn in Virginia, and then bring it on straight back here. We don't want y'all out on the roads during the dark hours. You'll have plenty for food and fuel. I know the lady who owns the barn in Virginia. She knows y'all are coming and will be there, but I have told her to leave you be. You'll go down the Plains Road south and then up Sidehill Road and it'll be the first open barn at top of hill on right. It's all in your directions there. Pull in and close the doors. Make sure y'all hit the can at a truck stop before you get there. No wandering out to pee or squat.

"She'll be curious of course. But she's smart and will leave you be. She's a good friend and a fine person and I do not want her able to identify you. She has a great big dog named Barney who is nothing but sweet and only wants to play and get patted. If he comes around, try not to play with him. He's kinda irresistible. Do y'all understand?"

"Yes."

Curt looked at Eddie and said, "Jesus, a big dog. Oh, good." His tone was flat.

"Any questions?"

Rise looked at Kenny who nodded. Rise said, "What happens if we get stopped? Get caught?"

"Name, rank, and serial number only. Give only your name as it appears on your driver's license. Tell them you want a lawyer, that you do not know anything about anything and that you want a lawyer. Sit tight and keep your mouths closed. And that's it. You'll get one phone call. Call me here. And if you don't get me here call my cell. Rise, Kenny, y'all know the drill. Don't forget it now! And Patty, how about you cut a check for 4.K cash? I'll sign it and then you can go down to Wachovia and get it greened. Will need to pay Leon his balance owed."

Eddie continued. "Everybody go home and do their homework. Curt, would you review with them for a while? We'll see y'all in the morning. I'm very, very proud of you all!" The meeting broke up.

Eddie looked at Patty and Mikey and said, "All right, my warrior women. Let's see where we're all going to be sitting when Alph arrives at three. I want to maximize the effects of y'all's luscious pulchritude on his libidinous brain while I read him the indictment. Is Pussy Preacher ready to start review and extraction? Yes, good. We'll start on that next once we've picked our staged places and Patty can join us once she's back from the bank. Y'all come on in here."

Eddie led them into his office. "Our plan is to put him in the box and make his head swivel. Patty, you're to his right. Mikey, to his left. We will all be in here when he arrives. He'll call out a 'hello' or some such and I'll bring him in. Y'all will be seated. Do get up when he comes in. I want him to get a good look at both of you. Shake hands, be gracious, take notes, give him legs and skin. It'll make him crazy. His beady little eyes will be flitting back and forth over you even as he tries not to. This isn't going to take long, I don't think. Everybody got it? Good. Patty bring me a check, please, and Mikey, let's you and me go on in the big conference room." Patty brought Eddie the check. He signed it.

Eddie seated himself at the center of the long side of the conference table. Mikey was at his arm and they began to go through the file and its subparts, one by one, slowly, and methodically. Eddie would scratch out a note now and then. Sometimes he would ask Mikey to make a copy of something or to set something aside on the far corner of the table, such as documents, photographs, trial exhibits, and the like. They would ask each other questions and give answers, all to the effect of putting the strongest, most convincing case together. After thirty minutes or so, Patty returned, handed Eddie the envelope with the cash in it, and joined them in the mutual effort.

At 1:30, Eddie asked, "Anyone hungry? I sure am. How about a lunch break and then wind-down time before Alph gets here."

The girls agreed and the three of them walked down the hill to the Jury Room Cafe which sat across the street from the county courthouse.

At 2:45, they heard the front office door open and Alph's high pitched nervous falsetto ask, "Halloo. Is anyone home?"

Eddie looked his troops over and asked, "Game time?" They smiled and nodded.

He went and got Alph and brought him into the warm and comfortable slaughter pen and then it was on.

Patty and Mikey stood though Eddie had missed their need to ply Alph's mind with longitudinal flesh. Eddie stood corrected, with Patty reintroducing herself, and Eddie introducing Mikey as his newest legal assistant from Montana. They all shook hands. Alph was paying close attention. He eyed Patty closely to see if there was any hint of his Lee Ann moments of a few nights ago. If left to his own devices, he would have pretended it never happened.

"Uh, Patty, I hope you are well. Nice to see you again. And, Miss Mikey, is that right? Now, how did a pretty gal from all the way out in Montana end up here in little old Winston-Salem?"

"Well, Mr. Baron. It's a long story and a short story. Eddie was out in southwest Montana on a vacation. We met, took a liking to one another. Guy accosted me. Eddie beat his ass. He invited me to come back with him. I accepted. He put me to work here. It's hard and interesting and fun. I'm learning a lot. I like it here too a lot."

"Well, if that's the short version, I would love to hear the long one." The hints of assignation gushed and frustrated Alph. The picture of Eddie beating someone's ass was troublesome.

She smiled sweetly. "Well, that's pretty much between me and Eddie, and besides, we really don't have time for that this afternoon, do we?"

Eddie motioned for all to sit and they did, the girls primly balancing their legal pads and pens on their knees. Between Patty's voluptuous bosom and Mikey's hourglass everything, Alph was fighting his focus.

Alph was looking back and forth and trying not to look back and forth. Alph had pieced it together. Eddie and Mikey were an item just like Eddie and Lee Ann had been. He was bailing as fast as he could and it occurred to him that on every front before him, he was in trouble. His world was becoming a sieve. And this was even before Eddie set the table for the afternoon's agenda.

And then Eddie began the liturgy and Alph paid attention. This was straight-up Lawyer Land. This was going to be the whipping he was unsuited for. Alph steeled himself and sat up straight and braced. The President of the North Carolina Bar was getting ready to be flogged. He knew it. Patty and Mikey looked at him in self-warm pleasure and he knew he was castrated before the knife sliced.

"Alph, you know why we are here, right? Oh, would you like something to drink? Coffee, water, a drink of whiskey?"

"Oh, thank you. I'm fine." His little chuckling, that little false giggle had shrunk.

Alph, remarkably out of context, thinking ahead, vaguely wondered what bars he could slide into from here on out with second-string-no-count-whatever serving of cheap booze. The revelation came to him now starkly as it had before subtly for decades. The law and his big desk and prominent letterhead and power and prestige and all the legions who took his call were fine, but none could top liquor and pussy, and now he was going into the desert. This was regrettable but he was frozen now in a vice of salacious beauty and irrefutable evidence against his clients whom he had overpromised and also, he had bullshitted himself into ignorance and danger. In his arrogance, Alph now understood he had run himself into a box canyon. The due bill was arriving. His eyes flinched and he gave an involuntary twitch.

They watched him. They knew.

"Yes, Eddie, I believe I know why I'm here."

"Good. Alph, now tell me how this is all going to end and let me add, end quickly for if it does not, there is going to be hell to pay and the payment that will be made will not be coming from our end." Eddie spoke softly, directly, hypnotically.

Patty was steel-eyed and comfortable. Mikey involuntarily reached down and slowly stroked her crossed leg and did so intentionally. She realized that it was her job to help make this poor, smart but stupid, overmatched man go into a place where he could not escape. She'd done it before, just this time it involved fine suits and ties and more money than she could picture. The South really was a weirdly fascinating place and she already knew she was on the right side. Patty winked at her. Alph was blind but still could see. Eddie leaned forward and looked straight at Alph.

"Now, Alph. What is your proposal to resolve this disaster? I am certain you have a solution in mind and have conferred at length with your clients and have explained the case in specific detail with them."

"Eddie, I think we can work this out. This, of course, is an unfortunate thing. No one wanted this to happen."

Alph tailed off lamely. He had nothing with which to play for time or space to maneuver.

"Alph, you and I know that we live in an imperfect world where the best and yet so flawed manner of addressing a problem like this and making things right is with the poor substitute of money. This is an unfortunate thing and, of course, no one wanted this to happen but it did. An attractive and promising young life has been negligently snuffed out and either you have brought me an acceptable number today or the suit against your law firm clients will be filed on Monday at noon and the local press will have it soon thereafter. You and I both understand this, don't we?"

Alph nodded.

"You have not, after all this time, reported this to their liability carrier, have you?"

Alph took the loaded inquiry straight on. "No, Eddie, we have not. We felt that this could be worked out between the parties on a gentlemanly and reasonable basis."

Eddie shook his head back and forth very slowly as he stared a hole into his target.

"I'm afraid that the Emily Post Miss Manners Good Old Boys Club approach is not going to be helpful here. We are going to find the strike price here pretty soon or the gloves are going to come off. So, now, what is your authority?"

Alph paused, then said, "I am authorized to tell you that my clients offer one million dollars to resolve this matter, due and payable in three months."

Eddie stared at him. Patty and Mikey glanced at each other. They all sat very still.

"Alph, that's not an unreasonable start but we're not here to bargain today. We are here to have this case settled within twenty-four hours or we are heading straight to the courthouse to file. Now, here's what has to happen and be agreed to real quick by the end of business tomorrow. Five p.m. sharp. I will explain to you in due course. This will not take long, so please listen carefully."

Alph nodded slightly and waited.

"Our demand and the only demand on this you will ever get from me is three-and-one-half-million dollars. And I'm going to now walk you through it and will give you what you need to convince your people to do, as y'all so often say, the right thing."

"Eddie, that's pretty outlandish," Alph whined.

"No, it could be a whole lot worse and I'm certain that if this case ends up in front of a jury, once they've digested it, they will blow your doors off. And let me promise you, if we are not done by 5 p.m. tomorrow, there will be no further discussions about settlement. None. I'm going to give you a baker's dozen of reasons, plus one bonus reason why this is to be over in short order. Again, please listen carefully."

Patty and Mikey knew the bonus reason was the nuclear mystery bomb they'd been waiting on. They were excited.

Alph realized the broadside was beginning and he sat frozen in apprehensive anticipation. Eddie pulled out his stack of red file cards and began his planned litany.

"First, Reynolds was a high value, target defendant and because of y'all's massive screw up, you are now an even higher value, target defendant. You know how the public generally feels about lawyers. They don't like them. You know all that from the gazillion surveys y'all look at down at the state bar offices all the time.

Second, Zach will be portrayed accurately as an immature, clownish, loosey goosey, irresponsible might-as-well-be-a-kid kinda guy. You've known him and his family your entire life. At best a goofball, at worse dangerous with his impetuosity. Thirdly, easy to say, Zach just was not and never was going to be the sharpest knife in the drawer."

Eddie snapped each card to the desk's surface as might a Vegas dealer.

"Fourth, he liked being the Pied Piper. Hell, all his play pals were mostly neighborhood kids, mostly boys. Pretty creepy, don't you think? And you know the rest of the story of the Pied Piper, don't you, Alph? It's not pretty either."

Alph shook his head in the negative. "Tell me, please."

Eddie thought that was a good sign. Alph was thinking and learning.

"The Pied Piper of Hamlin was hired by the little village to drive all the rats out. A price was agreed upon. The Pied Piper did his job. The villagers declined to pay him. So the Pied Piper of Hamlin, in revenge for the villagers welching on the deal, lured all of the children out of the village, all of them, and those children were never seen again. Many think the Pied Piper was a child molester and serial killer. So there you have that." Alph winced again.

"Fifth, we know from our far extensive investigations, that while Zach was earlier known to be a noteworthy stunt pilot, we know he had not been out at Smith Reynolds to practice in over a year. We got a sneak peek look at the airport's log flight books. He was very rusty and stale.

"Sixth, at the crash site, he was found by the FAA to have been in the left-hand seat, the pilot's seat. That eliminates any question or speculation that somewhere along the short way of the flight, he let one of the boys take the controls. The boys were guest passengers. You know the law.

"Seventh, his pilot's license had expired more than a year before and he had not made any effort to renew it. Now we are getting into areas that would call for jury charges on gross negligence and an award of punitive damages.

"Eighth, we know he had a bad back—probably why he had not practiced or renewed—and at autopsy was found to have significant opioids in his system. We also know that he took them regularly and that his prescription was current and active. Flying while doped up is again punitive damages land."

Alph Baron began to sag little by little. This was wearing on him. Mikey stretched and arched her back. Patty did pretty much the same. Alph just wanted to look at them. He couldn't shake his libido, although his self-doubts were closing in on it. Eddie noticed this with pleasure and reined him back to attention.

"Stay with me, Alph. I'm almost done. Ninth, there is no question that lawyer Whiteside was trolling for the case under the guise of being a helpful and sympathetic neighbor and friend. And his handling of it within his offices really does smack of deceit and greed. Hide the ball until he gets to be king. How stupid. Also calls into question how the firm kept track of cases and ongoing work. Smacks hard of sloppy and half-ass, doesn't it? This sort of laissez-faire practice would not be tolerated at your shop, now would it? No need to answer that. We all know the answer.

"Tenth, I've just handed you the letter from my expert. Read it. And now you have already seen the opinion letter from our expert down in Charlotte. It's very powerful. He nails your people on their negligence, labels it 'blatant' among other things and as for the case within the case, says there is no doubt that had the claim proceeded against Zach's estate in a procedurally proper and timely fashion, he has no doubt that the plaintiffs would have prevailed. He doesn't say they would 'most probably prevail.' He says he is certain they would recover.

"You know the guy. He's as smart an aviation disaster lawyer as there is around, is regarded by all as a real gentleman and fine, organized witness; he works both sides of the street and is recognized for his sagacity, veracity, and impressive knowledge of the law. And when we get to the courthouse, you all will have no expert witness that can even lick spittle his boots. At best, y'all will have to hire a whore whom I look forward to undressing piece by piece, if you will.

"Eleventh, on every level, the conduct of Zach Reynolds and of your law firm clients scream out recklessness and failure of oversight and there will be charges for gross negligence and punitive damages. Now, there is no doubt."

Eddie took a deep breath. "Now, just two, yes two cards to go."

Alph pulled out a handkerchief and mopped his forehead and rustled about a little. He was mentally in the pit and he knew there was no way out.

"Number Twelve. The failure to notify their liability carrier will, at best which is improbable, means that once they are called in, any defense will be tendered under seriously restricted reservations of rights. More likely, they will refuse to defend on obvious grounds of failure to timely notify. All the partners are targets and are vulnerable. All will be named. All of this will be part of evidentiary presentations at various stages along the way. And by the way, your complicity in the little scheme of trying to work all this out 'on the side' could very well pose some ethical dilemmas, problems, and punishments for you if anyone were to make a complaint to the state bar and as you well know, a good lawyer is required to relay all options to clients."

Alph Baron felt ill. His repartee of banter and false good humor had evaporated.

"Eddie, I think I've got it. Really. Can we talk a little bit?"

"No, I really don't think you do, not yet anyway, but you will soon. Of that I'm very sure. Remember, I said a baker's dozen, the bonus card, if you will, so now I will finish. Number Thirteen, you and I both know that if this thing gets public, the adverse publicity will in all likelihood destroy the law firm, taint every member of it, ruin many careers of both the young and the old and as noted above, your involvement is going to blow back on you hot and hard."

Alph groaned. "I know. I know."

"Now, I promised you a bonus card. Here it is." Patty and Mikey leaned forward aggressively, all pretense of just standing by long gone.

"Alph, did you know that when Whiteside was in law school at Wake Forest, he was on the Law Review?"

"No, I didn't know that."

"Well he was. And he wrote an article that the law review published. I'll bet you can guess what the topic he wrote on was."

Alph paused and pondered. He knew the pin was out of the grenade and he was really trying to think hard. And then it came to him. He blurted out, “Claims against decedent’s estates in North Carolina?”

Eddie nodded and simply said, “Bingo. ”

“Oh, Jesus, Joseph, and Mary. Christ Almighty. You’re kidding, right?” He knew Eddie was not, but he was in the throes of the involuntary last flail for hope.

“No, I’m not kidding. And interestingly in the article, he not only gets the six months statute of limitation correct but he warns his readers to be very aware of it as it is very different than the so-called regular two-year limitation. Here, I have a copy for you with the cover sheet, dates, volume, and all. And the volume is being held at the checkout desk at the library with your name on it, if you are so inclined to go down the street and do some reading with the very book in your hands, though I’d bet your clients have the actual volume over at their place as well.”

Alph was a blown tire. He took off his glasses, rubbed his face with both hands, blinked repeatedly, looked about disoriented. He had even lost interest in the pretty ladies. And then he shook his head, cleared it, and snapped to.

“Okay, Eddie, okay. Oh, shit. I understand. I’m going to recommend the number. If they go for it, they’ll need time. I’m worried that their old, prideful selves will buck at the number. What would you do to get them to go along?”

“Thank you, Alph.” Eddie’s tone was gentle. “Here’s what I think would be helpful. I’m going to give you this set of red note cards and this law review article. You can use one of our phones. Hell, use this one right here. Call their office now and tell Webster that you have just met with me and you need to have an all hands-on deck meeting with all the partners right now, that time is of the essence. Get right on over there and go through each of these things just as I have with you. We are happy to give them time. All agreements will be totally confidential and must all contain the personal guarantees of the firm and its partners. They’ve got the money. Some can come out of the firm; some can come out of the partners’ pockets. They got plenty of assets. They’ve been around a long time. They’ve piled plenty up.

“The first million has to be paid within one month, the next million within three months, the last one and a half within six months. I’m going to charge a fee of five-hundred thousand and pay whatever expenses there are from the fee. That’s about a 14-percent rate. My clients will receive three million clear. I'm doing this as another reason to illustrate to your people that I'm not hunting the usual fat fee that rolls off a fat case like this. I'm doing it this way because your people really fucked up and my people should be properly rewarded. And Alph, let's not dress this up. You're a lot older, lot wiser than me. I've danced with you a few times and plenty also too with the boys and girls over at your shop. I truly respect you and always tried to give you and your crowd my best, if only to make me better and to earn y'all's respect.

"Now, not only are your clients in deep shit, you're up on the edge of the ledge too. I hope you can get this done so your ass gets out of the vise too. Alph, this needs to get done. You've been a fine, effective, brilliant advocate over the years. Go do it again, please. I do not, repeat, do not want to take everything down, you, them, everything, but if they don't come along, then as they say, cry havoc and loose the dogs of war. Please help us all. Please." Eddie was a little surprised by his fervency.

Alph was stunned by the sincerity of emotion from Eddie.

Mikey was in awe of her man. Patty knew that Eddie just had beaten the dog and now was patting it gently, evoking its gratitude.

"Eddie, how about I go make the call privately to Webster from another phone in here so we can talk and get the ball rolling. May I, please?"

"Of course. Mikey, please take Mr. Baron to the little corner office off the big conference room. Please close the door once he's in. Alph, come back and see me please before you go."

Alph nodded and followed Mikey. The small pleasure of watching her high hatted ass helped a little. His little head was still alive. His big head was on fire with dread.

Patty whistled. "Well, I've seen a lot over these years but I'll have to admit, that was quite a show. If it had been a prize fight, it would have been stopped on a TKO about two thirds of the way through. You broke him. And good. In half, no, into pieces. To pick him up would take a broom and a dustpan. Jesus! Do you think he can sell it to that set-in-their-ways bunch of old buzzards?"

"Well, thanks, it was fun. I think Alph will rise to the occasion, stiffen his spine, and go over there and get it done. Remember, his ass is on the line if he doesn't. As is their entire law firm. And ruination from that far on high is simply not acceptable to a fellow like Alph. Lot of 'em at this stage of their careers would just say 'fuck it,' take a swipe at it, see what happens and if it fails, it fails. Not Alph. He has big ego, big pride, big skills, and miles to go. I say he gets it done."

"Okay. What's next?"

"Let's wait on Alph and Mikey to get back, which shouldn't be too long. Then we'll reinforce the marching orders. And then it's on to other things."

They sat quietly waiting now, and in a few minutes, Alph walked back in with Mikey. "Did you get your meeting, Alph?"

"I did, Eddie. I did."

"All hands on deck?"

"Webster says they'll all be there."

"Good. Alph, I meant every word I earlier said. The deal has to be sealed by 5 p.m. tomorrow. You can stop back by here. Just call me first. I'll be here. I'll need a brief Memorandum of Agreement signed off on by the partners. It won't take long to get everything, releases, etc., drafted and signed off on. And I strongly suggest you go gentle with Whiteside."

"I will. I understand. I need to be going now. Wish me luck. Ladies, I must admit it was very nice to have seen you." There was a wry smile on Alph Baron's face. He had perked up a bit.

Patty and Mikey nodded kindly in his direction.

"Of course. Bring us all good news please. Good luck!"

And Alph Baron went out to do Eddie Terrell's bidding.

It was about 4 o'clock, Eddie asked, "What y'all want to do? I'm kinda tired. Leon's bringing the bus tomorrow." He trailed off in wandering thought.

Patty said, "With Pussy Preacher on deck for next Wednesday, we got plenty of time to tune up for that mediation. Let's get Tom Wills, the mediator, a quick list. None better. We can get the memo together tomorrow after the bus arrives. I vote that we knock it off for today. It's been long and time to be hopeful."

"I agree. Let's shut it down and all go over to Shober's and have a few. I'm buying. But first, Patty, how about you call our clients in Pussy Preacher and tell 'em we want 'em with us for the proceedings next Wednesday? Tell them you'll have their plane tickets for them to pick up if they need them on Monday—they may want to drive—but whatever, and also, we'll line up a place for them to stay one of two nights in Charleston. They need to all be there by late Tuesday afternoon. We will all need to go to dinner and do last tune-ups Tuesday night. Book them all reservations, including two more for us, at The Mills House. It's got a good bar, The Best Friend, it's dark and quiet and the restaurant is perfectly fine. Plus, it's within walking distance of Tom Wills' office."

Patty asked, "All three of us going, not just you and Mikey?"

"Hell, yes, all three of us are going. Duh!"

"So how we getting there? Drive down Tuesday morning?"

"Nope. Get Atlantic Aero over in Greensboro on the phone. We want a small jet, two pilots. They can take us into the Charleston FBO, we'll get a cab to hotel, they'll go back wherever and be good to go next day when we call. Flight ain't long either way. Just make sure that we make enough allowance for the Wednesday afternoon hold and go."

Mikey tilted her head, eyes wide. "Jesus, Eddie. Isn't that going to be a small fortune?"

He grinned a weary grin. "Yup, but let's emphasize 'small.' We're after a much bigger number than the expense of the flight. Plus, when the folks on the other side ask, as they surely will, 'how'd y'all get here?' the 'modest' answer will be a hard and confirmatory signal in a very real way what they already know or at least ought to know. We got heavy resources, we don't shit around, and we will come after them hard if they don't get this done promptly."

Patty nodded as she took notes on her steno pad and said, "I got it. Will make some calls. Y'all go on. I'll get this done right now and then be over to meet you. I need my car anyway."

"Fair deal. See you there."

CHAPTER THIRTY-SEVEN

I GET THE JOB DONE

Chill Bump

THURSDAY MORNING ARRIVED with all six team members, three white, three black, at the office by 8:30 a.m. They drank coffee and smoked and chatted and checked their watches constantly, nervously. Patty had brought a box of a dozen simple glazed Krispy Kremes. This delighted Mikey and she offered that such was a good omen.

And at 9:30, they all stood on the porch watching the little school bus turn off of Cherry Street and move smoothly into the back of the firm's parking lot, gleaming with its new paint job and signage. It looked very official. It pulled up and parked next to the big barn-like garage at the far back end of the parking lot. Its front fan doors opened and out bounded Leon. It was obvious he was pleased with his work.

"How do you think she looks?" He beamed as might a proud parent. He already knew the answer.

"Damn good, Leon. Damn good! Thank you!" Eddie happily shook his hand and handed him an envelope with the balance enclosed. Curt stood a few steps back and then circled the bus, looking at this and that, inspecting, a smile blossoming on his face. A rare expression.

"Leon, you have done yourself proud. This is one chill machine! Nice work!" He patted him on the back. Kenny and Rise and Mikey and Patty just watched and smiled.

A small car driven by one of Leon's mechanics pulled in. Leon waved at the fellow and said he'd be right there.

"Well, folks, my ride has come to take me back to work." He held up his fat envelope.

They all laughed and Leon was zipped away. Leon was one of the good crooks. The group circled the little bus a few more times, pointing out to one another the extra touches here and there that Leon and his boys had applied to help lift its regularity of being. The lettering and signage were precise and crisp. Its swing gate was government issue as was its caution placards. Its lights were consistent with current usage. And it carried a State of Virginia Government permanent license tag that was a knockoff but a very fine thing. Leon was no fool. He could have lifted one but instead he did no such thing. His machine shop was as good as the tag shop at Central Prison down in Raleigh and he, good magician that he was, created one from oblivion with no heartburn for anyone.

"What now, Eddie?" asked Rise.

"How about this? Rise, you and Kenny hop in and crank her up and take her for a test drive. Both of you can drive a stick, right?" They nodded their assent. "Curt will come with you as your backseat driver. Get you used to it. See you in forty-five minutes or so."

Patty, Mikey, and Eddie went back in the office and Eddie said, "Okay, we're waiting to hear from Alph. It's distracting enough but I'm thinking positive and hope y'all are too. I don't expect to hear from him until at least mid-afternoon. Let's put time in now on Pussy Preacher. They'll be back in a little bit. So later, grab some lunch and then back to P-squared.

The ladies went to the conference room and continued their dissection of the file, while Eddie went into his office and fooled around, reading case reports and newspapers. He was just killing time, building himself up for the two main events that were within hours of consuming his thinking.

After a while, the bus rolled back in and Rise was at the wheel. Eddie went out and opened the shed doors. Rise swung wide in an elegant sweeping curve and deftly slotted the bus in the open space. He told them to report for duty at 6:30 tomorrow morning.

Returning to the office, Mikey had had the receiver to her ear and had said nothing. She just listened, nodding her head. Finally, she spoke. "Yes, Mr. Baron. Eddie is on his way to his office to take your call."

Everyone's eyes got wide and big. It was barely past noon.

He walked into his office and shut the door. He exhaled fully, sat down at his desk, and picked up the phone.

"Alph, to what do I owe the privilege of this call?" His accompanying laugh was genuine, grim, and ironic.

"Well, Eddie, the task you gave me is akin to wrestling a family of alligators to the ground and extracting all of their teeth with a hammer and a screwdriver while they writhe and fight. Not exactly easy." Alph was then silent save for his nervously giggled high falsetto.

"Go on." Eddie's voice was flat.

"Well, I tried and tried and tried, but the haters hate my guts and they have fired me."

"Which means what? That you have not accomplished your task, that your mission has failed? Jesus! I'm sorry, Alph. I really am. We will prepare the suit and file it first thing Monday morning. Let them know, though, now you have already been kicked to the curb, they can expect the sheriff to be coming around mid-morning to effect service. And promise them I am going to name every damn one of them. Bunch of damn arrogant fools. I expect this thing is going to get radioactive and, as you know, you're going to get sucked into the quicksand. Damn, I'm sorry for you. Sorry for my clients and sorry for me too. Was so hoping for so many reasons we could get this mess cleaned up quietly. No reason not to be honest about it."

Eddie's voice tailed off and he sighed deeply. Alph giggled again.

Eddie cocked his head inquisitively, "Alph, I know you laugh a lot but this doesn't seem like the time or place for it." Eddie was beginning to steam.

"I'm sorry, Eddie. You know it's my nervous habit. In good times and bad ones too. I apologize. You're right."

"Well, I guess we haven't got anything else to talk about. I wish you well but this is going to be a rough ride. You know that, don't you?"

"Yes, I do. I really do. And I appreciate your expressed sentiment. But there is one more thing I need to tell you."

"What's that?"

"Yes, they did fire me and also said they would not pay me one red cent, that my billed hours were worthless as far as they were concerned."

"Well, I'm sorry to hear that too. And I know you tried hard. Fair to say, I appreciate that."

"Yes, they are going to fuck me over, but I'm a big boy and will take it like a man."

Eddie said, "Good luck on that too. Well, goodbye, Alph."

"Not quite yet, Eddie. While they've fired me and will fuck me on my fees, they have agreed to your demand. All of it."

"Say again?"

"They will meet your stated terms on the time schedule you have laid out. You win." Alph giggled again.

"No shit? I mean, the way you started just now had me going into the biggest pig shit ditch I could imagine. You really got me, Alph. Damn! Now, you are for real, right? They're going to do the deal, right?" Eddie was nervous, agitated. Alph had played him perfectly. Eddie was instantly exhausted.

"Yes, they sure are. I have a piece of paper with all of their signatures on it, laying it all out. I want to bring you the original and, of course, I have just enough extra copies. And I'll tell you this too. I don't mind getting fired and getting stiffed on my fees. I was terrified by this thing. I'd gotten in way too deep. I had been foolish. I'm glad this is going to be over soon. Lord, let this cup pass from my lips! I'm going to make a full, albeit cleaned up, confession to my partners too once all this dust settles. Would you mind if I came over to give you the document and the signatures? I can be there in ten minutes."

"Oh, of course, sure. That would be fine. Thank you, Alph. Hell, we all fly too close to the sun sometimes. It's going to be okay. I'll see you soon. Oh, Alph, one more question, well, a sort of a jumbled few. What was it like, giving them the demand and the reasons behind it?"

"It was rough, real rough. Lot of anger, lot of sadness too. I'll tell you in detail once I get over there, fair enough? I'm on my way."

Eddie hung up. He sat there. He was shaking inside. He shuddered involuntarily. He needed to compose himself. He took a few minutes and did so. He opened his door and went out to the girls.

He slowly walked out into their workspace, his lips pursed, his brow furrowed. They looked at him intently.

"Well?" Patty asked. Mikey was scanning him, trying to divine the message received on his face.

He moved slowly and stood in between their two desks.

He looked down in well-feigned despair. He steepled his hands under his chin, his eyes cast down.

Patty snorted, "Well, fuck him and fuck them. Let's nuke their asses! This will not be a complaint that's tough to draw up and fucking fast at that!" She was mulish, annoyed, daring.

Mikey kept looking at Eddie, studying him, slowly rotating her head back in forth so as to not miss something.

She wasn't convinced that there had been a systems failure. She balanced on the tightrope of doubt and surety.

"Hang on, Patty. Hang on. I think he's gaming us. So, Eddie, spit it out. What's the story? For real now..."

Eddie stood silent, holding the beat of his doubtful face just a little longer.

He cleared his throat and then spoke in a low, mournful voice.

"Well, I'm sorry to report that...I have disappointed you. That it has come to this."

He paused. They looked. This wasn't Eddie. They could smell it coming. And he did not let them down. Suddenly, his bleak mask of a face turned devilishly, delightfully happy and he leapt into the air and clicked his heels.

"I'm just disappointed that I couldn't fake y'all out any longer! They took the whole deal. They swallowed it all, hook, line, and sinker! Our poor clients are gonna get a pile which will help some and we're gonna get a plenty nice lick and a whole bunch of it! Alph Baron is on his way over here in a few minutes with the sign offs. Y'all, please, please make over him big time. He deserves some serious adoration. I expect he did some heavy, heavy lifting over there. And I think y'all were a big part of his sales push. He wanted to save his ass, theirs too, and he wanted to impress y'all, to show y'all he could still play, still sell on a big-time stage. I'm convinced of it. I'm proud of y'all, very proud of you both! I gave him the reasons, y'all gave him the motivation! There will be serious bonuses as we count it up. I promise!"

Patty lit one up and leaned back and laughed big as a volcano of silver smoke tsunamied out of her mouth and nostrils.

"Eddie, you are just a shit-eating, rotten, fucking up, goof ball son of a bitch. But I love you for reasons unbeknownst to me, to God, and to the beyond. Jesus, it's all a big, crazy circus here. How in the hell did I sign onto this clown car parade where everyone gets an Oscar while their nerves are being hard skinned with a dull knife? Jesus! By the way, Mikey, good call on this rat's ass SOB!" She pointed at Eddie.

Mikey just smiled. "Why, thank you, Patty. I think I'm beginning to read him a little better and a little better each day. Eddie, I'll deal with you later." She gave him a come hither look that clearly showed cards coming off the bottom of the deck.

"I surrender. I am complicit. Indeed, I surrender to you both."

He was happy. And he had more ideas too.

"Let me go back to my office and unwad my panties and wait a few more minutes till Mr. Alph Baron gets here. Before y'all bring him to me, please do some serious goo-goo juju on his deserving ass. Over and out. That is all."

And he turned and started toward his office as Patty hard laughed again. Directly, Mr. Alph Baron opened the front door of the office and called a hesitating "hallo."

Patty and Mikey instantly came for him, wreathed in comely smiles and suggestive curves.

Mikey asked, "Mr. Baron, I'll take you back to Eddie's office now. Might I get you something to drink?"

"Oh, thank you very much but I'm going to save that pleasure for a little later in the day. I'm ready whenever you are."

"Yes, I understand. Right this way, please."

Eddie stood and came around his desk and embraced Alph.

"First, here is the original sign off and two extra copies." He handed them across the desk.

Eddie took them and took his time reading them over. Alph understood. It was quiet.

Eddie looked up. "Thank you, Alph Baron. Well and precisely done."

Alph replied, "Eddie, that's the strongest case for legal malpractice I have ever seen. It would never have gotten done were it not for the way the facts lined up for you and the way you layered them in. Like a guy mortaring a wall. Jesus! Those little red flash cards were poison to them, especially that damn law review article. Talk about a noose of their own making!

"Lemme tell you how it went down. One look at them when I walked in told me this was going to be rough sledding at best and a bone dry corncob up my ass at worse. They all knew why they had been summoned and they were not happy. They were sad, scared, angry, wrought up. Real restless. Old man Webster knew there was point of the pencil trouble but in his highed-up dignity and snoot didn't help me a bit. I guess when you've been fancy that long, it's about impossible to get off your high horse. Obviously, I almost got there myself. Hell, barely dodged that bullet.

"Whiteside sat there like a dead man, his face pale and still, staring off into what obviously was a painful place. Fair to say, none of the others looked anything but hateful. But, that's another big part of why we were able to get home."

"Why's that?"

"They knew by then there had been a massive screw-up. The younger ones got it long before the old ostriches. They didn't want to be skinned early on in their careers and they let the old farts know it too. The red card litany of pressures really marched it into line. I walked through it all with them. One by one by one, drip, drip, drip. There were a few questions but not many. About autopsy results, lab tests, our expert lawyer from Charlotte, the FAA report. That sort of stuff. Terse. Short. When I got to the law review article, there was an audible gasp from some. Not all, but some. You see, the kids knew the law. They didn't know about the article. Lot of Demon Deacons in that crowd. The older ones hadn't given it a thought in years. Collectively, it bit a hole in all their asses bigger than all their asses."

"What was next?"

"I told them too it might all work out if they made the deal. I told them if they did not make the deal, they would all be sued and served first thing Monday morning. I told them that under all of the attendant circumstances, I recommended they make the deal. I again told them none of this was negotiable, to not even think about it much less propose something else. I told them once I left the room so they could discuss, I'd be back in once an hour had passed or until they called me back in.

I told them again in no uncertain terms that the demand was not negotiable. I told them if they rejected the deal, it would be in the press quickly, that there would be a trial with no further discussion or negotiation and that the punitive damages alone could blow them all the kingdom come. I told them it would be the biggest courthouse spectacle in the history of Forsyth County. I told them that there was no wiggle room or escape hatch. I told them I had to bring you an answer by 5:00 p.m. today. I told them I was sorry but there it is. I asked for questions. There were none.

"Then Whiteside stood up. Very formally. Broken. It was heart-wrenching. He offered his resignation. Said he asked respectfully that they accept it."

"Oh, damn, what happened? Jesus!"

"I responded immediately and forcefully. I stood up. I did tell them at that point and with strong emphasis that you had specifically asked that Whiteside not be made a scapegoat, that this was a firm problem, that Whiteside had given them his good works, his lawyer guts for years and years and this was a mistake, not a life sentence and could be rectified, as best could be, by proper payment of good faith money, that there but for whatever go all of us and told them again, look at me, I'm your lawyer and I have not only failed, I have sinned too. Whiteside just sat down and resumed his dead man stare. The rest were blank, like zombies.

"Anyway, there was nothing more to be said so I went to the far front of their offices, way away from that conference room. I knew there would be raised voices and bickering and caterwauling, and I just didn't want to hear it. It was upsetting enough as it was. I just sat and stared out the window. After about twenty minutes, Webster came and sat down next to me. He said, 'Alph Baron. You have a deal. We understand the gravity of the situation and despite the fact that we abhor all of it, we will comply as to what is instructed. Here is a sign off sheet memorializing all of it. Along with some extra copies of it. It's signed by all partners, including Whiteside. Obviously, this is especially difficult for him. May we shake hands on this, please? I've got some comforting to do back in there.'

"And we shook hands and as he went to go, he turned and said, 'Oh, Alph Baron. We are also in agreement with you that you have not served our interests very well and so, we are discharging you as of right this moment. We are disinclined to pay any of your fees. I trust you understand.'

"I told him I did and that I appreciated his directness and candor and wished him well in calming the roiled waters that awaited him. And I left, went to my office, called you, and here I am."

"Christ. Fuck. This is tough. God knows I love the money, but Alph, this is a ball buster."

"God knows we love the civility of the courts, we really do, but things like this come up from time to time and they are very difficult, very hard. Crushing. I know it. I hate this one for so many reasons, I can't begin to count. It's too damn early for a drink but I sure want a stiff one now."

"Alph, will you do this for me? I know it's a little crazy but in a few minutes, would you go back over to their shop and tell them we will accept their acceptance of the deal as long as it is promised that Whiteside is retained by the firm until his chosen retirement. All of this is confidential. There's no reason to have a self-inflicted tar and feathering run amok with his partners complicit in the torture. Pull Webster aside. This is a public service sort of thing. Tell him no hard feelings but we need him to sell this to his people. This is the compassionate thing to do. Then come back and see me one more time today. I have a couple of ideas that might appeal to you. I want to discuss them with you."

"Webster's an old ramrod but he's still got a heart. He showed it at the finish line. I'm on my way. I'll be back in twenty minutes."

Eddie sat very still. Mikey came to his door and asked, "Everything all right?"

"Yes, I'm pretty sure we're good to go. There is just one loose end that Alph is going to tie up. He'll be back shortly."

An hour later Alph returned with the news that Whiteside was back with the firm. Eddie asked them all to sit down in the conference room.

"Alph, again, thank you for all your help here. It occurs to me that even as you have been discharged by Mr. Webster's outfit, there are substantial and important settlement documents and releases and guarantees and confidentiality agreements that need to be drafted and put into place to finish the total underpinnings of the case. Candidly, we are not very good at all with that kind of stuff and almost always depend on the defense to put the drafts and so forth together. Would you be so kind as to put all that together for us? I am happy to compensate you at your usual hourly rate and I see no conflicts of interest. As we raced toward the end of the line everyone at the end was pulling on the same oar. And you can schedule with the ladies here when you'd like to work on it. No need, I think, to let your old outfit know you are over here doing scrivener's work. This is all confidential as far as we are concerned. So, what do you say? I hope it's a 'yes.'"

"Eddie, I am deeply complimented and accept your kind offer. I am happy to help get these materials together for you."

"Thank you. That's great! We have a couple of comfortable chairs and would enjoy your company from time to time." Eddie winked at the girls. They understood and smiled knowingly back at him.

"Why, Eddie, thank you so much. I do think that's a good idea. Be a lot less telephoning and back and forthing. Plus, this sure seems to be a fun and interesting place to get some work done. I'd like that. Yes." He happily emphasized his "yes."

Patty drolled out, "Mr. Baron, you don't know the half of it." They all laughed.

"All right, folks, I need to call our client and share the rewarding news that we settled their case for three-million dollars and won't be going to court for a trial." In his office, Eddie sat still for a few minutes before placing the call to Mrs. Wilson. He thought to himself, *How sad. How damned sad. We've helped get them a damn big pile of money, the green poultice, what the high and mighty insurance companies and arrogant defense lawyers call it. And still, it's not over. It'll never be over. There will always be a giant, aching hole in their hearts, for the rest of their lives. What was it Faulkner said? "The past is never dead. It's not even past." How inadequate we all are.*

CHAPTER THIRTY-EIGHT

LET'S GO

Def Leppard

THE EARLY MORNING came even earlier. It was impossible for any of them to sleep. All had lain fitfully awake that dark night, each in their own fashion.

Eddie was still, his eyes cast toward the ceiling, seeing nothing, sensing everything. Mikey was curled up in the crook of his side. She would ask if he was okay. Eddie would tell her he was. He wasn't sure. He just hugged her to him.

Patty stayed up late and paced and smoked and drank a few big belts and then restlessly tried to no avail to get in her bed and make that create the salve of sleep. It did not.

Rise wrestled with what all this was going to be like. Her imagination fluttered and flew all over the place and her great bulk would heave this way and that as the different scenarios played across her eyes' stage.

Curt never belied a conscious doubt in his Spartan rooms, but all night long he pondered if he had done enough, instructed, and taught enough, ingrained in his rookie troop what was needed to be done to pull this off. Always steely organized, he made to-do and contact lists for himself as the dawn came on.

Kenny was simply excited as the little kid would be the night before Christmas. He was ready to go. He wasn't worried, only apprehensive. Could he address his responsibilities and help Rise and bring the little bus on home safe and sound? The legal niceties never crossed his mind. He wanted to warrant their respect. He craved their approval.

And then, it was a pretty Friday morning. They all gathered, and the little bus was backed out of the building. Rise and Kenny looked very sharp, very professional.

Patty and Mikey looked on with a mixture of wonder and concern. It was impossible not to worry. Eddie asked, "Do y'all have all your directions, guides, enough money, locker keys?"

Curt replied, "Check to all. We went over everything again just an hour ago before we came over here. They're good to go. I'm proud of them."

Rise looked at her toes as Kenny grinned. They all shook hands.

Eddie said with a big smile, "Okay, girls and boys, then let's light this candle! Rise, y'all please call me once you've got matters in hand and are on the way to Virginia. For God's sake, please don't make us worry. Should be about four o'clock or so. I'll be here next to a phone all the way until y'all are back."

Rise said, "You got it. How about I take the first shift?"

"Good by me," replied Kenny. They clambered aboard, two big people making the steps up quiver, the bus cranked life. They shifted her to go, waved, and went out the parking lot and down the street to the interstate on-ramp.

As they disappeared around the corner, they just looked at their watches. Eddie and Curt shook hands again and nodded to one another. Curt drove away.

Eddie said, "Patty, please hold down the fort. I want to take Mikey to get her car. We'll be back in a little while. How about you please call Meyer Richie out at the BMW place and tell him we are on the way?"

Eddie took Mikey's hand. "Come on, kid. First I've gotta make a quick call so please wait here and then it's time for you to get your ride."

She kissed him softly behind his ear. "I've already got my ride."

He imperceptibly shivered with happiness, no storm clouds yet to be held at bay.

Eddie went into his office and dialed Risty's number up in the Northern Virginia horse country.

"Hey, Risty, my crowd is early. They should be at your place late this afternoon. I hope that's not too big a pain in the ass for you." He squeezed his eyes shut in guarded hope.

Risty paused and answered, "No, we'll adjust. I'll have Juan get the doors open now. Remember, first big barn on the right at top of the hill across from the main house. And I know. I won't go snooping them."

"Oh, Risty, I really appreciate it! I really do."

"I'm sure you do, Eddie. But, remember, there is one thing attendant to all this."

"Yeah?"

"You need to come up here sooner rather than later and tell me all about it and I do mean ALL about it."

"Yes, I recall that condition and I will meet it. Thanks, Risty."

"Eddie, I'm not sure I'm gonna thank you back, but I will note, times are never dull with you."

"Honey, I'll take it as a compliment and I'll see you soon. Take care of yourself."

"Goodbye, Eddie." The line clicked off. Regret was always lurking around out there, somewhere.

Rise and Kenny, she hovering on the wheel and he too large rocking in the seat behind her, slid onto I-40 heading east toward Greensboro and then quickly exited and headed to Highway 158 and headed north. Rise was humming her repertoire of hymns and Kenny was looking around, looking out, nodding as her metronome. They moved methodically, mindful of their orders. Nothing to see here, move along. They had initially been tense but were now watchfully more relaxed.

"Rise, you think we really gonna do this?"

"Sonny boy, we really doing it right now!" She quick turned and grinned at Kenny.

Now that they were off the speeding lanes of the interstate, the pace was more slow, halting, with stop signs at many crossroads, farm equipment, slow moving country folk, narrowing two lanes lined by fields with cows and sheep, modest homes, and farms.

Not too far along their travel route, near Midway, they were held up in a line of cars and trucks by an old maroon mini-van, a battered Plymouth, that had somehow managed to get itself sideways into a deep roadside ditch next to a small, red brick nursing home, a place that looked more like some sort of modest, rural adult day care.

A big Ford Dually had its drag chains on the van, and with the help of five pushing, gee and hawing country boys, it was slow lurching its way out of the ditch's muck, red clay mud smearing its rims and low panels. A single county sheriff's deputy, a hefty, running to fat fellow, Ray Bans glaring blank in the light, his cruiser parked off the side of the road with its strobe popping in the sunlight, was halting and directing traffic as the extraction progressed.

"Rise, should I get out and help?"

"Hell, no! No need to take that kind of chance," she hissed at him. "Just sit tight. When it's our turn to pass all this and move on, just smile and wave. Hell, give 'em a thumbs up if you like. I know I will. Just a normal school bus with two big fat black folks tending to it."

And as they moved up at the direction of the deputy, they were then next to the mess and saw two old ladies up on the bank next to the ditch, hopefully worrying about their saggy, old, muddied up ride. Kenny waved to them and they waved back. Kenny was pleased.

Rise got in on the good feelings with a quick couple of horn toots and a thumbs up which the deputy, grinning, returned.

They were waved on through and thus confirmed. They could do this. This was not just possible. It was probable.

They kept moving through and up the countryside, the sun's shining only slightly interrupted by a few scudding clouds. Near Reidsville, they hooked onto Highway 29 and were a straight shot onto Ballymore, The Charm City.

Rise looked quickly at her maps and directions. They were on time and in sync. They were soon to be in Virginia.

CHAPTER THIRTY-NINE

SUSPICIOUS MINDS

Elvis

THE BUS ROLLED on in the nice weather. They crossed into Virginia, passing Danville, then Chatham, and onto Gretna (Town motto: We ain't no big thing but we growin'). The land was lovely, undulating with the beautiful Blue Ridge Mountains covering to their west. Lynchburg and then Charlottesville.

They stopped at a large gas station with a convenience store in Charlottesville to top their tank, use the facilities, grab some snacks and a drink. There was a large historical marker on the curb proclaiming that The University of Virginia was just ahead, founded by Thomas Jefferson, the third president, drafter of the Declaration of Independence and so forth. Kenny and Rise studied on it for a minute.

Kenny asked Rise, "That mean anything to you? You know anything about him? Looks like he done a lot of shit."

"Yeah, does don't it. He kinda rings a bell, but I really don't know. Matter of fact, I don't give a shit one way or another. Let's get going. We on schedule and Mr. T.J. up there ain't gonna help us snatch the goodies we going to pick up. Let's get moving."

They were moving further north. Traffic was all right. No delays so far. Every now and then, a highway patrol cruiser or a sheriff's deputy car would pass them but that was just that. Nothing. They were innocuous, virtually invisible. They got up into Fauquier County near Warrenton and there was marker after marker after marker addressing much that had happened during the War Between the States.

Rise and Kenny just glanced at them as they sped by.

"Rise, you know anything about that war? Looks like there was a lot of fighting and killing going on in these parts way back then."

"A little bit. Just a little bit. Back a long time ago, the South states split off from the Yankee states. They started fighting over slavery. Kenny, you know about slavery?"

"Sorta. Not really."

"Well, back then, white folks owned black folks like us. Flat out fucking owned us. Bought and sold us like we nothing but a can of beer or a pack of cigarettes. We had to do what the whiteys wanted us to do. They beat the shit outta us. Whipped us like dogs. Anyway, it was a big war. Lots of people killed and all fucked up. Finally, the Yankees from the north won and they set the slaves free. That's why you see pictures of Abraham Lincoln in a lot of black folks' houses and in black churches too. He was the white president that freed the slaves. He's kind of a hero to a lot of black folks like Dr. King is."

"Okay. I guess I've seen his picture out there here and there. So that's who he is. I always kinda wondered. I do think I know who Dr. King is." Kenny chuckled. "Now, I haven't been in a church in a coon's age so I wouldn't have no idea about that."

Rise just shook her head in tolerant affection.

"Kenny boy, you really don't pay too much attention to much of anything, do you?"

"Hell, Rise, I'm paying attention to this, to what we're doing right now."

"Fair enough."

"Rise, do you feel free right now?"

"I guess but not so much right now. What we're doing right now, we might as well be chained to this old bus."

"I got it. At least no one is beating on us now."

Rise pursed her lips and looked straight ahead. "Not anymore. No, not anymore."

They were coming into more city, more urban areas. Things were denser. Traffic a lot heavier and manic. Washington, D.C. was near. They swung through D.C. Here and there, they could see the Washington Monument, the dome of the Capitol and large, impressive government buildings. Wide streets.

"Kenny, I've never been here before. And I know you haven't either. Maybe one day, we could come up here and look around, really check the place out. It looks pretty neat."

"Yeah, that'd be nice I think. You know, you get out traveling and you see all sorts of stuff. I've never been anywhere much. Greensboro a couple of times, Charlotte too. And of course, there was my time down in Raleigh at Central but that was no fun at all. Really boring most of the time unless some prisoners wanted to fight or fuck with me or with somebody else and then, I just held my ground or got the fuck outta the way. Yeah, would be nice to come back up here sometime and be, what do you call them, people that go around and look at the sights?"

"Oh, you mean tourists? That's them. Tourists. They tour about."

"Yeah, that's it."

They lapsed back into silence. With the traffic heavier, Rise picked her concentration up. She mumbled to herself, "No time to fuck this up now." Kenny ate some Nabs and pulled on his Coca-Cola. They moved out of D.C., up into Maryland. Near Ellicott City, they picked up U.S. 40 and headed east toward Baltimore. They were on the home stretch of the pickup leg.

Kenny suddenly exclaimed as they were passed by a long Peterbilt tractor and trailer.

"Rise, look at that shit! That's funny!"

The back of the cab read, "Ain't nothing sweeter than a long nose Peter."

Rise glanced and scolded, "Kenny, that's nice but we ain't into amusement time now. We be close now. Look sharp now. Cut the cute shit out, got it?"

Kenny, chastened, still laughed and laughed, "Rise, look at me. I am looking sharp, sharp as shit!"

Rise laughed. "Okay. Okay. Yes you do. Now, pull out those maps again and let's make sure we nail this." It was 2:15 in the afternoon.

Patty and Mikey had laid Pussy Preacher and Blockhouse out on the big conference room table. It was too bad that the Bible thumpers from Indiana did not get up on the high line for top billing but they just didn't bring as much fun and bizarre to the story as it hatched out. They were at best plain vanilla compared to the other villains—though they indeed did have nice, hefty, workable liability insurance policies so there was merit there. And too and then again, all three targets did. The compromised good Christian Hoosiers' end of the catastrophe was simply the denouement of a solid, seedy, drunk and hurt induced, inebriated hard slog across the asphalt and cheap construction of South Carolina's scenic Sodom and Gomorrah, scenic if cheesy high rises, crummy food, and trashy behavior that fit that bill for whomever.

It was put-it-together time. As always, the files were disassembled and deconstructed for analysis and the creation of that delicate alchemy of mix and match, sorted facts that would maximize their impact as they blossomed forth out into the flaccid, pallid faces of three sets of defense counsel and their insurance adjuster handlers, though in eternal truth, the allegedly handled would most likely be the drum majors. Big cases made lots of chicken hearts grow in the breasts of the tough talkers from not around here.

"Okay, Eddie, ready to take a look? Oh, I see you gone off to Eddie World again. What you thinking about this time?" Patty lit up a big menthol.

"Ah, you caught me again."

Both girls looked at him, waiting.

"Shit, Eddie, sometimes I think you ought to get a dog but then the dog runs the show and then what?" Patty had amused herself and was choking on a hard drag.

"Serves you right, disparaging me. Arf fucking arf. Like Harry Truman said, 'You want a friend in Washington, D.C. Get a dog.'" He winked. "No, nothing like that. I'll explain it later. Stuff from when I was a kid. Let's get to it.

"First, our clients and their injuries? And they are lined up to be in Charleston on time and looking good, right? And we've all got rooms and there will be no gaps, right?"

"Right. All lined up. Now, our three clients and their injuries."

Patty handed Mikey a 5x7 index card and Mikey read it.

"Number One-Dooley Johnson, age twenty-four, Upper Montclair, New Jersey, UNC Lax; lacerations, stitches, multiple broken bones in hands and feet, torn ACL, surgical repairs, concussion, multi-day hospital stay at Grand Strand, physical therapy, medical specials in excess of $175K. Claimed lost wages, potential, north of 60K. Multiple photos in file.

"Number Two-Fishers Marks, age twenty-five, Manhasset, Long Island, New York, UNC Lax; lacerations, stitches, broken ribs, right hand amputated above the wrist (He was right hand dominant), bruised liver, surgical repairs, physical therapy, minimal but apparent closed head injury, medical special in excess of $300K and will be climbing. Claimed lost wages north of a 100K.

"Number Three-David Shelvin, age twenty-four, Babylon, Long Island, UNC Lax; lacerations, stitches, broken left femur, shattered left shoulder, ruptured spleen, surgical repairs, physical therapy, medical specials of 250K and will be increasing. Claimed lost wages, north of 65-70K.

"Eddie, as you know, we have Dr. Bahnson as our forensic economist doing all the three workups. Those will not be ready in time for mediation next week. Also, Sarah Lustig on Life Care planning. Again, not ready by next week. And same for Dr. Haynie with alcohol analysis."

"Patty, for our purposes next week, that's okay by me. All are superb, virtually impregnable. The defense knows we got them. Aces to eights for them. We will need compilations of each individual set of medical records, highlighted, and marked for the strongest components—let's keep it simple—ER records, Admit and Discharge Notes, Surgeons Op reports, Discharge Summaries—that'll be more than enough like reading flip cards—and the itemized medical bills. So let's get that cooking.

"The folks on the other side of the table will get it, no matter how they'll act like it's all smoke and mirrors. Hell, I remember when I first got started working on these kinds of cases, if you talked with adjusters about 'pain and suffering,' they'd just laugh at you and blow you off. 'Pain and Suffering?!' they'd snort, 'That's just hocus pocus bullshit dreamed up by the plaintiff's bar. You can't touch it, you can't see it, you can't count it.' And we, like lambs, acceded. But then, people began to network and piece things together and share ideas and theories and began to work to illustrate the horrible reality of bad injuries. Today, there is not a major hospital complex in the country that does not have an active and comprehensive pain center, manned by anesthesiologists. And you can take the itemized medical bills and extrapolate a lot of P and S from them. Easy example, the pricing of pain killing or minimizing drugs. That sort of thing."

"Right."

Eddie pulled the boys' photos out of the envelopes and stared at them, shuffling through them, looking at the before and the after. "Nice looking guys," he mused aloud. "Quite a contrast. Healthy young studs in team pictures, playing for a nationally-ranked lacrosse powerhouse. Handsome, confident, likeable. Big futures. And then. Look at this, broken and cracked and dismantled. Lives and looks pretty badly fucked up. A long, a very long road back, if there is even a road back. Damn, easy road behavior busted up by just sloppy, craven, don't give a shit behavior."

He shook his head. "All right, let's get these worked up with a tight-ass one page bullet point summary sheet on cover. Next, who are all defense counsel, liability carriers, their reps if we know and what are the liability policies in play?"

Patty cleared her throat, wiggled and waggled the card as her smoking butt hung from her lips and intoned as if it were a game show. "Okay. Here we go. For the Jim Nabors crowd, back home again in Indiana so to speak, we've got counsel Mills Gaines out of Columbia. We've worked with him before. Their adjuster is Jack McKinney out of Indianapolis, don't know him. Company is Indianapolis General. They've got 500K primary, plus a two-million-dollar umbrella."

"Nice start. Mills is a good guy and will help the carrier to see the light. Next?"

"Next up for Thee Doll House is John Winkler out of Myrtle Beach. Again, we know him, have seen him across the tables many times. He's a funny guy, smart too. Adjuster is Deborah Mynyrta Roth out of Atlanta. Don't know her either. Carrier is Chubb Special Lines with a flat ten million in coverage."

"Very good. Like the size of their package. Helps to have enough seed to feed the trough. Winkler is a pretty wide out guy, can work the edges and center of the field with good, effective skill. Guarantee you he's done his own, probably more than a few, field inspections of his client's ground and I'd wager he did his surveying with an ample supply of table dance dollars. Perfect match of client and counsel. Hell, might as well have a little fun before the toilet flushes. The pressing of the flesh before time is called.

"And, the adjuster. Roth? Female? Atlanta? Don't mean to stereotype but think I will anyway. Here's the way I see this. Just a little uptight, a realist, a pro Jewish lady with real good manners and a fairly cold, detached way. Handed a heavy file with a tawdry, trashy enough client, already a heavy reserve set and she's coming up to play in the Bohemian Grove Boys Club of South Carolina with all the back slapping, misogynistic bullshit that goes with all the 'wink' other shit that goes on in these types of cases. She'll not be fighting back, at least not much in public. She's got the biggest policy which, when enough of it is released, will grease the skids nicely so she'll be penurious at first until our mediator and Winkler get her respectfully loosened up. That'll be around midafternoon as she won't want to miss her flight back to the big city; last one goes at 6:15 p.m. I recall. I expect then the cherries will begin to light up.

"Winkler can be a bad boy but he has a nice touch with people and can be very well-mannered and thoughtful. He has a nice touch with people. That's why on close cases, be careful with him as juries can come to like him. It'll be like Sadie Hawkins Day in the old cartoon strip, *L'il Abner*. They'll chase her until she catches them.

Patty grinned. "And last but surely not least, on behalf of our friends at the Blockhouse, we have the inimitable, the memorable, the most fraudulently mulish jerk that can rapidly come to mind, the one and only Wallish Marcus, also out of Columbia."

"Now, Patty, let's be charitable," Eddie joked.

"Bullshit. Those words came straight out of your blowhole years ago and still ring in my ears. And hell, I've seen that jackass in action. Ain't nobody missing the mark there. Even to a man jack, his colleagues in the defense bar revile him. He makes their skin crawl."

Mikey said, "Y'all tell me more, please?"

"Oh, honey, Eddie will in just a little bit. Talk about a round peg in a square hole!" She harrumphed and blew smoke out her nose like Ferdinand the Bull does when he sits on the bee. "Now let me wrap up this part of their team's roster. His adjuster is Sampson D., always Sampson D. Jenkins, also from Columbia. They've got farmers. Good company. Generally play fair and are happily realistic. They've got five million primary and five million in umbrella. Again, good numbers."

"Okay. There we go," Eddie intoned. "And we've got a great mediator, Tom Wills, who is not just a really good, fine guy but he is damned effective and respected across the board. I love him. He's fun to be with, smart, perceptive and stays with it.

"Now, just a little more flavor on Marcus. We call him 'Wailing Wall Wally,' the king of 'Woe is Me.' Nothing is ever his clients' fault or responsibility. Nothing. And when he is called out on it, he sniffs and looks away in false anguish like The Little Prince. He acts so high and mighty and is always just begging that he be recognized as the mighty martyr he play acts every single damn time. He hates me because I call him out. And I promise I will twist his tail. He hates public excoriation. Not me."

Mikey said, "Wow, he sounds pretty twisted."

"Yes, he is but now, let me tell you a little about Sampson D. Jenkins. Talk about these two being an odd couple. Sampson D. a very big, fat, lumbering man. Corpulent would put him on the thin side of the description. He is bright, kind, considerate and has a playbook that has exactly and I'm not kidding, two plays.

"We all say his name really should be Sampson D. P. Jenkins, the D being for Delay and the P being for Pay. He will, without a doubt next week, call both plays and he doesn't ever alternate or switch things up. For a long while next week, he'll go right along with Mr. Self-Righteous Wailing Wally and will and when Wally says no or balks or nickels and dimes, he'll be right there nodding along with him, a sycophant metronome."

"Damn, Eddie, we need a damn Boy Scout with a compass to follow your scattered ass all over."

"True. This is how it will work. First office is Wills' big conference room where we will open up the proceedings. Tom makes a short introduction, 99 percent of it for benefit of clients and adjusters. He pleasantly makes it very clear he is king dog and do not mess with his proceedings. Then he'll invite me to speak. I will decline, simply will say, 'We all know why we are here. I'm sure y'all will say y'all are all real sorry about all this disaster and wish it hadn't happened, but the fault lays with these young whippersnappers and so forth so how about stuff it and save it.' Tom will smile and invite the other side to inveigh.

"They'll mumble the same old tired shit I will have already exposed and then we shuffle off to our respective, our hot box rooms, my second office. This is where, to me and the others, Wills will begin to level things out, start turning the screw once the money shows.

"My third office is everywhere else, hallways, front rooms, empty offices, hell, a damn broom closet where I can screw around, crack jokes, collar someone in a corner, call a football play, ask about folks, even sneak someone off to the sidewalk outside; the world is my oyster and things are always either public or private. Being a chameleon is sometimes fun." Eddie winked.

"Now Wailing Wally, high and mighty prince that he is, avoids this sort of plebian riffraff and rubbing elbows with lesser thans. When he ventures forth from his sequestered chambers, he is efficiently direct and curt and above it all. He does not pause to chat. He does not pause to visit, to inquire about other's families or firms. His nose truly is up in the air as if there is a bad odor just below it. It is as though his modest beginnings snotty below the salt face was designed to sneer at those nasty commoners that vex him, swatting them away mentally like fruit flies. He is an in and out guy. Everybody knows it, notices it, is bemused by it, and they all call each other's attention to it.

"And finally what is going to inevitably happen, Wills will make one of his stop-by individual visits, as he does with all participants, to Wailing Wally and Sampson D. and he'll crack the code by getting good old Sampson to beg, plead, cajole Wally into his first offer of significance and thus the march of a thousand miles begins with its first step. And from thereon out, Wally, with Sampson D egging him on, will feed the same amount in over and over again as all the others share in the momentum of moving toward a compromise. Of course, we are graciously reducing our demand, trying his mid-points consistently along the way. And Wills is working us all to get this done. And he is effective. Let's see if my prognostications hold meat on the bone next week. I'm sure y'all will hold me up to the hot light on them."

"We have the players, but what's the goal?"

"How about, again, a one page cover sheet for Wills that simply lays out all parties and counsel for all, plus adjusters and carriers and amounts of coverage? Obviously, no need for my editorializing. I'll do plenty of that when Tom and I are in private. Well, maybe a little bit early. Happily, Wills makes me laugh and I help him laugh too. Takes a nut to know a nut. Make sure too you put in there that both of y'all be coming with me and let's remember our effective dress codes so y'all can make some eyes pop in wonder and envy, I shit you not! Let's get those medical sheets ready and then identify the parties, and overnight them to Wills and to all counsel and carriers. Let me take a look at them before they go, please."

Patty and Mikey sat back and watched as Eddie mentally tossed the bouncing ball into his mind's roulette wheel and let it pop and hop and skitter about as he thought about how he wanted these things to come out. The ball settled into a red slot, a black slot, it mattered not. What mattered was the ball settled and stopped.

"They've got an aggregate of north of twenty-two million. More than enough to get this done and let them all save a little something, maybe a little more than a little something. We're going to make a composite demand of twenty million to open and work from there. I feel strongly, and I think his friends will concur, that the Marks' kid who lost the hand and has the closed head injury, treatable though it appears to be, should get a million, million and a half more than the others. We will cover this with them all the night before. Everybody coming in the night before, right?"

"Yes, Eddie, yes. For God's sake, don't be going over-anal on me right now. We got this. You just think about how to get the money. I'll think about how to get us there. Jesus."

"You're right. I'll go internal. Also put on the sheet that identifies the parties and all that our collective demand for compromised resolution at mediation is twenty million. Make sure I initial it before it goes. Please and thank you. Also, make sure all defense counsel know and understand that their clients and principals are required to be present at mediation. That's the court's rule; that's Tom's rule and remember for these purposes he is an assigned officer of the court and no one gets to be excused until Tom says so and these proceedings are closed."

Mikey asked, "What's next?"

"Make sure our boy Truck Tinker meets us at the Mills for drinks and dinner and that he is there with us at mediation. Tell him there's gold in them thar hills for him. That'll move his ass."

Eddie laughed. "Truck's like those goats that fall over when someone yells 'Boo!' He gets around some good-looking ladies who will show some flesh and smell real good and he goes nearly catatonic, but that is only after he blubbers out his promise to leave home and hearth for the birds and his fervent marriage proposal to any and all within earshot. Jesus!"

Mikey and Patty giggled. "That bad? He sounds like such an amateur."

"Worse. He'd grovel on the floor to see more of anything like that. He was raised strict and the libertine life is such tempting forbidden fruit to him. Married real early while we were all still in school, never played, never strayed, loves his wife and kids dearly but never got to play, never was allowed to sow a wild oat or two. No kidding, but he's a good guy and he's gonna help us put their balls in a very tight vise.

"Now, let me go over all this by myself and I'll make a one sheet to be transmitted separately overnight to Tom Wills. It'll be a précis of how we're gonna hang 'em all. Y'all can go get going on the other stuff. Oh, please get five copies made of Pussy Preacher that we will take down there with us. Like they say on TV, 'Lovely parting gifts for our contestants.'"

They looked at him as though he were a laughable alien. They left him.

Eddie took out a legal pad and wrote in caps across the top of the page.

N.B.
IT IS PROBABLE THAT AN AWARD OF PUNITIVE DAMAGES WILL BE MADE IN THESE CASES IF THEY GO TO JURY. RECKLESS, WILLFUL, WANTON MISCONDUCT. HANDLE WITH CARE OR THE SKY IS GOING TO CAVE IN

In order:

1) Thee Doll House-Pussy Preacher Video to be provided to all at mediation, shows three clients getting served and served some more, shows them clearly intoxicated as they get served and served some more. Multiple withdrawal receipts from in-house ATM, plus credit card receipts, all timely, from Daddy's Amex and Visa; also, direct eyewitness testimony from TDH working gals as to how they are charged with making money for the club, "Get them to drink TOO MUCH and show them as much of the goods as you can and keep them drinking and keep at it. Lots of smiles and winks. The money always comes. It's simple. It works." (Direct Verbatim Quote) We have the girls' names and IDs. When the boys left there about dusk, they were directed up the street—they staggered—to their next destination which was...

2) Blockhouse that bills itself as a private club but our three were allowed in and drank fully there for almost an hour, despite being clearly drunk. We have a forensic toxicologist whom I'm sure you know, Dr. Janice Haynie of national and statewide reputation—all the defendants know her and have used her

so any of their whining is useless. She has done work-back, retrograde extrapolations from all three ER blood draws and clearly show all three to be intoxicated in the extreme from the just about the get-go. Both at TDH and now at Blockhouse. At their time of departure from BH, they all read out at plus .20, i.e. falling down drunk.

Their private club gambit of screened shielded protection doesn't fly. While I was dining one evening at the Patricia Manor with a friend, who is also an eyewitness as to both the TDH and BH, we were approached by a nice young man who offered us passes at minimal expense—buy a 30 day "membership" for $2.50. Love that initiation fee for entry to the Blockhouse. He explained that he had arrived at the Patricia on his bike, being not old enough to have a driver's license. He had hundreds of these passes. We bought a couple of hundred of them from him. I'll bring a handful when we meet in a few days.

I enclose one for your perusal. He explained that he was part of a network of youngsters who worked the nicest hotels and resorts on the beach. This group of teenage solicitors hand out thousands of these things each week. We have the kid's name, of course. Not only is this bad bad bad against the law in South Carolina, it also includes the state ABC Board, goodbye licenses, using minors improperly, etc. So after being served while drunk in this most public of private clubs (Sorry, Tom, such bullshit! And by the way, not one of our three had the "magic" admission card—they just let three stumbling drunks in), my guys are kicked out the door with no assistance, no ride, no taxi, no nothing. They are wandering about in a staggering clot trying to figure which end is up in the dark in a gravel and dirt parking lot next to busy Kings Highway. And so they have their last encounter with those I name

3) The Indiana Bible Thumpers, who can't get their stories straight. They are in Myrtle Beach on a church golf outing. God Bless the Christian Goodness of Golf... One of them says they were pulling into the club, two others say they were leaving. No matter. Eyewitnesses have their truck visibly speeding.

They struck our three all at the same time. Field tests by SCHP clearly found they had been drinking but there were no DUI charges, but there were charges as to reckless driving and failing to give pedestrians right of way, failing to keep a proper lookout. Those fines have already been paid by the driver, ergo pleas of guilty to South Carolina safety statutes. (Tom, I have to laugh at all this mishmash of a cluster fuck. Good Christian Gentlemen on a quest. Can you imagine how all this goes down if it gets with their tight ass wives and families? Get the rope! Love sanctimony! Hell, come to think of it, I dated sanctimony more than a few times. Nothing but begging and rejection.) All three of our guys end up at Grand Strand Regional with very bad injuries as described on other materials you have been sent contemporaneously with this sheet.

Tom, I think this gives you a pretty good look at where things stand.

As for your first piercing inquiry next week. "But, Eddie, they got drunk and had a ball? Isn't that comparative?"

I'll say, 'Sure, Tom, but they all went out of their way to get them shit-faced and in the second place, the Blockhouse, not only welcomed them and poured them good, they've already broken so many rules even the ghosts of Strom and Wade Hampton and his Red Shirts can't save them. The guys from Indiana will fold first. I'll help you.

Please make sure your VCR player works. The Pussy Preacher video is alone worth the price of admission! Not long but you'll wish you had more.

I look forward to visiting with you in a few days. If in the brief meantime, you have questions or comments, please don't hesitate to call me. I send my very best regards. It has been a while! Eddie T.

Eddie tore the sheet off carefully and walked it out to Patty. He was deliberate in all of his actions.

"Here you go. Let's get it all together and transmit overnight today. I want to initial where appropriate. Should be four sets. Only one liability cover sheet to Wills. No video copies to anyone. Want to hand out at the day of reckoning. They'll piss and moan but then they'll piss themselves and maybe even better."

"Will do. You're a sneaky one, aren't you?" Both girls leered in high fun, trying to lighten him.

Then face falling quickly, Mikey asked, "When do you think we'll hear from Rise and Kenny?"

"Hopefully, not too much longer. Let's stay busy." His face was taut. They knew he was wrapped up tight.

Patty smoked and just looked off into her cloud. It calmed them. But they all did not at all want to look at each other so they were furtive.

CHAPTER FORTY

BALTIMORE

Randy Newman

BALTIMORE, ALLEGEDLY THE Charm City, had outskirts that were pretty grimy at best. And as Highway 40 became Edmonson, one of the main arteries into the inner city, things just got worse.

Rows and rows of bleached-out, blank-faced buildings, habitations of the poor, the apathetic, the beaten, the sad and preyed upon lined the way in, all interspersed with strip clubs, bars, taverns, cemeteries, convenience stores, head shops, gas stations, and churches. All were slapped and squeezed close together by what appeared to be some perverse gravitational force that sealed all these slapdash, falling down, rusted, and tattered hovels into a gray, amorphous urbanity.

And everywhere, there were clots and singles of slow-moving people, almost all people of color. They stood about, leaned back in alleyways, crouched against walls, stared vacantly away, argued, yelled, gesticulated, shot dice, played cards, got high, flapping their poor clothing about the cracked sidewalks littered with garbage and trash.

Rise pulled the bus into a small gas station. "Kenny, I want you to drive now. We've got good directions and I do read better than you, so let's switch places and you'll be on the wheel and I'll be your map-reading guide dog. That okay with you?"

"Sure. That's a good idea. Rise, look at all this. This is a for sure shitty-looking town, ain't it? I've seen slums but nothing to top this."

"Yeah, this is like being on the planet of the zombies. Like they've all been stun-gunned. Okay. Let's keep going. We're real close."

Kenny carefully turned the bus back out into the street and Rise had her maps.

"Let's take it easy now. We're looking for West Mulberry. Shouldn't be far."

On they went. Rise called, "There it is. Turn right onto West Mulberry. And then we're looking for North Fremont. That's it, right down there. Take the turn there and this will take us down around the curve to West Lexington and there should be a couple of guys down below the curve to wave us on in where they want us."

Rise and Kenny peered down the way and then appeared two young fellows wearing identical white shirts and black watch caps who started signaling the bus to turn into an alley. They ran out in front of the bus, waving them along until they signaled stop and crossed arms. They were stopped next to a large warehouse where a corrugated metal door was rolled up and open. In the doorway stood Pee Wee and another man. The bus's engine kept running.

Rise swiveled the bus door open, stood up and bounded down the steps, Kenny in a close follow. It was old home week.

Rise exclaimed, "Pee Wee! Son! Look how you've grown up. Oh, I am glad to see you!"

"Same here, Rise! Same here, Kenny! Y'all are a sight for sore eyes!" He jumped down and they all gave each other big hugs and bigger smiles."

"Y'all, this is Punch, my assistant. I know we don't have much time. Punch, would you please bring these two old friends of mine what they've come to get? Those other two out there who led you in are Screw and Lennie. They're some of our front-line scouts."

Rise admired Pee Wee. "Son, just look at you. You surely have come a long way from Camel City and east Winston. Nice clothes, nice everything. So grown up! Looking good! Damn, I'm proud of you! Kenny, aren't you too?"

"Yeah sure. I remember you good when you were just a pain-in-the-ass whippersnapper. Now, you are The Man. It's cool."

"Thank y'all. It's been a lot of hard work. But the pay is good and the hours aren't too shabby either." He winked and laughed. "Just try not to get a fat head about it. There are plenty of folks who would like my job, so I keep my head down and my nose clean. There can be some plenty dangerous parts to this if you don't pay attention. Hell, y'all know about good old Ballymore –guns, murder, and drugs. Just part of the deal. Been shot a couple of times but so far, I've been lucky."

He pulled his shirttail up and gestured to a ragged scar that ran down near his appendix and then he held out his left hand which showed a through and through scar down his left palm. He paused. "Oh, I wish we could have a real visit but this time around, we don't have the time. Are y'all doing all right down home?"

Rise and Kenny nodded. "We got enough work. We be doing all right. We're helping Mr. Curt Minor out on this."

"Yeah, I know. Had a couple of visits from him over the last few weeks. Please give him my best regards. He seems like a very good man, a straight shooter. Here comes Punch and JoJo the Helper with the goodies. Rise, I understand the bus has some hidden compartments. May I have the keys to those, please?"

"Here you go." She jangled them and handed them to Pee Wee who in turn handed them to Punch.

Punch and JoJo went up into the bus with a large bottle of Clorox and some towels. They opened the three carry spots and rinsed each down with the bleach and then wiped them dry. Then they got the kilos and placed two in each compartment. They then tight wrapped and taped them in very stretch cellophane. They locked the compartments and handed the keys back to Rise.

"Nice seeing y'all. Have a good trip back." Punch and JoJo went back into the dark of the warehouse.

Pee Wee noted, "As you can see, these kilos are a little larger and heavier. They've been bag-sealed and completely dip-coated in a light but im-pene-tra-ta-ble layer of concrete. About a quarter to a half inch. The blow stays nice and dry. To get to it, just a few light hammer taps and there it is. Makes it all very secure. Now, y'all gotta be going. Sorry this is all so short but this is business after all. Y'all be safe and tell everyone old Pee Wee says 'Hey!'"

Rise stood back and took one more good, long look at Pee Wee and then enveloped him in a big hug. A few tears were leaking from her eyes. She brushed them away. Kenny stepped forward and shook hands. "Pee Wee, I really am glad to see you. Man, take care of yourself."

"Hell, y'all come back and see me soon. Now, Screw and Lennie are gonna get you backed out and on your way. Same way out as you did in."

"Kenny, you drive and I'll be map reader again." It was five minutes after three. "And, we need to call Eddie Terrell and let him know we on our way to his friend's farm. Let's get on road, find a payphone, get gassed up, grab food and drink for the evening and find a bathroom or two."

"Good plan. I'm ready."

And they were waved back and rolled back into the street and moved on.

CHAPTER FORTY-ONE

ON THE ROAD AGAIN

Willie Nelson

"RISE, DO YOU think it's strange that here we are, riding along, disguised as a school bus, with six kilos of cocaine in the back way up under the seats, acting like we know what we're doing?"

"Well, yeah I guess so, but it's not so bad and it does look to me like we know what we're doing and we sure did sign up for this damn rodeo, didn't we?" She laughed as the bus rocked gracefully on. Kenny pursed his lips and nodded in accord.

They were heading west on US 40 toward Frederick and they soon found a big truck stop near the junction of 40 and Interstate 70. Kenny eased the bus into the large parking area way off the side and Rise found a bank of pay phones and dropped in some quarters and called the operator, gave her the number to the office, and asked to have the charges reversed. Patty answered and accepted the reverse.

"Rise? That you? How are things going?"

"Fine, Miss Patty. No problems so far. We are on our way to spend the night in Virginia."

"Good. Let me get Eddie for you. Hang on."

Mikey was listening and hopped up and went and got Eddie. He quickly came out to Patty's desk and took the receiver.

"Hey, there. Y'all okay?"

"Oh, yeah. We're fine. On the way to your friend's place. Should be there by around five or so."

"Good, she's expecting you but will not come say 'hey' or bother you. Remember, you'll go up Sidehill Road off the Plains Road. Pull in the first dark-colored barn on the right. The doors will be open. Once in, pull them closed. Want you on the road first thing in the morning. Say by 7 a.m. It's about a five-hour drive so I hope you can be back here by noon."

"Got it. We'll leave at 6:30 to give us a little extra space."

"Be safe. I'll have Curt here at noon. We are all counting on you now."

Rise got back in the bus and reported the brief conversation to Kenny. As they were talking, a Maryland State Trooper pulled up beside them in the lot. Rise and Kenny's eyes got big and their breathing got shallow.

Rise said, "Big Boy, Just look straight ahead, straight ahead."

They waited and still took quick, darting glances to their left.

The trooper got out, stretched, looked around, looked at the bus, paused and turned and ambled toward the C-store.

Rise and Kenny exhaled. "Let's hope he's just going to get a pop and a snack and take a leak. We'll know soon enough. Just be still." After ten minutes, the trooper came walking out across the lot with a can of Mountain Dew and a candy bar. He looked up and caught Kenny's eye and pleasantly said, "How y'all doing up there?"

Kenny did not hesitate. "We're fine, officer. Hope you are. Been in D.C. on a school field trip and now going to pick up some of the kids at a farm down in Virginia. Sorta moving a lot of them around."

"Well, that sounds good. Nice day for it. Where down in Virginia?"

Rise leaned over and waved and said, "The Plains, Virginia. One of our teachers has a friend with a nice farm there."

The trooper nodded. "That's real pretty country down there. Lots of rich people too. Horse people. Well, y'all take care. I'm back on patrol. Watch your speed, please."

"We will. Thank you." And Kenny tapped the bill of his hat in salute. And the trooper responded in kind, got in his black and white, revved the engine and curled out of the lot and onto an entrance ramp to the interstate and was gone.

Kenny and Rise looked at each other silently for a moment and then both giggled.

"Damn, Kenny! That was great. What a line of bullshit and nicely done and delivered too!"

"Thanks, Rise. Once him and me saw each other, it just come out of me. Damned if I know from where. And you were great with your lean in too 'cause I was running out of air fast!"

Rise chuckled. "School field trip...farm in Virginia...hell, son, you been taking acting lessons?"

"I guess just being in this uniform and hat and all and riding around in this school bus has done got me in the mood to play the part."

Rise nodded and then her face went thoughtful. "Kenny, you know what? We look normal. As long as we don't do anything stupid, we might as well be invisible. Ain't nobody paying much attention to us. We'll be home before this time tomorrow, so let's get to it and get covered up for the night. Let's go get some food and drinks and fill our tank up and hit the restrooms and keep on rolling."

"Yes, ma'am."

After pumping the gas and buying Vienna sausages, saltine crackers, sardines, potato chips, candy bars and a cold six pack of Mountain Dew, and then getting their bladders good and empty, they set out on the next to last leg.

Rise was back on the wheel. They turned south down Highway 15 toward Leesburg, just taking it alertly easy. They were tired and there wasn't a lot of talking. They wanted to just get to the lady's farm. They passed Aldie where there was another big history marker on a gravel pull off next to the road. There had been a running three-day cavalry fight up and down outside the little crossroads, fought in good part on foot.

Rise read it out loud to Kenny. "More shooting. More killing. Lord, these people surely did hate one another."

"I wonder if they still do. Seems like most of this is really old stuff."

"I dunno, Kenny. You know how people be where we live. A lot of people walk around with a lot of black hate in their hearts. It's too bad. Meanness, I mean."

"I know. Well, really not so much. It's that kind of stuff I try not to think about. You know, when I shot at Bo back a long time ago, I did hate him at that moment, but once he went down and I knew he couldn't fuck with me anymore, that hate just lifted right up and out of my body."

"I think I can understand that. When Ben was beating me up all the time, I came to hate him too, but now that he's gone on, I don't hate him anymore."

Kenny nodded his head and looked away from her.

"Kenny, it's okay. I understand. I got it. I understand."

They kept moving.

CHAPTER FORTY-TWO

WAGON WHEEL

Old Crow Medicine Show

THEY RAN INTO a little curvy narrow road, not even worth calling a highway, Road 601. They followed into the northern side of the crossroads of The Plains and then on to The Old Plains Road. They turned left and slowed to look for the side road signs. In just a bit, there was a tall, green sign that read "Sidehills Road." They took the right and headed up the hill. As they crested the rise and swung over to the right, there was the large, dark-colored barn with its door yawning open. Across the way, there was a neat, low slung white house with green shutters tucked down in a gentle swale. There were pretty horses out in a big field over to the left.

And standing in the drive was a very attractive, tall blonde lady with a great big furry brown and black and white dog on a leash. The lady wore a big floppy straw hat and her head was wrapped with a bright scarf. She wore jeans and riding boots that had mud on them. They both, the lady and the dog, looked nice and friendly. The lady made a little wave. Rise made a little wave back. The big dog looked like he was sweetly grinning.

Rise knew she was supposed to go straight into the barn and get the doors closed, but the lady and the big dog were easily walking toward them. The lady was smiling. The big dog was almost prancing at her side. He looked happy, about the size of a small pony. Rise decided to stop at the front of the barn. She knew she wasn't supposed to but she just wanted to so she just did. Sitting high in her seat, she knew the lady was coming below her. She waited for the lady and the dog.

The lady said, "Hello. How are y'all? I know I'm not supposed to visit with you and I expect that rascal Eddie has told y'all not to visit with me. And we're not supposed to look at each other too. That's why I'm all covered up like this. I apologize. Not very hospitable, I know. But I just had to come say hello. Curious too, I guess."

Rise leaned out the window and looked down and laughed. "Lady, to be honest with you, we're pretty curious too. From up here, all I can see is the top of your hat and your dog. And you're right, that nobody says anything to anybody rule was preached to us strong by Mr. Eddie. But when I saw you coming over, I felt like we should say 'hey' to you. After all, you letting us spend the night here. We appreciate it a lot. Thank you."

The lady said, "You're very welcome. Let's make sure nobody knows anyone's name. But I need to ask you two questions, neither one of which is asking about whatever this bus thing is all about though one day I'd love to know. Eddie and I used to go out. He drove me crazy but he is a good guy, a sweet guy. He was just restless. And we're still good friends. Maybe one day I'll get him to tell me."

"How about that. Eddie was courting you? Looks to me like he should have stood his ground. Nice, real nice place you got here. Maybe he should have stayed around a little longer. Sorry to hear it didn't work out. And so, go ahead on the two questions. Shoot."

"First of all, do y'all need anything? Blankets, water. Anything. It sometimes gets chilly up here at nighttime."

"Well, we got some blankets and pillows but wouldn't mind a couple more. And a jug of water would be great too. We've got food and soft drinks so it ain't like we ain't gonna make it through the night, but some water would be welcomed."

"Okay, no problem. Doing some rule breaking here but it's not my first time doing it. I'll get them and leave them next to the bus door. I won't be peeking. And will make sure my dog here is put up, kept in the house."

"He seems like a nice dog. He sure is big!"

"He's a good dog, loves to play, and is real gentle. He'll go in the house with me soon. I guess we could say he's curious too so need to keep him out of the way. Now, here's something else. What about needing a bathroom? I'm happy to let y'all..."

Rise broke in. "No, ma'am, that's not gonna happen. We appreciate it but that's just be some serious Mr. Eddie-rule breaking. If he found out we'd been in your house, he'd be madder than a wet hen. You got some nice, deep woods right over there behind this barn. They'll do just fine."

Kenny nodded in accord.

The lady murmured, "I understand. And too, there's electricity in this barn. There are switches for the overheads on the far wall."

"Thank you. Now, what's your other question?"

The lady paused and then looked up and asked, "How is Eddie? How is he really? Is he all right?"

Rise could now see the lady still had feelings for Mr. Eddie Terrell. She understood and decided not to tell all of it.

"He's good. Real busy with his law work and other things. He travels off sometimes it seems but that's almost always for business. Like you say, he's restless, real smart, real good with what he does but yes, he's restless."

"Does he have a girl?"

Rise hedged and fudged. "Sometimes it seems, kinda off and on, he has trouble settling down I think but that's just me."

The lady kept looking up lost in thought. Then she snapped out of it and said she was going to get the extra blankets and water. She and her big dog went into the house and quickly brought the extra supplies out. It was close to 5 p.m. She put them on the ground next to bus door. She called, "If you need anything, just knock on the door. I'm sure y'all are all right. I hope you have a good night."

"Thank you, ma'am. Nice sorta meeting you. We appreciate it. We'll be leaving at sunup. Hope we're not too much trouble."

The lady just nodded and went back into her house and closed the door and turned on the front porch lights. Kenny grabbed up the supplies just out the door and Rise carefully slipped the bus in the barn. Kenny pulled and shut the old doors that sagged and creaked. They tucked in for the night.

Risty Emiligia sat down in her office, just off her kitchen, her desk a veritable blizzard of paper and mess. She picked up the phone and called Eddie's office. A female voice answered. She asked for Mr. Terrell, said it was Miss Emiligia, an old friend calling. After a few moments, Eddie picked up.

"Hey. Everything all right? They there?"

"Yes, they're here. Everything is fine. As they pulled in, I went out just to say hello. I had to. Would have been bad manners not to. I'm curious. That's a cute little bus. Have to wonder if that fits with attorney Eddie Terrell but that's for another time. We visited just a little bit but no names and not really any looking at each other. I got them some extra blankets and water. Never talked with the big fella with her, just talked briefly with her."

"Risty, curiosity killed the cat and satisfaction brought him back. That was all nice of you to do. They're nice people. Just want to keep this one quiet and moving."

"I understand, I guess. They say they will leave at dawn so should be back to you by about noon. And Eddie, just by the way, do you have a girl?" She was quietly blunt.

He paused. "Well, yes, sorta, for now, but you know how that goes."

She felt her face redden. She felt instantly stupid for having asked.

"Yes, I do know how that goes. Okay, just wanted to let you know they're here and safe and sound. Come see me soon."

"Thank you, Risty. I appreciate it. I will." The line clicked dead.

Risty silently called herself a damn fool.

Eddie just pushed old memories away. They were getting closer.

Rise and Kenny settled in, ate and drank, and made spaces for their blankets and pillows on the running length of bus's middle aisle. They both, taking turns, went out the small back door of the barn once it was dark to use nature's plumbing. Both rumbled into their makeshift floor beds.

"Thanks for coming with me, Kenny. It helps."

"Thanks for letting me come, Rise. I'm glad to be along with you."

They uttered their goodnights as the wind picked up a little bit and the Blue Ridge Mountains got cooler in the ending of the season's night. They slept quietly and well and almost restfully.

The sun started to come up, its golden rays knitting through the slats of the old barn's walls. Kenny and Rise, like so many who pay attention with built-in antennae, had internal clocks and they were already three-quarters awake when the light became brighter, and they then easily snapped to alert, quickly arose, and prepared to go. Again, they, in turns, went out to the back and watered the weeds.

They gathered up their soda cans and snack wrappings and stuffed them in a paper bag. They were good scouts and policed their campsite to make sure it was left in good order. They folded the extra blankets, splashed some of the remaining water in the large jug on their faces, poured the rest out and left the borrowed items neatly stacked by the doors.

Kenny pushed open the big doors and Rise cranked up and carefully backed the little bus out onto the graveled drive. He leaned into the barn doors and closed them tight and hopped up the steps to sit at Rise's right. Rise backed on out a little further and then shifted into drive and began a long sweeping turn past the house and down the hill to the road.

The pretty lady and her big dog were standing at the door as they went slowly by. All waved at one another and Rise called a "thank you" and the pretty lady called back with a "good luck." They were down the hill and on their way. It was a little before 7 a.m.

They followed their directions carefully. Finding their way to Highway 29, it took them south through a long swath of the Old Dominion state for a good while, seeing much of the land and places they had rolled through on their way up and then outside Greensboro. They hooked onto 158 and then 311 and followed the signs back into Winston-Salem. They knew the way from there. They both sighed in relief and nodded at each other as they pulled into the parking lot of Eddie Terrell's law office on Cherry Street. They had done it. It had been an uneventful and interesting ride, but not without the constant current of adrenaline-driven tension and watchfulness. They were happy and very tired. It was almost noon.

Curt's car was parked next to the garage shed back in the corner of the lot and Curt stood leaning on its trunk. Rise made a three-point turn so the bus's hinging door would be facing Curt's trunk. She eased the bus up snug enough.

Eddie, Mikey, and Patty emerged from the office and quietly, all with big smiles, walked purposely across to where the two vehicles were virtually joined. There was lots of nodding and hand-shaking and hugging, and quiet congratulations were offered all around, but they were all in an efficient hurry.

Rise and Kenny led Curt up into the bus and unlocked the compartments and handed him the first of the six kilos. He held it, feeling its heft.

"I can smell the Clorox, and of course there's the wrapping, but where's the extra weight coming from?"

Rise, now informed, was pleased to explain. "Curt, they've been dipped in a light concrete to completely seal them. Drug dogs can't pick up the scent. It's a thin coating. Like rolling the chicken in the batter before frying. A few light taps of a small hammer will release the bags. Ought to help as you transport, I'd think."

"Damn, that's cool. Have never seen this before. Yeah, for sure, this is a nice touch. Good."

"And Pee Wee sends you his best. Punch too. They think you're solid. We do too."

"Thanks. Same here. Now, let's get these in my trunk and I'll be on my way."

Curt's trunk was already sectioned and buttressed as the six kilos were slotted securely in along a brief bucket line handle so each of the six could hold the same weight in consistent rows. Curt slammed the trunk.

Eddie stepped forward. "Curt, you got it all? Everything okay? You good to go?"

"Yeah. It's all good. I've got calls and visits to make now. I'll be back in two or three, maybe four days."

Curt grinned. "So far, it's been damn good doing business with you. Let's see if I can help punch up the pot now. I'm outta here."

"Good luck, Curt." Eddie waved and Curt moved on. The rest just stood there.

"Y'all okay?" Eddie asked Rise and Kenny.

"Yeah, we're good. That was, well, that was kinda fun."

"Good, let's lose the hats and the school bus paraphernalia except for your shirts and pants. Here, Patty, take this stuff from them and trash it. Now, y'all need to take the bus back to Leon right now. Tell him to rip the compartments out and then to quick sell it to some nice rube at a low-ball price and call me when it's done. Tell him to take a 50-percent commission on the deal. I'll stop by to pick my cut up when he does call me. No, fuck it. Tell him to take it all. No problem, keep it clean. He'll move fast on it so it won't be too long. Patty, how about you follow them over there for the drop off and then take them home? I really appreciate y'alls good help on this.

Hopefully, soon enough, we'll have something soon to spread around. Dear Baby Jesus... Y'all get going now." They did.

Eddie and Mikey watched them all go on. They had their arms around each other, joined at the hip.

"Eddie, is it almost done? It seems like a dream. Do you think Curt can finish the job?"

"Yes, it's almost done. Curt will come through. Sweetheart, let's go grab a little work to take home with us and mess with. It's Saturday. And truth be told, I'm pretty tired. How about you?"

"Honey, Eddie, I'm really, really tired. It would be nice to take a day and a half or so and just do nothing. Just do what we want to do. We've all been doing a lot and these last days have been pretty intense. Yes, let's go be tired for a little bit."

"I agree. Good idea. It's out of our hands for now. And Tuesday we go to Charleston for what should be a pretty good shot and show. Yeah, let's go have some downcycle time."

The mutual admission of their weariness was reflected instantly in their physical bearing. They sagged, held on to one another, almost holding one another up. Their shoulders slumped. Their eyes were tired. They wanted to go home.

They walked slowly back up into the office and then Eddie looked around and said, "No more work for a few days." Mikey nodded gratefully. He took Mikey's hand and led her back out to the steps and closed the door quietly behind them.

CHAPTER FORTY-THREE

TAKIN' CARE OF BUSINESS

Bachman-Turner Overdrive

CURT HEADED OVER to the Walgreens drug store down below the big Baptist Hospital complex. He made a few notes in his head, ordered them, reordered them, and then strolled in. What he was looking for were disposable flip phones and he found them all in plastic cases locked up behind sliding glass doors behind the main sales counter. Leaning behind the register was a lumpy, zit-faced teenager with a nice smile. At his appearance the kid did then stand up straight and appeared pleasantly alert.

Curt's head swiveled toward him. Curt knew his resting face held a useful, hard look so as he turned, he intentionally softened his face and nodded a tight-lipped but non-threatening smile.

The kid nodded. "Hi, mister. What can I help you with? Pretty nice day, isn't it?" This was all part of the all over the place, newly emergent sales concept of positive customer engagement, the purposeful relaxing of the consumer.

Curt started to grunt out a terse affirmation but caught himself instead responded with a respectful nod and what now appeared to be a genuine smile, though in the manner of the crocodile.

"Why, yes, young man. Yes, it is. I hope you can help me."

"I'll sure try. What do you need?"

Curt looked around and quickly noted aside from some shuffling blue hairs here and there who were tortoise-like with their little shopping carts moving slowly and carefully along the long aisles handling and inspecting the useless, the place was virtually empty. The Muzak played Bobby Brown's "My Prerogative" of all the weird things.

"Pretty slow for a Saturday afternoon, huh?" Curt said.

"Yessir. It is. It'll pick up around four when folks realize they need beer and wine and chips and candy or cigarettes or whatever for the night. It's always like this when it's nice out like this."

This was a good thing for Curt. There wasn't anyone around who might squeeze up behind him in the checkout line and wonder about the transaction going in front of them. And now, he was getting ready to soften the salesclerk up.

"Here's what I'd like, please. Five of those flip phones up there on the top two racks. In different colors if you have them. Please. Those are disposable and can be prepaid, right?"

"Yes, they are. Wow, mister, that's a lot of the same thing."

"Yes, it is, and I will tell you why I want to get them." Curt leaned forward on the counter, getting nearer to the young man.

With a kindly conspiratorial grin, he continued. "It's my eleven-year-old granddaughter's birthday party tonight. We're having a few cousins and little friends over for cake and ice cream. The missus and I thought it would be fun to give each little one their own phone for a little while with just a list of the numbers and no names and they could play hide and seek out in the backyard and try calling each other and seeing who they get on the other end. Pretty neat idea, right? My wife came up with it and I think it's pretty cool. Don't you? Now, I'll admit my idea was the different colors. Makes it even more fun, right?"

The scene he painted was so benignly bucolic and did lend itself to one of those Hallmark card family moments, even as Curt was lying through his teeth. He could even picture the sweet camaraderie of it all while recalling that none such sweet shit as that ever happened when he was a dirt poor kid, always running from his drunk, mean-ass daddy and his passively hysterical momma, and that was before the alleged family imploded and he was sent off to live with mothball-smelling, disgruntled auntie near Carthage in Moore County.

The kid clerk agreed, nodding his head. "You know that does sounds like a lot of fun. I like that. Never thought of that one."

"Well, good. Let's see what you got, please?"

"Never can be too careful with this kind of item. People will steal these like crazy. We have to keep them locked up. I know it's an inconvenience, but if we didn't, the bad guys would clean us out. Same thing with stuff like Sudafed and baby formula. Can you imagine? People make meth drugs with those!"

Curt agreed gently. "Yeah, there's no telling what folks with bad reasons will do."

Wouldn't it have been amusing for Curt to share with the clerk that he was actually assembling these items to contact a few of his dealer buddies to set up the cocaine buys? He had previously been in contact with all of them upon his return from his second Baltimore foray and now it was time to mark the time for the meets and greets and gets and goes.

The kid arrayed the phones on the counter and waved his hand over them like a game show hostess might.

"These colors okay? I have others."

"Naw, these are just fine. I'd like each loaded with twenty dollars of call time. You know little children, right? They do like to jabber and squawk away." Curt grinned paternally.

"Yes, sir. That I understand." He did the math out loud and then said, "That comes to $183.75 total. Cash or charge?"

Curt pulled out his wallet and lifted out four crisp fifties to hand them to the kid. "Thanks very much. How about you load them up and keep the change, please?"

"Thanks, mister! Gee. Appreciate that. Would you like your receipt?"

"Yes, please." No reason to leave any paper trail. In the parking lot, he would put the slip in his mouth, chew and swallow it.

While the phones were being prepaid, Curt wandered over to kill time and peruse the magazine rack. There was a lot of Brittany and no *Jet* or *Ebony*. It didn't surprise him. He was in Whitey Land. No reason to have much of anything that would appeal to people of color.

Just out of curiosity, he took a stroll down the aisle labeled "Hair Care." As suspected, no Queen Bergamot, no Jheri Curl. Hard to imagine the tight ass rich bitches of Buena Vista up the hill greasing their locks down. The thought of it made him laugh on the inside.

The clerk called to him. "Hey, mister, I've got you good to go." He held up a white paper bag. Curt took it and drove across town to his place.

He walked in, turned on a few lights, clicked the television on to a college football game and, at the break, went to his refrigerator. He pulled out two cold Schlitz beers and then went up top to the freezer. He removed a Swanson's fried chicken dinner box. He set it on the counter to thaw a bit and while it did, he sat in front of the screen and mindlessly sipped on the first beer and gazed blankly at players on the screen. Once he had finished the beer, he turned the television off and went and got the Swanson's box. Carefully, using his thumbnail, he unsealed the thin strip of clear tape that closed its back end.

He tilted the box and out slid a small leatherette address book. He slowly folded the pages over and again, making sure none were stuck together. The book was sectioned alphabetically. He studied the many names and numbers that were neatly written in boxy letters.

The bag of phones was on the floor beside his foot. He reached in, brought a phone out and dialed a number in Raleigh. A voice answered and Curt spoke quietly for just a few minutes. His last remark was, "Okay, see you Tuesday. I'll call when I'm ten minutes away." He pressed the off button and set the phone down on the floor.

He repeated the process with another new phone one at a time, calling then in further succession Durham, Chapel Hill, Greensboro. The talking was always the same: terse and brief. The last call was to Charlotte with Wednesday the day of the week noted and the number two used instead of the number one. Otherwise, all was the same. As he called, he wrote the recipient's number on a piece of paper. Once done with the five calls, he put all the phones back in the bag along with the short list of numbers and walked it to his car and locked it in the glove compartment. He idly recalled that he thought the green phone was good looking, had some professional edge to it. He had no idea why he thought that.

Once back inside, he locked the door and pulled the window shades down.

He placed the address book back in the box, carefully re-taped its edge and returned it in the freezer compartment underneath a Swanson's meat loaf and a box of Sealtest vanilla ice cream. He took the other beer and opened it and took a long pull. He stood at his short kitchen counter and rolled himself a tolerably large joint and lit it. He took a long pull on it too.

Curt turned the television back on, pulled his chair up close to the screen and began to watch the game more intently now. He enjoyed his beer and his dope. Later he got on his couch and took a long nap. He needed to rest. Though it was only Saturday afternoon, Tuesday would be here soon and Monday was his day to attend to his drink houses.

He ordered his mind carefully and quietly and slept on into the night and all the way through.

Mikey and Eddie went home, took a long walk around the lake, kicking the fallen autumn leaves before below them as they shuffled along. It was getting cooler. The sky was blue and purple gray, filled with scudding streaks of clouds. The colors of the season were bright beneath their feet before their inevitable browning. They held hands, moved slowly, and did not speak much. After their walk they ate together in quiet, gentle companionship, and soon enough, they turned all the lights off and leaned on one another into bed.

Rise had been staying with Kenny and had decided to get his place cleaned up enough in order for it to escape its description as a hovel.

Kenny was slouched in a chair, watching football, saw his sister bustling about and sincerely asked, "What you up to? Can I help?"

"Naw, Kenny Boy, just enjoy your game. I'm good. Thank you."

This was a good Saturday afternoon project and she threw herself into it determined and distractedly. She took the sheets and towels to Tommy Chester's laundromat, Top Sheets and Ts, just down the way from them, stuffed quarters into a couple of washers and turned them on heavy duty. She had then walked down the street to a local 7-Eleven where kids on little bikes hung around outside at the entrance, sucking down Slurpees and gnawing on candy corn and off-brand chips. They parted dutifully as she came on to buy enough beer to last the weekend, along with chips, little cigars, packs of cigarettes, Brillo pads, Pledge furniture polish, air freshener hangers, a double deck of Bicycle playing cards, a triple roll of paper towels, a big container of Comet, a bottle of Joy, a wrapped set of heavy-duty sponges and some paper pads and some pens. She hefted the two big brown paper bags home.

Moving all about and all around Kenny, she had swept and dusted and wiped all the horizontal surfaces down. She straightened the blinds and plumped up the ratty cushion pillows and arranged the furniture in some semblance of order. She washed and dried all the dishes in the sink and scoured the shower and tub. She addressed the toilet with an especially intense ardor. Although a big woman, she did not lumber about. Instead, she moved like an outside linebacker with quick purpose. Her tasks were lined up before her and she knocked them over in quick succession.

She went back over to Tommy's and put the wet linens into two industrial-strength dryers and turned them up to "high cotton." She admired the place. Ten big washers, ten big dryers. Sorting and folding tables. Well-lit, clean, no lint balls and dust bunnies flitting about. Tommy, a kind, silver haired older man, ran a good ship.

Rise then went back to the 7-Eleven and bought a dozen eggs and a flat of bacon, some butter, a loaf of bread, a jar of Peter Pan, a jar of Garner's grape jelly, many cans of Campbell's chicken noodle, tomato and mushroom soups and a box of Ritz crackers. She marched that home, put it in the cabinet and turned and started back to Tommy's.

"Damn, Rise, you be the damn lady tornado of Mr. Clean!"

She laughed. "Damn straight. You keep watching. I'll keep on keeping on." And on she went.

She returned with the bed clothes and towels, all neatly folded. She hung the towels and made the beds with tight military corners and plumped the freshly covered pillows up in the two bedrooms as well.

And lastly, she laid the decks of cards out of the battered so-called coffee table along with the pads and the pens. She cracked a cold beer, an Old Milwaukee, and sat down next to Kenny and said, "Now that's better. Much better."

She looked around. "I'll make us some soup and a sandwich in a little bit and we can watch some more and then get some sleep. I think we should sleep late tomorrow morning and have friends over to play cards and watch the football. Get some more rest later and then hit Monday running. What do you think?"

"I think you are right, Rise. Thank you. Thank you very much."

Eddie and Mikey arose Sunday morning around 8. It was a beautiful, crisp morning. They lapped about the kitchen, drinking coffee. Eddie asked, "Well, tomorrow we are back at it hard and on the move Tuesday. What would you like to do today? Maybe more of the same like yesterday?"

"Well, yes, that would be nice, but there's one thing..."

"What might that be?" Eddie cocked his head in curiosity.

She walked over to him and looked up into his searching face.

"Eddie, I'd like to go to church this morning. I'm feeling like it's something we need to do. I dunno. It's a strong feeling I have. Honestly, I haven't been to church in years.

Slowly, Eddie contemplated this very new component that had just deftly cat-walked into their lives. He paused, looking at her. "Well, why not? That's a nice idea." He wondered to himself as he spoke as to whether or not that was true or just pandering, but he had assented and they were now going to church.

He added half in jest, half is seriousness which meant he was about 99 percent serious, "Honey, you know I don't think I've been in a church except for a funeral or a wedding here and there for a long, long time. As a worshipper, probably not since I was a kid and then, Hell, I had no idea what I was doing. Considering my sometimes pretty shaky ways and especially what I have recently set into motion with this cocaine deal and my studied inexperience with all this faith and religion and Jesus stuff, aren't you worried when I walk in, the whole place is going to be struck by lightning and crash down on top of us? Ain't you worried about me as a potential lightning rod?"

"Eddie. It'll be all right. This is something I think we need to do. You are a good man. I'm a nice person. We need to be doing some filling in on our insides. There's something in church that I've been thinking we need. We might just find something. I want us to go. I want us to go real bad. Not every weekend, not all the time and don't worry, I'm not looking to become a holy rolling hand-waving Baby Jesus church nut but considering our lives and our needs and where we are, I think we need to go today. I think we ought to go."

"Fair enough. Let's go."

She crossed her arms, studied him and kissed him sweetly on the cheek.

"Thank you, honey. Let's get dressed."

He was clean shaven, handsome, and simple in a dark suit and somber tie. She was demurely and innocently lovely in a light fall dress and simple tan flats with just a little bit of makeup. Her hair was pulled back into a tight ponytail, making her look as a teenager. They were both nervous.

They discussed which church they should go to. Should it be the big massive Centenary Methodist, the soaring gothic rock pile that Eddie had been raised in, where he had been baptized and of course, that pretty much was the entire short trajectory of his walk of faith. Eddie well knew that his faith was in himself, that he was self-contained and isolated within himself. He had never felt that to be inadequate until this morning. Eddie was not an alcoholic but he carried the great fear of all alcoholics. Eddie was his Higher Power, so there wasn't really a need for another. But, maybe there was?

Should they attend the elegantly smaller St. Paul's Episcopal up on the top of Summit Street, classically Anglican, where his daddy had faithfully attended? His daddy never made much of a big deal about his comings and goings there, but it was always known that he enjoyed going and was always buoyed up and happy when he returned from services. He never judged those who did not go, which of course included Eddie's mother.

It made them all laugh as she had made it clear a long time ago that there really was no need for such transformational travel. She was living a good and Christian and generous life—just ask her—and had it on solid information that her entrance into the Pearly Gates was a 100 percent lock.

Or should it be another church, one he knew nothing about. An obscure, a not known place where the chances of him knowing anyone would be lessened. It occurred to him this was some piece of shame in him, akin to Adam and Eve discovering their nakedness in the Garden of Eden.

They talked about all this. Since she was the stranger, she deferred and asked him what he thought. He thought, looked at her, looked at her gentle loveliness and decided.

"Let's go to St. Paul's. I think it fits you. To me, you look like a St. Paul's girl."

"I'm not sure what that means but let's go ahead."

"Trust me, honey. It's all good."

They went to church. It was very nice. It was calming and inspiring. It felt good. And it was comforting which affirmed her and surprised him. Eddie saw a few folks that knew him, nodded to them and that was that. There were no shouts or expressions of surprise that the infant terrible trial lawyer Eddie Terrell and his unknown, mysterious pretty gal pal had suddenly appeared to bathe away their certain iniquities. The hymns and the choir were glorious. The altar flowers and the candles and the pomp and grandeur and power of it all were moving. The homily was short and to the point. The priest spoke about there always being a new beginning just around the corner from a failure, using Christ's crucifixion and his rising from the dead as his hook. On their way out, they along with all the others in attendance, were quickly greeted at the big doors out by the clerical staff with true smiles, a firm handshake and a thank you for coming and too, a please-come-back.

They had both knelt and prayed toward the end and asked God, reading the Book of Common Prayer, to forgive them their "wicked and manifold sins." As they deepened their efforts as they went along, they became more fervent in their askings.

Asking for forgiveness, asking for guidance, asking that things turn out all right, asking that they be safe. Eddie asking especially for forgiveness and that they get away with it all. Mikey asking for some way, somehow, she and Eddie be held together and for a future filled with good and not bad. At the end at the benediction, they watched the others and then they clumsily crossed themselves.

They held hands and walked quickly to Eddie's car. He wanted to get out of there, away from there. There was no distaste, just the urgency to return to the old normal. It had been good and it had been frightening too. The steady blocks of underneath support had been shaken.

"What did you think, Eddie?"

"Well, that was pretty nice. I'd like to try again, sooner rather than later. I don't think I'm quite right for this but I'll try if it makes you happy. I'm afraid I've got a long way to go in the praying department. I gotta admit I prayed for the success of our current adventure. Yes, Lord, thy will be done."

Sunday, Rise got in touch with Curt, using the phone booth in the scabby yard outside Kenny's door. She invited him to come drink a little beer, smoke a little weed, play cards, have some snacks, and watch the game. She asked him to bring a couple of friends. Curt accepted and he arrived a little past noon with Leon and Leon's son, Leon the Three. Rise asked what happened to "Junior."

Leon laughed and answered, "Junior makes him sound like a punk. The Three is solid with me!" They all laughed and sat down and had a good time. During a break in their entertainment when folks were getting up to use the can and grab a beer, Rise looked at Curt and mouthed, "When you going?"

"Tuesday and Wednesday. On your way into work tomorrow, how about you let Eddie know?"

"Will do."

Sunday passed on a nice note. They had fun and let their labors and worries subside for a few hours. The Redskins were as usual awful but the backdrop they provided was just right. All were grateful for the time. Just before all were stretching and the game was over and it was time to go, Rise mused out loud, "Kenny, in the morning, I've got one stop to make at Eddie T's and then onto work at City B. You're like always gonna go rattling about looking for short-time piece work, scratching for a car wash here, a trash hauling there. I'm thinking it's time for something more permanent for you. What do think about my asking Mr. Harry about a place for you?"

"I guess that'd be okay by me. I can drive and make deliveries and I'm a good hauler and stacker and all, but I do not want to make things thin for you. He's been good to you. Don't worry. If you do ask, make it little please. I'll find something after a while. Hell, I've got a strong back and a weak mind and according to the screws down at Central, that's the winning combination." Kenny laughed at himself and they laughed with him. After all, he was a sweet guy.

It was a small table that they'd played gin rummy and tonk on and it was easy for Curt to lean in and concentrate and listen with interest. It was as though in her comments, Rise was indirectly soliciting other inputs. These two had been good and faithful to him, had brought the fatted calf on home to him whole and safe. He was now genuinely fond of them.

Curt raised his hand as if in sixth grade. "Rise. Kenny. May I?"

Rise said, "Sure." Kenny watched. He knew he was with his elders and they were, he was sure, far wiser than he.

"As y'all mostly know, I've got some work to do over the next few days. If the Lord wills it so, then it will be predictable work and I will bring something back to those who have trusted me. I would suggest waiting a bit to see if my efforts bring forth fruit. For if I am able to do so, the recipients of those efforts will be pleased. I respectfully suggest we, y'all wait a little while."

Curt looked around the table at them all. Leon nodded slowly. He was no fool. "Son, I believe you were raised in the church. Isn't that right?"

"That would be so. Yes."

"Curt, you could have been a preacher. Of course, you're not but you bring value in other ways. Rise and Kenny, knowing next to nothing and hoping I know less as time goes by, I think Curt's thinking is worthy."

They all nodded in accord and that was that.

"And also one of y'all let Eddie Terrell know that the bus is cleared, cleaned and gone. Stolen it does appear." Leon smiled thinly in the fashion of the Cheshire Cat. They all rose together to end their afternoon.

Leon and his boy were gracious and well-mannered on their departure. "Thank you for having us. This was fun."

"Please come back anytime. You too, Three!"

Curt hung back and watched the Leons get into his car.

He turned to Rise and Kenny. "That was nice. Thank you. Rise, you got this dump cleaned up good. Nice work. Kenny, now you know that I know you didn't have nothing to do with it." Curt gave Kenny a playful, soft poke in the ribs.

Kenny grinned and murmured, "That's right. That's right."

Curt continued. "Everybody look sharp and behave. I'm on the move first thing Tuesday morning and then again Wednesday morning. If all goes according to plan, I will be back in good shape by Wednesday. Again, please let Eddie Terrell know and that I'll be in touch. And also, don't forget. This coming weekend, I'm gonna have both my drink houses up and running and I'll need y'all running and working them. I'll be back and forth checking and so forth. But y'all will be boss in both. Have to say it's been years since that damn fool Bo Diddley bought the farm and still don't miss him a lick. What a meddlesome smart ass he was. On the other hand, I sure could use

Pee Wee back here. He was solid good from the get-go. A real natural. Did y'all have a nice visit with him? I hope so."

"We did. It was too short. Kenny and I talked on the ride about maybe going back up that way one of these days after things calm down."

"I think that's a good idea. I like that. We'll talk about that some more later. I'll see y'all this Friday night. I gotta skip now." Curt winked and all were soon gone, and the cool evening began its crawl to dark.

CHAPTER FORTY-FOUR

DELIVERING THE GOODS

Judas Priest

CURT GOT UP with the dawn on Monday morning, checked his messages, found nothing of import which was usually the case. If somebody really needed Curt to know something, it was face to face. He dressed and went on over for coffee and cigarettes at an old hole-in-the-wall off Patterson. The smell of eggs and sausage and bacon and butter floated around the silent heads just waking up and enjoying this little, modest home away from home, actually in most ways better than home.

There was little conversation, mostly looks, glances, and blank stares. There were no women. They liked it that way. He glanced at the newspaper. There wasn't much else there either. But he checked some scores, scanned the headlines and the comics, and finished his coffee and ground out his glowing butt.

He was a smart man and while not formally educated, was informed and perceptive. He did not linger and soon headed to the same hardware store he had often visited in the past. Owned by and operated by garrulous, helpful white people, he was recognized and assisted without judgment. It made life a little easier. Curt bought six sturdy, long, zippered canvas totes, each the size of a small, thin briefcase. He figured he would only need a couple but at the same time, he was hoping Eddie would need more. It was a hopeful expediency.

Curt thought, *What the hell, why not?* Their best use was normally for brick masons to use in carrying their trowels and short levels and break bars. He tossed them onto the floor well of the passenger's seat. He then went out driving toward Liberty Street to check on his two drink houses. One was in a short-tailed cul-de-sac called Talley's Corner, the other a couple of blocks north of the first on a side street marked Jimmy Landing. Both were deep into east Winston and a short walk from one another. That helped with roving supervision.

At Talley, he met up with Ravon and his paint and work crew. They were a good outfit, knew how to do good work and do it efficiently. When they hit a place, they covered it up like the Sherwin Williams paint commercials. After their greetings, Curt gave him the keys to two of his drink houses.

"The cold weather time is coming along and I want them both comfortable and right for the season. I'd like a fresh coat of paint on the full interior of each. As long as the paint is white or light gray, I don't care. Also, please check all the electricals and fix whatever needs fixing. Make sure all the strings and other bulbs and lights are working good. Please check all the plumbing, including the bathroom sinks and toilets and also stoves, refrigerators, and all appliances including the coolers. Make sure the locks are secure and if you see anything that needs light carpentry or just basic fixing, just tend to it and make a list of everything. Let's do a quick walk through on each and then I'm going up to Gore's Club for an early lunch and a few hands of cards and some chewing the fat, and then I'm home to rest by midafternoon. Will be traveling next few days so I want to be, how do they say it, bright-eyed and bushy-tailed."

"Yes, sir. I'm following you."

They went into Talley and inspected each room carefully, one by one, pointing out this or that along the way. Ravon would from time to time make a note on a small pad he carried with him. His men, numbering three, followed along, gesturing or whispering quietly. They then walked over to Jimmy Land as it was called and did the same. It was about eleven.

Curt said, "You know, Ravon, nobody thinks much about it 'cause these places are in a crummy neighborhood but they are important. Just like other people got businesses, so do I and if I don't keep my places up to grade, then folks gonna go someplace else and that hurts me, hurts me here in my heart and in my pocketbook too which is even worse. White folks don't get it. It's like we are invisible except when we are not."

"I know, Curt. Believe me, I know."

"Thanks, Ravon. How about you come find me at Gore's about two, no later than three, and give me a progress report? How about we get square later in the week? Or if you like, you and the boys come by Friday and I'll toss in some complimentary refreshments too. Like I said, I'm not gonna be around tomorrow or Wednesday."

"Works for me. I'll get you word as to where things stand in a little while. Come on, boys. Let's go get our stuff and get to it."

Curt was bored and cocked and primed too. He was ready to go but it wasn't time to go. He knew that straining at the bit did no good and was actually a bad thing. It burned up energy, mental energy that he needed to have, both at the forefront and in reserve when the next few days came. He knew if he leveled his breathing out and concentrated on inhaling and exhaling, slowly the anxiousness would pass. In a nicely, and he knew it, unhealthy way, smoking helped with the needed repetition of it all.

When he walked in, off to the left was a tired baby grand piano that was well past any chance of being seen at Carnegie Hall and at that piano sat Johnnie Gore, randomly picking out some notes here and there, the pidgin English of the ivories. He was a big, square of a man with a lovely smile and a full head of hair that was brushed and pomaded back in oceanic waves. He wore, as he always did, one of his customized, gaudy dinner jackets, a crisp white shirt, baggy jeans and as a nod to the increasing vagaries of age and balance, heavy, black crepe rubber-soled Velcro-strapped shoes.

Gore saw Curt and nodded in greeting. Curt returned the gesture. They had known each other a long time.

Curt sat at the bar at Gore's and had a bowl of vegetable soup and a chicken sandwich. Curt nursed a couple of beers, visited reservedly with a few of the place's regulars, played a few hands of gin rummy, talked sports and politics in an affable, low key, non-confrontational way, and flipped through old magazines.

About 2:30 Ravon came in and lively hopped up on the stool next to him. Curt saw him in the mirror, turned to him and kindly said, "Well... how are things?"

"Hey, boss. All good, boss. We're rolling along nicely. Haven't run into anything much except for some loose flooring, boards in the kitchen at Jimmy. Need some new, stronger struts on both counters, at Talley and at Jimmy too. I'd like to switch out the front porch lights at both places. And I'm gonna suggest you hook some stronger speakers to the jukeboxes, again both places. Can get quick and easy."

"Sounds good. You want a drink? I'm gonna have one more before I go home. What's the damage?"

"Damage not bad. About three grand max. Working cash sure cuts the bullshit. Sure, a drink would be nice, thank you. We'll be done by six. Want me to bring keys by your place when we finish?"

"That'd be good, thanks. Appreciate your help. What you drinking? And how about I pay you up Friday?"

"Works fine. Thanks. How about a big shot of Old Grand Dad?"

"Good. I'll join you."

Monday morning, Patty and Mikey carefully ordered and loaded two bankers' boxes of Pussy Preacher and Blockhouse Club files, while Eddie was back in his office not doing much of anything beyond playing with rubber bands and paperclips, refining his trash can shot with a steady mediocrity.

They'd gone over the case ad infinitum and Eddie was full. He was about sick of it but that was a good sign. He was immersed and knew it up one side and down the other knowing how to play it. He had them by the short hairs. His engine was slow idling. He was going to machine gun them and if they didn't like it, tough shit. He would try the case and never speak to them again.

Earlier, Rise had stopped by very briefly to tell Eddie that Curt would be on the move tomorrow and Wednesday and would be in touch on Thursday. Eddie cautioned Rise to tell Kenny to be quiet, not to go hunting odd jobs or drinking. Loose lips sink ships. He would let them all know when the time was right. Eddie also explained that all three in the office would be away for all of Tuesday and Wednesday and thus would be out of pocket then. He explained that they should not fret. She left and went on over to City B.

Patty, Eddie, and Mikey heard the office front door open. They had not been expecting anyone.

A familiar voice called an unmistakable "halloo" from Alph Baron. They all went to the front to see him.

"Hey, Alph. Hey there, stranger! Good to see you!" Hugs all around.

"Hey, y'all. Glad to be seen. Just came by to see if I could start getting to work drafting on those settlement documents. Would that be all right? I hope everyone is well."

Alph shook hands enthusiastically with Eddie and eyed glowingly the pulchritude of Patty and Mikey.

"Well, Alph, that sounds good to me. Patty, would you gather up the settlement files and memos and orders of need for Alph? We'll plant him in the back corner office with the good sunlight and he can get started. Alph, remember to keep good track of your hours and..." And then Eddie paused.

"No, no, I've got a better idea for now for the effective use of your manifest talents. We've got plenty of time for those documents. I've got what I think is a better idea. That is, if you're game for it and feel like you can play with us. Plus, I've got a feeling it will be effective and fun and a nice experience for us all."

Alph looked curious. The girls saw it coming like Hank Aaron sitting on a seventy-mile-per-hour fastball. Alph, having not a clue, looked even more curious and cocked his head in his wonderings.

"Eddie, you have surprised me so often recently and it has all worked out pretty damn good so I'm all ears."

"Alph, the three of us are flying down to Charleston tomorrow morning to have dinner tomorrow night with three clients and a key witness. Dinner will be to make sure everyone is singing from the same page in the hymnal. Clients are young, once recently big-time college athletes, now all gone. Cocky then, chastened now. This is a big damages, strong liability case. Then after a decent night's rest, Wednesday, we're going to have a mediation right smack in the middle of the beautiful Four Corners of The Law in Tom Wills' offices. Can play crazy goofy with the best of them while he tightens the tie string around whomever's nuts need a squeeze. Lassoed my ball sack more than a few times over the years. Has superb judgment. We'll fly home Wednesday afternoon or evening. We either settle it all for some ridiculous good numbers or we come home and ask for a day certain setting and get ready to blow their sorry asses out of the water. The cases have a couple of really interesting twists that I think you'll enjoy it all. Most of the defense lawyers are good people, the adjusters probably so as well. Whaddaya say? Come with us?" If he could have busted his buttons in pride and happiness, Alph would have made that happen.

He beamed and said, "My goodness! Oh, yes! Oh, damn! I'm being invited to watch from the other end of the telescope. Never have done that before. And all of y'all are coming? Please let me call my office and my wife to let them know I'm going on quick trip to Charleston. Is that okay? This is so exciting!" His delight was palpable. It was as though he had just been released from a long prison sentence.

"Of course it is. Patty, please call the hotel in Charleston and get Alph a nice room. Mikey, please make Alph a copy of our mediation précis and package that we sent Tom Wills. I know there's plenty of room on the jet so there's no problem there."

"Jet!? You're kidding?!"

"Yeah, we figured why not? It's a Citation from Atlantic Aero over in Greensboro. Plenty of room. Might as well be comfortable and we're kinda figuring our traveling in style will set us up for success. Go make your calls and Mikey will get you the mediation materials, and then please come in my office and come sit with me and we'll go over it all so you're decently tuned in. We're glad you're here."

An hour later, after Alph had read over the materials, he whistled low and observed that this case was a complete cluster fuck for the other sides and he was glad, very glad to be included.

"Good. Alph. How 'bout be on the ramp by say, 10:15? Just an overnight bag with a power suit and power tie. Please bring a very bright tie. Their eyes cannot resist it and it's one more distraction. We take every edge we can get. And Alph, please make sure your shoes are shined." Eddie winked. Alph giggled.

"You got it. Gee, this is like being a kid with a new bike in a candy store!"

"We're glad you're coming! I've got your room lined up. We're all staying at The Mills House. It's pretty nice enough," Patty explained.

"Always nice to take a trip to a nice place." Alph giggled again and zipped out the door on winged feet. Patty laughed once he was gone.

"Jesus, you are just bringing him right down the pipe on a wiggling lure. I like it."

Mikey nodded her assent and admired her man.

"Let's get some stuff done now, and then how about we meet at the airport about ten tomorrow? We'll check in and wait for Alph."

They went about their business until later, when they dispersed to have a few drinks at the old, ratty and lovely Sir Winston down in the basement of the O'Hanlon Building, a beloved dump with cheap, flaring red, faux leather booths, rented and torn with the stuffing leaking and oozing out. They shot the bull, gossiped, drank close to too much and then scattered and went on home to grab some dinner and then get a good night's rest.

Curt was up before his alarm. He dressed neatly and plainly and watched the news and weather while he had some instant coffee that tasted like cardboard but had that good caffeine pop. He went out and slowly, carefully raised open his trunk to make sure each of the six vessels were there, which of course they were. He thought about slipping a .38 in the glove compartment, just in case, but quickly ditched the thought. If things get fucked up, no reason to add insult to injury. He thought he'd go ahead and be a little early and so headed east on Interstate 40 at 6:45. He had a full tank and a full trunk. He had his flip phones. No rushing now.

About two hours later, he was topping his gas tank off at a station just down Oakwood Avenue in east Raleigh. He waited a few minutes, looked at his call list, took the corresponding phone and punched in the number.

"I'm ten minutes away." He was told to come on. He went to the trunk and removed one sealed kilo and was on his way. He pulled in the back behind the Saint Augustine's College historical chapel, a lovely old building, old, built by freedmen during the beginnings of the Episcopal effort to educate the released slaves after the War Between the States.

A SAC campus maintenance services truck awaited him. It was positioned so they were side by side at the driver's open windows. They were screened by two large dumpsters.

An older man, one Evans Gee, with a shining brass-toothed grin said, "Good morning, friend. Here you go." Gee was a long-time fixture on campus, knew many of the students on a first-name basis and was trusted and benign. He also knew plenty of back-of-the-house workers and more than a few students up and down Hillsborough Street over at North Carolina State. The network had always been there. Students and some faculty for sure did love their blow. More than a few mommies and daddies funded the highs. Nice of them, though most had no idea. So it goes.

Curt handed him the odd-shaped cylindrical brick and Gee reciprocated with a sealed heavy-duty book mailer envelope that weighed a little more than two pounds.

Gee asked, "It's all there?"

"I'm sure. The seal is lightweight concrete. A few light hammer taps will release it once you're ready to prepare it for retail."

"Thanks. See you around. Don't be a stranger. Then again, why not be a stranger? Makes more sense." They both laughed.

Curt pushed the envelope under his seat and pulled away and headed to Durham.

Within a half an hour, he was again parked behind dumpsters at the soaring Duke Chapel on the campus of what was often referred to, much to the consternation of the Blue Devil faithful, as the Million Dollar Buck Duke Ego Tower on the campus of The University of New Jersey in Durham. He made the alert call. He had earlier removed another kilo for efficient delivery and it sat beside him, mutely waiting. A university campus police car sidled up next to him.

Thomas Finn, a thin, handsome man in late middle age, a long-time master sergeant in the service of the Methodists looked Curt over and said, "Been a long time, Curt. Ready to do some business? I got a bunch of little and big Dukies and lots over at N.C. Central who have hankerings." He smiled calmly.

"Yes, it has been awhile. Hope they and you enjoy." He again explained the seal. They exchanged containers.

"See you around."

"Be safe. Be square."

As Curt was leaving Durham, Alph Baron, Patty Cherry, Mikey Riewy, and Eddie Terrell climbed aboard a Citation Two which had shuttled over to Smith Reynolds from Atlantic Aero in Greensboro. There were two pilots in the cabin, stereotypical with their buzzed haircuts, short-sleeved, emblazoned, starched-white pilot shirts, and the ever-present Ray Bans. They were good humored, reticent, and well mannered. They assisted the happy, excited party of four up and in, got them settled and hauled up briefcases, two bank boxes of documents and exhibits that were most likely rarely to be opened, and small, overnight bags. This was a speedball trip with no need to overpack.

They buttoned her up, fired up the engines, and sat on the tarmac for ten minutes as the mechanicals reached proper revolutions and temperature.

Mikey held Eddie's hand, squeezed it firm and whispered in his ear, "My God, Eddie, will it always be this much fun? I've never done anything like this. I'm in a dream and I have no interest in waking up!"

Eddie bussed her cheek, smiled at her. "I sure hope so."

Alph grinned an enormous grin, looked around surveying their comfortable decadence and declared, "What a damn fool I have been! Should have gone plaintiffs from the get-go! Ain't this a kick?!"

Patty just smiled and nodded. "Mr. Alph, don't tell anyone, but this really is how we roll."

The co-pilot came back and told them to sit back and relax. It would be about a one-hour flight, pretty much an arc up and an arc down. The Citation was simply a powerful bullet in the skies. Once they came into Charleston airspace and were handed to Charleston tower, they'd circle a bit in deference to commercial flight's schedules before being slotted for landing at the FBO. The weather was fine. It would be a nice ride.

The plane nosed in a tight semi-circle and hesitated at a slight braking, then rolled down a long runway and turned back into a slight wind out of the south.

The engines revved up and hard whined and then the brake was released and the plane lurched forward, roared down the runway and hurtled into the beautiful air in a steep and breathtaking climb out. They were on their way. Eddie closed his eyes and refined his game plan for tomorrow. It was a simple, three-step assault of plain, unorthodox daring.

Curt took the quick interstate, flying west, always with the careful speedometer in his cocked eye, past the new, big, messy, jammed up Southpoint mall exit and then hooked it off to the right and swung west toward Kenan Stadium and the Dean Dome and began to slide up the hill to the Hill. He began a slow crawl, cross walked stopped, students wandering oblivious past the old Carmichael Arena and the student store and the gray, ugly, monolithic chemistry building. He made his "I'm almost there" call.

He cleared the intersection in front of the Navy ROTC building with the Carolina Inn to his right and goosed it gentle up McCauley Street and swung left into the back lot of the Phi Delt fraternity house, crammed up with well-to-do white boy late model cars.

The back kitchen door open as he pulled in and the legendary Jeffrey Spencer, better known as Uncle Buck, came out and stood at the top of the steps. He snaggle-tooth grinned and waved at Curt and Curt returned the courtesy. They'd known each other a long time. Buck was older than dirt, had the lazy energy of a happy cub, took care of everything at Phi Delt, and never let any alcohol waste away. He was known to, on early Saturday and Sunday mornings as he dusted and vacuumed, pick the drowned cigarette butts of the now gone prior evening's festivities from their plastic cups, toss them on the floor to be sucked into the Electrolux, and then with a grimace of pleasure, swallow swill the liquid residue. Football and basketball weekends were his favorites. Crowds and parties burgeoned his wealth. He stayed nicely drunk and nicotined high, as pleasant a gentleman as could be found. It was his bonus time. People just handed him money in fascination and revulsed appreciation.

Curt went up the steps, shook Buck's hand and spoke quietly to him. Buck went back into the Phi Delt kitchen and returned with two large bags of sandwiches, one of which layered the money. The two walked to the back of Curt's car, opened the trunk, and discreetly settled the bag with the cash next to the spare tire and placed the vessel of blow in the other. They shook hands again and said their goodbyes. Buck winked and Curt moved on. Three down and one to go for this day. So far so good.

Curt headed down 86 and got on interstate to Greensboro, a short ride no more than 45 minutes. He took his time. He made his contact call soon thereafter and pulled into the far parking lot of the tattered, abandoned Aggie Inn, once the very nice residence for visiting North Carolina A&T visitors, friends, and alums. Now, it was but an abandoned dump with the chronic look of ever-worsening disrepair, trash blowing across the parking lot, dead weeds sprouting, and many windows cracked and broken.

No one had paid attention to it in years and as such, it was a good place for an exchange. Curt parked up the hill, waited, tapped his steering wheel to the quiet beat of some innocuous R&B. Directly, a late model, modest blue Chevy with sparkly rims rolled up next to him, driven by a young black male with an enormous, mushrooming afro.

"You Sammy's man?" Curt asked.

"Yessir, I am. I think you have brought Sammy something. I've been sent to get it and hand you some tribute."

Curt looked him over and asked, "Before we dance, tell me what Sammy looks like and who is his favorite team?"

"Yessir, I understand. Sammy has a really big mole on his right cheek, looks like a dime, and his top two front teeth are shiny gold. He actually has two favorite teams, the Redskins and the Tar Heels. That help you?"

"Yes, it does."

They both looked around, saw not a thing and effected the handoff through their opened windows. There were plenty of college kids in town who soon would be rolling dollar bills and snorting and jerking their heads in shock and pleasure.

"Thank you. Give Sammie my regards. By the way, how do you know him?"

"My mom is his sister. He's my uncle."

"Good. Be safe out there."

"Good plan that." And they were gone.

Curt drove back to Winston-Salem, thinking that he now had $400,000 in cash under his ass and wondering how often this kind of shit went down. He thought a lot more than most folks recognized or figured. Keep it small, keep it simple, fly under the radar. Good way to get well.

He went straight back to Gore's, put the four packets of dollar bills in one of the canvas mason bags and walked in. A hundred thousand in one-hundred-dollar bills that weighed a little north of two pounds so the load was easy enough.

Gore was sitting at his piano plinking away.

"Gore, can we go in your office and talk real quick."

"Sure. Come on."

Gore hoisted his big frame off the piano bench and led Curt in.

"I think you'd like to close the door, right?"

"Yeah that be good. Thanks."

"What's up?" Curt held up the bag.

"Gore, in here is real valuable. I've got to make one more trip tomorrow down south and will be back tomorrow afternoon. Would you please lock this up for me today in your safe and whatever I bring you tomorrow as well? I'd really appreciate it. I'm happy to pay you ten grand for the courtesy. I'll pick everything up on Thursday."

Gore looked him over. "Curt, you've never been an extravagant man. That's a right big number for babysitting a couple of no-count canvas bags. I didn't fall off the turnip truck yesterday. I got an idea of where you are. I'm happy to lock your stuff up safe and sound in my gun safe but only for a couple of Gs please. You're renting a little space for just two days, right? Pay me when you come to make your final pickup. That all right with you? I hope so."

"Yes, it is, and I thank you for your courtesy. I guess I'm a little antsy. That was a high offer, wasn't it?"

"Yeah, but it's okay now and I understand. Give me that bag and let's put it in the safe dark."

Curt handed Gore the bag and he walked over to a closet door in his office, opened it, spun the tumblers on a big gun safe and pulled the door open. Over Gore's shoulder, Curt could see rifles, shotguns, pistols, other bags similar to his, and even a couple of ornate jewel cases. Gore placed Curt's bag on a shelf and closed the door and spun the tumblers into a tight, clicked lock.

"I think we're in good shape now. Lunch?"

"Thank you very much, Gore. Like I said, I'll be here tomorrow with one last bag and then I will get all and go on Thursday. And yes, some lunch would be nice, thanks. I'm buying."

"Bullshit on that. Last time I looked this is my place. Let's go out and have a beer and a whatever and catch up. No need to talk about this anymore today."

"Fine with that, good."

The jet whooshed comfortably into Charleston a little before noon. They all disembarked, carrying their things. It was, even for it being autumn, hot and humid in the Holy City. The captain leaned out the cockpit window and told them to just give them a couple of hours' notice tomorrow and they'd be back to get them. He thanked them for using AA. As they walked into the FBO offices, the little jet had already turned and was headed back to North Carolina. They all crammed into a taxi and headed into town.

They were before check-in time at The Mills House, so they left all their things with the bellman's station and walked down Queen Street to the venerated and venerable 82 Queen. They sat in the back open-air courtyard, which was all garlanded up in threading ivy and palmetto trees and painted in a rococo Pepto Bismol pink where the enormous Albert, an ebony obelisk of a man shucked oysters and cracked beers and poured cold wine. The men shed their jackets and the ladies laid their sweaters aside.

They talked about this and that but not about the case much at all save for brief review of the folks who would be present.

They would do this again later that evening when their clients and Truck Tinker would join them for dinner at 7:30 at the hotel. After their pleasant lunch, they were able to get into their rooms a little early. They all changed into comfortable shoes and took a collective stroll across Broad Street and down Meeting to the High Battery, admiring the lovely homes and gardens. It all had a fairyland feel to it except when they spied a palmetto bug scampering away on the cobblestones. They stared out across Charleston Harbor and studied the low silhouette of Fort Sumter well off in the distance to the east.

Eddie recalled before them all like a history museum docent that before all hell broke loose, Fort Sumter on April 12, 1861 was three high stories of massive brickworks. The first shot fired by the South to initiate the conflict was a star shell that perfectly exploded a few hundred yards above the fort and illuminated the entire structure so the Confederates could dial their guns in. And they did so well. That first lanyard was pulled by the rabid secessionist Benjamin Butler with a grim delight. Some years later, when Butler realized that things were not going to work out for the butternut and gray, Butler killed himself rather than countenance living under Yankee rule.

For two full days, the Confederates battered the place, and despite there being no Union casualties from the hot firing, the fort was shrunk to but one story of torn up rubble. When the Union finally capitulated, their troop was allowed to formally strike their colors and fire cannon shots in tribute to their bravery. It was during that when the first casualties of the

War Between the States occurred. A defective shell load exploded prematurely in the barrel and killed one artillerist and gravely wounded another.

They followed Eddie intently not blinking. Alph and Mikey were intrigued and asked, "How do you know all this stuff?"

Patty laughed. "Hell, he reads everything. He's a bug on lots of military history. Got it from his daddy who was a tank commander in World War Two. Plus, he ain't exactly stupid either. This is the God's truth. I once heard him tell an opposing counsel who he dazzled with some obscure shit he whipped out during a pre-trial conference that there was no way he had time to die, that he had too many books to read."

Eddie half-smiled and they kept walking down the Battery and wound their way back on East Bay Street and then up Queen to The Mills House. It was a sweet walk. They went back to hotel to rest until they would all gather in the Best Friend Bar at 7 p.m.

Alph said, "I need to get back down here sooner rather than later. What a gorgeous place!" They were all in agreement on that one.

When Mikey and Eddie were back in their room, she asked him, "You okay? You good to go? I worry about you, you know."

"Honey, I'm good to go. I'm a little wound up but that's fine. Pre-game butterflies. Perfectly normal. You've seen it before now. As you know, this is a pretty high stakes deal. Fun to play for big numbers, don't you think?" She came to him and held him close.

"You are something else, Mr. Edward Terrell."

"Thanks for that. Want to play a little bit before showtime?"

"You bet! Let's cut some tension." And so they went about it.

At the Best Friend Bar they were soon joined by their clients Johnson, Marks, and Shelvin who had just checked in and Truck Tinker who followed in about 10 minutes later carrying a large plastic cup, redolent of the scent of a tasty bourbon.

"Hey, y'all! I wasn't supposed to bring Horty, was I? I sure as hell did not want to!"

"No, no, no, Truck! It's just right you are here by yourself. Don't think Horty would bring much to this little pre-business meeting. And, Truck, you know I'm gonna buy you a couple of drinks. No need to be brown bagging in here." Eddie laughed.

Truck grew sheepish. "Whew, Eddie, you know how I worry about protocol all the time. Guess I'm a little nervous too, stirred up. This ain't exactly my primo line of work. Not a lot of serious business gets done here in Charleston after dark. And when folks gather, it's almost always with spouses and significant others." He gently snorted and mumbled, "Glad she's not here."

Then he noticed that he did not know most of these folks standing before his musings and reflexively began to introduce himself to the young clients to whom he was sympathetic and courtly respectful, as well as to Patty and Alph, and lastly, to Mikey. He paused and admired her.

She murmured, "I help Patty. I'm with Eddie."

Truck grinned appreciably. "How could I not know that!? Good job, Eddie! And good job, Miss Mikey!"

Truck had been loosed by his early brown water and was a tad too garrulous. Eddie knew Truck was nervous. Anything that was even distantly close to courtroom combat weakened his knees and his will. Eddie, with his tone, just a bit strident and monotone, sharpened everyone's focus quickly. Truck knew it was meant for him. And although no Carrie Nation, Eddie also made sure all had a drink or a beer if they wanted it, which they all did. Truck traded his cup for a short glass, making sure the no-nonsense reining in was delivered.

Eddie told his clients he would appreciate it, no check that, it was clearly an admonishment of ruling that they each needed to hold it to two beers max this evening with no post-prandial forays out into the lively and tempting streets of Charleston. The television sets in their rooms worked just fine. And too, stay out of those honor bars up in their rooms. They did not need to look hung over or shitty the next day. Such foolishness could and probably would cost them significant money. And as that was all they could seek tomorrow, the waste of same would be a real shame.

He complimented them on their timeliness and appearance, acknowledged how battered and hurt they had become, reminded them they still had the disciplined minds of fine athletes and that he needed them to rely on the game plan. This was a competition and they needed to be sharp. They all nodded. They heard him. They understood him. He could see it and thanked them and told them he trusted them.

Truck and Alph looked on in quiet admiration as Eddie went over tomorrow's order of battle. Eddie was swimming effortlessly in his element. Patty and Mikey each beamed.

Lots of small talk ensued, encouraged by their ringmaster, their master of ceremonies, Eddie.

"Now, come on, y'all, talk a little bit about sports, politics, life, travel, money, dating, whatever. This ain't a blowout, but it sure as hell ain't a wake either, so let's pleasantly loosen a bit." Hesitantly then engagingly, they all pitched in.

The maître d'hotel came and escorted them into the large, lovely, high-ceilinged dining room. The walls were a continuous wave of light gray and silver velvet, brocaded with gold lanyard. It was what they all imagined old Charleston must have looked like "back then." Golden candlelight pushed by the lazy, slow overhead fans splayed on the walls like a clutch of fireflies. The table was substantial, accommodating their eight comfortably without crowding, the chairs just right high enough and plush without being sinkers. Menus were handed around. A young man in a white jacket poured water. Another older gentleman with a crimped brush of silver hair appeared at Eddie's shoulder, told them his name was Percy, that he was there to serve and help them and asked what he could bring them from the wine list or from the bar. He waited at comfortable attention, his hands gently clasped together.

"Thank you, Percy. We will get with you in about ten minutes or so. We need to go over some business first."

"Of course, Mr. Terrell. I'll be just right over there. Just wave when you're ready." He unobtrusively moved over into the shadows. It was the kind of old time, quiet hotel where there were still shadows in its common rooms.

Eddie leaned forward and said, "Here's what it's gonna look like tomorrow. But first, take this instruction to absolute heart and do not break these rules. No one, and that includes me, is to be rude, make faces, be disrespectful or gloat or grimace, make speeches or talk out of turn. Of course, I'm gonna rip here and there but no matter what, y'all sit real still.

"I ask you all to be ladies and gentlemen all the time. Poker faces are the faces of the day. Implacable and that goes with when we are alone with our mediator Tom Wills. I get to bullshit with Tom. We go way back. But no one else. Bad or ill-mannered behavior could change some thinking and I want them thinking only about the strength of these cases. Y'all got that?" They all nodded.

"And that also goes even if someone on the other side goes nuts, ballistic, whatever. Give them no response. By the way, if and when that might happen, such a non-response will drive them crazy and weaken them. Now, here's the layout which is the deal as well." Eddie pulled out a few pages of notes.

"Y'all pay attention now. We really won't have time for too much of this in the morning. Let me set the scene. Think of this as a stage being set up for a play and when the curtain rises, all the characters will be on the boards in full view and ready to go. Imagine you are standing well above it all and you are looking down on the field of rooms and players. Wills is a real good mediator and runs a good show. We will meet at 9:15 in the morning after breakfast to head down to Tom's offices.

"Tom will then make his opening comments, emphasizing that he is neutral and his only interest is in getting the case resolved. We will all sign off on a confidentiality sheet agreeing nothing that is said in mediation can be quoted in any later trial. Sometime folks make admissions or say things that could hurt bad at a trial. This signing off eliminates the threat of that and encourages full candor. We will each be invited to make an opening statement. Tom has already been provided by us and the others small summaries of positions on liability and damages. Usually those start with the plaintiffs, that being us, and then we go around the room and each group will speak to their positions on their cases.

"Sometimes, when a case is technically complex, medical or accounting or some such, opening statements can get pretty long with exhibits and charts and the like, but I do not expect that here. What I do is expect is that everyone is sorry about what happened, that everyone bears some responsibility for what happened, and that we are all here in good faith to see if we can't get these unfortunate matters compromised and resolve. Very plain vanilla.

"By the way, there is plenty of liability insurance on all three pikes so that doesn't hurt. Now, just because they got it, doesn't mean we're gonna get it all but we're gonna get a chunk of it and they know it."Eddie paused. Randomly, Curt and Rise and Kenny wandered through Eddie's mind's eye. He paused again. He wondered about them, how Curt was doing. He was very still for few moments more and let them all pass through. They were then gone, wisps leaving tiny contrails. Mikey had been watching him and saw the flickers come across his eyes.

"And so then we'll get started on the mediation. Tom will go back and forth visiting with, gauging, encouraging, scolding each group. I've always called it The Anglo-American Shuttle Diplomacy of English Law.

"A last few notes before we choke and chew. All of the lawyers on each side are good and competent and know what they are doing. I hesitate to draw attention to one individual but feel like I need to as he is a bit different and I think it's best y'all have some information so he'll not be a distraction as the matters move forward. And I will also tell you I'm thinking I may have a bit of a plan for myself which might be a little disruptive but I'm still working on it.

"Here we go. There are two lawyers who represent Blockhouse. One is a strange fellow named Sampson Jenkins. He's a really large, round man. He's kind of innocuous but he parrots the other one, the lead lawyer I'm going to soon tell you about, parrots him all the time and then, until he doesn't.

"But the other guy, the one I want to tell you about is a guy named Wallace Marcus from Columbia. He's tall and strikingly handsome and one of the most arrogant stubborn jackasses I have ever run across. He is snotty, he is haughty, he is better than the rest of us put together. He is rude, dismissive, and curt. Pay attention to him as he really is quite entertaining, but for God's sake don't laugh. It won't help and I'm not kidding. His poseur skin is thinner than a pig's heart valve. Now, one last thing and this is an offering of mine that I have given a lot of thought to. I mean to cause no consternation or upset but it's on my mind and feel if I don't speak to it and have some concordance, I won't be able to speak to Wills about it either. And I feel like I need to. Please pay close attention here." They all leaned in.

"Dooley, Fishers, David, y'all all got beat up badly that night. All badly hurt. Y'all understand they're gonna blame you in part because of your drinking and that's fair. But our position is they let y'all drink and drink some more to the point where y'all were blind drunk and exposed to harm like pitiful, defenseless babies. So we'll be kicking that one around as we go down the road tomorrow.

"But, here's what I'm thinking. I have to make judgment calls all the time. I gotta size things up and try to get them in the right perspective using all the facts and the law and all the tools I have at my disposal. First, I think Fishers here is the worst of all your beaten-up guys. And secondly, I think he ought to get more money than y'all, Davis and Dooley. Now, we're gonna leave here with money. I'm hopeful a good sum for each of you. But I'm thinking Fishers ought to get a bigger bump. And I also think they're gonna be thinking along those lines. I hope, truly hope I have not upset any of you. Y'all are old enough to be considered adults in the eyes of the law so this kind of decision lays with y'all. Mommy and Daddy love y'all, but it's up to y'all individually and together who are gonna scratch the marks on the board."

There was a rustling, quiet pause. Fishers spoke up.

"Mr. Terrell, I appreciate all that but that isn't necessary. I'm a big boy. I'll make my way just fine without an extra crutch. I promise." He looked off into the distance.

David looked at them. "Fishers, you've always been such a hard ass. I like the idea. Why not see if you can't get you a little extra juice? Hell, you've lost your hand and had your head rapped pretty seriously. I think we ought to help you if we can and it appears this is the only way we can do it. Hopefully, it will make your life a little easier over time. I'm all for it." David crossed his arms and nodded at Fishers.

Dooley was quiet for a moment, then spoke. "I'm for it too. I like the idea but just not too much!" He winked. "Hell, get him the biggest pile. He's been through the biggest pile of, excuse my French, shit."

Fishers held his arms up, the missing hand so obvious in its absence.

"Okay, okay, okay. No mas, no mas. I ain't gonna fight y'all. Whatever happens, happens. I appreciate it. I hope you know I do." He misted up and looked away. The table went quiet.

Eddie spoke, "That's it for now. Let's eat and drink and get some rest. And if as y'all think on it later on, somebody has different thoughts, if anybody wants to talk with me about it, get me in the morning. I'm think we should do breakfast at 7:30. I'll be here in the lobby at 7, fair enough?"

They all agreed and nodded. Alph exhaled deeply and approvingly, "Professional all way around."

Truck was trying to keep up but he knew he was on the better team no matter what.

The ladies looked at each, smiled and secretly held and squeezed each other's hand under the table. Mikey appraised Eddie radiantly and quietly. He noticed, nodded briefly.

Eddie looked around the table. "Let's eat." And he turned and waved to Percy to come along.

After finishing their first rounds, they began their evening's decompression and accepted some relaxation, some comfort in one another. They each carefully counted from one to two and had another. Truck had a big bucket of ice water with a useless lemon in it and laughed sweetly at himself, reminding them all in good humor that they should remember he had jumped to the front of the line in the beginning. He was adorable, a teddy bear, and some of them applauded and clapped him on his broad shoulders.

They mellowed carefully. They knew they were safe, that tomorrow would be interesting, not without some intrigue, but surely they were in good hands and in good shape. The smiling presence of Alph Baron was an unexpected troop of reserve, another real pro, and a heavy-duty older guy too. That lent a wonderful contrast as between the two. It was so obvious Alph and Eddie really liked and admired each other, that they were sort of a one plus one equals ten, a hand in glove deal, making an imposing fist.

They each knew their roles, imagined their lines, saw themselves delivering. They did more asking about one another, learned more about each other, learned a little more about themselves. They were all climbing into their crowded foxhole and kindly shifting, becoming a small platoon of well-heeled misfits.

They ate well but were not piggish or sloppy. Good cheese biscuits, salty, fat oysters from just up the intercoastal beds, shrimp and grits, crab cakes, sweet bene wafers. They all watched their table manners, their people manners. Then they let the little fog of full fatigue begin to drape them and soon, folks began to excuse themselves.

Eddie and Alph sat comfortably and watched them all ghost away, shaking hands, kissing cheeks. The last to go up was Mikey who came around behind Alph and then Eddie and hugged their necks and kissed their cheeks and stood her beautiful well hewn dark-tressed self straight up. It was impossible to not look at her intently.

"Alph, I hope you have a good night."

"Well, Mikey, not sure how it could ever be better but thank you. I hope the same for you, y'all as well."

She deep curtsied, right leg laid out long as a praying mantis pinned behind her, the toe of her five-inch heel sleek stacked on point.

"And you, Mr. Terrell. I presume you'll be along as well?"

"Yes, dear, of course, but I would like to spend a few minutes with Mr. Baron before I come on, if indeed he is amenable."

Eddie looked at Alph. Alph nodded that he was indeed amenable and asked, "Is that acceptable with you, Mikey, just a few minutes?"

Mikey nodded, smiling, and turned and strutted slowly, one foot planted in front of the other, walking her own red carpet, her beautiful backside, tremoring as the first fissure of a small earthquake, and strode into the elevator without ever turning to look back.

"Well, Eddie, how do I say it? This is all so crazy good and please forgive me, but if I didn't watch that, they'd have to take the windows out of all the department stores!" Alph spoke impulsively, involuntarily, rapidly, hoping that if it were offensive, Eddie would just blur through it.

Eddie heard every bit of it and was simply happy. She confirmed all recognitions. He was a fine lawyer. She was a finer marker. It could not be helped.

"Alph, no offense taken. No, she's...how to say it? Transcendent...maybe... or just hotter than a cherry bomb in July. Might you spend a few minutes with me? Let's talk a little. Please." Eddie and Alph, the haze of camaraderie and an obviously enticing future, ambled into the little bar, took seats at the counter and each ordered a brandy.

They talked of the tomorrow's proceedings and how nice the young men were, and they also spoke about getting the Reynolds/Law Firm debacle and its paperwork tidied up and cemented. They talked about life in general, the fragility of it all, their pleasures, and woes. And their snifters slowly sipped away until there were a few long-necked drops in the bottom of each.

"Eddie, in truth, it's time for me to go find my beauty sleep. I've enjoyed this evening immensely and I think I'm gonna enjoy tomorrow as much if not more. Please tell me what you need me to help you with. You know I'm game."

"Fair enough. I've been thinking. As you well know, these things really have only two parts, the beginning and the end. The middle is just a lot of sitting around and waiting for the numbers to move and move they will I'm pretty sure. The middle is just desultory, just being patient. Liability is so strong and I'm sure they've all written memo after memo to their carriers warning them to set adequate reserves. All these lawyers and their adjusters are older, weary. They don't want to burn all the time and energy it's gonna take to get this thing to the courthouse. They're worn out even if one of them doesn't know it." Eddie winked.

"The guy? That guy? Wallace Marcus?"

"Yeah, him. He thinks he's hot shit but he doesn't get called 'Wailing Wall Wally' for nothing. So, here's what I'm thinking. The beginning is going to be the 'shock' and you'll see that soon enough. I've settled it in my head."

"You gonna tell me what it is?"

"No, but I think you'll enjoy it. Now, the end is going to be the 'awe' and I'm not gonna tell you about it either, but I'm gonna set you up with one or two lines at the end that should strike them mortally hard and help get the job done. I expect Wills will help us too. I'll explain when the time comes."

Alph snickered. "Okay, boss. I'll await my further orders. Should we head on upstairs now?"

"Yes, sure, I've got two things to say to you, if you will, please."

"What's that?"

"Alph, long ago you earned your spurs and earned them well. I've just watched you in middle of a bad, bad storm that came about in great part because you had so much confidence in yourself and your plan. Very much like Lee on the third day of Gettysburg and Pickett's Charge. Lee had his blood up and his men, his plan as it were had never failed him. Up they went and were destroyed. And Lee kept going. He led his people no matter the rough going. He stayed with it. For himself and for them.

"Alph, you didn't panic or go fetal or ostrich when all this shit hit the fan. You stayed with it and moved and maneuvered with the wind and the weather and helped salvage what could have been an absolute disaster. You are to be commended."

"Thank you, Eddie. I appreciate your saying that, very much. But now remember, they can still file a complaint against me and that could cook my goose but good." Alph looked away, ashamed but not fearful.

"Alph, your four decades of sharp and effective skill, of the best kind of lawyering, your leadership in the bar, statewide and nationally, your great reputation and more all adds up, in my mind, to a lot more than your getting thrown in the ditch by the fellows that fucked it up in the first place. Listen, if they had any damn sense at all, they'd leave the whole stinking mess alone, call it a day, piss on the fire and call the dogs in. The state bar could do some bad blow-back on all of them, bad juju spilling out everywhere.

"I want you to know that if anything like a bar complaint against you comes up, please know I'm gonna stand up with you, for you, and explain to the powers that be how it all went down and how you, with lots of courage and brains and plenty of brass balls, pulled it together and salvaged a train wreck of others' doing. If anything, anything at all happens when all the dust has cleared, I expect it will be nothing more than a very, very private slap on the wrist." They were silent for a moment.

"Oh, Eddie, thank you. Thank you so much. That means so much to me. Boy, you do think it through, don't you?"

"We'll see."

"And just to show you I have been paying attention, I'm curious. What's the second thing?"

"Alph, I'd like you to join my firm as my Of Counsel."

"Eddie! Eddie! I'm floored. Really, I am. I am very complimented. I never saw that one coming!"

"Well, whatever. Look, you have fun with us. We all like each other. We have already shown we can work well and effectively together. You could be released from all those 'want to kill yourself' partners meetings, firm retreats, your monolith's rule books and policies and procedures handbooks and politically correct bullshit. You can be comfortable, flexible, hell, even decorate your office exactly as you'd like it. I think we can make proper arrangements for a nice monthly or quarterly stipend, plus you'd get to eat what you'd kill and just on the idea of your reputation and draw, there would be plenty to feast on. Give me a while. I'm sure I can think of lots more."

Alph was smiling, a serene faraway look in his watery blue eyes.

"Alph, think of the shock waves that would flow from Manteo to Murphy and well beyond too. It would be a big deal, a really big deal. I think it would be so much fun. And those over there that you are still close to will quietly applaud your willingness to pull the ripcord and go do something new and freeing. I hope you'll think it over. No rush. No rush at all."

"Man, Eddie, you make a helluva effective case! I really need to ponder on all this. And will do once we get done tomorrow. I promise."

"Deal. Let's hit the hay."

They rode up in the elevator in silence. As they got off at the fourth floor, they shook hands heartily.

CHAPTER FORTY-FIVE

WRAP IT UP

The Fabulous Thunderbirds

CURT SLEPT BETTER than he thought he might and was initially relaxed when he opened his eyes and stretched. And then, of course, his awaiting, appointed tasks elbowed their way into his rapidly fading peacefulness and shoved it roughly aside and he was now alert. He dressed quickly and got an empty shoebox from his closet.

Before he went out the door, he clicked on the television, checked the news, weather, and sports. He really did like knowing what was going on out in the world. He sat there and made himself slow down and pay attention for a while. It also helped him center himself and be quiet in preparation for the day.

Now satisfactorily informed, he opened his car trunk, pulled the last two small bricks out of their resting slots and topped them into the shoebox. He put the box on the front seat next to him, slid in, started the engine and started on his way.

Curt stopped at an old Shell station in Clemmons on his way out of town to fill his tank. He grabbed a Coca-Cola and a Butterfinger for breakfast as he paid. Then he moved back onto the interstate and headed to Charlotte. It was about an hour and a half ride. It was another nice fall day, about nine in the morning. He circled around the city's perimeter and came in from the

South Carolina side. He had needed to burn off some time. He wanted to arrive at just about 11, so the spot for the pickup was just opened for lunch but not yet busy and crowded.

When he got into the developing South Park area, he pulled into a 7-Eleven parking lot up on the corner next to the sprawling mall and made the last of his "I'm near, I'm almost there" calls. He waited five minutes and then pulled away. He passed expansive lawns, long, deep driveways and large brick homes set well back from the road, many with columns and silent, stone lions guarding the entryways.

He stopped at the traffic light at the top of the hill and then turned left and headed down Providence Road. The growing, imposing skyline of Charlotte was a straight shot in front of him, tall buildings and construction cranes sprouting out and upward like bursts of weeds. Banking and business were the lures, along with a world class and busy airport. Charlotte was a city on the make. Young professionals were pouring into the place and they had money and a yen to spend that money on luxury and fun when they weren't toiling away trying to make vice president or partner or more bucks than they had ever dreamed possible.

Down the way on the left was P Road Sundries, a long-time hangout for the locals and the invading newbies, but now the demographics had moved from mostly old-timers to mostly young WASPs with coats, suits, and ties, and plenty of cash and plastic in their wallets. The place was old, had been around a long time and had originally been billed as an ice cream and soda shop. Demon rum had long ago run the sweet treats off.

Girls and boys crowded in as each day wore on to laugh and listen to loud music, eat greasy burgers, and cut up and drink too much and lower their inhibitions to enticingly delicious levels of bad behavior. It was the perfect play for quick, point-of-sale transactions.

Curt pulled into PRS right on the button at 11 and on past the building into the back parking lot. There were a few cars here and there, but the place was surely not going to be crowded. He walked back to front door, shoebox tight under his arm, and walked in. The long bar stretched away off to the right. There was a tired old guy down at the far end nursing a tall boy Bud and a whip length Slim Jim while a whorl of smoke lifted lazily from his cigarette, his ash tray already filling.

And that was the sum total of the visible patronage at that moment. Curt could hear some pot clanging and banging and low voices going on back in the kitchen as they readied for the day, but the swinging kitchen doors were shut, all the tables and booths already having been set up with napkins and glasses and bendable, aged sets of cheap silverware. A Motown song played softly.

Behind the bar, toweling glasses and humming and quietly wah-wahing along to the Temptations was Jersey, a tall, burly black man with a shining, bald head, and a full beard. He looked like Teddy Pendergrass sans coif, had a sweet smile and narrow eyes. His very bearing called out that this was his place.

Curt stood at the door and said quietly, "Hey, Jersey. How you doing?"

"Hey, Curt. Right on the money. I've been good. How about you?"

Curt and Jersey went way back in the time machine. Jersey had been born and raised in Winston-Salem, and he and Curt had run the numbers and butter and eggs for their elders when they were little kids. Now, hiding in plain sight, Jersey ran a tight and successful operation of demand, thus supply from his bar keep's perch at PRS. His regulars loved him for his skills, his friendly gruff ways, his constant willingness to pour just a little bit more, his encyclopedic knowledge of sports and local history, and his subtle ability to gather and distribute snow and grass at reasonable prices and basically always, in a one-stop shop setting.

"I believe you've come by for an early in the day take-out order."

"That would be so."

"I have your two bags with the order tickets stapled to them."

Jersey lifted the two, innocuous white takeout bags from behind the bar and placed them on the counter. Curt leaned over and looked at the tickets, marked for cheeseburgers, chili dogs, fries, and two chocolate malt milkshakes.

"Nice. A good look. Thanks."

Curt slid the shoebox back across the counter to Jersey who in the barest blink of an eye, shoved it up deep under the counter's bottom shelf. It would leave with him later in the day for further processing.

Curt quickly explained the packaging nuance and Jersey nodded.

They shook hands and Curt left with his lunch money.

Eddie had been down in the lobby drinking coffee and reading newspapers, awaiting all to assemble. There were no questions or further comments from any of the clients as the discussions of the night before. All had a quick breakfast sitting together. The group was quietly gregarious.

A brief morning sprinkle now replaced by a beaming sun had the streets of Charleston shining. Eddie and his squadron walked down Meeting Street past the high sitting Hibernian Hall and the old courthouse, waiting for the lights to turn at the four corners of the law, scooted across Broad Street and then down to Tom Wills' offices. The place was typical, lovely old Charleston and had been decorated and upfitted in classic good taste. And too, as it was typical old Charleston, the entry way and the waiting rooms and the reception areas were all tight little rooms, a series of rabbit warrens with low ceilings.

For today's main event, clusters and clots of lawyers and adjusters and clients milled about in tight-smiled good humor, introducing and shaking hands, some making old acquaintances, many new. There was a guarded anticipation to the group.

In perfect form was the standoffish Wallish Marcus, who shook hands reticently, nodded slightly, and who looked as though he had been trapped inside a stinking hog car bound for the stockyards of Chicago. His face was skeptical, pained in the visage of a man who was going to have to deal with the dregs of human offal this day. Sampson D. Jenkins ran interference for him, sort of a distorted conviviality to him, his efforts at good manners attempting to leaven out the sourness of his colleague.

That set was joined by a nice-enough fellow, the adjuster for Farmers named Frost. He was handsome and looked smart.

Tom Wills, possessed of a big, useful brain, the patience of Job and an enormous reservoir of laughter and an appreciation of the comedic, appeared and by good humored direction and instruction herded the groups down some tight, low ceiling stairs to a very large and long conference room. There were plenty of seats. All settled in, the rustling quickly abating. Wills asked everyone to again introduce themselves to the group and passed the sign in sheet around for all signatures, pledging the confidentiality of the proceedings.

Eddie noted the large color television set in the far corner with a tape deck player plugged in next to it. Wills made his basic remarks and then asked for opening statements, first starting with Eddie on behalf of the plaintiffs.

"Thank you, Tom. Just a few introductory remarks and then I'd like to make my more substantive remarks, and I promise they will be brief and to the point, after everyone else has spoken. Is that amenable to you, I hope?"

Wills looked at Eddie with a wondering smile and said, "Not the most unusual thing I've heard over these many years so I have no problem with that."

As by court order, Wills, the mediator, was the boss on this ride and his word was law. A definitive example of his preeminence in these proceedings was no one was ever allowed to get mad, get put out, pick up his ball and walk out. Such fits of pique could get one a nice, fat contempt charge. No one left without Wills' permission or until he called an impasse, meaning wherever the negotiations were, they all were at a pause or stopping point.

"Anybody got any heartburn over that?"

As it did not behoove anyone to rankle with the mediator this early on, all shook their heads in the negative. Wallish made a grumpy face but it could not be discerned if it was done in disapproval of the request or just another of his regular tics.

"Let's start. Eddie, give us your basics and we will wait attentively for your concluding remarks in just a few minutes, I expect."

"Thank you, Tom. First, we are glad we are all here. Hopefully we can get this matter resolved. Obviously, there are big damages here. We promise to work hard with Tom and you all to make good progress. It would be nice if we could go home this afternoon with this matter wrapped up and concluded." Eddie introduced all of his associates starting with Alph and concluding with his witness, Truck Tinker.

Tom Wills gestured. "All right, John Winkler on behalf of Thee Doll House. Please have your say."

"Thank you, Tom. Hello again, all. I think we all agree this is a matter that warrants our serious attention today. We are real sorry all this happened. With all due respect, we feel these obviously nice young men contributed in some serious part to their current plights. No need to linger on that now. Miss Roth is here with me from the Chubb offices in Atlanta, having flown in this morning. We are here in good faith. That's all I've got for now. Thanks."

Ms. Roth did a little ass squirm in her seat.

"Thank you. Next up will be Wallish Marcus and Sampson D. Jenkins on behalf of the defendant, the Blockhouse."

Wallish Marcus started. "Jenkins will speak for our clients."

Jenkins looked a bit lost just for a moment, realizing that Marcus had just called a play and handed him a ball he wasn't ready to receive. No matter. They weren't going to say anything of value any way. He composed and took the thread. "We're here in good faith. Mr. Frost from Farmers is here with us to help if he can. And, well, we pretty much agree with what John Winkler has just said. No reason to say more now."

Tom nodded and spoke. "Mills Gaines joining us from Columbia. Again, Mills, nice to see you. It's been a while. Tell us what you'd like to about this on behalf of your client from Indiana."

Gaines laughed. "Tom, always nice to see you. Love what you've done with your offices. Now, I'm not about to sing out of a different hymnal than my learned counsel have thus far used this morning, but I am authorized by our adjuster here Mr. Jack McKinney to say we come in good faith and we would really, really like to get this one done today. We admit we are going to have to spend some money here. This is a serious money case. We trust and believe that everyone in this room knows that, understands that, and understands that they are going to have to write sizeable checks too. To do otherwise would be not only a serious waste of time, it would be dangerous and potentially negligent, and we've already got too much of that on this table right now. Once we break out into our sequester rooms, we will initiate, hopefully, an early breaking of the logjams that so often eat up the first many hours of these exercises. There, I'm done."

Gaines looked at adjuster McKinney. "Anything to add?"

McKinney paused for a few seconds and then hesitated and then continued, "No, well said Mills. People buy insurance to escape risk. That's exactly why we are here. I know our just-now stated position is generally unusual in these settings, especially at their beginnings, but we need to get moving here and eliminate all the puffery and posturing. Bluntly put, we are here to deal but everyone needs to come along and that includes the plaintiffs."

Tom Wills spoke a heartfelt thank you to the last group and Eddie nodded toward them in true respect. Marcus looked sour; Jenkins looked hopeful. Ms. Roth looked both relieved and discomfited at the same time.

"All right, Mr. Eddie Terrell, you're requested time has come. Please speak to us now."

"Thank you, Tom. Appreciate y'all's patience and forbearance with me. I'm going to first address Mills Gaines and Mr. McKinney.

"We take you at your word and deeply appreciate your stated intentions. We know your client and his friends have anguished over this and I think we can all agree that by the time the Hoosier state folks got into the mix, just so many things had gone wrong, that it seems it was inevitable that there would be one more big domino to fall and it surely did. We look forward to working with you. I assure you we have room within which to work. Thank you for being here."

Sitting behind his representatives was the named defendant driver, Mr. Nestor Banks, a mild and miserable looking fellow, slight and owlish in his glasses. He was an assistant rector at a little Methodist church up near Terre Haute. He stood up and asked to speak.

"You sure?" asked Mills Gaines, his hand gently on Mr. Banks' arm, some light restraint if needed.

"Yes. I'm sure. I'm fine." He gulped and looked around the table, paused and continued, directly addressing the three young men with such bad injuries.

"Fellows, I'm just so sick about this. I am so sorry about this. Please accept my apologies. I am so sorry I hurt y'all so. We were just out having some fun, blowing off some steam. We had no idea...I had no idea. I'm a fool. Such a fool. I'm surely at fault here. I don't know much at all about these legal goings-on. Mr. Gaines and also Mr. McKinney have tried to keep me caught up, but as best I can tell is that I hurt y'all and that's why we have insurance. Again, I am so sorry about all this. I really am." He was tearing up just a little bit. He sat down quickly; his eyes cast downward. Gaines patted his arm softly.

"Again, Mr. Banks, we appreciate your being here and your sentiments, certainly, your sentiments as well. Mills, for purposes of these discussions today, please be advised that we will not be seeking punitive damages against Mr. Banks. His actions were stupid and even a bit reckless but there was no intentioned, planned misconduct on his part."

Eddie turned his attention to the others and then spoke in a quiet, conversational tone. There was no hint of anger or righteousness in his voice but there was no doubt the chits were getting ready to be called in.

"As for Thee Doll House and the Blockhouse, I cannot give y'all any such assurance as to prospective jury charges as to punitive damages. As the smart man says, 'Y'all paid your money and you took your chances.' You both acted well outside what the law allows and did so for a very long time and did so willfully and intentionally."

The assistant manager of Thee Doll House, a greasy, squirrely type looked off into the distance with the Alfred E. Neuman "What Me Worry?" gaze.

Eddie was glad to see him there. He had less value and input to the proceedings than a dried-out houseplant. All decisions on that side of the case were in the hands of garrulous John Winkler and Ms. Deborah Mynyrta Roth whose appraising look at her defendant's nasty representative could only signal revulsion and a need to flee. She was a handsome woman with graceful posture but her tightened eyes were giving her away.

"Now as to Thee Doll House. First, I'll show you a tape. By the way, we have copies for all of you once we are done today, sort of like lovely parting gifts for our contestants. It's titled, please excuse the rude title, *The Pussy Preacher*, and it features the comedic talents, you will allow such license of one Willie Whistler, from of all places, my and our hometown of Winston-Salem, North Carolina. It was made on the day these young men had stopped in for many drinks and more and they were immediately stage side as Mr. Whistler did his shtick for a videographer. And of course, during the course of this forty-six-minute run of absolute vulgar hysteria, you will see the repeated drink runs made by the buxom, barely clothed young ladies, and y'all know we have the ATM and credit card receipts for multiple purchases and cash withdrawals. Patty and Mikey have all those over there with them if anyone cares to take a look."

Patty nodded and held up a box. Mikey sat next to her, nodding too, a lovely distraction often welcomed in rooms like this when all the shit is sliding downhill onto somebody else's head. Mikey thought this was crazy shit that these people do.

Eddie continued. "It is pretty obvious to me that by time we get to the last ten minutes or so, that all three of these fellows are stumbling about and swaying and hanging on to wherever to steady themselves and y'all keep right on serving them, visibly intoxicated. Watch for the last round as Slinging Willie takes his nasty bows and joins our guys in a round of shots. I've got the ticket for that one too, four double Rebel Yells I recall it was."

Eddie pushed the tape in and hit play, turned the volume up and the group drew close and watched in a very pained silence. Ms. Roth watched intently, her head shaking briefly, here and there along the way.

Marcus looked distantly pleased, his breathing was sibilant as a serpent might present; Eddie read him to think this display of vulgarity would take some pressure off him. He was wrong. He was going to make his peace today with a generosity until now unknown to him or he and the Blockhouse and the Thee Doll House were going to mount the scaffold together. Either all pay out now or be dragged to the gallows together, yoked in the bonds of reckless, irresponsible behavior. There would be no dismissal of one without the other.

To boot, and this was delicious to envision, Mills Gaines from Indiana was a good guy, fun and nice to be with. Marcus was a sour, snotty jerk. If they did not already understand it, they soon would come to appreciate that the two of them would come to detest one another and at counsel table, that is a visible debacle. Juries aren't stupid. They'd figure that dynamic out fast.

The tape came to an end and everyone looked about vacantly or busied themselves with some note-taking or whispering with one another. Eddie let it sink in for a few minutes.

Alph leaned over and whispered to Eddie. "Jesus, where'd you get that? That's a ballbuster. And I know I shouldn't admit it, but a couple of those lines were pretty funny." He winced as he made the cheesy admission.

Tom Wills was suppressing a deep, buried laugh.

Eddie cleared his throat. "I suppose someone in here might want to know where I got that tape. Pretty simple answer. Before I allowed myself to be retained here, I went up to TDH a couple of times to see what I could see, do a reconnoiter or two if you will. On one of those visits, I purchased at fair market value that tape. Which now leads me to my other visit, on which I was accompanied by my friend Truck here." Truck reddened slightly but his jaw was steady and his blue eyes very clear.

"Truck, did you bring your brief note you made when we were there? The one that you made within three minutes of our parting company with Carrie and Carol?"

"Yes, I did. It's right here."

"Again, folks, this was but a visit late on a gray, dreary Myrtle Beach afternoon. Truck and I had a few beers and had a nice, very informative visit with the aforementioned Carrie and Carol. Yes, I have the receipt for that too. No shenanigans, no table dancing, no lap dancing, none of that stuff, but we are happy to tell you, those are some very pretty gals up there; it's hard to figure in which direction to look. And by the way, we did not drink with those ladies. We asked them to have one with us. A test we figured they'd pass. They did. They declined as they were on the clock. So there goes the 'get the witness drunk' defense.'

"Anyway, we were there not so long. It was pretty quiet. And I asked them both, together, straight up, how did they make the good money, not the kind of next to nothing they were gonna get from us, but the good, count it out good and long green money that they worked so hard for. Truck, please read your note. Read it loud enough so all of us in this big room can hear."

Truck cleared his throat and then warbled it out steady in the voice of the command presence naval officer he once had been before the Navy's JAG Corps had ensnared him into the law.

Truck stated, "And I quote, 'Yes, Carol said, 'the playbook is a real simple one. Get them to drink too much and show 'em as much of the goods as you can and keep at it with a smile and some winks and you'll do fine, honey.'"

Mills Gaines nodded in an agreeable agreement. Ms. Roth looked at Gaines with a knowing curiosity. The assistant manager, dullard that he was, tossed his head in happy assent. Ms. Roth was basically disgusted.

"Oh, of course, once we are adjourned today, all can get a copy of this and also, Truck is available for his deposition as can be conveniently agreed upon. Thank you, Truck. Y'all mind if Truck goes on? I'll keep the original here."

There were no objections and Truck slipped out of the room.

"Now I will continue on with our last defendant, The Blockhouse, before lunch; is that all right with you?"

"Absolutely. We have a couple of platters of sandwiches and salads on the way and of course, there are plenty of waters and coffee and tea and soft drinks out on the big table in the center hallway. Eddie, please continue."

"Thank you, Tom."

Marcus glared at Eddie. Mr. Jenkins looked hungry and worried. Mr. Frost looked interested. There did not appear to be an establishment representative with them, but whomever that was would have been a useless appendage save for being yet another whipping boy.

Eddie reached into his jacket pocket and brought out an inch and a half stack of what looked like white stock business cards, wrapped with a rubber band. Eddie just stood there, staring at Marcus, snapping the rubber band on the little stack over and over again. Marcus did not like being stared at. *Tough shit*, thought Eddie.

Eddie quietly asked, "Marcus, am I correctly informed that you are a member in good standing of the, shall we say, exclusive and very private Carolina Yacht Club here in Charleston?"

Wailing Wally defiantly thrust his jaw forward in prideful arrogance and hissed his response out.

"Yes, I am. What on God's green earth does that have to do with anything involving this matter?" His dudgeon was up.

Eddie smiled patiently at Marcus and said. "Let's study on that now, why don't we?"

About the time that Eddie began his evisceration of the Blockhouse and its waterboys, Curt pulled up in from of Gore's in Winston-Salem and stepped inside, carrying his two white take-out bags with him. Gore was at his station on the piano's bench, a steaming cup of black coffee next to the stacks of sheet music he loved to mess with.

"Why, good morning, Curt. Take-out this morning? In here? Now, you know good and well we serve many a good, decent meal in here. No need to be bringing your own picnic."

He stretched himself up off his seat and smiled at Curt.

"My guess is you'd like to put these bags with the other things you brought yesterday?" Gore arched an eyebrow without accusation toward Curt.

"Yes, please. I'd really appreciate it. I'll be back late tomorrow morning to take it all away. I hope that's all right."

"Of course it is. It is always my pleasure to be of assistance to a friend, loyal patron, and fellow businessman. Don't you worry about a thing. It'll all be here waiting for you tomorrow." He was courtly and gracious. It was how people ought to be to one another.

The tumblers clicked, the bags went in, the big door closed tight.

"Come on, Curt. How about a drink and a sandwich?"

"Thank you, Gore. I accept."

Curt did not know where everyone was. He was lonely. He was glad for Gore's kind company. He missed his crew.

Eddie stretched the fingers on his left hand. And he walked slowly around the long left side of the table. He held his big paw up, centering it on the faces of the entranced. They all watched him.

"First, both TDH and Blockhouse got them, helped these three young men get all drunker than Adam's house cat. And knew it while they did it. That's against the law and y'all knew it before this sorry run out." One finger out.

"Two, TDH is already good and nailed to the wall as is poor Mr. Banks." A second finger out.

"Three. So let me now focus my attention on the Blockhouse." A third finger out.

"Mr. Marcus obviously takes great umbrage to what he perceives as my insolent inquiry as to his membership, long-time membership in the exclusive Carolina Yacht Club. That's unfortunate. I would think, as his client, the Blockhouse, is also a fine, exclusive private club, there would be some helpful parallels there.

"Isn't that right, Mr. Marcus? The Carolina Yacht Club is very exclusive, no? No room for the flotsam and jetsam of riffraff there, right? No chance that some nasty, intrusive plaintiff's lawyer like me would be invited for entry. Of course not!"

Eddie grinned pleasantly. "Of course, in one of his many moments of wisdom, the great Groucho Marx once observed presciently that he was not at all sure that he would want to belong to any private club that wanted him as a member."

Many in the room laughed a little and most smiled. Even Mr. Jenkins did until Marcus's withering glare knocked his jaw back to rictus. "Additionally, my research has developed the following additional information. Mr. Marcus here has served on the yacht club's board of directors, its admissions committee, and has acted as general counsel as well. Fair to say, you know what it's like to help run a very private club."

"Now, wait just a minute. I'm not on trial here!"

"No you are not but your knowledge surely is."

"Now, just to be sure, the Blockhouse is a fine, private, exclusive club too, right?" Marcus just glared.

"And because it is a private club, it is exempt from these petty travails I have burdened you with. Right, Mr. Marcus?"

A fourth finger out. Grudgingly, Marcus muttered, "Yes, that's right. That's our position."

"Well, all I've got left is my thumb, so let me thumb something out of this little stack for you and Mr. Jenkins and Mr. Frost."

Eddie pulled three slips from his little deck and handed them very slowly and respectfully to his three oppositions at the end of the table and then stepped back.

Wills knew what was coming and looked down into his lap with a barely suppressed grin. "Mr. Marcus. Mr. Jenkins. Mr. Frost. I am of the opinion that none of you have ever visited your client's club, have you? That's too bad. Y'all might have learned some things during such a visit." The three looked dully at Eddie, giving no answer.

"Well then, I ask that you read what I have handed to you and once you have finished, please let us know. Thank you."

They read it and Marcus balled up the card and tossed it aside.

"This is ridiculous. This is just bull..."

Tom Wills interjected with a raised palm and a "No, not here, never. No time." He along with the rest of the room was fast tiring of Wailing Wally's attitude and his bloating puffery.

Eddie continued. "Would one of you three like to read what the little card says to the rest of us or should I?"

There was no response so accommodated by their collective silence, Eddie read the card that started with "WELCOME TO THE BLOCKHOUSE, MYRTLE BEACH'S FINEST PRIVATE CLUB. FINE FOOD, DRINK, AND LOVELIES."

Jenkins and Frost looked worried. Their brows were furrowed and their lips were pinched. Marcus just sat and seethed. He knew his defense had just been defanged. Now, Eddie decided it was nut-cutting time.

"You know how we got these cards? And by the way, I have a couple of hundred. And I know how to get more. By the way, wouldn't we all like to know how they came into my hands, and too, wouldn't we all like to know what the printing bills and run numbers are for the continued creation of these things?" Eddie narrated he and Truck's trip to the Patricia Manor Hotel and his encounter with the young salesman in great, flourishing detail.

"Now, don't y'all think down at the State Alcohol Licensing Board they'd have a lot of interest in all this? How about the State Department of Labor? How about the Myrtle Beach Police Department? How about the Horry County Business Licensing Department? How about the Horry County Solicitor's Office? The list could just grow and grow, don't you think? TDH and the Blockhouse let these gentlemen drink in there without so much as offering a cup of coffee or the calling of a taxicab, and then toss them unceremoniously out the door into a dark and confusing parking area where they each got nailed, badly hurt by Mr. Banks.

'No other way to put it. Y'all all broke the civil law, some of you the criminal, and now it is time to pay the piper."

Tom Wills said, "Thank you, Mr. Eddie Terrell. That was an unusual presentation but a helpful one, I think."

Wills looked hard at Marcus when he said that. Wills knew who would be the obstinate one as the day wore on.

"Lunch is here. Let me show each group to its own room and then everyone can grab some food, buffet style. Considering the size of the Terrell group, let's let them stay in this room. As we have our lunches, I'll start my rounds, starting in here with the Terrell group."

A little later as Eddie and his cohorts pushed their salad and sandwiches around their plates, Wills appeared and dropped in a seat, his plate balanced in his hands. He began to eat and yet spoke lucidly as he did.

"Eddie, what we got here? It appears to me you've got them with the vice grips and now we have to find the money and make this all go away. And by the way, Mr. Baron, nice to make your acquaintance."

"Please call me Alph. Nice to be visiting with y'all today. This is pretty interesting."

"Oh yes, it usually is. We do have a lot of fun, most of the time. Don't see enough of Eddie. Things usually get right spicy when Eddie comes to town." Wills and Eddie chuckled.

"Now, all the rest of y'all, young gentlemen and ladies, please don't think I'm ignoring you but most of my dealings and conversation will be with Eddie here. I think we have plenty to work with here. Eddie, by the way, how did all y'all get here?"

"The fellows here drove in last evening. We were all able to have dinner together. We're staying over at The Mills House. Even Truck got a free meal out of me. I'm hoping we can get this business done today so we can scoot on home later on."

"How you gonna get home? How'd you get here?"

"Oh, yeah, I chartered a Citation. They'll come back and get us with about 90 minutes' notice."

Wills grinned and whistled. "You are a showy one, that's for sure."

"Tom, how 'bout do me a favor?"

"What do you need?"

"Make sure Marcus and his crowd know about the jet. It'll stick in his craw and signal to them all that we ain't willing to just play popgun here. You and I both know it's the Blockhouse crowd that's gonna have to be roped and tied."

"Yes. True. Fine. Good idea. Now, what's your demand?"

"Something explosively exorbitant."

"Like what?"

"Let me lay it out this way. Indiana has 500K primary and a two-million-dollar umbrella. TDH has 10 million. Blockhouse has five million primary and five in umbrella. That totals 22.5 million in insured exposure. I can see a sizeable award of punitive damages.

"Indiana has pretty much already laid his head on the block and TDH's adjuster looked like she was gonna puke as the tape played. I think she'd pay for us to give her a ride home to Atlanta. You need to let her and John Winkler know, either everyone's gonna settle or no one's gonna settle. I need Winkler and Gaines leaning on Marcus but good. By the way, as much as Winkler enjoys the ladies, he and Ms. Roth don't appear to have any chemistry on any level other than disdain. I expect she can smell the baby powder on Winkler from his obvious multiple scouting visits up that way. He's a randy one, he is. Knew him from years back. He's as obvious as a big fart in a small closet. One more reason I think they'd both like to get this one put to bed and now."

"That's all good information and will be helpful. But, Eddie, what's your damn demand?" Wills was smirking.

Eddie asked him, "Did you hear the one about the two nuns?"

"Now, dammit, Eddie, don't start that shit on me." Wills giggled. They all did. Wills looked at the others and explained, "We've known each other a long time. We are taking this all very seriously, but it helps to have a nut like Eddie around to keep the game grounded sometimes." He looked back at Eddie. "Okay, tell me later. Now, tell me the damn demand."

"I will now and I need to walk you through my thinking."

"Fair enough. Now go ahead. Shoot."

"Our demand is twenty-million dollars." Eddie smiled benevolently at Tom.

"Oh, good God! Jesus, Eddie, you're not serious. That's crazy! That's bullshit! Christ! Now tell me your real demand." Wills was both exasperated and amused at the same time.

Patty leaned over and said to the clients, "Y'all just hang on. It's gonna be a good ride, I do believe."

Mikey asked, "Is that crazy or is this going somewhere?"

Alph murmured, "I believe this is going somewhere. Let's just watch."

"Tom, you've known me a long time and you know I don't bullshit around too much, and I can see the incredulity in your face so let me walk through this with you. You might want to take a note or two cause rather than hold a bunch of cards close to my chest, I'm going to lay our deal out and let you go to work. You ready?"

"Yes, you damned crazy-ass fool." But Tom Wills was still smirking.

"Indiana has two and a half aggregate. We'll take two and leave them half a million. I'd go to them first. Work them any way you like, as many shuttle visits as you like. You can make it up as you go. They're begging to be set free.

"Same deal with TDH. And I'd go see them right after you start with Indiana. Think it would be helpful to pile up a good aggregate number before you wade into sourpuss incorporated. Puts pressure on them and as we all know, Wailing Wally Marcus does not like to be kept waiting. It will make them antsy.

"Now back to TDH. Back and forth, up and down and all around, you write the script, say it all as you please, all as you think will move the ball and be effective but four from them is the goal. They save a savage beat down, get to keep a bunch, and that would get us to six. And lastly, the Blockhouse. Same suggested approach. They've got ten total. We'll take four and no need to tell them I'm doing them a favor. They are already pissed off enough at me as it is, at least Marcus sure is. But he's got nothing but his pig-headed stubbornness going for him. Try to wait us out. Fat chance on that. If he starts pulling that shit, tell them it's a waste of time. I'll camp out at The Mills House until hell freezes over. His defense is gone. In its place is a fraud, a scam with a bunch of little boys acting as their damn admissions committee. Get old, sweet S.D. Jenkins on the generous train and that'll help roll the ball. I can't imagine the adjuster Mr. Frost came down here to say 'no.'

"And so, that gets us to ten. At trial it's all gonna be joint and several liability anyway, plus a whopping big punitive number, so as the guy in the Fram oil filter ad says, 'You can pay me now or you can pay me later.' So, Mr. Tom Wills, what say you?"

"Eddie, the way you lay it out sounds so controlled and easy. And of course, it isn't. Goddamn you. Jesus H. Christ. What the hell. Here I go. I'll come back around in a while and report."

And so, the wiggling and convincing and pushing and pulling began. The Terrell crowd finished their lunches and settled in to wait. Eddie and Alph chatted back and forth as did the ladies, and then all would lapse into silence and then start up again. The clients asked a few questions that warranted answers and explanations, which Eddie was happy to provide. But they understood the drill. This was not a Rubik's Cube of mystery. This was a moneyball straight shot. The three clients had been badly hurt. Now the only question was how willing these defendants were to buy their way out of the uncertainty of a jury verdict which might just blow all their doors off. This just did not look like a low money case, and from the Pussy Preacher video to the 'private club admission chits' and so much more, there were a lot of landmines out there.

After a while, Eddie wandered out into the hall to grab a cup of coffee and check out the lay of the land, to see if there was anything, anyone to be seen. It was getting on toward the middle of the afternoon.

He saw Wills go back into the Indiana room and as he went, he gave Eddie a nod and the waving arms of a symphony conductor. Eddie took this to be a good sign, a sign that Tom was making a little music and that meant progress.

Then as Eddie poured a good, strong cup of black, Ms. Roth came up beside him and poured a cup for herself.

Eddie nodded and asked, "How are you doing? I know this is arduous for everyone. I'm sorry about the nastiness of that videotape but I think you understand it had to be played. Obviously, it was very crude."

"Yes, I understand. I appreciate your nice manners about it. I'm fine. This is the kind of work I do. Have been doing it for a long while. I must note that this territory here in Charleston is very different than what I'm usually up to in Atlanta."

"How so? We a little rough and tumble out here in the Lowcountry?"

"Yes, something like that. Shall I say a lot of good old boys in these parts. I usually don't mind it, but the combination of it with that awful tape really has made my skin crawl today."

"I understand. I'm sorry about that." Eddie was sincere and she knew he was.

She turned to go back to her waiting area and said softly over her shoulder, "We already put two on it for Mr. Wills and are ready to move higher. Will probably have to make a couple of phone calls back to Georgia but we are here to get it done if we can. Act like you don't know when he comes to tell you."

"I will. Thank you."

Wills came around the corner. "Okay, let's go in and assess where things stand."

Now back in the conference room with Eddie and his group, Wills started, "I've made three rounds so far, three with TDH and Indiana, two with Blockhouse. As we all saw and figured, Indiana is in full retreat. They're at one and a half so just another shove or two and they'll get to where you want them. TDH put a half on to open, then on second visit, a full million and just a little while ago, added another half. They're clearly willing to keep moving. Once I got to beyond three, I went to see the Blockhouse."

"This ought to be interesting."

"No surprises so far but they look weak in there. They've put three-quarters in so far. The interesting thing is Marcus ain't talking. He looks upset. All the talking is being done by the adjuster Mr. Frost. Mr. Jenkins is being affable. It's as though Marcus has either gone AWOL or has been invited to zip it by his employer. So we're at four and a quarter and plenty of room and time to go. So let me go on and get back to it."

"Thank you, Tom."

"You're welcome, but you and I know it's your ridiculously fat set of facts that's driving this."

"True, but thank you just the same. Without you, it would not be moving. My sword and shield!" Eddie made bowing, praying hands at Wills who responded with a merry-mouthed "Fuck You" and zoomed out, jumping back up on his carrousel.

"You know," said Alph, "That fellow really seems to enjoy his work. Makes him so much more effective."

"It's true. Let me tell y'all something very interesting about Tom Wills. In his office up toward the front, he has a life-sized, dressed and decorated to the nines statue of James Brown. I kid you not. Why it's there I have no idea. I ought to ask him about it but haven't ever gotten around to it. I think that says something about his approach and mindset about all this. What that is I have no idea. Let's resume our patience within our impatience."

At about 3:45 p.m., Wills pounded back into the Terrell stables. He was on the verge of breathless. He was also laughing.

"Okay, what you got, you nut?"

"Here's the deal. I've been back and forth pretty good and we have more progress to report. Indiana has fully caved so there's two million. May I please when I go back to them in a little while assure them you will not seek anymore from them as of this day as long as we get it all finished with everyone?"

"Yeah, sure, and the message of all or none needs to be spoken loud and clear to the others."

"I've also shared that very pointedly with TDH and they get it. I have not done so with the Blockhouse just yet as I want to have my basket of arrows plenty full when I do. Blockhouse has come up to one and a half again with negligible whining or posturing by Marcus, though as I was leaving he did say to the others that this was just throwing money to drunks. Impressive, no? Guy has the heart of a cow turd in a freezer. TDH is up to three and have indicated they'll make a call for one more big pop but that'll be their top-out. So in total, we are at six and one half, climbing soon to seven and one half which ain't bad."

"No, but now it's time to squeeze the Blockhouse's balls. How about you go see the Blockhouse again and I bet they put another half on it? Then it's time to try for both barrels. You know who just might be a big help?"

"Who?"

Eddie said, "The sultry Ms. Roth. She really wants to get on out of here and I have a feeling we can motivate her to snap and slap hard at Marcus and his bunch. In the meantime, let's see what you can get next. How about you go get Roth to make the call? I don't sense that you are sensing any pushback from Winkler on any of this?"

"None at all. It's her show."

Once we get Roth's call, the full number four agreed upon, and we know where the Blockhouse is, come back and let's formulate a little plan."

"Okay. I got it. Outta here."

In about twenty minutes, Wills was back.

"Roth has made the call. Their four is solid. The Blockhouse has added another half so they are at two for a total of eight. You know, we're getting close here."

"Great, Tom. How about you go get Ms. Roth and Winkler and let's me, you, and Alph and them all talk in your office? It's neutral territory. And I wanted to see your James Brown again. Before we do that, how did that remarkable thing come into your possession? Always been meaning to ask you."

"Hell, I did some mediation work for a couple of his record labels and in addition to paying me handsomely, they gave me the thing. It's pretty funny and pretty cool too, but my wife said there was no place for it in our so-called dignified house so in my office corner it went. When I sit at my desk, the Godfather of Soul watches over me. Inspirational, right?" Wills grinned.

"Okay, let me go round them up and I'm gonna go get Indiana as well."

Alph and Eddie went out in the hall to wait for Ms. Roth and Winkler. Wills led the four of them to his office. There, of course, was Mr. James Brown as well. Tom shut the door and told them Eddie had a plan he'd hatched and turned it over to Eddie.

"Thank y'all for your help today. You two defendants have done all that we expected and hoped of you and your fairness is appreciated. Here's where we are with Blockhouse. They are at a grudging two and we need them to get together another two and as the afternoon is getting on, I'm suggesting the equivalent of a double-barreled dynamite charge."

"Please explain," said Winkler.

"Alph, please pay close attention as I know you will. First, I'd like Tom to take Alph down the hall and pull Jenkins and Mr. Frost out. Explain to Marcus that there is no need for him to be troubled with this brief gathering as he has clearly, for whatever reasons, checked out of the proceedings. It will both insult and shame him. Deservedly so. Fuck with his pea brain, big deal ego mind. Small balls, smaller sense of the world.

"If he wants to visit with Alph, fine, but wouldn't surprise me if his pouting pride signals his recusal. Either way, Alph, make it short and sweet. Explain to them that you've known me a long time, explain to them we are not amateurs, and explain to them we would just as soon try this case if we can't get this finished up by 5:30 or so; but most importantly make it very clear to them that I am about half crazy, which is true, and wouldn't mind blowing this whole thing up anyway. Explain to them you have tried more big deal civil litigation from the defense side than just about anyone and that if it were up to you, this matter would have been over before lunch. If all this fails, it will make his update letter to Farmers with your weight in the mix fall heavy on his inabilities to relate and get it done well clear of liability limits. Will hurt him down the line with them and they are not a cheap shit outfit. Try to engage Jenkins and Frost especially. Jenkins can, once properly motivated, pull the pin.

"Then, Tom, take them back in and see what else you can drag out of them. This is when I think you need to tell them that everyone else is topped off and done and if this mediation collapses because of their penury in the face of overwhelming facts, it's gonna be on them. Then come back and tell us all.

"And after this next round with them, I think it would be good and helpful if all lawyers and adjusters for TDH and Indiana go down there or get everyone up here or wherever and let's go for the jugular. And Ms. Roth, if you would be so kind, speak for the group and wither and shrivel them but good, quiet, and cutting. Would you please do that for us?"

"Why, yes. I'd be delighted. I don't know if you all picked up on it but they really are jerks, especially that Marcus twit."

The consensus was sealed and put into motion.

Alph went with Tom and met with them all, Marcus stiffly and haughtily joining them. In a very low key, affable, experienced, and savvy way Alph laid it out for them, playing predominantly to Frost and Jenkins, signaling that Marcus had taken himself out of the game. He emphasized his long experience of success and that if the day's proceedings did not conclude successfully, he would be coming into the case as pro hoc vice and that they were bringing heavy loads across the board.

Alph shook hands with each of them. It seemed to ease them noticeably, the toxins beginning to drain, running its course. He went back to join Eddie and the others. Tom Wills went back into their room with them.

He implored them to get this thing done. He was making it up on the fly. He told them that as to their 10 million in liability coverage, Eddie had reduced his demand to seven, that they were at two so some legitimate compromise would get them close to done. He stated emphatically that a couple of extra miles per hour and some different biomechanics might have brought them to three wrongful death suits and that the Blockhouse had the last chance to avoid all this save for a taxi ride, but they had failed miserably.

Tom stated, "Yeah, I'm a neutral advocate for the conclusion of the case, but for God's sake, your crowd really screwed the pooch here. And don't think I haven't noticed there is no personal rep here for the Blockhouse. Inexcusable but too understandable. God forbid any of us would ask him a question, in private of course...more damn stupid hide the ball."

They asked what the other two defendants had done. Tom said that he had no permission to speak specific figures but that both the others had put up substantial money and that they were not going to put up anymore and nothing further was being asked of them. The final ball was in their court.

Wills reminded them again that it was all or none today. He reminded them of the enormous expense that lay ahead of them all if things did not work out today. Expert witnesses, depositions, travel, every billable hour a treasure and a burden, evidentiary hearings, procedural hearings, not to mention an easy week plus in the courtroom at trial. There was certain potential fallout on licenses, and did anyone in here really think they could keep Pussy Preacher out of the show? And what would the trial judge think and say once he or she learned that all of this could have been avoided had Blockhouse just stepped up to the plate well within its policy limits and conceded its obvious responsibility? There could well be a judicial vendetta within the nightmare of a trial and a riled-up jury.

"And you guys are smart and know and can think through these things, I can only hope," Frost said. "Okay, we get it. We need to talk. How about give us a few minutes?"

Wills resisted. "Sure, but don't take too long. The clock's ticking and if I have to call an impasse here, I am going to be good and unhappy, and you boys know I've got a long memory."

Tom went straight back to his office and waited, not stopping by Eddie's room.

In a few minutes, Marcus knocked on the door. "Tom, we'll go to two and a half. Will that get it done?"

"Not quite but you're sneaking up on it."

"Okay." Marcus sighed. He looked tired. "How about three?"

Tom looked up at James Brown. "Godfather, what you think? Nope. I thought so."

It was an enormous sign of crumbling, them now bidding against themselves.

"Nope, you ain't there yet. I appreciate your getting back in the game. Now, get back in the game harder. You want out of here? Move! Let me go report this to Terrell and we'll be back to you soon."

Resignedly, Marcus went back down the hall. His body language was that of one awaiting the coup de grace.

Wills waited a few minutes and went and told Eddie that Blockhouse was at three and they had not said "that's it."

"Let's round up everyone and bring them all in here. I think a good talking to from a smart lady will get us there or almost there." They were soon assembled. All of them. A cavalry charge was arrayed before the Blockhouse. Tired, hot, almost angry eyes burned before them.

Tom announced that the day was getting late and not mincing words, said it was time to shit or get off the pot. Marcus looked at his shoes and nodded. Jenkins looked at anything and everything but the others in the room.

Frost had his hands steepled under his chin, paying close attention to Wills and no one else.

Eddie waited as did they all for Ms. Roth to read them the riot act. She was indeed a good-looking lady, with a strong and fierce presence. She crossed her legs, smoothed her skirt, cleared her throat, and began to speak quietly but firmly. At first, they all leaned forward to hear her but then collectively realized if they just settled down, they could hear her fine. She never raised her voice.

"None of you know me at all. Even my assigned counsel John Winkler has no idea as to who I really am. You know how it works. Cases appear, get assigned, we get paired up with one another, we exchange communications and thoughts, regular status reports, even talk on the phone from time to time but it all has the depth of a shallow puddle. It's as we all know just about the money and what our chances are from either end of the telescope.

"Now, I think it is expected of me to sit here and blow you, the Blockhouse bunch out. Cuss you up one side and down and move this thing to the finish. But there is no need for that and that's really not what's in my wheelhouse.

"I will say that, Mr. Marcus, you could really use some attitude adjustment in the direction of recognizing there is humanity out there beyond your very narrow, short-sighted self-loving appraisal of yourself. I think if you could work on that, you'd find this world to be a far more pleasant place. Why in the world would you invent yourself as the biggest turd in the punchbowl? Makes no sense to me. You can do so much better. You would become a much better, more effective lawyer.

"Mr. Jenkins, you're nice enough and in this case it is obvious you have tried hard to compensate for your co-counsel's ill-mannered shortcomings. That's appreciated I guess but goes to little effect. I have over these last hours come to wonder if you are really a lawyer, a trial lawyer or just a court jester, a sycophant. You seem very bright and very nice, so why not give the lawyer thing a try? Mr. Frost, you work at being inscrutable and do a fine job of it. I am familiar with the posture as I have to be a cipher most of the time myself. We've got the money and we sit back and dole it out in phases, often stingily to frustrate the green grabbers on the other side. Many of the cases we work on aren't worth a bucket of warm piss, to quote the forgettable John Nance Garner, but I think you and I can agree, this one here and now is a different, more dangerous creature. This one can eat you up if you are not careful and you know it.

"I'm a Jewish girl and was raised on enough Yiddisms and sayings and parables to last all of us a lifetime. Here's one that has come to mind from the beginnings of this awful train wreck of a case. 'Strain on a gnat and swallow a camel.'

"Y'all have already swallowed the camel. You've put three on it and we're at the finish line and yet, with just a little ways to go, y'all are dithering about whether to go any farther and you've got a pile of reserves backing you up. You're straining on a gnat. Well, here you go.

"All of us are all in. We've all swallowed the camel and the gnat too. If y'all can't get this done, everything is all for naught and when this case gets tried, I will be there to tell the court in no uncertain terms about your foolish intransigence which has led to this wasteful, very wasteful exercise. I promise I will burn you down."

Her voice and gaze were simply out there, quiet. She was riveting. She was put together in every way one might think of.

"I will say this too. I am the mother of two beautiful, wonderful little boys. If anything were to happen to them like this, it would tear my heart out. I expect you have children as well. At the end of the day, where is your humanity? Surely you haven't tossed it in the garbage can. It was your insured who had the last, real clear chance to keep this from happening. There is a lot of blood on their hands, certainly on ours, but Good Lord on your hands by proxy too. And of course, in the twisted ways of our legal, insurance, risk-filled world, if you don't get this done now and you get blown up at trial, there will surely be a claim for bad faith which will be a nightmare for you all professionally and individually. Me too, and I promise I'll make sure you get crapped on heavy then. No doubt.

"Now, it's almost time for me to go, for us all to go. I'm asking the three of you to help us all finish this. Please. I'm done."

The room was silent. Wallace Marcus deferentially raised his hand.

"How much to conclude it?" There was no contempt, no starch in the ask.

"One more," Roth replied.

"That's it?"

"Yes, that's it. You never have figured that out? Gee."

"Well, apparently not. Guess I got lost. No one would tell me anything. I guess I know why. Sorry. Four million from us ties it up, right?"

"That's right."

Marcus looked at Frost. Frost nodded his assent.

And from the level eyes and lovely lips of a stranger from Atlanta, some decent, good sense finally broke through. All stood and shook hands.

Tom Wills filled in the blanks of the Mediation Settlement Agreement and all signed it.

Wills said, "Good job, people. All agreed upon funds to be paid must be available within ninety days. Defendants will prepare settlement documents and releases. All know this settlement is enforceable by the court. No turning back now, right? No buyer's remorse. I will split my mediation fee charges four ways. In the end, y'all did just fine."

They all signed up and started gathering up their belongings for departure. The dusk was coming. Eddie spoke up.

"Tom, please bill all your mediator's charges for all of us to me."

Marcus shook Eddie's hand again. "Thank you."

"Happy to help it along. An example of good faith and fair dealing. Look forward to seeing you again on down the line."

"Me too, though might I say, 'Oh I bet.'"

"Tom, may we use your phone to call our ride home? I've a dead battery again."

"Sure. Your jet? Can I get a ride?" He laughed, his bonhomie having replaced his seriousness.

"Not this time but soon enough. Which does though call to mind... Ms. Roth, may we give you a lift back to Atlanta? It would be our pleasure."

"I am running pretty late and probably will have to take the 9:30 out of here now. Are you serious?"

"Yes, ma'am. Patty, how about you call Atlantic in Greensboro and tell them we're ready to roll home but we need to make an intermediate drop off in Atlanta? Which airport from down there did you come out of?"

"Hartsfield, Delta."

"Patty, please get her ticket and call Delta too and cancel her return. We'll have you there by 7:45. Please tell AA to alert ATL FBO of our quick stick in."

Patty got it all done in a few minutes. "They'll be here by 6:30."

Eddie gathered his group, inviting them for a drink at The Mills House before heading to the airport.

They said their goodbyes and thank-yous. Wills was beaming. "Glad y'all came. Glad we got this done."

"Couldn't have done it without you, Tom. Hope I see you again, sooner rather than later."

Out on the sidewalk, Eddie hugged Patty. "Can't do without you! Thank you!" Patty fired one up and laughed and observed, "We do right well together, don't we?"

Eddie pulled Mikey close to him, kissed her forehead and her lips and nuzzled her neck. "My good luck charm, my precious, smart good luck charm."

"You telling me it wouldn't do for me to be too far from you?" She grinned.

"Yes, you're a genius too." He looked at Alph.

"You been thinking about what we talked about last night, I hope?"

"I have. Let's talk about it once we get Ms. Roth home."

"Agreed."

Patty and Mikey wondered about that.

"Come on, Ms. Roth, let's go have one before we have to go. By the way, may we call you Debbie or Deborah?"

"Debbie is fine. I appreciate it. Ms. Roth is starting to sound downright schoolmarmish."

"Tough crowd, right?" She nodded.

They reassembled in the Best Friend Bar and ordered all around.

Eddie addressed the boys. They were smiling and pleased. "Dooley, Fishers, and David. We just achieved a very good settlement in there. And in no small part due to the strong and straightforward efforts of Debbie Roth here. She dragged the wagon across the finish line. I hope y'all understand how vital and critical she was, she is. We may have been at nine but that was just a wish, a figment. Once she got us to 10, things got real. Now, having heard no objections as to what we discussed last night; we will structure the money accordingly. I will reduce my fee to 25 percent. We will take care of all costs advanced out of our pocket. None will be charged to y'all. Don't worry about the jet. That's on me, just for fun."

Fishers asked in amazed delight, "How did you all just do that?!"

Eddie winked at them all. "Damned if I know. But you dumb asses getting hurt are, sorry to say, not hurting my life. I hate it for y'all but do enjoy it for me. Just another paradox.

"Now, here's the deal. I think y'all should stay here again tonight. It's getting late. I expect y'all want to sow a wild oat or two. I don't want any nonsense. Y'all are still in my charge as far as I'm concerned. On the way out, I'll speak to the front desk and will get everything taken care on my ticket. But dammit all, you and your families have been through so much. I want y'all safe! You understand that?!" There were "yes, sirs" all around.

"Okay, bottoms up and let's grab a cab. Y'all ready? Boys, we will be in touch. First come with me."

Eddie zipped around to the front desk, spoke quickly to the desk clerk, gestured at the three and then said, "I want them all on my chit this night too. Toss them out gently in the morning. Please add 30 percent. I want them safe. I want them to have some fun but not too much. They've earned it. Send them over to 82 Queen. Please have the Bell Captain walk 'em down and walk 'em back. Their curfew is midnight. If they miss it, I want to know. If they are gonna get dog drunk, I want them in house here and I would ask that they be walked to bed. They may not need it but then again. Okay, kids, let's blow this pop stand."

Eddie handed the guy two crisp Bens, one for the ask, one for the assistance.

He shook hard, hearty hands with each of them and Eddie held Marks' stump for more than briefly in tribute. There were a few tears but they all looked away and rolled on.

At the airport, they had but a brief wait before the plane arrived. Its wing and nose lights swung wide, drawing hanging yellow curves on the blue-purpling board of the coming night as it rolled to the pickup, the engines not yet shut down. The co-pilot opened the hatch and released the stairs and came down to greet them as they came out of the building to embark.

"Good evening, y'all. Miss Patty, when she called, said y'all have had a right successful day. Congratulations! Come on aboard. We've made sure we're good and stocked up with wine and beer and whiskey and snacks, even some champagne if you like. Y'all celebrate some. You only go round once and we're to get that done for you so please, have at it. As I understand it, we'll run over to Atlanta FBO real quick and then back up to Winston. That's the plan, right?"

"You've got it, Captain. Thank you."

They settled in and puttered about for a cocktail of choice and a bag of chips or crackers. The jet lifted like a silver arrow into the night sky. They all were tired so the conversations were neutral and friendly. They found out that Debbie Roth had been at it for over twenty years and admitted she had a rep as mean bitch but it was all mostly role playing, that she was a marshmallow at heart, that she was married to a stockbroker, a good man, and she grew orchids and liked to fish and go to the beach when not working. She was attractively normal. She's taught first grade for years before she jumped at another, fatter hook.

Patty admitted that she had a rep as a mean bitch and that indeed, she was a mean bitch. They all laughed. Eddie and Alph talked quietly with each other.

Alph said quietly, "It's a big break, a big step, Eddie. I'm tempted but just can't pull the trigger just yet, I don't think."

"Just don't give up on it, just stay with it, please. I think it can be good."

Mikey just sat close to Eddie and drank it all in. Her eyes would close and a little sleep would drift over her and then she'd start back to consciousness, open her eyes, and then close them again. The insulated roar of the jet's engines was the sound of the ocean breaking and it was soothing. It was a clean, clear ride to Atlanta and soon they were there.

"Here we are. Debbie, do you need help with your things? Do you have a ride?"

"No, no, I'm all good. I'll call my husband and wait for him to come get me. Thank you so much for this nice, quick treat. It was wonderful. Thank you."

"The pleasure was all ours. Glad to be of help. God knows you helped us out big time back there a few hours ago. That was a class act across the board and we are in your debt. Thank you!"

"Guess we could call it a win-win-win or something like that."

"I think you're right."

"Don't y'all know you can always get more flies with sugar than you can with vinegar?! Y'all are from the south. You know better than that." And she waved and was gone.

The plane buttoned up again and lifted again into the dark night flecked with stars.

"Now, she is a real lady. Hard not to like her. Impressive." They all agreed.

Eddie looked around, freshened his drink, helped everyone else with the same and then leaned forward and said in an important tone of voice, "I have something to tell Mikey and Patty."

They paid attention. Alph sensed he was getting ready to be roped. He was right.

"Last night after we all broke up, Alph and I went back to the bar at the hotel and kicked a lot of stuff around. While having just one more small one, I formally offered Alph the position of Senior Of Counsel to our law office. I think he would be a fine and fun fit and we all could be of great help to one another. He's been thinking on it but hasn't committed yet. It's a big move for him but one that I think and hope would be a terrific way for him to finish off what we all hope is a still longer and still and forever will be a distinguished career as a true and able trial lawyer.

"I need you ladies to help convince him to come and be with us. He did know I was going to let y'all in on it later on but he had no idea I was going to do it this way, at this time. I suppose we've ambushed him. Ladies, what say you?"

They needed no further prompting. They jumped into the seats on either side of Alph and held his arms and his hands and implored him to come be a part of the fun and the work. There was no pretense in these happy women. They had grown fond of this elder and cute and smart statesman. They did not quite gush over him but it was close. They chattered at him as children do in the manner of "please, please, pretty please!" with Santa Claus.

Alph blushed and drained his drink and paused only briefly. "Yes, you've all won me over. Yes, I'll do it. It's about time I did something new and different and God knows y'all are something new and different!"

The ladies squealed and hugged him and made all over him. Mikey even tousled his hair. Alph giggled. He and Eddie shook hands. "Alph, I'm thrilled and delighted. Thank you so much!"

"Thank you, Eddie. I am too. Ladies, I very much look forward to working with all of you. It has been quite a ride from here to there. It really has."

They all leaned back.

Eddie said, "Let's all go home."

Upon landing, they all stood on the tarmac and watched their ride puddle jump back over to Greensboro.

Eddie pulled Alph aside and told him, "Now don't you worry. You're gonna get paid well, gonna get a nice signing bonus. After all, you had a big hand in this giant success we've had today and you will have every benefit you had at your old shop, a good car of your choice, your office decorated as you like it, your name in big gilt and gold lettering on the front door and all the signage. Hell, we'll have a fine, big party to introduce the new you to the bar. This is gonna be fun, I promise."

"Eddie, I'm all in. Don't you worry. You have got this old head spinning. Feels like I'm on a hot roll with butter! I've got to get home. How about I check with you in a couple of days?"

"Perfect. Go on now, get some rest. Again, thanks for everything! Alph headed to his car.

Eddie turned to Patty and Mikey. "Isn't that great?" They nodded enthusiastically. "Now, time to find Curt and once we do, round up Rise and Kenny. Let's see if we can zip this other adventure up."

"Patty volunteered. "I'll be at the office by 8:30 and begin the round-up. I'll call you at home once the contacts have been made. If I'm successful, want to say 11:30, before lunch?"

"Yes, that's good. Thanks. Okay, we're out of here. Good job, everybody. Let's get some rest. Let's all drive safe, would be the smart thing to do."

They parted.

Mikey and Eddie were walking in the cool night air, each enveloping the other.

"Thank you so much for all your help on all of this, honey."

"Well, thank you, but I'm not sure I was all that helpful though I sure am learning a lot. It's like drinking out of a fire hose. Eddie, what do you think about Curt? How do you think it's all going? You haven't heard from him since last Saturday, have you?"

"No, I haven't but that doesn't surprise me. I am working under the assumption that no news is good news. Hopefully we'll see tomorrow. Are you hungry?"

"Some. Let's go home and I'll make us some spaghetti and you can open some decent red and we can build a fire and watch an old movie, and let's just be calm and normal for a night. I think we're gonna need a few hours to downcycle here."

"Good idea. Can we throw some back rubs and smooching in there too, just for good measure?"

"You bet!" She leaned over and nipped his ear lobe. "Come on, mister. Let's go home."

CHAPTER FORTY-SIX

SPECIAL GIFT

The Isley Brothers

THE PHONE RANG. Eddie looked at his watch. It was 8:45. He figured it was Patty. He cleared his throat and grabbed the receiver. "Patty?"

"That's my name and deception is my game." She was in high spirits and her voice mirrored it.

"Hey. What's going on? You sound fired up." He laughed.

"You bet. Curt, Rise, and Kenny will all be here at 11:30. Curt says he has presents for you."

"That's great. Good! Damn good! We'll be there by eleven. Thank you!"

Mikey was up on one elbow and of course had been listening in.

"Is it done? Is it really done?"

"Almost, honey, almost. How about some breakfast? Let's get dressed and be down there at eleven. Patty says they'll all be there at 11:30."

"You got it." She grabbed him and kissed him hard and fast. "Guess I should have brushed my teeth." She smiled coquettishly.

"Not a problem." He winked. They held each other closely for a few seconds and then leapt from their bed.

Curt got hold of Rise and Kenny, told them he had good news and he would pick them up at 11, suggesting to both that they should dress neatly.

He also suggested that Rise call Harry Davis at City B and let him know she wouldn't be in until afternoon, around 12:30 or so, but she expected to be bringing some good news with her.

Curt showered, got cleaned up and dressed and went down to the hole in the wall for breakfast. There was a snap in his step and he was very alert, not agitated, just keen eyed and sharp.

At around 10:30, he drove to Gore's. The place did not open until 11, but a knock on the door brought the big man to the window. He smiled and let Curt in.

"Good morning, Curt. Are you picking up today or delivering again? I know, I know. I do recall that this is a pick-up. Come on into the office and let's get you squared away."

"Thank you, Gore."

They went in and Gore closed the office door behind them. He opened the safe and brought out the small canvas bag along with the two larger food take-out bags and set them on a table in front of his desk. He closed the big safe.

"Here you go. Nothing has been touched or messed with, I promise you."

"Thank you very much. I'm sure that's right. You've been right kind to me these last few days, Gore, and I appreciate it. I want to pay you now. Uh, may I have a little privacy now? It'll just take me a minute to get my money for you together."

"Of course. I understand. I'll step out now. When you're ready just come back out to front. You know where I'll be. There's no one here right now but the kitchen staff and they're busy getting ready for the day."

"Yes, sir. I'll be there in just a minute."

Gore went out and closed the door. Curt opened one of the white food bags and brought out two small stacks of $100 bills, ten to a stack. They were less than an eighth of an inch in depth. He folded them and tucked them in his pocket. He picked up all the carryings—they did not weigh much—and went out the door.

Gore asked, "Coffee?"

Curt slipped the fold into Gore's big hand. "Thank you but not today. I got places to go and people to see."

Gore smiled. "That I understand too. Good luck, Curt. Now don't be a stranger."

Gore opened the door and as Curt went out, Gore warbled nicely in the style of Nat King Cole, "I've grown accustomed to your face."

The three arrived at Eddie's office at 11:20. Eddie and Mikey had already arrived. Eddie had been looking out the window for Curt, Rise, and Kenny. He went and got them, escorted them and as he did, called to Patty and Mikey for all to go into the big conference room.

They assembled.

"Good morning. How is everyone?" Everyone was fine, good, copacetic, and better. Their collective anticipation was palpable.

Curt looked pleased as he laid the deliveries on the table before Eddie. They were all seated around him. Curt pulled up a chair too. He had also brought along the extra masonry sacks that he had bought earlier.

Eddie told them all how proud he was of them, that they had acted as a brilliant, cohesive team and that he was going to now hand out the proceeds, that everyone was going to get something that Eddie thought was in keeping with this success.

"Curt, how much are in these white bags?"

"The one with the slight tear in the top corner has 98K. I guess that should be mine. The other is a hundred. The one that is light is because I paid a friend to hold all this safely for me until I was able to round it all up and get it here to you. That 2G payment is on me, my deal with him, out of my cut from the proceeds. He's a good guy and was real fair with me. I think you'll understand."

"I do. Sure I do. So you have your hundred less your two. Would you like me to safe keep it for you until you know what you want to do with it?"

"I appreciate it but I'll be taking this on with me today. No offense intended but I know what I'm going to do with it and I want to have it with me."

"No offense taken. I promise. Good luck with it. Curt, you've been great, a real champion."

Eddie counted out fifty thousand and handed it to Rise. "This is for you and Kenny. I know y'all will be fair and good to one another about it. Y'all have been real pros and taken some heavy chances about all this. I hope y'all think this is fair."

Rise and Kenny just smiled so big and murmured their thank-yous and stared at the money in Rise's hands.

Kenny whistled out a happy, "Holey Moley!" but it was all very low key, almost solemn.

Eddie cautioned them to not talk about this to anyone, to keep quiet and go about their daily business, and that went for everybody, all of them. They all nodded. He told Rise and Kenny that he would be happy to keep their money in his safe if they liked until they could figure out what to do with it.

Rise replied that she thought that was a good idea. Kenny agreed but asked if they could both each have one thousand for pocket money. Rise thought that was a nice idea. Eddie told them it was their money and of course they could do with it as they pleased. He did hope they would do something useful with it. Rise peeled off a G for each of them and handed the rest back to Eddie.

"Now, as to the other fifty in this set of bills, I'd like to propose that Patty and Mikey split it fifty-fifty. Patty, as you know I'm pretty good with bonuses from settled cases and we have recently just successfully landed two whales. You know you'll not be forgotten at early Christmastime. That work for you?"

"Absolutely. Jesus. Thank you!" Her eyes were big and bright. "Oh, and if you don't mind, I'd like to take mine with me at the end of the day. Maybe I'll sign up for a stop smoking workshop and get my hair done. Naw, good luck with that."

They all laughed. Patty burned another one and blew a big smoke ring for effect. It was a beauty too, big and fat, floating along. They were all floating along.

"Now, Mikey." Eddie turned to her. Tears were rolling down her cheeks, her face was flushed. She was shaking. She choked out a weak, "Eddie..."

Eddie took her hand and squeezed it and brushed her tears away and gently, pushed her hair back, physically soothing her. "Honey, please don't be upset. We are all here for you."

"Oh, Eddie, I'm not upset, not upset at all. I know what we've done is against the law but it sure isn't murder, and you've done it and I'm just amazed and I'm so proud of y'all and how cool and calm everyone has been. I guess it's all just gotten to me now that you're at the finish line. And, Eddie, I don't want any money. You're too good to me now as it is."

"Well, it's no secret to any of us here in this room how I feel about you. When I first talked to you about all this out in Montana, I expect you thought

I was pretty much bughouse. But, you took a huge chance, a huge leap of faith, hell, and you came South with me and you trusted me and bucked me up and by the way, you are turning into a fine legal assistant."

Patty nodded vigorously and patted Mikey's knee.

"Mikey, I want you to have your own stuff so here is some stuff for you to have. It will give you a sense of independence. After a while, I'll show you how to set up your own brokerage account and then as time goes by, you can add to them and watch your stuff grow."

"But, Eddie, what about you? You're getting nothing. That's not right."

"I got more than anyone can ever imagine. Remember, I told you way back when I just wanted to do it, do something different, to see if I could do it? And we have. That's my payment and that's fine by me. You understand that, right?"

"Yes." She sniffed and threw her arms around him and kissed him about twenty times and pulled back, threw her shoulders back and steadied herself and said, "Yes, okay. Thank you. Thank you so much. What's next?" They all looked around.

Curt said, "Seems to me, you got some more delivering to do. Here are some extra bags. Think you'll need four all total."

"That is so. Rise, how about go call Mr. Davis and tell him we'd like to come see him in a few minutes? Ask him if he could get hold of Mr. Siddon too. You and Kenny ride with me. I've got to go make two phone calls. I won't be long. Thinking we can take a ride down the hill in about ten minutes." Eddie sighed. "Curt, I expect you'll be moving on now. Again, I can't thank you enough. You are one strong player. Feel free to check in with me, come see me anytime."

"I'll sure keep it in mind. Thank you. How about I wait for Kenny and Rise until y'all come back from down the street? That okay with you? I'll take them home."

"Sure. Thanks. That's real kind of you. I'll see you later." Eddie went into his office and closed the door. First he called his brother down in Naples and told him he wanted to come visit.

Grass said, "Hmmmm...so soon after your last visit. You must miss me." He laughed and followed it with a hearty, "Horseshit, of course. When you coming?"

"I'm thinking in a couple of days. Gonna drive down, split trip in half. Spend a night at Sea Island, then come on down and across to you."

"Sounds good. Keep me posted. Anyone traveling with you? Mother says you've found quite a nice looker."

"Yes, that's true. Yes, Mikey's coming with me. That okay?"

"Absolutely. Y'all gotta spend one night with me at least."

"Fair enough. Thank you. I'm planning on leaving tomorrow so I will see you day after. That okay?"

"Works fine. I'll look forward to seeing you then." They hung up.

He then called the next number. It rang a few times and the lovely voice of Gigi Faye Erin answered with that voice of sultry silk. It made Eddie blink.

"Hey, Gigi Faye. It's Eddie."

"Eddie who?" she teased. "You dummy. I know you. Where have you been and what's up?"

"All around and the price of eggs," he lamely teased back. "Listen, can I buy you a drink this evening after work?"

"Sure. That would be nice. Where you want to meet?"

"How about the scene of the crime."

"The Alley or the Quiet Pint? Sure. You pick. Good spot and we did do good in both. Good karma. What time?"

" Let's go with the Q.P. Five o'clock?"

"You got it. See you there in a little while."

They hung up. He put three little masonry bags together, each with a full $100,000 in them. The rest he locked in his office safe.

Eddie went out front to where the others were. Patty said, "Mr. Davis and Mr. Siddon are waiting for you."

"Good. Patty, please call The Cloister in Sea Island, Georgia, and get us a nice big room for tomorrow night and then another for the two days after. I didn't explain that so well. Tomorrow night we'll be in Georgia, then we're going down to spend one night in Naples with my brother, and then the day after that, we'll go back to The Cloister for the night and then come on back here."

Mikey asked, "I'm going?"

"You bet! Okay, ladies, we'll see you soon. Curt is going to wait in the parking lot so when we get back, he'll give Kenny and Rise a ride home. How about please go out there and check on him and see if he wants something to drink or some crackers or something?"

Mikey said she'd attend to it.

"Rise, Kenny, let's go." They rode down the hill to City B. Eddie locked two of the carryalls in his trunk. Bing was at the counter when the three walked in. "Hey, y'all. Daddy said for y'all to go on back."

Harry and Syd stood as they came in. All shook hands and Eddie introduced Rise's little brother Kenny.

"Hell, if he's little, then I don't know what big is. Well, this is a pretty quick return visit, all things considered. Y'all please sit down wherever you can find a chair or a box or whatever." Harry Davis eyed them with a glimmering, amused curiosity. He seated himself at his desk.

"Mr. Davis, I want to return your investment to you." Eddie paused. "And also bring you all your return on that investment as well." He handed the canvas sack to Davis.

With Syd looking on, Davis opened it, whistled, and began to count the wrapped packets. He was used to handling cash money and his fingers rolled through the money like a Vegas dealer. In a couple of minutes, he looked up with a smile of delight on his face. "Syd, by my count and guess, this is about a hundred grand. Is that right, Mr. Terrell?"

"Yessir, it is exactly one-hundred-thousand dollars."

"Damn, boy, you do have your way, don't you? Damn, ain't this something! I have no questions about anything. Wouldn't be prudent. But I can surely say we are real pleased, right, Syd?"

"Damn right! Good work, Mr. Terrell."

"Appreciate that, Mr. Davis. I do have a question for you."

"Go right ahead."

"Obviously Rise here has been away for a bit here and there. She and her brother Kenny have been helping me on this project and they've been a big help too. I know Rise is a good and appreciated employee of yours."

"That's very true."

Eddie continued, "Her brother Kenny here doesn't have regular work, scratches around for odd jobs, works drink houses, mows lawns, that sort of thing. Would there be any chance he could get something steady with you? He's honest, reliable, strong as an ox, and polite and respectful, can drive a truck or a car, takes directions well..."

Harry held his hand up. “Say no more. He starts if he wants tomorrow at a decent hourly wage. We’ll watch over him and see how he does. Rise, will you get him here?”

“Yes, sir, Mr. Harry. We’ll be here.”

“You know, I expect Syd can find him things to do out at his place as well. Whaddaya think, Syd?”

“No doubt on that. We can probably back and forth him with all the mess the two of us have going on.”

“Son, Kenny, you want to do this?”

Kenny smiled big. “Yessir, I do, I really do. I appreciates it.”

“Anyone want a drink? Seems like we ought to each have one before we part for today. And, Rise, don’t worry about the rest of this day. We’ll see you tomorrow.”

“Thank you, Mr. Harry.”

Davis called, “Bing, bring me six small Dixie cups, please.” He pulled a big bottle of brown whiskey from one of his desk drawers. Bing handed the cups to his daddy who placed each one on his desk and poured about two ounces in each. He handed them about. He raised his as did they all, “To...well, to a damn good day! And just for good measure, here’s to you and here’s to me and if that doesn’t suit, then to hell with you and here’s to me!”

They all slung the drink back, shuddered, and sighed. Bing had no idea but was glad to be a part of whatever it was. They all shook hands, and then Eddie, Rise, and Kenny left.

Harry said to no one in particular, “You never know, you just never know, do you?”

Back in the car, Kenny and Rise thanked Eddie enthusiastically and graciously.

“Glad to do it. Please show them it was a good decision to make. Don’t let your sister down. Don’t let me down either.”

He dropped them off for Curt’s kind ride, shook hands with them all again and said he’d see them soon. They drove off and Eddie went into the office seeing Patty and Mickey working hard. Mikey said, “We’re trying to stay focused but it’s tough today.”

“I know. I’m going back in my office to make some calls, make some notes, review our case lists, and do some reading. I’ve got a meeting at five out of the office and should be home by six.”

"Who you seeing?"

"An investor. I'll tell you all about it this evening, I promise."

"That's fair."

At 4:45, Eddie headed further back down the Burke Street hill, and carrying a canvas sack he found Gigi Faye sitting in the very same booth at The Quiet Pint where they had busted Madge Roberts' girls. It was good karma indeed. And there stood their server from before, the really very gorgeous and leggy, leggy, leggy Mary P. who was no shrinking violet. She came to them and said, "Remember me? Mary P.? Nice to see you both again. What's your pleasure this evening? And do y'all have any more beautiful jewelry to show me. That was a neat thing that night. Y'all pretty much hollowed those two out but good. And I'm curious. Are y'all an item? Y'all look good together."

They both smiled in response.

Gigi Faye said, "Eddie, Mary P. is machine-gunning questions this night. Can you carry the ball for us?"

"Absolutely. I'm sorry but we have no beautiful baubles for you to look at today. Instead in the little carry sack, I have some very dull and also important and too absolutely confidential legal documents for Miss Erin here that deal with a case we have been working on. Boring as all get out but critical to getting a big part of the case finished.

"Well, what kind of case is this one.?" Mary P. was a real magpie too as she sought information. She liked shiny things but that interest could not be sated today.

"It's insurance fraud. The same kind of stuff we always work on together. Today's topic is nothing but money and how it's moving in this particular manner. That's all I can say about this. And because we're having some good success here, how about you bring us two nice, big glasses of champagne?"

Mary P. made a frowny face. "I hate that it's not interesting like that other thing. Oh, well, come back again and bring something juicy then. I'll go get your bubbles now. It's not the best in town but it'll do the trick."

"Okay, thanks. We will try to be more interesting next time."

They watched as she went to the far end of the bar, well out of snooping earshot.

Eddie pushed the canvas across to Gigi Faye and told her to put it right away in her purse. She did so and looked at him inquiringly. "What is it?"

"Your investment has paid off. It's a hundred grand."

Her mouth fell open. “You’re kidding. Eddie, this is a joke, right?”

“No, it’s all there. That extra loose and lost jewelry paid off nicely. You’ve got a safe at your office, right?”

She nodded. She felt a happy dizzy buzz in her head. She knew she was lopsided grinning like a goofy kid.

“Put it in there right after you leave here. Understand?”

She nodded again and said an attentive “Yes.”

“Ah, here is Mary P. with our refreshments. I was just explaining to Ms. Erin that it was very important that she take a good look at the documents this evening and that they be secured in her company safe.

Mary P. put two beer mugs of champagne down before them.

“Sorry we don’t have champagne flutes around here. Hope these buckets will do. You said ‘big,’ right? And that case you’re talking about sounds like spy stuff. Is it?”

“Mary P., you do have an extra special antenna, don’t you? Yes, it is all quite secretive and we have to keep it that way.”

He handed her a $50 bill and asked if that would take care of the drinks.

“Oh, good Lord yes!”

“Good, now you keep the change and leave us be for a bit so we can share more secrets, Okay? Go work over some of your other customers. Please.” Eddie and Gigi Faye smiled at her and she happily and swiftly walked away.

“Don’t forget to say goodbye when you go!” she called out in haste over her shoulder.

They clinked mugs.

“Wow, Eddie, I had no idea. How did you do this?”

“Well, I can’t really talk about it now—you know, the old ask me no questions and I’ll tell you no lies thing—but I truly would advise you to keep this confidential and locked up. Use the money little by little if you want to but keep most of the transactions small. Things like paying the house painter or gardener or buying yourself something nice now and again. And if you want to do some larger amount purchase like buying a car or investing it, call me and I’ll help you get it all legitimated. And I can’t visit long now. I’m going down to Florida first thing in the morning to see my brother.”

“I understand. I will get up with you later on it. Thank you so much! This is, to say the least, a real shocker, a real nice shocker. Thank you again. And I didn’t know you had a brother in Florida. Where is he?”

"Naples. He likes the pace of the place. He's a really good guy. Sort of a funny, grumpy sweetheart."

"What's he do for a living?"

"Stockbroker. Money manager. That sort of thing."

"Hmmmm...sounds interesting. Does your trip down that way have anything to do with all this?"

"Might."

"Eddie, you get more interesting every time around the block. Fascinating. One more question, please?" They had put deep drains into their champagne.

"Sure, but then it's time to go."

"Are you still seeing that gal?"

"Yes, we're pretty tight still."

"Rats. And what the hell. In one way I hope it works out for you and in another, I hope it doesn't. If it's to be the latter, I hope you will call me quick."

"I will. I promise. You are a doll. As pretty and smart as you are, I find it hard to believe you aren't already knotted up with some good guy."

"I know. I just like 'em good and bad and you fit the bill better than anyone else so far."

Eddie grinned and bowed his head.

Eddie got home by six and he and Mikey packed their bags for three days away. Mikey kept asking, holding up various items of clothing, "Does this look right? Does this look good? What do you think?" And Eddie told her she'd look perfect in a paper sack.

The Cloister was the grand dame of southern hostelry and hospitality. Verdant beyond description, she was draped and decorated in the highest and most comfortable of taste. Money and good manners oozed from every nook and cranny of the place. The staff was impeccable and kindly, attentively efficient. They valeted the car.

Because the weather was still warm, after they'd checked in, they visited the pool, which wasn't crowded since school was still in session. That would not be the case day after tomorrow as the weekend would be upon them and families and homeowners would come rolling in. In addition to the hotel itself, this was some of the most high end, good taste real estate in the country.

They soaked in the water for a while, had a couple of glasses of wine, and lolled on the chaises in the sun. They walked quietly about the grounds near the pool and then out to the beach. In years past, it had been one of few not so great things about the place, but now it had been expansively nourished and was a lovely spot for a stroll. The ocean was calm and there were no crashing waves. Their view to the horizon was unfettered. It was quiet and still, and their batteries were gently recharging.

They went back up to dress for drinks and dinner. There was a stillness, a calm about everything. When they spoke to each other, they spoke in low voices. They were in an absolute cathedral of fine culture.

Mikey did wink at him as they bathed and dressed. "Don't you worry, mister. I haven't forgotten where I put your groceries. I believe you'll be well fed later on tonight."

He adored her. While she was fixing her hair and makeup, he called his brother at his office.

Pablo the Grass suggested that they sleep a little late, have a nice later breakfast, and just come straight to his place out on the river. If they left at 10:30, they'd be there by 5:30 or so and that would be perfect. They'd have a fun visit filled with drinks and grilled steaks.

Eddie concurred and asked Pablo to tell Shay "hey" and that he was looking forward to seeing her. Pablo's wife was a firecracker, pretty and funny and kind, someone who loved to chat and visit. She was a professional in that regard.

Eddie and Mikey went downstairs to the bar off the lobby. Like the rest of the place, it was classy and cozy. They had a glass of champagne and went to dinner. The food was lovely and they ate modestly and moderately. They walked around the hotel for a while admiring its glitter and light and furnishings and appointments. It was a palatial, dreamy place where you held your liquor well and stood up straight and looked people in the eye. And plenty of her visitors paid close attention as Mikey passed by.

Then Mikey whispered in Eddie's ear. "I hear there is a lovely, very attractive evening buffet in room 1405. Might you be interested in a snack or two before bed?"

He grinned wolfishly. "You know, it's the damndest thing. Suddenly I'm absolutely starving. Let's go see." And they did. It was a feast.

CHAPTER FORTY-SEVEN

THAT'S ALL FOLKS

Porky Pig

THEY ARRIVED AT Pablo and Shay's condo just as the sun was starting its descent. There were big hugs and happy heys all around. Shay rustled them all quickly into the bar off the kitchen to mix up libations and get them all out on to the deck to watch the beautiful day end over the Golden River.

The sun obliged them in spectacular fashion, turning the bay and the marina and all the surroundings more golden than the river for which it was named. It was nature's alchemy and it was glowingly lovely. The weather was perfect and comfortable. Light sweaters all around would do the trick nicely.

Grass had already loaded the grill with briquettes and there were four gorgeous filets, gleaming in their rareness, streaked with little lines of fat on a large platter in the kitchen. Shay had made twice-baked potatoes that only needed to be heated up, and the green salad full of feta and tomatoes and homemade buttered croutons wanted only for a good toss. Grass suggested freshening up their drinks and firing up the steaks, but Eddie asked that they first talk business in his office.

Shay called to them, "Now don't be boring and business stuffy too long. We don't have them for long and I want to enjoy them real good while they're here." Then she and Mikey visited and visited some more. It was obvious they had gotten off on a very fine and formidable footing.

On the way to the office, Eddie stopped off in their guestroom and grabbed the canvas out of his bag. They stepped in and Grass closed the door.

"Is this what I think it is? Is this what I think this is going to be about?" He had a knowing, bemused look on his face.

Grass took the canvas and pulled the zipper and peered inside.

"Eddie, how much money is in there? Just curious, you know." The sarcasm was not meant to be hurtful.

"It's a hundred grand. Your twenty-five in and another seventy-five for good measure."

"Damn, son. How'd you get to this? No, never mind, don't tell me. I know you aren't going to tell me no matter what."

"That's true. You know I won't. But please notice when you pull it out, it's all old money, none of it new, none of in sequential order. None of it crispy."

Pablo nodded. "So none of it can be traced, right?"

"Right. Now I expect you have trusted resources that can provide further laundering."

"Yes. Yes, I do. Of course I do." Pablo was chuckling and shaking his head. "Amazing. Fucking amazing! Eddie, you are something else. You've got brass balls the size of Godzilla. What in the hell...damned if I know. Well, let's just let it be a mouse as mother says. I'll go put it in my safe now."

He walked over to his credenza, popped a three-numbered button and a door swung open to display a heavy duty Steelcase, bolted to the floor. He knelt down, spun its door open, zipped the canvas back up and put it in and closed it tight.

Absentmindedly, he noted, "You know, I'm not sure Shay even knows this thing is back here, much less the combinations. Had it installed one afternoon when she was out shopping or playing bridge or something. Now, let me ask you something."

"Let's see if I can answer it."

"You know Mother called me, told me about her investment with you, told me that she had invested with you because I had invested with you."

"Right. I figured she would."

"Is this the same kind of packet she's gonna get, when? Soon I presume."

"Yes, unless you have a better idea."

"I just might. Do you have hers with you?"

"No, it's locked up back at my office."

"I figured that would be the case. Let me think on this. And let me tell you thank you, thank you very much. I don't know how this all works and surely don't want to know, but whatever you've done and however you've done it, this is one hell of a return on investment. I'm amazed, shocked and grateful. Thank you, Eddie."

Pablo gave Eddie a big brotherly bear hug.

"Let's go get a drink and fire up those steaks. I'll think on this and we can talk some more in the morning. Oh, when does Mother expect to have some return on her investment?"

"Next two or three months, I think. As rotten as she thinks my business acumen is, I would not be half surprised if she figures I blew it and so it goes. She'll say I had no head for business or money and so forth. Oh by the way, she wanted me to tell you to buy her some Ford Motor Company and some IBM."

"Great. Oh sure, I'll make a note on that and she and I will discuss. Well, you've given me something to work on. A germ of an idea. And of course, until we figure this out, I'm not telling her anything other than we had a nice visit and that your new girl sure is a pretty thing. And she is, in spades."

"Thanks. I'm hungry and thirsty. Let's get on back to the gals. You really do have your work cut out for you now, don't you?"

Grass grinned. "So, what's new?"

They went back. Grass grilled the steaks to a juicy perfection and they sat on the deck and chattered and jabbered and gossiped and laughed and laughed some more. They ate like trenchermen and told stories and teased and kindly jibed at one another on this pretty night where the boats filled the bay.

At one point, Grass teased Shay about something she had said. "Shay, you are just like my mother."

Shay's retort brought down the house. "Pablo, you are your mother!"

They all howled. Mikey was in a thrall. It was the family she had never had. She clung to every word and studied and looked for cues and clues in the words and began to pick the flow of the repartee. The realization came to her that Eddie's brother Pablo was every bit as smart and sharp as was

Eddie, just in a funny, grumpier way. He was a sort of sweet Uncle Scrooge. Eddie was a tough guy with a heart of gold. While Shay could flat roll a conversation along. She was sneaky smart. Questions poured out of her, each leading to more information and more entertainment.

They had a wonderful time, a wonderful visit.

And like all such happy times, it wound down as a slowing clock and they all helped clean up and straighten up, and then shared fulsome compliments and said their good nights. The girls headed on to bed.

Grass just looked at Eddie with a smile and shook his head. After Eddie went to bed. Grass sat again on the deck, watched the slow-moving water, and did a few more algorithms in his head.

As Eddie slid into bed, Mikey's warm length magnetized him and he held her in both arms. She wrinkled herself comfortably and happily in the midst of her coming sleep and in a soft purr said, "That was so nice. They are such nice, fun people. I hope we can come back soon and have another visit, and I hope they'll come see us too. You are very lucky. They're great."

"Yes, they are. And so are you too. They like you a lot. And I love you and don't you ever forget it." They snuggled together even tighter.

Now a little more alert in the dark, Mikey asked, "Can you tell me what all you and Pablo were talking about earlier?"

"I'll tell you all about in the morning once we're on the road. We've hit a bump in the road, a bit of a snag about mother's investment. Pablo is sorting it out. It'll be okay. He's working on a plan. I'll know much more in the morning. Now, gorgeous thing, be still and shut your eyes and sleep."

"You too. I love you, Eddie. And don't you ever forget it."

They locked themselves up in one another and slept a good sleep.

The next morning as the sun was coming up, Eddie's internal clock went off and he popped his eyes open and quietly slipped away from Mikey and padded into the kitchen where Grass was having a coffee and doodling on a pad. After saying their morning hellos, Eddie asked his brother if he had any further thoughts.

"I think so. Eddie, you're a pretty successful guy, right? I mean, your practice generates plenty of fees, cash, and checks right?"

"Yes, that's true."

"I presume you have three accounts."

"Well, yes, that's right. A general operating account, a trust escrow account, and lastly what I call the 'Eddie Account' where I keep a stash for rainy days, fun and the like."

"Now, as I understand it, the one account that needs to be kept absolutely pristine is your trust account. That's the one the state bar auditors swoop in on without notice and make sure it's always perfectly balanced in and out, right? And if it's not, then you're fucked, right?"

"Oh, yeah, that's other people's money that is commanded, directed to be used for their benefit. It's totally fiduciary. That's one not to be messed with. By the way, I've never had my trust account audited. I think usually what sets off a rectal exam is someone waves a red flag or a trust account check bounces or a client blows the whistle about something not happening when it should have happened, that sort of thing. And of course, there are randomly selected audits, but the chances of getting a visit from the bar staff is small and stretched out and they've got more than enough complained of hanky panky to keep their plates piled high with projects. Like the rest of the world, unfortunately plenty of lawyers are not angels."

"Oh, don't worry. We're not going there. You're a sharpie but not a thief, right?"

Eddie grinned. "Sharpie, huh? And no, not a dipper. So what you think?"

"Here's my plan. You need to go home and take 25Gs in wrinkled, old beat-up bucks back to Mother. Tell her the deal didn't work out. Tell her the people you were dealing with were real estate investors, old codgers up in the mountains of West Virginia who were hot after some coal mining leases, real cash players, and tell her they couldn't get the deal to go so this is how they gave everyone their money back in cold, greasy cash. Tell her you came down here to give me mine back, same shape. Tell her, you got yours back just like this too. You can admit defeat and disappointment but don't go overboard. You don't need to don sackcloth and roll in the ashes. The deal just didn't go down. That's all and everyone got their initial juice back. She doesn't know any of the others, does she?"

"No, she doesn't."

"Good. She'll get a kick out of a bag of cash. It'll be like the old days when she kept that big cigar box full of Daddy Joe's gambling and betting money under the bed. For fun, you might go get a great big Hav-A-Tampa box and return her stake to her in it. It'll remind her of the good old days."

"Like that. Good idea. Now what about Mother's 75G?"

"In about a month, you and Mikey come on back down here and bring it to me. Ordinarily, I'd just put it in her account, but she birddogs her statements pretty good, always sniffing hard on the bottom lines even though she doesn't understand half of it. But, as you know, she's the smartest person in the room. Just ask her." They both laughed.

"With your permission and our agreed understanding, when you come back with the balance, I'm going wash it together with mine and hang on to it safely and at the proper time, somewhere down the road, we will go together to her with it. She's not getting any younger and will grow infirm and weak in due time. She will be less resistant, less questioning, and it'll be a nice surprise for her. She's always been ridiculously comfortable, and so this little bit is insignificant in the great scope of things. Nothing goes into your accounts, nothing comes out. You're clean. Safe and everybody is either happy or will be. What do you think?"

"Thank you, Grass. Works good for me."

"What about your other investors? How'd this all work out for them?"

"Let's see. There were four others. They're all pleased, all been fully fed."

"Does Mother know any of them?"

"Do you remember Harry Davis, Daddy Joe's old bookie? He and his partner Syd Siddon took a flyer. They can handle the burden of a nice lick of wrinkled cash. She doesn't have anything to do with them and hasn't for years."

"Good. Who else?"

"An insurance fraud investigator and a drink house operator who is a smart and successful under-the-radar hood–both good people. These are people she has never known and never will."

"Good. So are we decided on this plan?"

"Yes, thank you. Knew your money mind would pull the cat out of the bag. Thank you." They shook on it, had some more coffee, and waited for the girls to come yawning on along.

In a few hours after breakfast and last agreeable visits and so longs, Eddie and Mikey headed back up the road to Sea Island. There were more folks, more families, and children but it was still idyllic. It was a warm late autumn day. They swam and strolled, played bingo and shuffleboard, and drank good wine and enjoyed big, gooey ice cream sundaes. They loved each other well, while looking elegant and fitting into the place perfectly.

When they checked out the next morning, Mikey took Eddie's arm. "Eddie, this place is perfect. When can we come back? It's so wonderful!"

"Honey, I agree with you. How about we make it back down this way again in about a month? Would that suit? You're turning into quite a southern belle, aren't you? Quite something to see. Need to come back and see Pablo and wrap up some more family business. Maybe spend a few more days next time around. What do you think about that?"

She just smiled and kissed his cheek. He blushed. The desk clerk laughed approvingly.

"Ms. Terrell, it's fine. This place just has that effect on folks. Hope y'all travel safely and indeed, we hope you do come back soon."

On the way up the road, Eddie explained the conundrum of his mother's ill-gotten gains and how Pablo had formulated a very reasonable and sound plan to address it.

"You and Pablo work well together, don't you?"

"I think that's right."

"Y'all are lucky to have each other."

"Yes, we are."

It was a pleasant and easy drive home. They got back to Winston-Salem around dark. They went out and had a couple of drinks and split a steak at Town Steak House, went home and went to bed. It had been a wonderful and tiring few days.

The next morning, Mikey and Eddie went by the pharmacy and Eddie bought the biggest box of Hav-A-Tampa cigars he could find. They quickly stopped at the office where pulled his mother's pouch, opened the cigar box and dumped its contents in the trash can, counted 25Gs out and laid it neatly in the cigar box and then tapped the little lid nail down tight with his shoe heel.

At his mother's house Camara appeared in the front hall. "She down in her room drinking coffee, watching the news."

"How's her mood?"

Camara shrugged. "Pretty good, I guess."

They walked back, Eddie holding Mikey's hand.

He peeked around the corner. "Hey, Momma. I brought you a visitor."

She didn't look up from her paper. "Hey, son. Who did you bring me?"

"It's Mikey."

"Oh, Mikey! What a nice surprise. Come in. Come in. Sit down, please. Let's have a visit."

"Yes, ma'am. That would be nice."

"Camara, bring us three coffees and some of those nice little breakfast biscuits Mrs. Slick brought over the other day."

"Yes, ma'am."

"Now, how was your trip? Mikey, did you like The Cloister?"

"Yes, ma'am. And Pablo and Shay are so nice."

Eddie added, "We had a really nice time. And I have to say, I've brought you some good news and some not so good news as well."

"Is this about our investment? I spoke with your brother about it you know." Eddie nodded.

"Well, Mother, the deal fell through."

"Is the money lost? Oh, Lord. Eddie, have you lost our investments?"

"No, ma'am. Here is your original investment, albeit in a different form." He handed her the cigar box. She took it, shook it, rattled it, smelled it, and then gingerly pried the lid open.

She studied the layered cash in it for a good while and asked if Pablo and Eddie and the others had each gotten their money returned to them in this very form.

"Yes, ma'am, I've gotten everyone their original money back, all in this particular format."

"Eddie, what was the deal, this investment supposed to be about?"

Camara brought the coffee and biscuits in and served them all and left the room. She saw the box of cash in his mother's lap and her eyes said, "What the hell?"

"Well, Mother, we were trying to buy some coal leases up in West Virginia. Uncle Vernon had birddogged the deal and put a bee in my ear and so I ran with it. The fellows we were dealing with are old hillbillies up in the mountains, real old timers, and they, smelling, I think, city rubes took our money and then doubled the price. I told them that just wasn't gonna work out and we wanted our money back right away and that the deal was off. They were fine with that and then sat down and counted it all out this way. They're strictly cash-and-carry boys. I don't think any of them have a checkbook. I'm sorry it didn't work out. We gave it a try." Eddie looked glum. "Mother, I'm really sorry."

"And my full twenty-five thousand is all in here?"

"Yes, ma'am, counted it out three times before we came over here."

"Mikey, did you have any part of this nonsense? Were you there when the fellows up in West Virginia tried this shakedown?"

"No, ma'am. Eddie just told me about it when we were on the way to Pablo's."

"Well, that's just too bad." She looked at Eddie. "I keep hoping you'll turn out to be a real businessman like your brother, but I expect you better stick to your law business and stay out this kind of thing. You just don't seem to have an aptitude for business. You are very lucky those fellows up in West Virginia didn't clip you clean. Very poor judgment. Very poor, indeed."

Eddie hung his head. "Yes, ma'am, I expect you are right."

"I don't expect I'm right. I know I'm right."

"Yes, ma'am."

"When it comes to this sort of thing, one piece of advice. Don't get involved in such at all, ever again!" She shook her finger at him.

"Yes, ma'am. I won't."

She made a big harrumph sound, paused, and then said, "Well, you know what this reminds me of? Your Daddy Joe kept his gambling money in a big cigar box just like this, kept it under this very bed. Maybe this is a good sign. Eddie, take this thing and push it up under there. I'll pull it out later and count it out and think about what I ought to do with it. Of course, I am going to call your brother. He'll know what to do. He's good with money. You, not so much."

"Yes, ma'am. I did remember to tell Pablo to buy you some Ford Motor and IBM."

"Well, now. Well now, he just better. So, what are you doing with yourselves today? Better get on back to your office and make some money in a way you know how to make it. Mikey, I'm sorry this visit wasn't a good one. How about you get him straightened up? I'm sorry to scold him in front of you but it just needed to be said."

"Yes, ma'am. I understand. It's all right."

"Now I'm aggravated and agitated and need to calm myself. Y'all go on now and come back and see me in a few days. Just let yourselves out, please."

She purposely then instantly ignored them. The audience was concluded.

They rose. Eddie kissed her turned cheek. They went back down the hall.

Camara was there waiting. "Everything okay?"

"Oh yeah, all good. I'm a stupid businessman. So what's new...we gotta go. See you around."

"Oh yeah."

At the front door, he paused and cocked his ear.

He could hear his mother clearly as she spoke into her telephone.

"Pablo, did you get your money back from that damn fool? Did you try to talk some sense into him? I never in my life..."

Eddie grabbed Mikey's hand and as they went out the front door, Eddie laughed and Mikey said, "What?"

"Perfect. It's just perfect. That's all."

ABOUT THE AUTHOR

E. VERNON F. GLENN had no idea he would become a lawyer, much less a trial lawyer when he wandered out the doors of his beloved University in Chapel Hill way back when. His love of sports, gambling, and trying cases before both judges and juries has immersed and marinated his mind in the sharp-eyed calculations of strategy and tactics, strengths and weaknesses, human nature and chance. He went to work digging ditches in 1961 at the age of eleven for sixty cents an hour and knows that the sweat of work along with a good dose of brains is the curative dose.

In 2019 he released his first novel, *Friday Calls*, a work of fiction based on true events, which Kirkus Reviews called "a lyrical Southern tale of rippling effects." Vernon hangs his hat in the beautiful Lowcountry of South Carolina and in the re-emergent phoenix of his hometown of Winston-Salem, North Carolina.

If you would like to book Vernon for an author event, please email Hannah Larrew at hannah@spellboundpublicrelations.com.

CPSIA information can be obtained
at www.ICGtesting.com
Printed in the USA
BVHW071404060521
606648BV00003B/492